# THE PENTHOUSE ON PARK AVENUE

# THE PENTHOUSE ON PARK AVENUE

A HOUSES OF CRIME MYSTERY

JENNY DANDY

*First published by Level Best Books 2025*



*Author Photo Credit: Walter Dandy III*

*First edition*

*ISBN: 978-1-68512-958-3*

*Cover art by Level Best Designs*

*This book was professionally typeset on Reedsy.*
*Find out more at reedsy.com*

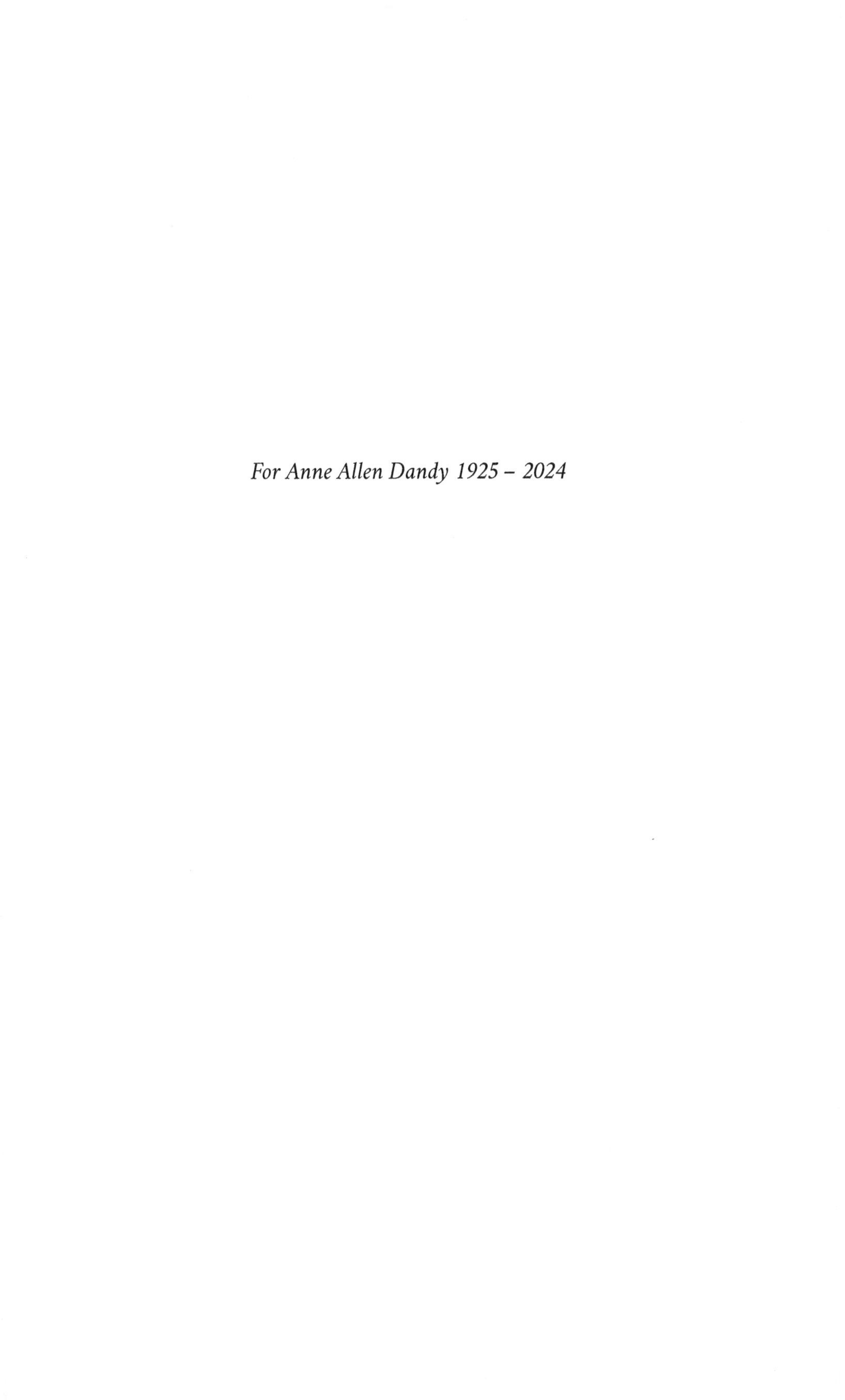

*For Anne Allen Dandy 1925 – 2024*

# Praise for The Penthouse on Park Avenue

"Jenny Dandy's *The Penthouse on Park Avenue* sets FBI agent Frank Jankowski and reformed thief Ronnie Charles against a professional money launderer in a story showcasing Dandy's talent for intricate plotting and well-honed dialogue. The relationship between Frank and Ronnie deepens, Frank's search for his missing daughter grows darker, and the stakes grow deadlier. *The Penthouse on Park Avenue* is top-floor entertainment from a gifted writer on the rise."—James D.F. Hannah, Shamus-winning author of *Because the Night* and *Behind the Wall of Sleep*

"*The Penthouse on Park Avenue* grips you from the start, never letting go through the twists and turns as Ronnie and Frank pursue a money launderer for the Mataderos Cartel. Jenny Dandy's characters stay with you long after you finish the book."—Abbott Kahler, *New York Times* bestselling author of *Eden Undone, Where You End,* and *The Ghosts of Eden Park*

"Jenny Dandy's new novel delivers everything you crave in a mystery—hardboiled-yet-scrappy protagonists, high stakes, suspense, dry humor, and true villainy. Written with compassion and an appetite for justice, *The Penthouse on Park Avenue* lures us even more deeply into Dandy's *Houses of Crime* series. I can't wait for the next one!"—Erika Krouse, author of *Save Me, Stranger*

"*The Penthouse on Park Avenue* sneaks up on you, comes alive, and won't let you go. Whether Dandy takes us to high end restaurants or low end diners, penthouses or homeless encampments, we're along for the ride. You'll care deeply about what might happen to Ronnie and Frank, eager for the next in the series."—Diane Capri, *New York Times* bestselling author of the Hunt for Jack Reacher series

"In her follow-up to *The Brownstone on E. 83rd,* Jenny Dandy continues the escapades of quick-witted Ronnie Charles, now working as the butler in a Park Avenue penthouse while simultaneously going undercover as a confidential informant for Special Agent Frank Jankowski, who perseveres in his quest to find his missing daughter. Adding impact to the story, Dandy introduces a villainous but charming drug lord and his malevolent accomplices in this page-turning whodunnit."—Cynthia Swanson, *New York Times* bestselling author of *The Bookseller, The Glass Forest,* and *Anyone But Her*

# Chapter One

"You're overqualified for this job."

*No*. Ronnie Charles shook her head, opened her mouth, closed it. This was her last chance. She had to get this job. What did this Lisa Cranberry person want?

"I'm thinking you'll find this position boring after your previous one." Lisa eyed her over her reading glasses, as if measuring her for a coffin.

If she didn't hire her, then that was it. Back on the streets, useless to Frank, to the FBI. Ronnie moved to the edge of her seat, sucked in a breath. She couldn't sound desperate, and she had to say the exact right thing to land this job.

Lisa was already talking. "Do you always dress as a man? Are you one of those gender fluid people?"

Could she ask that in a job interview? Yes, she could. Because what was Ronnie going to do about it? She was applying for a job as butler in the household of a suspected money launderer for a Mexican drug cartel. Though none of that was in the job listing.

"My previous employer liked me to dress like a man when I was her butler. And she bought me these suits and everything, and this is the best I got, so I wore it."

"Whatever." Lisa Cranberry glanced down at her resume again. Ronnie should've spent more time studying it herself after Frank, or someone else in the FBI, put it together for this job. Who knew she'd have to study up on her own life.

Lisa pushed a mass of curls off her forehead. "Did you really do all this for Isabelle Anderson? Why would you be looking for a job requiring fewer responsibilities?"

"To be honest," Ronnie leaned forward, held Ms. Cranberry's eyes, "she demanded a lot. Too much. Some days I worked 18 hours or more."

Lisa made a skeptical snick sound, tongue against the roof of her mouth. "So..." She drew the word out on an exhale, a heads up for the next question. "Were you there for the arrest?" She leaned back and crossed her arms, ready to be skeptical of Ronnie's story.

Ronnie stayed silent.

"Come on now, we all read about it in the papers. A society hostess like her, arrested for fraud. That's all the Upper East Side could talk about for days on end. I'm wondering, actually, why they didn't arrest you as well?" Like she thought the world would be better off if Ronnie were behind bars.

Frank had prepped her for this. "They questioned me, of course. Part of the household and all. But," she widened her eyes, innocence shining out, "I had no idea about any of that." Not the Oxy for the guests, not the fake charities, not the sex for blackmail, uh-uh. "I mean, how could I tell them anything when I didn't know anything about it?" This woman had to hire her. If she didn't land this job, she'd be useless to Frank, and he'd probably follow up on his threats and issue an arrest warrant out on her. No way she was going to prison. Jail had been bad enough.

Lisa tapped her pencil on the desk. Raised her head like she just thought of the question: "Tell me about Isabelle. What was she like?"

Great. No longer a job interview. They were now in a gossip session. "So, um, Lisa. Maybe I can fill you in on her later. Is there a written job description, duties, and all that?" Act like you're already hired, Frank had told her.

Lisa stared at her a long minute, eyebrows meeting. Probably didn't like being told "no." She let out an irritated breath and then started counting off on her fingers. Serving. Errands. Cooking on Chef's days off. Greeting at the door if there's a party, handling packages. Shining his shoes, brushing out his suits, getting things cleaned and mended. A wave of the hand: anything else Mr. Anthony may require.

# CHAPTER ONE

"When do I meet Mr. Anthony?"

A long silence. Just the tap tap tap of Lisa's pencil until Ronnie wanted to reach over and grab it from her, fling it—

"Look." Lisa waved the pencil at her. "I've never heard of a female butler, gender fluid or whatnot." Her eyes nailed Ronnie. "Even if you are built like a boy."

Most people liked Ronnie, but for some reason this Lisa person didn't, and she had no idea why. She gave a quick glance around the office, pocket-sized things jumping out at her. She caught herself and stopped. Her street brain wanted something she could pawn, some way to buy food because she was sunk.

"I mean, really. What was he thinking?" Lisa face screwed up in annoyance.

Ronnie gripped the arms of the chair, pushed herself up. Should she say, thank you very much for your time, or plead with her to give her a chance, offer to work for free on a trial basis, then they'd see how hard she could work, they'd be glad they hired her, in fact she didn't need a salary, room and board plenty—

"But he said he wanted to talk to you himself. Especially you, in fact." Lisa shoved back her chair, went around her desk, opened the door, went through it first. Looked over her shoulder at Ronnie. "Though why in God's name he'd single you out, only he knows. Are you coming?"

* * *

John Anthony's office, only slightly bigger than Lisa's, was dark, hushed, gleaming wood and thick green carpet. He said nothing while she sat, looked around. His office chair seemed way too big for him. She would have no trouble taking him down if she were that kind of person.

"How did you and Lisa get along?" John held his head turned mostly away from her, like his computer screen called to him, but he tried to resist.

She was still trying to figure out how to answer that, what he might want her to say, when he faced her fully and she realized why he hadn't done it before. A strawberry birthmark covered the left side of his face, like he'd been dipped in something. No scarring, but a whole bunch of extra pink on him.

She gave him a shrug. "I get along with pretty much everyone."

He cleared his throat, his Adam's apple bobbing in his skinny neck. "Okay, Lisa will tell me what you talked about, so why don't you tell me about what you did for Isabelle."

Ronnie opened her mouth to list her butler duties, but he stopped her.

"I already know the sanitized version. If you're going to work for me, I need full honesty from you." He paused, like her teachers would, to make sure he had her attention. "Tell me everything," he pulled a green and gold thing that looked like a knife out of a leather pencil holder. "Everything you didn't tell the FBI when they arrested her."

This guy didn't mess around. She shifted in her seat. "Everything?"

"I think that's what I said."

As Ronnie launched into a description of the roles she played in Isabelle's schemes, John toyed with the letter opener as it lay on his desk blotter. He turned it over and over, the gold blade catching the light, the carved jade handle pulling the light in, absorbing it.

"And how did Isabelle come to hire you?"

Well, not exactly a hire. More like indentured servitude. "She caught me removing her diamond tennis bracelet from her wrist at a charity ball." If he wanted honesty, she would give it to him.

He stopped looking at his letter opener and regarded her for a long minute. He didn't say anything, so maybe he wanted more explanation.

"She said I would work for her until it was paid off and she would teach me the long-con."

"Were you involved in the financial side? Handling the checks, the cash?"

She told Frank she couldn't lie. He said just embellish. "Yeah, sure. She trusted me with all that." Hopefully, a point on the positive side.

John Anthony nodded. He settled into his chair, the letter opener on his desk blotter, blade pointing toward her. "So tell me...why weren't you arrested? Why didn't Isabelle tell them all about your part in her criminal activities?" The letter opener was in his hand again. He hunched over his desk blotter and watched it as he stabbed the tip into the green paper. Thump, thump, thump.

Ronnie swallowed. "I don't know why she didn't tell them."

He looked at her without raising his head. Looked down. Thump, thump.

"I—I guess she felt protective of me or something. She was always saying things like we were family."

"Did the FBI feel protective of you as well?"

What the—she was never going to get this job. She sat up straighter in her chair. "Sir, I don't know what the FBI feels or doesn't feel. I just know that when they swarmed the brownstone, some goon took me aside and grilled me, and I must've convinced them that I had no idea what was going on, that I was completely shocked. That it was all Isabelle."

"Sold her down the river, eh?"

"If that's how you want to look at it. I like to think of it as what she deserved for kidnapping me and forcing me to work without pay." She sucked in her breath. It wasn't a lie.

He stopped brutalizing his blotter, laid down the blade. "So, Lisa told you what the basic duties would be?"

"Yes sir." Phew, easier question. Maybe she was passing his test. She listed the duties and finished with the way Lisa had: "And anything else that you require."

"As far as I'm concerned, that's the most important thing. That you'll do things for me as they come up. Things..." he looked around the office as if those things were sitting on the shelf, next to his accounting textbooks and framed photographs. "Things I won't be enumerating right now, not before we hire you, not before we know we can trust you." He studied her for a beat. "Lisa had you sign the NDA, didn't she?"

What the hell is that. "I'm sorry. I haven't signed anything yet." Ronnie swallowed. "Um, when would I start?"

"Let's not get ahead of ourselves." He pointed the letter opener at her. "You can sign the NDA after I talk to Isabelle. Get a character reference on you."

She willed herself not to flinch. She could feel her pulse in her neck, prayed that he couldn't see it.

* * *

Damn. Ronnie used the elevator ride to focus on returning her heart to a semi-normal rate. She nodded to the doorman on her way out. No sense in getting to know him. She and Frank were due to meet for lunch, and she was not looking forward to telling him she didn't have the job and probably wouldn't be getting it. If John Anthony really did talk to Isabelle, then no way she'd get this job. Damn.

Maybe she should pretend someone was following her, and she couldn't meet Frank. Naw. She wasn't that much of a liar. She did a few maneuvers like he had taught her, pausing at a store window to look for reflections of hovering people, getting off the subway just as the doors closed to see if anyone got off too. But mostly what she did was pray. Pray that the FBI had a different job for her.

* * *

She watched Frank over the rim of her Coke glass, took a sip. They were at a small place near FBI headquarters, far away from the Park Avenue penthouse. Frank sat with his back to the wall, arms on the table. She filled him in on the interview.

"But if he talks to Isabelle, I don't see how—do you think she knows I'm a—" Ronnie shuddered. "—I mean, that I worked with you?"

He uncrossed his arms, tilted his head like he was thinking about how to answer her.

"And plus, like John Anthony said, why didn't she rat me out?"

He shifted in his seat. Lined up his silverware. He shook his head. "Only God above knows what she thinks. But I need to get to her before John does and tries to find out what she thinks." He cleared his throat. "There are a few things we could do. Hate to, but we really need you in there, and this is the closest you've come to getting hired." He met her eyes. "After the last three fell through, boss is ready to drop you."

Ronnie didn't mean for her glass to hit the table so hard. "What? No! You can't do that. Everything I've done—"

"Easy, easy. I'm on your side." He cut a glance at her, then returned to organizing his knife and fork. "That's why I'm going to offer her a 5K motion. Even though I'd like to see her get the full sentence. At least the AUSA will be happy."

Ronnie sat back so the waiter could deliver her salad. Watched while he placed Frank's quiche in front of him. "I understood about three words of what you just said. Like, isn't 5K a race?" Better to talk about this than about failing the interview. At least winter was over, sleeping on the streets not so bad in the spring.

Frank put his fork on the table, placed his napkin in his lap. "A 5K motion is a way for a criminal to get his sentence reduced by cooperating with the government. Like maybe giving us enough to nail Philippe." He picked up his fork. "I rarely offer one, but in this case—" He gestured with his fork at her. "If she can make sure John Anthony hires you, then it'll be worth it. He's a much bigger fish than she is."

"Ha! Wonder what she'd say to that." She mixed around in her salad. "And what's an AUSA?"

Frank finished chewing, swallowed. "Assistant United States Attorney. They're prosecuting her. If she cooperates, maybe the whole thing will go faster. Get off their plates sooner. Move on to the next case." He pulled out his phone, poked at it. "I'll get that lined up this afternoon. I'll just alert Pete to make sure I'll have time to talk to her before John Anthony can get to her."

"Speaking of all this legal stuff, what's an NDA?"

Frank stopped stirring his iced tea with his straw. "You're just mentioning this now? Did you sign one?"

Ronnie managed to get a few lettuce leaves onto her fork. Shook her head. "Naw, he said I would sign one after he talked to Isabelle. But what is it?"

"Non-disclosure Agreement. Depending on the wording, it means you can't tell anyone what goes on in the house, can't take pictures, can't post on social media." He picked up his fork, said to his quiche, "Will wonders never cease." Shook his head.

"What?" What had she done now?

"Criminals requiring NDAs. What's next?" He gave her a little smile. "Hiring a butler?" He sliced off a bite of his lunch.

"So if I sign that thing, that means I can't tell you anything?"

He laughed. "Nope. Unfortunately for them, law enforcement takes precedent, so you can tell me everything pertaining to the case." He fiddled with his spoon. "Uh, while we're waiting for him to talk to Isabelle," his voice was low, "I was wondering if you could help me."

"Aren't I already helping?" But she knew what he meant. The never-ending search for his daughter. Cathy, sixteen. Someone had run her over, then she'd gotten hooked on opioids, then run away from rehab. She was out there somewhere. Ronnie always wondered if Frank decided to get her to be his CI because she'd once lived on the streets and could help him look for her. Pain passed over his face, and she dropped her teasing smile. "Of course, dude, you know I will."

Frank nodded a thanks, as if he couldn't bring himself to say anything out loud, then he sat back, folded his arms, cleared his throat. "Tell me about John Anthony. What's he like?

Back to safer territory. "I don't know. Kinda hard to read." Ronnie sipped her Coke, watched the ice settle as she put the glass on the table. "He played with this letter opener the whole time, gold, jade handle, looked kind of lethal."

Frank said nothing, studied her eyes, listened.

"In fact, that was really the only thing scary about him, that letter opener. Are you sure this guy's the criminal?"

Frank nodded, still said nothing.

Guess he did want every detail. "Okay, so one whole side of his face is this pink birthmark thing. He tries to keep it away, y'know, looks at you sideways the way a horse would, but you can't help seeing it."

"We know about the birthmark. I want to know about the person."

"Well, he didn't shake hands, just kind of looked me over, watched me sit down. He seemed pretty harmless." Ronnie wiped her mouth with her napkin. "I know he'll have special errands or something for me to do, not just shining his shoes."

"Tell me what he said, verbatim."

She hated that word. "He asked if Lisa Cranberry had told me what my duties were, I listed them off, and said, 'and anything else you require.' He said that was the most important thing, as far as he was concerned."

"Did he enumerate those things?"

Ronnie one-shoulder shrugged. Whatever "enumerate" meant. Second time she'd heard it today. "He said he'd tell me after I was hired, after they knew they could trust me." She speared her lettuce, a cocktail tomato rolling off to the side. "Um, can I ask—what happened to the last butler? I mean, how did this job come up right after I didn't get those other ones?"

Frank grinned a little, as if to himself. "We snagged him one day as he ran errands. Managed to persuade him that he should find employment elsewhere." Frank closed his mouth like he didn't want any more words to come out.

"Just for me, huh?" Probably more to the story, but if she asked, he wouldn't or couldn't tell her. She stabbed at a crouton. Missed. "Wait." She put her fork down. "How do you know the old butler didn't tell John Anthony?"

Frank took a sip of his iced tea, set the glass down. "He wasn't live-in, so we gave him a ride home. And we made it very clear that if he did say anything, we would know it and he would be a guest of the Federal government before he knew what hit him." The waiter came by and Frank asked for refills. "And no one wants to go to prison."

"Tell me about it."

They picked up their forks at the same time, then chewed in silence together.

"And what do you make of Lisa Cranberry?" Frank sliced off another bite of quiche. Ate it. "Is she in on the illegal activity?"

"Who knows? She did ask why I wasn't arrested along with Isabelle. So she knows my background, I guess." Ronnie gave up on her salad, put her fork down.

Frank swayed away from the table, paused while the server placed their drinks, took the empties, and left. "So, let me tell you in more detail what the case is about." He took a sip, put the glass down. "We told you John Anthony launders money." Frank rearranged the salt and pepper shakers in the middle of the table. "You'll be our eyes and ears, reporting back to us on everything. Everything, no matter how small. We need to show that the source of the cash he's moving around is from the proceeds of criminal activity. That's key to the case, showing the source of the money."

Ronnie felt like she was back in school and should be taking notes. She never liked school. She let out a long breath.

"This is important." Frank turned his iced tea glass around and around. "You need to know why you're there, what we need you to look for, what to pay attention to."

If she got the job.

"Because," he went on, "paying cash for things, moving money from one account to another, isn't in and of itself illegal. It's where the money came from that's the most important thing. The only thing."

"So, how'd you know to go after him?" Maybe this would be more interesting.

Frank cleared his throat, "Through Isabelle's donor list. He gave her cash, she wrote a check back, keeping a little for herself."

Lisa had mentioned that he had donated, but Ronnie had never heard of Isabelle writing someone else a check. The crust of the quiche stood on Frank's plate like the carcass of a ship. Ronnie wanted to reach over and grab it. Best part.

"We do know he's close to Mateo Rosas de Flores, head of the Mataderos Cartel. A relationship that goes back to when John worked at the prestigious Trust Bank of New York."

"Does this guy, Mateo, show up at his house? Is he scary, I mean, a drug cartel…" She poked around in her salad again. She didn't know why she'd ordered it. She put her fork down and eyed Frank's plate.

"Comes to the house, meets him in restaurants." Frank watched over her shoulder, his eyes tracking from one side of her to the other.

She half turned but didn't see anyone.

"Handsome, well turned out. You'd think he was just a high-powered businessman, to look at him."

Ronnie drained her drink. "Seems like this'll be an easy gig. Nothing to do but shine his shoes." Plus, if she got hired, they would let her keep her pay, John Anthony providing room and board so she'd have a nice pile at the end of it.

"Once you're in there, just keep your ears and eyes open. We'll meet as usual each week, in between if there's something you think I need to know." He sliced into the crust, breaking off a piece.

"So you're pretty sure I'll get hired?"

He ate the rest of his crust, pressing the tines of his fork onto the flakes on his plate. "I think after Isabelle and I have a little chat, you'll be golden."

"You don't look very happy about that."

"No, no, we want you in there. It's just the thought of Isabelle not getting everything she deserves." He folded his napkin, placed it on the table. "By the way, how am I listed in your phone?"

"You're still Linus. Though I was thinking of changing it to 'Dreads.' "

"What? Why?"

"Because that would be the opposite of you."

He raked a hand through his short hair. "Everyone seems a little obsessed with my haircut." He studied her for a second. "Just keep it as Linus."

Ronnie nodded at him. "I put a few other made-up people in there so you wouldn't be the only one. Like I really have friends."

# Chapter Two

This case… Frank stirred his coffee, put the spoon down, glanced at the door through which Ronnie had just left. Even though she'd said no one was following her, he'd ordered the coffee to give himself something to do so they wouldn't be seen leaving together. But he didn't really want it.

She was the most unusual CI he'd ever run. Formerly homeless, yet clean, a petty thief, but as honest as could be. Plus, all the time she'd spent helping him look for his daughter. Maybe not by the book, getting that close to her, but she worked hard, and he could count on her. He picked up his phone just as it rang. His partner, Pete.

"Hey."

"Frank. I got them to put her in the SHU until you can talk to her."

"Solitary? Good."

"Yep. She's not going to like it."

Frank examined his coffee cup. When had he finished that? "Maybe she'll be so happy to get out of it to meet with me that she'll do as I ask. Without a 5K motion."

The waiter dropped the check, and Frank headed to the door to pay.

"We just got word that Mateo is due in end of next week. Thought you'd wanna know."

"Damn. We need to get our friend in there fast." Frank ended the call, paid, then angled past the customers waiting at the door and hit the street. He squinted, the spring sun bright after the dark of the restaurant. The reek from the trash bins and piles of garbage bags waiting on the sidewalk for pickup hit him as he approached, receded as he went past. Mateo didn't seem to have a regular schedule for visiting John, so they really needed Ronnie to get hired pronto.

Frank sidestepped a woman who had stopped for her dog to pee on a Bluebike, the reek of urine already in the air. Other than a close relationship with Mateo Rosas de Flores, they didn't have much on John Anthony. Oh, they'd done the background research, of course, tracing his rise through the Trust Bank. His start as a stockbroker, eventually put in charge of an entire sub-dept that everyone unofficially called Department Mateo. Then John quit his job, set up an office in his penthouse, and donated to the Isabelle Anderson Foundation where he became known to the FBI. Since Isabelle had been his case, it seemed natural he would take on this one. He needed to talk to the AUSA, hurry up the 5K.

He reached for his Bureau phone just as his personal one buzzed, the caller ID unavailable. "Jankowski." Frank walked, careful, unlike most people, to be aware of obstacles on the sidewalk, not so absorbed by the phone that he ran into lampposts or pedestrians.

"You the guy looking for his daughter?"

Frank stopped walking. A rushing in his ears, an automatic assessment of his surroundings, a wall to lean against as he switched his phone to the other ear. "That's me. Have you seen her? Is she—I mean, have you—"

"I might know her." The man's voice was deep, smooth. Someone adept at selling, talking people into things. "Depends."

Frank's impulse was to pull out all the stops, declare he was an agent, demand the guy stop dicking around and tell him where his daughter was. He inhaled, long and slow, then let it out even slower. He stared out at the street without really seeing it. He decided that Ronnie would be better at this and channeled her for a minute.

"Dude," the word awkward in Frank's mouth, "what're you looking for?"

"A guy's gotta make a living, man."

Asshole. "Where can we meet?"

The guy gave him a street corner not too far away on the Lower East Side. Ask for Leo. "And don't be late or I won't be here."

He must be one of the dealers at Seward Park he'd given the flyer to. Frank launched himself off the wall and headed south, calculating the time it would take against the time the guy gave him for the meeting. He might be ten minutes early, and that would be fine with him. "I'll be there." He tapped "end," moved between the parked cars, and held an arm up for a taxi, hoped it would buy him even more time and not get him stuck in traffic on the way. He mentally palpated his pockets. He'd have to hit an ATM once he got down there.

* * *

At the corner across the street from where Leo wanted to meet, Frank surveyed the area. The low buildings down here allowed more sunlight to hit the streets, fewer shadows to move in. A tall, skinny, white guy with a Rasta cap seemed to own that corner, kids, bums, approaching him, the telltale palming masquerading as a handshake, eyes scanning the street, the exchange of drugs and money. As if the guy personally knew everyone who passed him by and had to shake their hand. A cruiser slowed as it came down the street, and the dealer nodded to them. This had to be Leo. Frank examined everyone around him, pinpointing the females for signs of his daughter. *The streets change you,* Ronnie had said, but surely he'd know Cathy anywhere, that bounce, that confidence, the smile—

He just had time to hit the ATM around the corner and then meet the guy. A line at the ATM, of course there was a line. He checked his watch. Would Leo really leave if he weren't there on time? Did the guy consider late five minutes, ten minutes? Damn, hurry up, line. All these months and months, each day he had searched for her, his third job when he was undercover, every night he could, now—a lead, finally a lead.

He stuffed the wad of twenty-dollar bills in his front pocket, hoped it would be enough because he'd hit the limit—on his checking account and on what he was allowed to take out. As he waited at the corner for the light to change, he watched the guy, the little silvery bags he handed out in the right pocket, the cash going into the back pocket of his jeans. Frank found he was breathing hard through his nose, so he opened his mouth, forced his brain to put the criminal activity in a different mental box. Today was personal, and today he was going to get one step closer to finding his daughter, bringing her home, back into a family that loved her and could care for her. She could return to school, finish up, forget this past year, forget—the people next him began to move and he did too, aware of the cars, always making sure nobody was running the light the way that car had, the accident that started this whole thing with Cathy.

He paused to let the dealer finish his transaction and then approached him, the guy analyzing him, then tensing, as if trying to weigh threat against possible sale.

"You Leo?"

"Who's asking?" The guy waved a customer aside.

"I'm Frank Jankowski, you called me about my daughter."

"I don't know about any daughters. Why don't you go on about your business, and I'll go on about mine." Leo, if this was Leo, stared hard at him as if his eyes could push him away.

Frank took a step toward him. "Listen, you called me. You said you might know my daughter, and to meet you here at—" Frank looked at his watch" —exactly 2:30. Which it is. And here I am, on time."

"This is some kind of trick. You think you can pretend you have a lost daughter and then arrest me? I'm not falling for it. And I'm not paying no cops no more money. Go away." Leo turned his back on Frank, beckoned to a ragged teenager loitering near a bench.

"Leo, look, I'm not a cop." Technically, he wasn't. "I'm just a father looking for his daughter." He put a hand on the dealer's shoulder. "Please—"

Leo spun around and caught Frank's wrist. For such a skinny guy, he had a pretty powerful grip. "You don't get to touch me. Cop, no cop. Father, no father. I don't care. If you're not a cop, why are you armed?" He eyeballed Frank's jacket. "And why do you have that cop haircut?"

Frank retrieved his wrist, let out a long breath, stepped closer. "Look," he spoke quietly into the space between them. "If I was going to arrest you, you'd already be on the ground in cuffs. I'm FBI, and I leave these crimes to the locals. Right now I'm just looking for my daughter, and you said you might know her."

Leo took a step away from him. "You're bad for business." He scanned him up and down, eyes narrowed. He seemed to come to a decision. "That Starbucks down there?" Leo gestured with his chin, then looked at Frank as if afraid he was such an idiot he might not understand. Frank nodded. "Go order something and sit at the counter facing the window. I'll be there in a minute."

Gauging the odds and making himself a bet as to whether the guy would show up at all, Frank walked away without looking back. He scrapped that bet as he walked around a homeless guy taking up most of the sidewalk, his grocery cart full of bags tied up, a smelly wool blanket half falling off the top. He bet himself instead how long he would have to wait for Leo, settling on seven and a half minutes, hitting the timer on his watch. Like it mattered. All that mattered was that the guy had seen Cathy.

* * *

Frank took his order to the window, brushed the crumbs off the counter facing the sidewalk. He chose a seat with the fewest tables behind him and watched the door in his peripheral vision. He entertained himself by folding each twenty into a little square and then putting them in his jacket pocket. After eleven minutes, forty-three seconds, someone sat down on the stool next to him, and Frank sized him up. Pale skin revealed all manner of freckles, acne, scarring. Frank prayed he didn't dip into his own stash, hoped he would be lucid and sane. Leo split open a wax paper bag to serve as a plate for a pastry, stale no doubt, this time of day. He pried the lid off his paper cup of coffee and took a sip, then took a bite of the pastry, put it down, stared out the window.

Frank put his phone to his ear. "Have you seen my daughter?" Without looking at Leo, he spoke to his phone as if on a call.

"I might have."

The guy was not going to make this easy. While waiting for him to speak,

Frank pulled three little squares of money out of his pocket, put them on the counter between them.

Leo didn't make a move. Frank put two more out.

"There's someone who comes by sometimes." Leo rested his forearm on the money. "She might be 16, long dark hair. Her eyes looked like the ones in that picture. But Bro," Leo sipped his coffee, a slurp as if he didn't care who heard him, "in that picture, she looks about twelve."

Frank sat up straighter, the phone still to his ear. "When does she come by? I need to see her. She needs to come home. Get cl—" He stopped because he could hear Ronnie saying that the dealer wouldn't want to lose a customer. "I could give her money. Whatever she needs." He cut his eyes to Leo, who stuffed the rest of the pastry in his mouth, flakes from it all over the counter in front of him. No small squares of twenties, though. He hadn't even seen him pocket them. Leo didn't say anything, just stared out the window. Frank put another twenty down. No response. Two more. Click. click. No response. A hundred dollars seemed to be his price, so he put another two down.

Leo cleared his throat. "I can't say for sure if I'll even see her again."

Frank put another five twenties on the counter between them. He almost didn't see them disappear.

"I might get a message to her the next time she shows up. She's not on any schedule." He set his paper cup down. "Not like I make appointments, Bro." He spun away from Frank as if to leave.

"Wait." Frank cleared his throat so his voice wouldn't break again. "Tell her—" So many things. They loved her. They wanted her home, no questions asked. They've missed her. They've always loved her and always would. They would help her, things would be different, she'd see. She could stay with Frank if she wanted, he wouldn't be hard on her, he would just be happy that—

Leo had made a move toward the door, and Frank put a hand out. Leo looked at it, and Frank showed him his last five twenties. "Tell her I'll give her all the money she needs. I'd like to know she's okay. She can call me, any time. Please." Frank put the money on the counter, and Leo returned as if to clean up his mess. His hand shot out, and the money vanished. This guy was in the wrong line of work. He should've been a magician.

"I'll call you if she says anything."

Frank stood up, his nearly empty cup tipping, the black coffee sliding its way toward Leo's crumbs. "How will I know it's her? I have to give the money directly to her. So I know it's her. Cathy."

Leo shrugged one shoulder. "I'll text you what she says," he said. "When or if I see her." He went out the door, left Frank to stare at the detritus of their meeting, a small earthquake of paper cups, lids, wax paper, crumbs.

* * *

Two days later, the AUSA gave the go-ahead for the 5K motion, and two days after that, Frank met with Isabelle, newly released from the SHU. Her time in jail had not been kind.

"She still tried to flirt, though."

Pete gave him a quick grin.

"As if she were in any position to try one on." Frank sipped his coffee, stared out the office window. Their coveted cubicles gave them sunlight and a view, twenty-three floors up.

"How'd she like the possibility of a reduced sentence?" Pete returned to his keyboard.

"She willfully misunderstood at first, trying to tell me I was letting her out. Because of course she was innocent."

"They're all innocent." Pete hit a final tap and swiveled to face Frank. "Have you told Ronnie?"

He nodded. "And I gave them the go-ahead for John Anthony to visit. I just hope he does it soon." Frank threw his cup in the trash, perched on the heat register that blocked half the window. "I'll let her know once he visits." He jutted his chin at Pete's computer. "So tell me about this other case."

"I've been looking into it, the way the guy uses Facebook to—"

Frank's Bureau phone buzzed, and he pulled it out. "Speak of the devil." He poked his screen. "Ronnie. Good to hear from you." He eyebrowed a question at Pete.

Pete shrugged, put a hand to his ear like he wanted to hear, too.

Frank put her on speaker.

"—so he called with the offer. I'm moving in, start the day after. Took him long enough."

"But he hasn't had enough time to talk with Isabelle."

"Yeah, I know, isn't that great? You don't have to do your marathon run thing. He said it was taking too long to get in to see her. Said since I worked for Isabelle all that time, it meant she trusted me. So he would too."

Frank let out a long breath. Exchanged looks with Pete. "That's great."

"You don't sound happy. I thought you'd be happier about this. Isn't it what you wanted?"

"Ronnie, this is Pete. We're both very happy you got in there. Congratulations." He gave Frank a poke.

"Yeah, really, congratulations. You did good." He told her Mateo was expected at the end of next week, and they would meet before and after, a prebrief and a debrief. "Glad you got the job. Talk soon." He ended the call.

Goddammit. He might never ask for a 5K motion again.

# Chapter Three

Ronnie was elbow-deep in polishing John Anthony's shoes that didn't need polishing. The shoe trees lined the table waiting for their brogues in a nice rhythm, though why they said John Lobb instead of John Anthony was beyond her. Maybe they were hand-me-downs.

The house phone buzzed. The doorman.

"Patrick. Bro. What's the word?"

"No word. Just a lot of shopping bags down here."

"No shit? Why tell me?"

"I am running out of room, man. And they keep coming."

Ronnie took several pairs of shoes and headed up the servants' stairs that let her out behind panels onto each floor. After depositing the shoes in J.A.'s closet, she hit the second floor and stuck her head in Lisa's office.

"Patrick just called," Ronnie told her. "A lot of shopping bags are piling up down there. He's out of room."

Lisa snapped her head away from her computer, her eyes wide.

"I'm just going down to grab them."

Lisa shot out from behind her desk, her long skirt fluffing around her. She made a bunch of moves that made Ronnie think of a chicken, darting here and there with no real purpose or result.

"It's okay." Ronnie backed out of the tiny office. "I'm on it."

"Oh God. I had no idea she was coming today."

"Who?"

"Mrs. Anthony," Lisa practically yelled. "She always lets us know when she's coming. Damn, damn."

"How do you know she's—"

"She comes to the city, she shops, she sends all the bags ahead of her. Then—" Lisa's face paled, her eyes looked pained, then scared. "Oh no." She raced past Ronnie, her "no, no, no, no," louder and faster until she moaned one long "nooooooooo" as she turned the corner to John's office.

On Ronnie's fourth trip retrieving the shopping, she heard Patrick say, "Good afternoon, ma'am." Behind his desk, Ronnie took up fistfuls of handles, brightly colored tissue paper rustling. Better not be anything more delivered this was plenty thank you very much. She straightened up in time to see a broad-shouldered woman with large sunglasses breeze past Patrick, heading straight for the elevator. She seemed to study her reflection in the brass surroundings, adjusting a few things on herself before the doors.

Patrick nodded at the now-closed elevator doors. "Mrs. Anthony."

"I guess I have to take the service elevator now." She headed to a hidden door next to the elevator. "If anything else shows up," she said over her shoulder, "just throw the bags in the dumpster." His laughter followed her as the door shut behind her, the passage to the back of the building so narrow she had to trail the bags behind her, a little train of expensive toys bumping her legs.

Ronnie took the service elevator straight to the top, the master bedroom and huge bath taking up most of the floor, a terrace surrounding it on three sides. She stowed the bags in Mrs. Anthony's closet, a space far bigger than her own room downstairs.

Halfway down the main staircase, Ronnie realized her mistake. She should be invisible, and who knows where the wife lurked right now. Ronnie made her quiet way to the panel which hid the servants' stairs, Lisa's voice loud in John Anthony's office, the door not closed all the way. *Cancel it.* A snake hiss, venomous and insistent. John's answering voice sounded almost whiny and Lisa spoke louder. *Mateo never comes when* she's *here.*

She paused. This could be useful to Frank. Lisa's voice was lower, so it was hard to make out. Sounded like *nicer...not here*. John's voice lost the whine. "She has every right to be here."

Ronnie couldn't risk listening to more. So, the famous Mateo was coming.

Sending Lisa into a little panic storm. And the Personal Assistant likes it better when the wife isn't around. She pushed on the wall, popping open the narrow door, headed past the other staff bedroom for the stairs.

She made it to the kitchen in time to pick up the buzzing house phone, Patrick telling her there were more bags. "Bro," she said to him, "I told you what to do with them." He laughed, called her "bad" and hung up.

* * *

In the elevator the bags at her feet glowed in party colors, and Ronnie moved aside some bright red tissue paper to see one small box, about as big as a bar of soap, taking up a tiny fraction of the space in the bag. Whatever floats your boat.

She stowed the hopefully last of the bags in the closet, prayed the wife didn't want her to unpack them all. Maybe there were still some leftovers she could have for lunch, that pasta stuff—Barbara Anthony stood in the middle of the bedroom, staring at her. Not quite unfriendly, but not smiling either.

"And you are..."

Ronnie recovered and gave a slight bow.

"Ronnie, ma'am."

The tall, strong-looking woman studied her for a long minute and then said, "The new butler."

"Yes'm. I was just putting your shopping away. I'm sorry, I didn't think you'd be in here." Ronnie edged towards the door, but Mrs. J.A. blocked it, practically taking up the whole space. "I'll just be getting out of your way." Always make it your fault.

"You may call me Barbara. I don't believe in any of this 'ma'am' stuff. Come over here and talk to me a minute." She headed to the windows where two low armchairs stood guard, a small round table between them. "Here, sit, sit. You can take a rest from your duties, can't you?"

Ronnie figured that the wife must be the boss as much as the husband, and she'd better do what she said.

"You're so much younger than our last butler. How did they find you?"

"I just answered the ad. I guess they liked me." Ronnie perched on the edge of the chair.

Barbara crossed her legs, a shishing of nylons and skirt. "And your previous job? Why did you leave it?"

Maybe she didn't trust her husband's interviewing techniques. "It left me, you might say."

"Really." A statement. An eyebrowed question.

"Um, well, do you know who Isabelle Anderson is?"

"Rings a bell, but I'm not—is she famous? Oh wait. The society hostess who was arrested for fraud? You worked for her?" Barbara uncrossed her legs and leaned forward, her face lit up, like something delicious was coming her way. "What was that like?"

Maybe the woman was just in it for the gossip. Ronnie stood up, gave a slight bow. She was starving. "I should be getting back to work. But I'm glad to meet you. Please let me know if there is anything I can do for you."

Barbara Anthony's eyes widened, both eyebrows went up. As if no one had ever said "no" to her. As if she might stamp her foot and start yelling, her face scrunching up, a sour, spoiled look.

"Mrs. Anthony," Ronnie softened her voice, "I'm sorry. But I never talk about the people I work for. Discretion is the better—"

"Yes, yes," Barbara waved a dismissive hand at her, "better part of valor. I get it."

"Well, I was going to say 'valet.'" She pronounced it so that it rhymed with "wallet." "Better part of valet." Thank you, Downton Abbey.

Barbara's head snapped up as if Ronnie had been impolite. But then the woman laughed, a great big belly laugh, her eyes crinkling and her mouth thrown open, the grey and gold of cavities and crowns begging for Ronnie to count them.

"Oh, you are a dark horse. Surely my husband doesn't need you at this very moment. Please sit a bit with me. Now I really want to know all about you."

The last thing Ronnie wanted to do was tell this woman all about herself.

It wasn't a good idea to let the lies pile up, but if she sidestepped, this woman would probably chase her down. And no way she could tell her the truth. She never told anyone about how she grew up. "There isn't much to tell. Grew up in Garden City, the job with Mrs. Anderson the first one I had." Ronnie stayed standing to emphasize their professional relationship. And make a quick getaway.

"And have you always wanted to be a butler?

Ronnie gave a shrug. "It's a good job. I like the work."

"Brothers and sisters?" At Ronnie's nod, Barbara had so many questions she interrupted herself: how old were they, where were they now, what were they doing, parents, how often did she see them—

It was rude to interrupt, but Ronnie had to stop all these questions. "We weren't what you would call a very close family. What about you?"

"Me? Oh, well. Me." Barbara studied Ronnie's face, hair, as if assessing—what? Maybe trust. Ronnie put on her interested expression. Maybe Barbara would focus on herself instead.

Mrs. Anthony settled against the chair, smoothed her hands down her skirt, her large knees peeping out. "I grew up in Minnesota, Edina, you know," she paused to see Ronnie's reaction, got an encouraging smile, and went on. "College in the East, job in New York. The Big City, if you can make it here and all that." She swiveled in her seat to face Ronnie. "Boy, was I naïve back then." She let out a sigh, memories practically visible in the air over her head. "But," she got up and went into her closet, the sound of rustling tissue paper and bags wafting out. "I did meet John." She came out with a pale green blouse in her hand. "And the rest is history." She held the blouse out to Ronnie, who peered at it, glad their little get-together seemed to be over. Glad she could go eat. "Could you get this cleaned? I want to wear it tonight, and I never wear anything straight from the store. Have you seen the factories where they make clothing? And they just throw the finished garment on the floor. Disgusting."

Ronnie took the blouse and headed for the door. The color was hideous and it felt like silk, a bitch to iron, so she'd have to take it to the two-hour dry cleaners. Which meant she'd have to go right away, maybe she could grab a protein bar or something from the pantry, and now she wouldn't get to the silver this afternoon, which Lisa would probably be mean about, so she'd have to—

"I'm glad we could have this chat." Barbara rattled some tissue paper.

"Ma'am."

Barbara paused next to her, her hands full of little boxes. "You're so much nicer than that Lisa person," she whispered, a nod toward the door as if Lisa hovered on the other side of it. "I think we'll get along just super."

* * *

With Barbara safely in her room, Ronnie figured she could risk the main staircase, but as she came out on the landing, she heard a hiss, sort of a "psssft," a sound you'd make if you were scaring off a cat. Lisa's office door stood open, and for a quick second Ronnie considered pretending she hadn't heard. But she figured Lisa was on edge and the last thing Ronnie needed was a pissed off Lisa Cranberry.

"Close the door." Lisa's whisper was fierce, her look caged. "What did she want?"

Ronnie gestured at her with the ugly green blouse, grabbed the doorknob. "She wants this cleaned. I have to go."

"What is she doing here? She always lets us know." Her eyes went over Ronnie like the answers were hidden somewhere on her. "What did she say to you?"

"She asked me to take this to the cleaners so she can wear it tonight."

"Tonight? Oh, no. Nothing's on the calendar." Lisa tapped on her keyboard, eyes darting up at the screen. "And John—"

Ronnie threw a second "I gotta go" over her shoulder and beat it out of there, took the narrow servant stairs two at a time, wondered if she should take the service stairs for the whole building all the way down to save time. How come these rich people had to have everything now or yesterday, no thought to the hoops you had to go through, or how hungry she was. Barbara Anthony had so many clothes she could wear something else, in fact, she should wear something else, this green would turn her skin yellow.

She burst out into the lobby, threw Patrick a look which he returned with a wise nod as she flew out the front door, turned left, found the traffic light, calculated the distance, and wondered why she wanted to work so hard for this woman she had just met. She could say the cleaners took too long, she could say this other blouse would look like heaven on you. She ran down to 77th. Her hands better not sweat all over the new blouse. She would have them deliver it. She didn't need to go through this marathon again.

As she walked back, she decided that maybe she had taken this errand so seriously, partly because something about Barbara Anthony made her feel a little sorry for her. She waited for the light to change, watched the traffic go by, the taxis, always taxis, a bicyclist with stacks of carryout on the rack over his back tire, a black car with the paint glistening in the afternoon sun, the darkened windows blocking the curious. She didn't know why she should feel sorry for her. Ronnie crossed Park. Barbara had everything, she had spent more on shopping today for things she probably didn't need than Ronnie got paid in half a year, she guessed. But there was something kind of sad and lonely about her, lost, even. The way her voice trailed off when she'd said "the rest is history" about her life with John. Like there was nothing more to tell, no more excitement. She headed uptown, spotted the dark green awning, Patrick out on the sidewalk enjoying the sun like so many other doormen down Park Avenue. Well, she'd report back on Barbara Anthony, but she spent so little time at the penthouse, she probably wasn't worth Frank taking a second look. In fact, the way Lisa whisper-yelled at her employer to cancel whatever it was, it seemed like the two of them worked hard at keeping Barbara out of his business. Maybe that's why she seemed so lonely.

# Chapter Four

"I thought you said Mateo was visiting." Ronnie sat next to Frank on the bench around the John Lennon memorial. "I mean, great getting the time to figure out my job, but—"

"He did visit." His eyes traced the mosaic pattern in the circle, followed the black and white tiles to the center where they spelled out "Imagine." Roses of all colors, still in their cellophane sleeves, encircled the space.

Ronnie shook her head. "Not at the penthouse."

"What happened?"

Ronnie's backpack nestled on her lap, and she hugged it to her. "Well, Barbara Anthony showed up and Lisa got upset because she hadn't told them she was coming, and she ran off to J.A.'s office, and I heard her yelling in a whisper that he should cancel."

"Interesting. They met at his hotel. Too bad. We were hoping to finally find out what they talk about."

Ronnie slid down on the bench, her chin buried in her backpack. "Even if he'd come to the penthouse, I don't think I'd be allowed to listen." She scuffed one black running shoe on the ground. "What if I can't..." She spoke so low the rest of her sentence evaded Frank.

A few tourists came up, a few left, someone sat down on the bench across from them, and unlocked a guitar case. "Not quite sure what you're afraid you can't do. But we wouldn't have put you in there if we didn't think you could do it." The guitarist strummed, twisted knobs, strummed again. "We've been trying for a long time to get someone into that Penthouse, and you're the first one to succeed. You're perfect for this job." The musician looked a little scruffy, a little dirty, the guitar case open in front of her. What if she knew Cathy?

Ronnie sat up straighter. "It's just that Lisa guards John Anthony like you wouldn't believe. I can barely say hello to him without her zooming in, talking over me."

"Well, let's run through your day. Maybe we'll come up with a way to circumvent Lisa Cranberry."

Ronnie blew out her breath, fluttering the bangs on her forehead. She listed the things that happened on a typical day, but nothing jumped out at him.

"You said he likes you, right? Even with Lisa's gatekeeping, I'm sure you'll find a way to talk to him." A group of tourists waded through the bouquets to stand on "Imagine." He had miscalculated the time he and Ronnie would have before a bus offloaded them for the typical stop. He ducked his head. "Time to move. Don't act like you're with me for a few strides." Frank turned his head away from the camera on the extension pole, headed south down the path, didn't look back. He lengthened his stride, and soon the path narrowed, the trees meeting overhead, the air noticeably cooler. He slowed. No one anywhere nearby.

"What happened?" Ronnie breathed hard next to him.

"Never mind. Tourists came early." Frank strode in silence. Had he missed an opportunity to ask the girl with the guitar? He cleared his throat. "So, is it part of your duties to clean in their offices?"

"No way. They lock the doors when they're not in them. I don't know what they do about dust and trash. There's a shredder. Sometimes one of them asks me to empty it. But they're always there when I do."

"What does that look like?"

"Confetti. Want me to bring it to you? You could have a parade."

Frank grunted. Pulling teeth. He gestured to a bench up ahead, the path still empty.

"As butler, don't you manage household expenses, hand out pay checks?"

"I think Lisa does all that stuff. She puts money in sealed envelopes for the household staff." Ronnie wriggled on the bench, settled her backpack on her lap again.

"So, each week Lisa gives you an envelope with your check..."

"Cash. That's how we get paid."

"Wait. Stop. Don't tell me." He glanced up and down the path, but he already knew it was empty. "I got the okay for you to keep what you earn, but really, I can't know the details." He wished he didn't know this much. Normally, after the arrest, it would be considered proceeds from criminal activity, but he'd gotten an exception, arguing that her information would be invaluable to them and cheaper for John Anthony to pay her than for the FBI. And it would be more believable to the suspect for Ronnie to act like this was a real job. But the less he knew about how they paid her, the better. Frank sat down on the bench nestled among the bushes, the air a little cooler with all the shade.

"Okay, fine. Whatever." Ronnie tilted her head back, looked straight up into the trees. Tightened her grip on her backpack.

Frank examined her. Probably kept everything in there. "So, I would advise that if, hypothetically, someone were amassing cash every week, that someone might want a lockbox or a good safe to store it in. Hypothetically speaking." He cleared his throat. "So. Back to the household routine. The chef, he goes home after the dinner is served, and you said he doesn't clean up?"

"Yeah," Ronnie stretched her legs out in front of her, twitched her feet as if to music. "But if a party or something runs late, he sometimes stays in the extra room, up the stairs from mine."

"Okay, not much there probably." He zipped his light jacket up. "Monday offer to dust their offices for them. Let me know what you find." Too bad Frank couldn't cook. Then he could replace Kerry, he'd be in the field, whisking sauces and wearing a white apron...

They sat in silence for a minute or two, three teenagers coming down the path, loud, shutting out the world and demanding it pay attention to them at the same time.

"Her dealer called me last week."

Ronnie turned fully toward him, her face lighting up. "Really? That's great. Did you see him? What'd he say? Dude." She sat back, smiling as if she was the one who had arranged the meeting.

Frank described the encounter with Leo, how he had to pay for the information, but he was hopeful. "And I think I owe you one."

"Yeah you do." Ronnie smiled at the air in front of her. "But why do you think you do?"

"For the advice on how to handle these guys. He responded well when I said I could give her money. I even called him 'Dude,' thinking about how you would approach him."

"Dude."

They got off the bench in silent agreement and headed east, the path then veering north and along open fields. An intense three-way Frisbee toss erupted in shouts when an airborne dog intercepted the disc.

"But Frank." She blocked his path, tilted her head to look him in the eye. "Listen. I mean, I need this job, I need to do something for you, you keep telling me. But there's nothing going on inside the penthouse, and you've got people watching anyway. Do you really need me?"

He studied her. What was this all about?

"But if you don't need me, then what happens to me? Out on the streets again?"

He nodded his head to a bench overlooking The Lake. Away from the shore, a squad of ducks followed a rowboat, the child in the boat tearing off bits of a sandwich to keep them coming. "Ronnie, look, we'll always be able to use you somewhere. But trust me, John Anthony launders money for the Mataderos Cartel, and we need you in there, getting the information so we can build the case against them. We've been watching him and Mateo all along, and that's not going to stop. That team complements what you're doing, and they're a safety measure, in case we need to rush in there."

"You'll never have to rush. Nothing dangerous is going on. The biggest thing I had to do was run a brand new blouse over to the two-hour dry cleaners."

"Even so. We're still around, and you should know that. Remember the escape code?"

She recited it like a robot: "*Oops. Gotta go exclamation point TTYL* Which is dumb because what if it's the first message I send?"

"At that point it's not going to matter, is it. But now that I think about it, it is a little long. What if you send something quick, like a smiley face?"

She rolled her eyes at him. A year ago, she didn't have a smartphone, and now she was the expert and he the Neanderthal.

"How 'bout an angry emoji, like the steam blowing off the top of my head? I'll never use that one accidentally."

"I'll be sure to log that. Now, tell me about Barbara Anthony."

They continued their walk around The Lake, along East Park Drive, heading uptown, Frank glad to listen, glad Ronnie had relaxed again.

"So she's your new best friend, huh? Why do you think these older women like you so much?"

"She's nothing like Isabelle, and Lisa Cranberry doesn't seem to like anyone."

"But Lisa's closer to your age."

"Yeah, but she acts like an old lady, all those long skirts and blouses all buttoned up to the very top."

"Is she in on it?"

"I'm not sure how much she knows, though the way she flew into John's office when she found out Barbara was coming, she's gotta know there's something to hide. Plus she puts the cash in all the envelopes on pay day."

"Please don't tell me any more than that. I'll note it for her probable knowledge and/or participation, but as far as you're concerned..."

Ronnie gestured zipping her lips together. She gave him a look, then unzipped. "You never answered me about what happens when this job is over."

Damn. Of course she wouldn't forget that part. "Look, Ronnie, I can't predict what will happen—I didn't know we could use you on this job until the last minute, remember? But I do know that the Bureau considers you an important—a very important asset. I'll always fight for you—I got them to agree to let you keep your salary after we take John Anthony down—and I'll do everything within my power to ensure you can continue working for us, and we'll continue to take care of you." They waited at the crosswalk for a break in the runners and bicyclists who had the whole road to themselves. "And the Bureau will put you up in that room between jobs."

"What a luxury."

* * *

They parted ways while they were still in the Park, Ronnie heading east, her backpack bouncing as she strode. He went south toward his apartment to work on all the little chores that kept his life running smoothly. Though maybe he should grab a bunch of flyers and keep at his search for Cathy. Vacuuming was never more important than his daughter. It always hit him in the gut, every single time, thinking about his sweet-faced daughter, what she was doing after she ran away from rehab…if only he could find her. She was only sixteen—he almost forgot. Her birthday was next month.

He stopped along the wall as he came out of the Park, pulled out his phone, hit the picture of his ex-wife.

"Frank, what's up?" Susan sounded rushed, a little breathless, but she'd answered in the middle of the second ring, so maybe not too busy.

"No news, sorry."

He could hear her let out her breath, imagined her cradling the phone to her ear, going back to whatever she had been doing before he interrupted. He heard a faucet turn on.

"Frank? You there?"

"Yeah." He let out a breath. "I'm here. It's just that—I just—"

"I know. Next month. She'll be seventeen."

They sat in silence for a beat or two, Frank examining the cobbled sidewalk, the moss growing between the stones, a pigeon walking toward a piece of food, others coming up to see what he had found.

"I look over every teenager I see come into Benedict House." Susan sounded far away. "Wondering if it's Cathy, wondering if they know her, wanting to grab them by the shoulders, beg them—"

"I know exactly what you mean. I got a call—"

"What?" The sound of running water stopped. "A call? From whom? When were you going to tell me?"

"I'm telling you now. It's a long shot." He paused for the whoosh and squeal of a bus stopping and then told her about Leo, how he said he'd let him know.

"Do you want me to—could I—I'd like to come with you the next time. When he calls you. Or texts. Whatever."

"If he even calls. As I said, it's a long shot. But I did tell him I'd like to give Cathy money, y'know, so he has an incentive to let us know."

He listened to Susan's end, the faucet noise replaced by dishes clattering. Probably their wedding china, picked out by Susan, given by her relatives, left by him when he moved out. He couldn't even conjure up the pattern on it now.

"Well, thanks for telling me. Hang in there, Frank. And let me know, okay?"

"I'll let you know." Though he couldn't picture her at a rendezvous with a drug dealer, the two of them walking up like it was Back to School night.

He pushed off from the wall and continued heading south, needing the motion to get all this stuff out of his brain so he didn't stop the next mom-type person and yell at them to appreciate their children, that they should be glad the only problem they had was making sure the dog didn't eat their orthodontic retainers.

* * *

The next day, as if telling Susan about Leo conjured him, he got a text.

*tonight*

Nothing if not terse. Frank texted back with an emoji of a clock and got a *10* in response. Must be very hectic, the drug trade, keeping Leo from making a phone call or clicking out full sentences.

Frank returned the phone to his pocket, but it buzzed again.

*Wear a hoodie dark*

Frank sent him a question mark, turned back to his computer, to the 302s, the endless paperwork the Bureau required. Maybe civilian jobs didn't have this much ass-covering. He surveyed the room, all the cubicles, the fluorescent lights, one flickering, the bulletin board with official notices over the coffee maker. He would hate a civilian job even if there was no paperwork involved, and he swiveled to the screen again. Nothing could possibly be more important work than catching criminals.

*Blend in better*

He might have one that didn't say "FBI" on it.

* * *

At 9:15 that night, after he put his shoulder holster on, took it off, put it on again, Frank left for Seward Park and a meeting with Leo, which he tried not to make too much of. But, of course he would hang a lot on this meeting. He hit the street and headed to the subway. Leo wouldn't request—demand—a meeting if it didn't have to do with Cathy. She had finally shown up. He would finally see her. She could come home, their family back together, she could return to school, come to his place on the weekends...

Though there were plenty of places to sit on the subway this time of night, he held on to the pole, his back to the door, the entire car within his vision with barely a move of his head, no one behind him. He tried to pretend to himself he didn't know how long she'd been missing, but he did know, and 257 was way too many days. Soon he could stop counting, soon they could have lunch at their favorite diner again, talk about how school was going. Her brain was so sharp, and he loved nothing better than to watch it at work as she explained key elements from her history class. They would be in a booth, Cathy sipping a milkshake and giving a dissertation on the French Revolution. He loved being a father.

Frank walked through the park, better to approach Leo from behind, scope out the situation before he got in the middle of it. He was right not to tell Susan about the meeting, it was too late, too dangerous, and it might scare Leo if two people showed up instead of one. He paused to watch the dealer, to watch the exchanges of drugs for money. So many customers, some he swore at and chased away, a gun on his hip if Frank read the bulge in his hoodie correctly. Others approached, the exchange quick, no words, Leo looking away as if the customer hadn't registered or wasn't worth a glance. No sign of Cathy, few female customers even. When Leo took a look at the watch on his wrist, the face of it glinting from the streetlight, Frank decided it must be time to say hello. "Bro."

Leo didn't even flinch when Frank appeared behind him. He gave him a glance over his shoulder. "Even in a hoodie, you look like a cop. Why don't you put the hood up?"

"Never mind that. Is she here? Where—can I see her?"

Leo scanned the street, up one way, down the other. He didn't look at Frank. "Easy, man."

"Isn't that why you called me? Look, *man*, you—"

Leo let out a long breath. "It's getting busy, kind of a bad time."

"And?"

"I can't leave this corner."

"Why did you call me?" Frank grasped his shoulder, shook it. "Tell me where she is."

Leo looked down at Frank's hand until he let go. "She only trusts me, man. That's the way it is."

Another customer approached, and Frank stepped back. His stomach tensed, so he expanded his chest with a breath, willed his muscles to let go on the exhale. A cruiser went by and Leo nodded at it, one short gesture of recognition, of reassurance.

Finally, Leo turned to Frank. "Okay. Come here. Stand in front of me." He looked Frank over as if assessing his strengths and weaknesses. The corner of his mouth pulled to the side a fraction, then he said, "Oh well." More to himself than to Frank. Quick like an animal lunging on its prey, his right hand shoved into the pocket of Frank's sweatshirt and out again. "Twenty dollars a bindle, no more, no less. No bindle without the money. No exceptions. I'll be right back." Leo melted into the dark recesses of the park, and Frank stood on the corner, his left pocket full of folded paper squares. "I know just how much, this time of night." Leo's voice, fierce, a whisper cutting through the air.

Frank faced the street, glancing around as if he'd just been beamed here, one minute a father looking for his daughter, the next minute expected to take over the corner, sell this shit that Leo put in his pocket. Well, he wasn't going to do it. He was a Law Enforcement Officer. Law and Order man. Felony possession. He clenched his jaw, his hand in his pocket counting, calculating.

"Where's Leo?"

The guy came out of nowhere, and Frank swore to himself, warned himself to be more alert.

"I don't know any Leo."

"Yes you do, I saw you talking to him." The man twitched, moved into Frank's space. Frank took a step away. The guy reeked.

"Why don't you keep walking."

"I know you got some. I got the money, right here. C'mon, man." He held out a crumpled bill in his dirty palm, the money so bedraggled the bank probably wouldn't take it. The guy shoved it closer to Frank's face, and Frank knocked his hand away, the pattern of dirt etching the guy's palm burned on his retina.

While the street guy bent over to look for his money, someone else came up, asked for Leo. Sweet Jesus, he couldn't let a crowd form. He looked over his shoulder for Leo, the trees and the grass of the park giving off a damp, gritty smell. More people approached, asking for Leo. Frank saw over one customer's shoulder the cruiser coming once more down the street. The last thing he needed was their attention.

"Okay, okay." He didn't mean to shout. "I'm Leo tonight." He took their money, gave them the drugs. "Here. Here. Here. Now go away. The cops are coming."

Frank pulled out his phone to look busy for the locals, turned a shoulder to the street as if to shut out the noise for his call. For God's sake, Leo better come back right now. He couldn't believe he had said that. *I'm Leo tonight.* Christ.

Without looking up, Frank clocked the cruiser slowing, passing, and his shoulders relaxed as the car kept going. Too awkward with the drugs in his left pocket, the palming all backwards. No one approached him, so he took a moment to shift the little squares to his right pocket, the folded and crumpled money to his left.

He was usually good at judging how much time had passed, but tonight that skill had left him. He was on edge, waiting for Leo to bring Cathy, and he didn't want to be taking care of Leo's customers who kept coming and coming, big, tall, short, mostly men, mostly white, all doing the same dance like it was choreographed.

Red and blue lights flashed, a quick whoooop of the siren, the two NYPDs walking straight toward him, the sidewalk suddenly empty except for him, his hood falling back, the air cool on his scalp.

"How's it going tonight, sir?" The cop on the left had his hand on the butt of his gun.

"I'm on duty and I'm armed." Straight out of his FBI training. He'd never had to use that phrase, and he wished he hadn't now. Because they immediately stood wide, drew their guns, and shouted "Hands up! Down on the ground!"

He gestured at them, palms down, an *easy now* bob of his hands. "We're on the same side. I'm FBI."

They kept shouting at him, so he got to his knees, held both hands up, but it obviously wasn't enough for them since the short fat one pushed him with a foot on his back, and once he was painfully on the ground, kept it there as if Frank might run. They yelled at him to put his hands behind him, then wrapped the Flexcuffs on him, tightening them until he felt the plastic bite his skin, cut off the blood supply. They pulled on them as if checking the fit, lifting his wrists up, his shoulders screaming.

"Officer, there's no need for this. I'm Special Agent Jankowski, FBI."

"I'm finding a gun, drugs, money, and no badge," growled the one who had gone through his pockets and patted him down. "Looks like a drug dealer to me."

"My ID is in my wallet."

"And my grandmother wears army boots."

Frank lifted his head to look for Leo, Cathy. The night air burned his cheek, and he knew he'd left some of his skin on the cement under his face. The foot was on his back again and pressing down, words of warning coming from one of the cops. He had to see Cathy. But she couldn't see him like this.

"My ID is in my wallet, take these off me. This is a mistake."

A blow to his side, another one coming as he turned his head, the little fat cop aiming for his ribs with his heavy black boot. A crunch, a sickening sound, and a sharp pain, an explosion of light behind his eyes. Why was it always the ribs? These guys were assholes and his brain smoked, what he would tell their superior, the dressing down, maybe suspension. He let everything go limp, as if playing dead would make the guy stop, as if he could move his lungs away from his ribs.

He wasn't on a case. He'd lied when he told them he was on duty. Rick, his boss, might or might not back him up, or he'd back him up to NYPD, and then he'd be in trouble, conduct unbecoming, the Integrity of Fidelity Bravery Integrity no longer part of his makeup. That, along with getting pulled—

They hauled him up by his arms, one on each side, leaning into him like they thought he'd bolt even with his hands behind his back. He felt his ribs on an intake of breath, and he thought about what he might do to the guy with the big foot. He was no longer so sure they were on the same side.

"Good evening, officers."

The cop, bending Frank's head down to shove him into the back seat, stopped, all three heads turning at the sound of the voice. Leo's voice.

"I think there's been a misunderstanding here. He's with me." Leo's voice was smooth, reasonable, in command.

"He claims he's FBI," said Fatty, not releasing his grip on Frank's arm.

"As I'd instructed him to."

The cops exchanged looks. It didn't make sense to Frank either, but if it got these handcuffs off him, he didn't care.

"He's got a gun," said the tall one. Once the cuffs were on, cops found it hard to give up their victim.

"So don't we all." Leo put a hand on Frank's shoulder, claiming him. "I know you have the snips in your car. Let's get these off him and see what else we have to discuss." The Bureau would find Leo useful as a hostage negotiator. The cops grumbled, probably to show themselves they were still in charge, but the cuffs were removed, Frank rubbing his puffy hands, his wrists, everything tingling as the blood came back into them. Leo gestured behind him with his head and Frank startled, took a step, looked a question at Leo, who didn't meet his eyes, just moved his head again, a silent *get going*.

He raced to the edge of the park. Maybe Cathy hid in the shadows by that bench, watching, eager to see him, his arms enveloping her, safe, with her family again…no one here. He looked around like he had missed something, saw Leo talking, laughing, clapping the fat cop on the shoulder. Watched him as he reached into his pocket in that practiced move, a closed hand coming out, probably all his money for the night going into the guy's pocket, a pat of the pant leg by Leo to underscore his present, their understanding.

"I knew you were a cop."

Frank looked up from where he perched on the bench, hoping not to bring on the knife stab from his ribs. "Where is she? Where's my daughter?"

Leo handed him his gun. Maybe Leo knew what an agent went through if he lost his gun, the repercussions worse, probably, than getting sprung from an NYPD jail cell. Leo sat down next to him but stayed alert, back straight, eyes scanning, scanning. "She bolted. You brought the lights and the siren, and she bolted like a little mouse."

Frank sprang up and made toward the park, wincing in pain, looking all around as if he could see her running even now.

Leo threw a laugh at him. "She's gone, man. Long gone."

Leo's eyes were on him as he returned to the bench, sat down, and tried not to breathe against his ribs. The drug dealer angled toward him, put his arm across the back of the bench behind Frank. His voice was deeper, quieter. "You cost me a lot tonight. I don't do favors, that's for suckers. But I figured she could use whatever money you gave her, and now I'm the one out the money."

Frank reached into his pocket and swore. "Those dirty cops kept everything."

Leo left the bench to make the exchange with someone. For such a skinny kid, he sure exuded authority. The way the cops responded to him, the way everyone knew he owned this part of the block. Frank sat up straighter, the sharp pain making him decide he should stand instead. Leo returned, Frank glad to note that he stood taller than the dealer, and he probably had about 40 pounds of muscle on him.

"Have you figured out how you're going to make me whole?"

"How is any of this my fault? You called me, they're your cops, and now I have no daughter and some broken ribs."

Leo regarded him, a once-over of his six-foot frame, a steady gaze into his eyes, no expression on his face. "That's how you want to play it." He shrugged and turned his back to Frank, a quick transaction, then he went to the street, stood between parked cars, looked down the street as if for a taxi. Not a taxi. A cruiser.

"Okay, okay," Frank called out as he headed toward Leo. "No need for that. I concede. You're holding all the cards tonight." Leo came away from the street, kept his profile toward Frank, but tilted his head as if to listen better. "There's an ATM around the corner, across the street." Frank spoke to the top of his Rasta cap. Leo didn't move, but Frank felt like an obedient school kid being encouraged by the teacher for getting the answer right. "It'll take just a minute or two. The limit is $500. That should be enough."

Leo shook his head like he was disappointed in his protégé, then straightened up, walked toward yet another customer. Leo stopped before reaching him, making the guy close the gap between them. Frank decided not to wait for him to finish the exchange. He wasn't going anywhere. He whipped across the street and around the corner, hit the ATM, withdrew the limit twice, the second time from his savings account. Dammit.

* * *

On the subway home, the night hit Frank without warning, and he fell into a seat next to a guy bopping his head in time to something on his headphones.

He was just tired, way past his bedtime. But his torso was on fire, each breath an icy pain, and, perversely, he was glad of it. Punishment, as it were, for the entire night. He hardly knew himself anymore. He thought he would be finally finding Cathy and he wound up nearly arrested. He began ranking each thing from bad to worse to horrifying and couldn't decide which belonged last: an FBI agent dealing drugs or the corrupt cops who hadn't arrested him. Or the drug dealer that rescued him. As for Cathy, he actually had hope now, especially since he told Leo to give her whatever was left over from what he thought Frank owed him. At least she could buy herself some food, and next time, next time, he would see her. He hoped, God, he hoped his ribs weren't healed by then, hugging her worth every bit of the pain that would sear into his memory.

# Chapter Five

"Mr. Anthony wants to see you." Lisa Cranberry's eyes flickered over Ronnie as if she had a dimension to her Lisa hadn't seen before. Or a tail. She narrowed her eyes at Ronnie. "Now. Go."

Ronnie pivoted in an about-face and went quickly down the hall, turning the corner, coming up against John's closed office door. The wood was dark, solid, the bottom of the panels full of dust. She ran a finger along an edge, sucked in her breath and knocked.

"It's open." The voice sounded annoyed, but Ronnie shrugged, turned the knob. She wasn't the one who had closed it.

His back was to her, and she paused in the doorway, watched as he searched through stacks of paper on the credenza behind his desk. His hands moved quickly, grabbing up papers, tossing them on the floor. He found what he was looking for and he swiveled around, scooted his chair up to his desk, a scowl turning down the corners of his mouth, his birthmark a dark pink.

"Yes?"

"Lisa said you wanted to see me?"

He put the stack of papers at the corner of his desk as if they might explode. He looked her up and down, eyes lingering on her shoes, running up to find her eyes.

"Okay. I guess that's okay." He cleared his throat. "I need you to run an errand for me." He watched her carefully, and Ronnie felt like a caged animal.

"Sir."

He scribbled on a piece of paper, handed it to her when he finished. "Memorize this. Then give me back the paper."

The Help Desk in the Port Authority, a *Finding Nemo* backpack left for her. Take it to the dry cleaners on 86th, leave the backpack, and get his three suits.

"And come see me when you're done." He continued appraising her, looking her face over, his birthmark back to a pale pink. She gave no reaction, which she didn't have to fake.

She handed the piece of paper back to him and paused while the paper shredder shrieked it into tiny bits. "No problem. What time am I expected?"

"Soon." He looked at the heavy gold watch on his wrist. "You have half an hour. I think you might have to run to the subway." He turned back to his computer and said to the screen, "In fact, you should run because he's going to leave it there and disappear. You don't want anyone getting to that backpack before you do."

No driver, then. Not springing for a cab, either. She mentally checked herself over. She'd grab her MetroCard and a twenty but leave her backpack. She didn't need to carry around two of them. She gave him a nod and left, hitting the stairs to her room. She'd have to run the few blocks to the station, but these shoes would survive that. She'd take the 6 train, change at Grand Central to the 7 across town, and pray she made it in time. She grabbed her card and cash and ran to the elevator, hit the button several times even though she knew that wouldn't help. Why couldn't whoever left the *Finding Nemo* backpack take it to the dry cleaners themselves. But, she shrugged at her reflection in the elevator doors, whatever J.A. wanted her to do, she did. She raked her fingers through her hair. She might have to get it cut soon.

* * *

She hit the doors of the Port Authority with about ten minutes to spare and glanced around. Two cops off to the side scanned the crowds, maybe the same ones Frank had given his daughter's picture to all those months ago. Glad Cathy's drug dealer called Frank. The big guy finally listened to her, talking to the dealer and not spending years searching the parks full of runaways and users.

She found one information booth with some dirty kids on the floor leaning against the front, their heads leaving grease spots on the poster under the window. Ronnie stood across from that kiosk, a broad walkway in between, and people passed in groups, or alone, or in pairs. The kids on the floor got up, new ones sitting down, the ones with stiff, clean backpacks hesitant, maybe asking directions, offering a cigarette, a dollar.

Whoa—a brightly colored kid's backpack leaned against the kiosk, on the other side of the kids. Like it sat there the whole time. She aimed for the backpack, and just like that a big group of people with suitcases streamed past between her and the kiosk, their luggage trailing behind them. She tried to go through them, make a beeline for the backpack, but these tourists were like a wall of rolling suitcases. Ronnie found a way around them, closed the space to the kiosk and—her shoes squeaked on the linoleum as she stopped suddenly, not seeing the backpack. Ohshitohshitohshit, where is it, she had just seen it, her heart pounding in her ears her vision narrowing, looking around, a flash of bright blue over by the exit, the orange fish in the center, a hammering of her leather butler shoes as she tore after it, the shaggy kid going through the door she had to get there before he hit the street, before he could escape into the crowds, down an alley. No way he was keeping the backpack.

She burst out the door, threaded her way onto the sidewalk. So many people, not only tourists but all the regular people on their lunch hour. She dodged through them to the corner, scanning up and down 8th, up and down 42nd, trying to figure out which way someone would go who wanted to disappear. Her heart pounded in her ears, and she made herself breathe. Think. Think. If she took it, where would be the best place—Times Square—no other place. The light turned yellow, and she darted across, hitting the corner in a blast of car horns, taxis showing off for their fares. She craned her neck, stretched, jumped where she stood, but it was useless.

If she blew this—if John Anthony fired her—she couldn't even think about what would happen to her...there he was near the opposite corner, the pack glinting in the sunlight, ridiculous looking over his army jacket, he pausing in the crowd, the crosswalk jammed with cars. She wove between the cars, slapping a bright green one that tried to inch her out of the way. She had to get to him before the light changed again, before the surge of people crossed the street. She ducked her head and made her way through the people, coming up right next to him. Her hand hovered over the strap, waiting for him to move so it would slip off more easily. She must've lost her touch, too long off the streets, because he took a look over his shoulder at her, grabbing the strap with his other hand.

"Light's green, Brodog." She gave the strap a tug. He tugged back, started to walk, and she went with him. "You know this isn't yours." She yanked on it, her job, her life, depended on the pack, a cop car across the street, siren giving a quick whoop, edging into the intersection, cross traffic not letting it through. In a well-practiced motion, she slid the flick knife she always carried out of her pocket, snapping it open as she did, ready to cut the strap, and if she cut him, then...

His eyes widened, then narrowed in anger. He looked from her to the cops, and ran, a weasel, the crowd closing around him, Ronnie shouldering the backpack and stowing the knife in one swift move, not running because she wasn't guilty, the cops would chase the runner. She ducked into a store anyway, headed to the back, pretended to look at a shelf, one eye on the door. Her stomach growled, the whiff of chocolate hitting it before her brain registered the smell, her eyes adjusting and taking in all the colors. Someone brushed the air next to her, reaching for a giant stuffed red M&M on the shelf in front of her. M&M pillows filled the display, all goofy eyebrows and knowing smiles, a kid on the floor screaming because he wanted one. Ronnie wanted to tell him to give up, the pillow not worth the sore throat, but what did she know, she had a *Finding Nemo* backpack slung over her shoulder.

She went out a different door, glad to see the green ball and wrought iron railing of a subway entrance down the block. She moved the pack around to her chest, clattered down the stairs, away from the traffic, the tourists, surrounded by people going about their business. People who couldn't care less about M&M pillows or *Finding Nemo* backpacks.

* * *

As she sat on the molded plastic subway seat, she fingered the backpack, squishing the sides a little, trying to find shapes inside. Whatever John Anthony had in here better be worth what she just went through. She almost knifed a stranger, risked the cops, then been assaulted by a ridiculous tourist trap store, and it better not be just for wads of newspaper. She sat back, hugging the prize to her, trying not to look around. Maybe drugs, not cash. She squeezed it tighter with her arms, but the hard plastic didn't give up any clues. As far as she knew, though, John didn't deal in the drugs, only cash. Turning cash into something clean, Frank said. But the cash came from drugs, so maybe there was—

Goddammit Frank. Put her in with a drug dealer. The brakes screeched, the train slowing into Grand Central, the people around her getting up, waiting at the doors. She never wanted to be a criminal—it was just something she had to do as a last resort when she and her brother lived on the streets. She sucked in a deep breath. She had to finish this errand, she had to help just this much, but she wasn't going to do anything more. Across from her, a dog stuffed into a tote bag hung his head out and panted. She should've told Frank no drugs. Anything but drugs. Well, maybe not a prostitution ring or whatever. And maybe not—dammit, anything she did for Frank would involve criminal activities by definition.

She followed the crowds out. This had to be a test, because why waste your butler on this errand. Maybe he had someone following her. Who knew how many people he had working for him, but no one like that came to the house. That she saw. The backpack was heavy enough, maybe it really was money. She hit the 6, the express, and watched the stations whooshing by, the white tile, the lights of the platforms, the dirt of the tunnels again as they went uptown, 68th street, 77th, the red and white striped band at the bottom of the walls, the people on the platform a flash and then gone.

She went over to the dry cleaners on 86th, put the backpack on the counter, got his suits, headed to Park Avenue, the penthouse, home.

* * *

"They said you almost lost it."

Ronnie still stood in front of his desk, no offer for her to sit down. "But I didn't, did I?" She stared at him, dared him to contradict her.

"He told me you had a knife."

"That guy was yours?" She sat down, even without the invitation, plopped into the chair, let out a long breath. She peered at John through her bangs. "Look, there's something you gotta know about me." She stood up again, better to be looming over him, make him look up at her. "You can trust me." She widened her stance. "I'm like a one-man dog. And since I'm working for you, you're my one man." He tilted his head at her as if curious. "You don't need to go placing roadblocks just to see how far I'll go to get the job done." She shoved her hands in her pants pockets, took them out, wondered what her fingers touched in the right pocket. "I will always get the job done. I'm totally trustworthy." She turned to go, a hand on the knob, then faced him. "And I need to be able to trust you. So I can always do whatever it is you need me to."

She walked out, shut the door quietly behind her, made a beeline for the backstairs, clattered down them, and practically dove into her room, closed and locked the door before she fell into the worn armchair wedged into the corner. Her body began trembling all over.

Godammit. Frank would kill her if J.A. fired her, but for chrissake, having that guy take the pack. She would've stabbed him, too. She took several deep breaths, slowed them down. Okay, maybe not. She always ran instead of stabbed, but all she could think of at that moment was getting the backpack no matter what. She guessed John wasn't the violent type, but he didn't seem to care much that she'd pulled a knife. She put her head on the back of the chair, stared up at the high ceiling, listened to the thudding in her ears. She knew she was right to stand up to J.A., to tell him he could trust her, but what if he fired her because of that, because she wasn't all, yes sir, very good sir, whatever you want sir. No, he needed her, needed someone used to the shadiness of the streets, of not doing everything legit. Otherwise, he would've found a butler through one of those agencies.

She launched herself out of the chair, paced the tiny room, bedside table, window, door, stopped to look out the window, a narrow thing looking into the airshaft. What was the point of having that, the narrow space in the middle of the building. Not like she could climb out or get some fresh air or any sunlight. She shoved her hands in her pockets, pulling out what her fingers had run into in J.A.'s office. What the—M&M's. The red, green, blue, yellow, brown disks crowding together in her palm. She had no idea how they'd gotten into her pocket. She threw them in the trash, examined her hand. Colors stained her palm, looking more like bruises and blood than candy. She went into her minuscule bathroom and washed her hands, splashed her face, water getting on the toilet seat. She stared at herself over in the mirror.

She had meant what she said: she was loyal. That was just who she was. She worked for him, and she would do whatever he required. He had to believe her. Because until she could convince Frank to find her another job, she needed the job to keep him happy. So she had to be as loyal as possible to John, so she could be loyal to Frank. Sheesh. She didn't know where that one-man dog stuff had come from. She rubbed her face with a towel, raked her fingers through her hair, looked hard into her eyes in the mirror. Woof woof.

* * *

Two days later, after not getting fired for talking back, Ronnie sat in the backseat of John's black Range Rover with a briefcase between her feet. Shiny black leather, gold clasps winking at her, the number dials next to them daring her to give it a try. She knew what was inside—she caught a glimpse right before he closed the top and turned the handle toward her, motioning to her to take it off his desk, run the errand for him. She tested the weight of it now, lifting it an inch off the car floor, setting it down slowly, not wanting to make a sound. Stupid, of course. This was New York, nothing but noise out there, the taxis honking, the trucks backing up and beeping, the construction workers jackhammering like artillery fire. The driver couldn't hear her put the briefcase down. And besides, Ronnie had no idea how much money weighed, how to do the calculation based on the weight. She had seen the stacks of green, but not what denomination. If they were hundreds, stacks of hundreds, row after row filling the briefcase...

If it were a million dollars, and if she could drive, she could buy a car and then...and then Frank would find her and put her in prison. The shame of it made her cheeks burn, and she cut her eyes to the driver, caught him looking at her in the rear-view mirror. She wanted to tell him to keep his eyes on the road, leave her alone. But Marc would report everything to John Anthony, and she needed John Anthony to know she was a team player, got along with everyone he employed. She went back to looking at the briefcase like it would suddenly leap out the window. It made her a little car sick. She figured this was her second test, and he better not have any more little tricks like someone trying to take it from her. He had given her the instructions and swiveled back to his keyboard, like however many hundreds of thousands he trusted her with was nothing.

She didn't really want to run anyway with this cash. Just a way to pass the time and, in a funny way, take her mind off how much was sitting there. Like if it was all hers, she wouldn't be as anxious. She guessed they were going all the way to Chelsea on 11th Avenue, and she took a quick look out the window, one eye on the briefcase, one eye noting the Mercedes Benz dealer. They must be halfway there. Soon they'd pass the docks she and Frank had sat at that night, watching the cruise ship being loaded, resting after stomping all over, looking for Frank's daughter. And wouldn't you know it, there was a Lexus dealer. Well, if she ever had a fancy car, and knew how to drive and had to get it serviced, she now knew where to go. The city emptied here, wider streets, lower buildings, room, obviously, for dealerships, the big windows showing off the cars inside. She whipped her head back to the briefcase as if someone might've taken it while she thought about owning an expensive vehicle.

Finally, Marc slowed the Range Rover, then stopped in the middle of the street, not even pulling to the curb for her. She got the feeling he didn't like her. The gallery, Waverly & Waverly, sat on the corner, all glass, wood, black metal framing the windows, inviting and unfriendly at the same time. As if it would only welcome you in if you were the right person.

"You'll wait for me, right?"

Marc looked at her in the rear-view mirror but didn't say anything.

"He told you, didn't he, that you were bringing me down here *and* back, right?"

Marc stretched his mouth into something he might have thought was a smile, but not because she had said something funny. He hit the button to unlock the doors, but still didn't say anything. Maybe he didn't speak English. Maybe J.A. liked it that way, so he didn't know too much about his business. How would that work, though, when Barbara went shop—

"Time to go."

So he can speak. She backed out of the car, dragging the heavy briefcase across the seat, straightened up, glanced at the gallery behind her. She knocked on Marc's window, made a rolling motion to try to get him to open it. She shouted through the window that he should park, pointed to a space right behind a delivery van. He stared at her through the glass, big brown eyes watching her until a semi behind him honked over and over, the truck driver leaning out the window to ask what was the matter with him and say unkind things about his mother. Or her mother.

She gave the truck driver a one-fingered cabbie salute and went to the door to the gallery, squaring her shoulders, broadening her chest. People seemed to respond better when they thought she was a guy. She buzzed the door. No answer. Buzzed again. She stepped back, looked over the building. He had said Waverly & Waverly, hadn't he? She looked up the street, turned around, searched down the other street. No sign of Marc. Maybe he dropped her at the wrong gallery, another stupid test. The briefcase weighed heavy in her hand, and she gripped it tighter. She didn't need to start sweating in this heat. Lose her grip as it were.

She leaned against the window of the gallery, though not much shade here. No way she could call John and say, they won't let me in. Admit to him she failed this second test, she was useless to him, then useless to Frank, back on the streets. She pulled out her phone, prayed she could find a number for the gallery. Slow going, poking her phone with one thumb while she held on to the briefcase—a sharp rapping on the window behind her and she almost dropped her phone. A woman with pointy eyebrows made shooing motions at her, and Ronnie stepped back, motioned to the door. The woman shook her head, crossed her arms. Ronnie lifted the leather briefcase to show her, pointed again to the door, then went to it. Pushed the button to be let in.

"Yes?" The voice sounded like she'd rather be swearing at her.

Ronnie moved her voice down to a lower register. "Ron Charles, on behalf of John Anthony, to see Mr. Waverly." Short and commanding. Worked every time. She gave her face to the camera in the corner, gripped the briefcase even tighter. Nothing happened. She buzzed again.

Finally, an angry return buzz, nearly too short for Ronnie to open the door before it stopped. The gallery seemed intensely clean, wide open, floors gleaming, huge paintings hung with expensive lights trained on them. It made her want to whisper. Or to drop a gum wrapper. The pointy-eyebrow lady raked her eyes over her, then told her he'd see her now. Ronnie followed her to the back of the space, watching her long hair move with her. Glad she didn't have all that hair to deal with, all the brushes and barrettes, an army of headbands. Though now that she looked at her head, it seemed this woman had tied her hair back with a pair of pantyhose, the legs in a bow, the toes hanging to either side. In another life, maybe she'd like this woman.

A man's voice called out, "Enter" at her knock, and the woman with the pantyhose opened the door and stood aside, letting Ronnie in, closing the door behind her as she left. The gallery owner gave her a glance, and Ronnie had no doubt he had already calculated the price of her suit and the amount of starch in her shirt. She said nothing. His eyes traveled over her again.

"You're new."

"Sir."

"And?"

"Mr. Anthony said he was in the mood for a painting."

Mr. Waverly nodded.

"That you would know which one."

Mr. Waverly peered into the briefcase, and the color of his eyes seemed to change. She'd seen that before, as if the person envied the object they already held in their hands. The black leather of the briefcase lid shone under the lamp.

"I'll have the painting delivered." He sat down at his computer and clicked the keyboard. A printer in the corner made a few tentative sounds, then spit out a piece of paper. He took it and handed it to her. "The receipt."

As Ronnie folded it to put in her pocket, she caught sight of an amount that was so much less than the cash in the case she thought she must've read it wrong. She slid the paper into her pocket. Not her monkey. Not by a long shot.

He opened the door for her and gestured for her to go first. "I think he'll be very happy with what I have in mind for him."

# Chapter Six

The bookstore was more crowded than Frank would like, but he soon found Ronnie at a table of books near the back. "I thought we'd agreed you'd let me know before you went on any unusual errands." He picked up a book and put it back down. He was not interested in forty ways to style his hair.

She shrugged without looking at him, pulled a green book off the table, cracked it open.

"I didn't know you were interested in Wall Street." Frank spoke into his book. He stood across the pile from her, acted like he was so into what he was reading nothing could tear him away. But please, this better not be another tooth-pulling exercise.

Ronnie closed the book, a profile of a guy in a top hat, *Reminiscences of a Stock Operator* on the cover. She turned it over, and back, as if she didn't know what the object in her hand was. She returned it to the pile and pulled out a book with a red cover.

"Remember you're working for me. You need to play by my rules, not his." He kept his voice low, nearly a hum.

Someone came up next to Frank, and he moved off, slowly though, pretended to read, figured she would follow. She'd better. He put the book down on a side table and went into one of the narrow aisles, between two tall shelves of books, scanned the titles. Of course he was in the Crime Fiction section. He couldn't stand reading this stuff. No author ever got it right, glorified the criminals often as not, the Special Agents always coming in to muck up the locals' cases, the local police resentful. In truth, the FBI never horned in on someone's case—they only came in when they were invited or when it was clearly a federal case, like kidnapping. The locals loved them. But maybe that didn't make for interesting reading. Fiction, after all.

He glanced around to see if Ronnie had followed, but couldn't see her. Damn. Get the girl a job, and she forgets which side her bread is buttered on.

"I was going to tell you." Her voice was low and seemed to come from the books themselves. He pulled a spine out as if checking the cover and saw the short, dark hair flopping over a pale forehead. "I didn't have time, and then I knew it was a test again, the driver barely watched the road, he was looking at me so much."

He pulled out the next book, her eyes meeting his. He grunted. "A UC always has time to text in. Next time—"

"Look. Fra—uh, I don't know about all the..." her voice dropped to a whisper so low he had to bend down, pretend to look at the lower shelf, put his ear at the gap. "I hate drugs. I don't want to be helping them sell drugs."

Frank straightened up. Grunted.

"Isn't there another job you can find for me?"

Why was she getting cold feet now? Way too much conversation required to parse this out, and a hole in a bookshelf wasn't going to cut it. He told her to meet him in the food hall at Whole Foods. He'd pay her back for whatever she got. Find a table with an empty one next to it, they could talk and pretend not to know each other.

* * *

At least she could follow those orders. He'd spotted her seated at the window, slumped in the tall chair. Looked like it was all high, group tables. Perfect. He sped through the salad bar, barely noticing what he'd thrown in his bowl, then silently urged the line at the cashier to hurry up. In his peripheral vision, his favorite CI looked a little forlorn, picking at her pizza slice, not looking up. Time for Frank to be the Ronnie Whisperer.

Just as he approached, someone was leaving, catty-corner to the morose girl with her boy haircut. He'd figure out how to handle this once he got her talking. He put his bowl down and used a napkin to wipe down the vacated space. His voice low, he told the table to pretend she was on the phone. She pulled her phone out, looked at the screen, swiped the screen, put it to her ear. That's my girl. He settled in, put his phone on the table next to his bowl, and pulled out his Bluetooth earbuds. Pierced a few leaves of lettuce, poked his own screen.

"Okay, talk to me." Frank chewed, listened, swallowed.

"It's just that—y'know. I mean, drugs killed my brother, and look what they did to your daughter—"

Frank grunted, took another bite.

"And even if none of that happened, I'd still hate them." She leaned back and folded her arms, a sullen teenager, sure she wasn't going to get what she wanted. "I don't want to be helping some horrible cartel sell them on the streets."

"Don't look at me."

"Okay, okay." She blew out a breath. "And I don't want to meet that Mateo guy." She shivered all over. "So can't I do something else for you? Something not involving drugs?"

Frank pushed his bowl aside. Why did he think those pickled hot peppers would be a good idea? He put his phone in his pocket. "Listen, Ronnie, I get it, I really do." Nearly a sing-song, a gentle lullaby for a skittish colt. "But I think you won't find Mateo as scary in person as in your imagination." He scrubbed his fingers with his napkin, balled it up, put it in the bowl. "Look, the way I think about it, the thing that helps me sleep at night is knowing we'll be taking down more than just the street corner dealer. Going after his money launderer is huge. You can't find anyone to do that for you on Angie's List. Especially not on short notice."

Ronnie took a bite of her pizza, wiped her mouth with the thin brown napkin.

"And your special talents got you in there when no one else could. We need you and we need your skills."

Ronnie chewed another mouthful. Swallowed. Sipped her drink. "But..." She turned her head, looked out the window. A disheveled guy put his face to it, banged on the glass. "But it's so hard. I have to do my job well to get you what you want. And to do my job well, I have to be one of them. Make them think I believe in what they're doing. And I don't. I can't. I'm so mad about this."

"And you were okay with what Isabelle was doing?" Frank raked his fingers through his short hair. Not that he wanted to dwell on that.

Ronnie shrugged, pulled a pepperoni slice off her pizza. "At least she wasn't pushing the drugs—they all wanted to buy it."

"But she did drug people against their will. Don't look my way, please."

"But, by then...I mean, she kinda kidnapped me. I didn't have a choice, did I? But don't I have a choice with you? I mean, if I don't want to be in that penthouse, what good am I to you?"

No way she took debate in high school. "Does it help to think about the end game? The resulting arrest?"

Another shrug.

"Maybe focus on the monetary aspect. It's not as if they're having you deal. And it's a cinch that he's not handling any drugs himself."

She picked up the crust, gnawed on it.

Frank piled his plasticware, his spent napkins in his salad bowl. "Maybe in a way, you need to focus on every little detail, the closeup view, while keeping in mind the end, the goal we're all striving towards. Ignore the in between." He scooted his chair back with a skin-crawling shriek. "Just concentrate on proof of the criminal source of the money, and then you'll be able to do your job." He picked up the bowl containing his miserable lunch. "Dontcha think?"

She folded her paper plate over the scraps of her own lunch. "I guess." She looked out the window again. "The pizza was five bucks."

* * *

Frank headed to the subway station in Union Square, the place filled with people enjoying the spring sunshine, a woman in a slip of a dress contorting herself to music, the sign in front of her donation tin announcing her name and "dance artist." Maybe he should take a quick stroll around before going underground, the square attracting people with nowhere else to go. Benches lined the shady walk, pigeons walking in front of him on the cobbled path like they knew they owned it.

Young people, old people, someone taking up the entire bench as he went through his suitcase, a breeze coming through, catching a white pastry tissue.

The hair on his arm prickled, and his whole body went on alert, every person around him in high relief, analyzed and dismissed faster than a blink. A girl sat on a bench in the shade as the path curved, and Frank stopped walking, let out a long breath. Her head hung down, the dark hair matted, a shoulder, a very bony shoulder poked out of the neck of her filthy T-shirt. A can sat in front of her with a sign that proclaimed, "Anything helps." She had to be the reason his body signaled him, a young girl, on the street—could she really be, finally be...Frank went over, reaching in his pocket for whatever change he might have.

"Cathy?" he asked the bent head, his voice so low the word rumbled. She didn't move, not even when he dropped the money in the can, but the clattering alerted the guy next to her.

"Thanks, man." The kid wouldn't look at Frank.

He knew it wasn't her. Couldn't be. She would never be this dirty. But something about her... "What's her name? Is it Cathy?"

The boy reached down and swapped the coins for a dollar bill, put the can down. "You couldn't spare something more, could you? Y'know, to encourage other people?"

Frank pulled out his wallet, flipped it open. "What's her name? How old is she?" He bent down to try to look at her face, kept his wallet next to his body so the kid wouldn't be tempted to grab it. She was bent over so much he couldn't get a good look, but there was no way this was his daughter. But she was someone's daughter.

"Everyone calls her 'Snickers.'"

"Really? Why is that?"

"Because she's sweet and she laughs a lot."

"She's not laughing now."

"She's just taking a nap, Dawg." The kid's eyes were on his wallet.

Frank pulled up a few bills but didn't take anything out. "Do you know where she came from?"

"Where does anyone come from?"

Frank started to fold his wallet up.

"Dawg, I don't know. Why are you asking all these questions? You a cop? I'm not doing anything illegal. We can sit here."

"Do you know how old she is? Because that might be illegal. I'm searching for my daughter, and she's only 16. So if this girl is underage, and she's with you..."

The kid took off from the bench like he was electrified. He wove among the dog walkers, strollers, and tourists, his baggy jeans sliding down as he ran. Frank sat down next to the girl, even though he was pretty sure this girl was a stranger. He tried talking to her in his coaxing voice, but she didn't respond, she was so out of it. Finally, he reached up and took her chin, tilting it up to see her face. She let out a moan but never opened her eyes. He eased her back, so her head was against the bench. Maybe that would be a more comfortable position. He was afraid that anything he left in the can would be stolen with her so incapacitated, so he folded up a twenty, slid it into her hand, and left, praying it wouldn't float away, praying it would help, figuring it probably wouldn't.

He made his way around the path which would take him back to the station. A sadness came over him that was so strong and so sudden, he nearly stopped walking. Maybe he should have tried to help her, buy her a sandwich, alert social services, take her to the ER, or all the way to Benedict House. He stared at the ground as he walked, thinking about all the young girls he had seen in his hunt for his daughter. He could spend all his time helping them, losing himself in their stories, investing in their welfare, and he'd never find Cathy, never have any time, or emotional energy to hand out the flyers and look in the tunnels. He could give everything to these girls and not have Cathy, not have anything left of himself.

He almost turned around, as if the girl would have become Cathy in the few minutes since he left her there. In a strange way, he felt relief that the girl hadn't been his daughter, he guessed, because there was still hope that she wasn't that messed up, that strung out. But, he was also very disappointed, plunged down so low he felt he'd never find her. This city was so big, the places to hide so numerous, the chances he'd run into her so minuscule. If he didn't start crying, he might start screaming, stand on this corner and yell until they came for him, locked him up. He glanced at the people around him going about their day, pretending they didn't see him or anyone else. Though in this city, he could stand on the corner and scream for hours, and no one would ever come for him.

# Chapter Seven

The painting arrived the next afternoon, and it was the loneliest thing Ronnie had ever seen, a young man with his back to the viewer, a plain white cube next to him, some other stark shapes, and he, evidently, stared out into the pastels in front of him, the back of his head telling her nothing about what he was thinking. John Anthony said to put it in the library on the first floor, where the Hamamoto was. He would be selling that anyway, so put this one up instead. She stood away to make sure it hung straight and decided no matter what the artist called his painting, she would call it "Nothing."

"When did John buy this?"

She squashed her jump. Damn these thick carpets. Barbara came up to stand beside her, and they each studied the artwork for a beat.

"I had no idea he was into Pimento." She sniffed. "He probably paid full price." She looked into her purse, snapped it shut, and headed to the elevator. Ronnie followed her. "If he wants another one, let me know this time. He can buy directly from Pimento and not have to pay the gallery owner his cut." They listened to the warm chugging as the elevator came up the shaft towards them. "On the other hand, I know the gallery owner too, so maybe we should go through him." The doors slid open, and she got in, held the door, and poked her head out. "If John's buying his work, maybe I'll tell Nigel Waverly to raise his prices. In fact," she released the door, her voice fading as they closed, "I think I'll drop by there today..."

Ronnie listened, though she couldn't make out the rest of the words, the elevator dropping Barbara down, down. As if she suddenly might jump out of the doors again, Ronnie waited until the light told her the elevator hit the lobby floor and then raced up the stairs to Lisa's office.

"We have a problem," Ronnie said to the top of Lisa's head.

"You have a problem, more likely." Lisa looked up from a battered paperback, her eyes flicked over Ronnie, returned to her book as if they'd found nothing interesting.

"You don't understand." Ronnie sat down in the chair in front of her desk, the same one she'd sat in for her interview.

"I hope not."

"Mrs. Anthony, the Gallery, Waverly & Waverly, she—"

Lisa raised her head again, turned the open book over, the cover giving Ronnie an upside-down view of an overbuilt man with no shirt, a fully dressed woman falling into his arms. Or out of them. "I know nothing about any gallery." She stood up. "And I'm not going to know. Whatever it is, take it up with J.A. Especially if it has to do with Barbara. In particular."

"Is he free?"

"He always is for me." Lisa picked up her book. "I have no idea if he will be for you."

Ronnie left Lisa to her paperback. All her warmth must come from romance novels because for sure she wasn't born with any. Well, now she really knew they weren't on the same team. Better to know.

John's voice on the phone trailed out through the crack in the door. Ronnie caught "...two point five, today. You can count on it," and no goodbyes, but no more conversation, so she knocked, light taps, a respect for her boss and how busy he was.

"It's open." He sat with his profile to her, the one without the birthmark, and he tapped away at his keyboard. "Yes?" John's clickety-clicking filled the tiny space.

"Um, I don't know how to say this, but—Please don't be mad at me."

He stopped, turned, no longer trying to keep her from seeing the bright pink side of his face. "Just say it. Usually the best thing."

She told him all on one exhaled breath how they were looking at the painting and his wife knew the artist and the gallery owner and was stopping to talk to him today and if she knew, then what—

John sat back in his chair, hands resting on the arms, fingertips and thumbs meeting to make a triangle, eyes on her. Ronnie's legs trembled so she sat down.

"Tell me that last thing she said? Verbatim." He must've thought she hesitated because she didn't know that meant, so he added, "Exactly as she said it. Word for word." He gave her a smile, encouraging, but maybe also laughing at her a little.

She swallowed. "She said, 'If John's buying, then I'll tell Nigel to raise his prices,' and then she said she was going to stop by there today." He didn't respond, so she told him the elevator doors had closed and she couldn't catch what else she said.

"That's it? The whole conversation?"

Ronnie nodded. His steepled fingers now bounced on his lower lip, the gears in his brain turning, turning. This was somehow her fault. Because of her, this avenue for moving cash was closed. She shifted in her chair, trying not to think of what would happen if he fired her.

"You're pretty close to my wife, huh?"

Ronnie nodded, hopefully a good thing.

"Oh, well." He studied the blotter on his desk. "I'm trying to figure out if you know just what it is that you've done here."

So. That was it. Ronnie got up. Back to the streets. Or jail. If she was no good to Frank, then…

"Doesn't matter one way or another, the result is still the same."

"Sir, I had no idea—"

"Yes, this will work out perfectly. In fact," he smiled as if to himself, "it couldn't be better." He gave a laugh, turned back to his computer, punched in some numbers from the keypad, and swiveled again to her. "Thank you so much. I think you may be getting a raise."

"Sir?"

"Listen, keep doing what you've been doing. No. Scratch that. Do more. In fact, the next gallery I line up, she's going with you."

"I'm confused."

"Look, go down and make us some sandwiches, that'll give me time to finish this up, and then we can eat out on the roof terrace, and I'll explain it to you." He swung around away from her and said to his screen, "Oh, Barbara!" Then he laughed again.

* * *

Turned out she and J.A. liked their sandwiches exactly the same way: good quality white bread sliced thin, generous on the mayo, and the meat piled high. A lettuce leaf or two to be healthy, a pile of ruffled potato chips filling the rest of the plate.

By the time she brought the tray up, he sat on the deck, at the table, now wearing sunglasses, a sweater, and a baseball hat. Ronnie liked the sun. She might even roll up her sleeves if that didn't seem too casual. He was extra chatty, and Ronnie was glad because she was starving. He told her how Barbara was always taking up hobbies, throwing herself all in, buying the clothes, the equipment, the classes, buddying up to the experts. She careened from flower arranging to ichthyology to pastry making to gardening to birding to throwing pots. She had had salons on the Great Books, and she had learned to blow glass and decorate cakes. At some point, she took up oil painting, and that was how he met Nigel Waverly. He didn't know she kept in touch with that crowd until today.

"So, she's going to help us, and she won't even know she's doing it." John bit into his sandwich.

Ronnie left three potato chips on her plate, not wanting to appear too greedy. She eyed the baklava still on the tray, wondering if he wanted any. "How do you figure?"

He put the sandwich down and wiped his hands on the cloth napkin. "I'm surprised someone as sharp as you hasn't worked that out." He cleared his throat. "She's going to tell the gallery owners how great these artists are, how we're going to make them into major players. And, because she can't resist it, she'll let them know just how wealthy we are."

He settled in his chair, tipped his face to the sun.

"I still don't—"

He turned his sunglasses to her. "Are you asking all these questions for a reason?" He kept facing her as if studying her behind his glasses. "I would have thought that after working so closely with Isabelle Anderson, after being involved in the financial aspect as you claimed, you would know how all this works." He aimed himself at the sunshine again. "So either you weren't as involved as you originally claimed, or you're wired up and asking all these questions so I'll incriminate myself." He lowered his sunglasses and gave her a look her teachers would've been envious of.

She wanted to kick the table leg. She straightened up in her chair. "Sir. If you like, you can check me for a wire, or you can take my word for it. There isn't one." She cleared her throat. "And Isabelle never dealt with all this cash—she ran all the checks through her foundation, and made the deposits herself." She stacked her plate on the tray, reached for his. "I thought it was your idea to explain it to me. But if you don't want to..."

In the silence, a siren started up, the whoop whoop putting Ronnie even more on edge. She might just cram three baklava in her mouth at once.

"No, no. Sit down. I'm just surprised that you don't understand how money laundering works." He removed his sunglasses, leaned forward, a helpful look on his face as if he hadn't just accused her of spying. "So, let's say you have a big pile of cash." He raised a hand over the table as if the bills sat in front of them. "And you can't account for them when the government takes a hard look at you." He dropped his hands, sat back in his chair. "So, you give the cash to Nigel, and then—"

"You have a weird painting."

He cocked his head at her.

Maybe she shouldn't have said that.

"That part doesn't matter." He waved a hand, dismissing her art critique. "He gives me a receipt for his cut, say, 25% of what you give him."

Whoa.

"Standard practice. Well worth it." John adjusted his hat. "So, I sell the painting back to Nigel, or to some other gallery, and because Barbara has hyped the artist, we get the money back, cleaned and deposited.

"So, because of Barbara, I'm happy, Nigel's happy, Mateo's happy." He beamed. "And you're brilliant. My wife hasn't liked anyone else before you, so whatever you're doing, keep it up."

"Okay, thanks for explaining it." She put a baklava on her plate. "Um, I wanted to ask you…does Mateo ever come here?" She rushed on. "And if he does, what should I do? What do you expect—" Ronnie willed her legs to stay still.

"—don't worry about it. When he comes here, he brings me wine, we discuss things in my office, we eat delicious meals, talk about all the lovely places he's visited. Nothing big. He's charming, he's easy to get along with, and you'll probably never see him, except to greet him at the elevator, usher him out again."

The honey syrup oozed from the baklava. Would it be too rude to lick it off her hands?

* * *

Two weeks later, when Barbara blew into town again, she found Ronnie polishing the silver at the kitchen counter, asked her if she could be ready at 11:30. She waved a piece of paper. "John's given me a list, and Marc will pick us up. We can go for lunch after. That all right with you?"

As they waited outside for Marc, Barbara rummaged in her purse, talking to herself. She snapped it shut and looked up the street. "Oh well."

"Ma'am?"

"That's all right. You can call me Barbara, you know. I must've left the list at home. But I remember it all right. I should. I know all these people." She waved her hand as if to brush away any doubts. The black Range Rover angled to the curb, and Patrick opened the door for her, leaving Ronnie to go around to the traffic side.

At Argus gallery, Barbara and the owner were speaking Greek. Or some kinda foreign language. They were saying things like "curvilinearity" and "virtuosity" and other weird, long words. On one wall, all by itself, a pair of wings made out of pieces of wood and rusty wire stopped her. No bird, just the wings, spread out about six feet wide, powerful looking. What it would be like to put them on, ride on the updrafts over the Hudson River, far away from all the crowds, the noise, the people, the horns honking and trucks reversing, a smell of salt and the sun warm on her head, gliding…

A shriek shook Ronnie, and she moved before she thought, first away from the sound and then towards it, her heart racing, her hands up ready to take on whatever had scared Mrs. A.

"Oh, but Henry, we must have this one. This is just too divine."

Ronnie stopped short, the adrenaline turning to anger, the anger to annoyance, her brain telling her fingers to uncurl now. Right now.

"Ronnie, don't you just love it?" She stood before a large photograph, black and white, and Ronnie's eyes worked on picking it apart, finding a fig cut in half, a dried leaf, a vase curving into shadow.

"I've never seen anything like it," Ronnie said. And that was the truth.

"Do you have more of hers? Oooooh let me see that one." She held up the next photograph, smaller this time, her arms straight out as if she wanted to get away from it and hold on to it all at once. Ronnie saw fuzzy colors and trees, a forest of people between trees, scarves hanging on trunks. She wanted to move closer, see what the people were doing, what lay beyond the trees.

"Now. You'll put all this on my husband's account? Send these on to us?"

Henry gave a little cough, looking uncomfortable, like he didn't know how to break the bad news. "Gallery policy is—we don't—credit is never extended—you know how it is in the art world."

"Oh. No, I'm sure." Barbara opened the huge leather bag on her shoulder and peered into the depths, saying into it, "I thought he had it arranged." She pulled out a tiny gold card holder and snapped it open. "You do take American Express, don't you?"

No. Damn, J.A. was going to be so apeshit.

"Sir." Ronnie squared her shoulders and expanded her chest. "Surely John Anthony has discussed this with you."

"I'm sorry, I don't know a John Anthony." Polite, yet firm.

"He didn't call you?" Ronnie looked between Barbara and the gallery owner. She must be in an alternate universe.

Barbara waved her American Express card like it was a golden ticket. "That must be the next gallery. I'm sure I mentioned this one to him. Never mind, we'll put these on the AmEx, go to the next one." She glanced at Ronnie. "Don't worry. He said I could get whatever I wanted."

Damn. She moved to the wall, away from the proceedings with the card and the wrapping of the pictures. She pulled out her phone, opened a game, switched over to text. As quickly as she could, keeping Barbara in her peripheral vision, she tapped out the gallery name, the owner's name, *"B's using AmEx,"* and sent it to John, switching over to her game as Barbara approached. She shot one of the gremlins down, then looked up at her boss's wife.

"Oh, this is just so much fun. I'm so thrilled J.A. is collecting. Did you text him? Is he on his way?" She handed Ronnie the wrapped artwork, which she had to take with both hands.

"Text—" Ronnie's heart pounded in her ears, and she gripped the packages tighter, prayed her hands didn't start sweating.

"Never mind, I see him there on the corner. Do you need him to help you with those?"

"He's here?"

"Of course he is. Marc is very prompt."

She waved to the gallery owner, saying something about seeing him again, and held the door for Ronnie, who had to tip her load sideways to angle it through. She threw a look at Henry, who smiled a not-friendly smile. Everyone in this city delivered things. Everyone but this jerk.

The next gallery went without a hitch, the owner nodding wisely to Barbara's observations, putting it on J.A.'s "account," promising delivery of her selections. She went for the oils this time, guaranteed she would skyrocket the artist's career, talked to herself about holding a salon, grilled the gallery owner about how he was promoting this young woman.

"Uh," Ronnie said, both of them looking at her as if suddenly remembering she was there, "maybe you should get another one of her works, if you think she's going to be that big."

Barbara gazed at her as if Ronnie had an ulterior motive. "Do you know her?"

"Oh, no. It's just that—y'know—listening to how much you like this work, how important you feel it is, I was thinking—I mean, why not invest in her more than just those two?" Maybe she'd overstepped, maybe Barbara suspected something.

"Right you are. Couldn't have said it better myself. Now," Barbara returned to the paintings, "I don't know if I like this one, or this one better. What do you think?" As if she could get a fair recommendation from the guy making a commission on these things.

"Why not both?" Ronnie was tired of this game, her feet were sore, and she was starving.

* * *

While Barbara was in the restaurant bathroom, Ronnie took out her phone to text Frank. He said he wanted to know when they went to the galleries again, so she sent him an emoji with googly eyes, no mouth, and the name of the next one on their list, along with a 3 to indicate the time, deleting the text as soon as she sent it.

Marc took them further downtown, the gallery all white and modern, floor-to-ceiling windows, and completely empty of people. Barbara threw her arms around the gallery owner, saying, "Michael, darling. It's been far too long. What's the big new thing? Who is the artist I just have to have?" She dwarfed the man in his fine suit, wrinkling the flowing silk stuffed into his top pocket instead of a handkerchief. He pulled himself away, beaming at her, patting at the pink and purple silk at his breast as if trying not to be too obvious about fixing what she'd crushed.

Ronnie sat on a bench in the middle of the gleaming floor, glad it was there, thinking this place felt more like a museum than a store. She found her game again for something to do, thinking she would've liked it better when she was eight. The door buzzed, but she didn't turn around, figuring someone coming into a gallery wouldn't be a threat, and she killed three more neon green things, looked closer at the screen to anticipate where they would pop up next.

"Is this his new one? It's a departure for him, isn't it?" The man's voice made Ronnie whip her head up, look for the source. WTF. She realized she had stood up, but she made herself stay in the middle of the room. Damn. An unnatural stillness came over her like ice, and Frank continued the conversation with Barbara as if he always talked about art and artists. The last thing she expected when she texted was that he would show up here. Maybe it was his way of reminding her she worked for him. She broke her freeze to glance around the gallery again. She'd stand against the wall by the door, go into butler-disappearing mode, pray he would leave.

The painting they were discussing, or rather waving their arms in front of, was all shadows and snow, maybe tree trunks, but it could be elephant legs, a rhythm of off white and smudgy blue columns. Maybe it was smokestacks and smog. Maybe she didn't know why they were so excited about it. Frank stood next to Barbara. They were practically the same size, he maybe a few inches taller, her shoulders were as wide as his. Maybe Barbara married the wrong man. John Anthony wasn't as tall as his wife, and so much skinnier she bet Barbara outweighed him by 30 or 40 pounds. And Barbara was not a hefty woman. Frank and Barbara stood next to each other, their backs to her, talking and nodding. They made a good couple. What would that be like, the wife of a criminal, the agent who took him down, Frank's tiny apartment with paint chipping on the windowsill…

"Ron, dear, I've just met the most amazing fellow art enthusiast. We agree on nearly everything."

Ronnie gave a slight bow without looking either of them in the eye, hoped she wouldn't be called on to do so.

Barbara bubbled on. "We almost came to blows, but he graciously let me have the new Randolph Eckerty. Whoever heard of such gallantry? Be a dear and make sure uh—" she waved in the direction of the gallery owner, "Michael here, knows where to send it and all of that. Tom," she turned toward Frank with a smile, "and I will go on to the next gallery and I'll send Marc back for you. Oh, this must be kismet!"

Ronnie looked around to see who Kismet was, but no one else was there. "Ma'am." She turned to find Michael before she had to totally take in Frank's grin. Shit-eating, someone would call it.

# Chapter Eight

Frank held the car door open for Barbara Anthony and smiled to himself. Ronnie had startled like a little pony. He could almost see her skin ripple. But she recovered like a pro. Thankfully, he didn't think Barbara noticed, though he would bet that raptor of an art dealer saw it. He would look into that guy, maybe a little extra carefully. Frank went around to the street side of the big black Range Rover and settled in on the fine leather next to his new friend. From what Ronnie had reported so far, he was pretty sure Barbara wasn't involved in the money laundering, but since she was visiting galleries and John was using cash to buy the paintings, getting close to Barbara might just pay off for the case. God, how he loved going undercover, getting this deep in a case.

The driver watched him in the mirror, and he offered him his profile as he remarked to Barbara something inane about the artist they'd just "fought" over. For a minute in the gallery, he wondered if he had miscalculated her, if her balance of competitiveness versus politeness tipped too far and she would cede the painting merely to be nice. And he would've been in real trouble, called on the carpet, the bellows from the boss rattling the windows. But in the end, her desire to win made it easy for him to be gracious, let her be the one to spend that ridiculous amount of money for a blurry painting, take home the Randolph Eckerty "Snow on Ice."

Of course, not clearing going undercover would also get him in trouble, but hey, the opportunity arose, and he had to take advantage of it. He assessed Marc out of the corner of his eye while he pretended to be absorbed in his conversation with Barbara. Marc eyed the rear-view mirror far more often than the road, confirming for Frank what he already suspected: the driver worked closely with John and wasn't only there to ferry Barbara around. He was far too nosy, suspicious. And he was built like a bodyguard, big neck, beefy shoulders, muscles developed far beyond their natural wont.

He tuned back in to Barbara, who was saying "…don't you think?"

He inclined his head and smiled generously, hoped he was agreeing to something he wouldn't regret.

"Oh, then," Barbara said, "I'll definitely put you on the list. Do you have a card?"

He patted his pockets and shrugged, gave her a rueful look. He pulled out the burner phone—he always made sure he had one for whatever might come up. He reminded himself to tell the Bureau the number for this current undercover persona. "What's your number? I'll call you, then you'll have mine."

They did the phone dance, and she pecked away at her screen. "So, Tom, what's your last name again?"

"Roberts. Tom Roberts."

"Why must everyone have first names as last names?" Barbara tucked her phone away. "John Anthony, Ronnie Charles, Tom Roberts. Maybe I should have kept my maiden name just to be different."

"Marc," Frank said to the bullet-shaped head, "are you part of this club? Do you have a first name for a last name?"

Marc grunted and slowed the car down, stopping on the narrow street. Barbara was on the street side this time, forcing Frank to get out before he finished his pursuit of a full name for the driver. He held the door open and waited for Barbara to slide across, automatically scanning the street, not seeing anything that made the hair on the back of his neck stand up. They were way downtown, the streets more convoluted, the old-growth trees tall and leafy, buckling the sidewalks, making the air a little cold, a little dank on this spring day.

* * *

In his apartment, Frank stood in front of his dresser, grinned at himself in the mirror. He toggled his cufflinks, slid them through the buttonholes, placed them in the velvet-lined leather box that Susan had given him as a birthday present from a one-year-old Cathy. The impossibly thin gold watch—which he should've returned to the Bureau when he was done going undercover as Peter Franks on the last case—that went in as well, the gold business card case nestling beside it. He should've alerted Pete that he decided to go undercover again, but there hadn't been time. He hung up the stiffly starched white shirt, pushed aside his other clothes in the tiny closet so the shirt wouldn't get squashed and wrinkled, and he could use it again before taking it to the cleaners. Sometimes the bureaucracy of the Bureau got in the way of the speed of a case, and you had to make your decision in the field. Pete would understand. What was it they said, better to ask for forgiveness than for permission. He never thought he'd be the kind of guy who said that, but in this case, he understood why some people did.

Time to be just plain Special Agent again. He put on his holster, unlocked his gun, unlocked his ammo, loaded the gun, snugged it into the pocket under his armpit, and snapped the tab down over it. He never wanted to unholster it, but he always felt better having it. Especially when he was going out to distribute Cathy's flyer among the drug-addled and the homeless.

Even though the weather was a little too warm, he put on a loose windbreaker to hide his sidearm and picked up the stack of flyers. Cathy's smile nearly made his eyes water. She appeared so young, so fresh, so trusting. A flaw in the reproduction gave her the hint of a dimple, and he brushed his finger on that spot. If she were home with him now, she'd be curled up on his couch, staring at her phone until he took it out of her hands, and they'd go out, maybe for street tacos in the park, or to that theater in Brooklyn with the wax museum and 1950's Bogart movies. Afterward, she'd have to lecture him on what a misogynistic genre noir was, sipping on her drink and then pointing her straw at him across the linoleum-covered table as if he were every misogynist on the planet.

He stuffed the flyers into the inside pocket of his windbreaker, on the other side from his gun, zipped up, straightened his shoulders with a deep breath and left, turned each key in the three deadbolts, wondered, as he pocketed the keys and headed for the stairs, if they kept out Cathy as well as the thieves.

* * *

He worked his way all the way down to the East River Park, the Williamsburg Bridge begging for another chance in any black and white movie on offer. His last flyer was in the hands of an impossibly skinny girl and her even skinnier male companion, the two looking like they could trade clothes and not look any different. He took a step away from her so she wouldn't feel like he hovered, though all he wanted to do was shake her shoulders and yell in her face. Because she seemed to know his daughter. She looked at the piece of paper so intently, whispered to her companion, dug an elbow into him, looked back at Cathy. He also wanted to take the photograph away from her before she tainted his daughter with her greasy hair, her dirty fingers.

The girl looked up at him, eyes narrowed. She threw a glance at the boy next to her and held the piece of paper out to Frank with a shrug.

"You do know her, don't you?" Frank asked, took a step toward her. He reached out to take the flyer, and she pulled it back to look at it again.

"I dunno."

She eyed his pockets.

He reached for his wallet. He had one more bill left, hopefully bigger than a one. His phone dinged. His Bureau phone. That he had to answer no matter what. No excuses ever unless he was dead, because if someone was calling him on this number, it was the only important thing happening at that moment.

He pulled the phone out instead of his wallet, the disappointment and disgust on the girl's face a magnification of the looks Susan used to throw at him when he took a call in the middle of something. He couldn't see the screen in the sunlight, but he could hear the pinging, and he could see the girl and her friend getting up from their bench.

"Wait, hold on. I—"

The girl threw a look at his phone as if to make sure it hadn't become his wallet and walked, leaving Cathy's picture on the bench where it fluttered as if she were laughing, slid to the dirt underneath, landed next to a crumpled paper cup. The faux dimple was absorbing a mysterious liquid, her face distorting and turning brown.

"Jankowski." Frank turned his back to the bench, to the retreating couple, to Cathy's ruined picture, the sun so warm on his jacket his back might spontaneously combust at any moment. It was Pete. "There better be a bank robbery or something going on, because I'm not even supposed to be working today."

"Rick said our namesake's—Peter Franks'—credit card popped up. He said it must be fraud and wants your ass on his carpet because he says you would've told me if Peter Franks was still in action." Pete chewed, swallowed, cleared his throat. "Why didn't you turn that in, anyway?"

"Oversight. And not fraud. I'm sure I told you I was going to…" Now, why did he just add a lie on top of deciding to go undercover without approval? Frank moved to the path along the river, maybe a breeze to cool off. He watched a boat chugging upstream, seagulls circling its wake. When Pete didn't respond, he said, "You couldn't cover for me, say you hadn't gotten to the paperwork, say it was a decision I had to make in the field?" Pete used to have his back. He leaned against the railing, still watching the East River. He glanced at his screen to make sure the line was still open. He returned the phone to his ear, and he heard chewing. "Pete—"

"Gotcha going there for a minute, didn't I?"

Frank almost hung up. He and Pete had been partners for so long, sometimes they were like an old married couple, finishing each other's sentences, or starting a sentence and not needing to finish it, pronouns sufficing for what they were saying.

Just the other day they were in a meeting and Frank said, "This sounds like that—" and Pete nodded and said "Yeah, when the guy—" and Frank said, "Of course, it's not—" "I know," Pete had said "It's kinda like the time—" The other two in the room, new guys, not long out of Quantico, looked back and forth between them and finally one of them asked, "Is this like something top top secret we don't have the clearance for?"

But now he was tired of Pete. His jokes, his ribbing, his constant eating. "Call me back after you've finished chewing," he told the screen and hit "end." He was sure that girl knew Cathy. If he could've given her some money, talked to her, gotten her to promise to call him when she saw her again. He headed north, runners breezing past him, nannies with strollers chattering away, someone bouncing a basketball as he strode along. He stopped under the bridge, the water lapping at the pilings, the shade welcome. Long time ago, this was where they dumped the bodies…

He mentally shook himself and turned to face Manhattan, the buildings, the cars, the sidewalks, the bicycles, the people. He couldn't let himself think like that. He was known for his dogged pursuance of a case, and he needed to treat his search for Cathy the same way. He wouldn't give up. She was out there somewhere, and he would find her. He would find her. He repeated that to himself in time to his footsteps, lengthening his stride, heels striking with each word until he left a trail behind him of certainty and conviction. *He would find her.*

# Chapter Nine

John had summoned Ronnie, and she stood on the other side of his desk, waiting.

"So what happened the other day? Why did you let Barbara go to the wrong gallery?" John faced his computer screen.

"What? Me? I didn't have the list. You gave it to her. She said she left it here, but she knew everyone on it."

He hit a key and swiveled to face her, his screen unreadable with some kind of privacy cover on it.

"Didn't Marc know where we were supposed to be going?"

John picked up his gold letter opener, passed it from his left hand to his right. And back again. He put it down, and they both stared at it. "Seems somebody mixed up 'Gargos' with 'Argus.' I don't know the guy at Argus…" As if he couldn't resist, he picked up the letter opener again and kept playing with it. He pointed it at Ronnie. "Do you know him?"

"What? No. How would I know him?" Ronnie put her hands in her pockets, and her fingers touched the flick knife she still carried for some reason. She breathed.

"What about that guy?" Her boss picked up a notepad, looked at the page, threw it down. "Tom Roberts? The one talking to Barbara at the Calfrida Gallery?"

"Was that his name?" She shook her head. "No, I don't know him." Never offer an explanation. Because then you look guilty, like those murderers in the TV shows who are too eager to help with the investigation.

John leaned back, his chair squeaking slightly, studied her. "Doesn't matter.

We'll look into him, as we do with everyone."

"Sir." Ronnie prayed her scalp didn't start sweating. Damn you, Frank.

"Okay. Now, I have an errand for you."

Ronnie pulled out the little white leather notebook she had to keep track of things. She flipped past the page that said *serve from the left.* She'd come a long way since she'd written that.

"Don't write this down. Don't ever write anything I say down. In fact, let me see that."

"It doesn't have anything in it, just notes from my last job."

He raised his eyebrows at her and then held out his hand. Like a teacher confiscating her gum.

"It's got some personal stuff too. Like my dreams." He still held out his hand like he would do that all day, still be sitting at his desk, elbow planted, palm flat, when Lisa brought him the pink newspaper in the morning. She handed over the little notebook and watched him riffle through it, squint at some pages as if he couldn't read her handwriting.

"So you used this to take notes about what to do on your previous job." He flipped through some more pages. Paused to read, looked up at her. "I'm not seeing any mention of Isabelle. Maybe you have a code name for her." He stared at her, as if he looked inside her, searching for the place she put the truth and the lies.

She held his gaze as if in a game of chicken. "Absolutely not." She shook her head. "No reason to write about her. In code or not." She gave him a shrug. "I just needed to remember which side to serve from."

He closed her notebook and handed it to her. "Okay. That's okay then. Just don't put anything I say in writing. Okay?"

She nodded, pocketed the notebook, felt it slide down, stop next to the flick knife.

"So today Marc is going to take you to various banks. He knows which ones. You'll make cash deposits, and you need to act like you do this all the time. You'll be visiting the same bank every other week, so you won't raise any alarms. Got that?"

Ronnie nodded. How hard could it be?

He turned around in his chair, his back to her, opened and shut doors in the credenza. "And you know, of course, the deposits have to be under ten thousand dollars."

Ronnie swallowed. Concentrated on relaxing her stance so it would seem like ten grand meant nothing to her.

He looked at her over his shoulder, and she nodded at him. Evidently finding what he was looking for, he placed a bound notebook next to his computer and turned back to his desk.

"Maybe wear something a little more casual. Because you're supposed to be some lowly assistant somewhere, like at a hairdresser's, or a T-shirt shop, or something."

She wanted to ask how many of these banks she would be bringing the under $10,000 to, but she didn't think she could handle thinking about all that money, where it came from, how many bindles of drugs they sold to have that much cash...

"I don't have to worry about whether you can handle this, do I?"

"Of course not. I was just thinking about my wardrobe." She turned to the door. "Uh, what should I bring it into the bank in? I mean, how do people usually do this?"

"Whatever you think. Backpack, shopping bag, pockets, anything." He swiveled to his screen, his birthmark a cool, pale pink. Ronnie noted where the letter opener lay on the desk, then left.

She went to her room and got the canvas duffle with the leather trim. She had no idea what it took to carry ten thousand dollars, excuse me, under ten thousand dollars, so she got some shopping totes from the kitchen as well, stuffed them in the duffle, zipped it up, and grabbed the brown leather handles. They seemed molded to her grip.

He hadn't said, so she hoped Marc already sat idling by the curb downstairs. She didn't even know how to call the guy. She came out the service entrance, no need to have Patrick the Doorman curious about what she was up to. At Park Avenue, she looked for the big black Range Rover, but Patrick spotted her instantly, giving her a small salute from the brim of his hat. Oh well. She made her way to the dark green awning where he waited for her.

"Have you seen Marc? He's supposed to be picking me up."

Patrick went to the curb, looked up the street, shook his head at a cab that angled toward him.

"My man, where the hell you been?"

Ronnie's stomach clenched, and she automatically turned away from the voice. This was not happening. Annie Anarchy got in front of her, so she was forced to look at her.

"What's in the bag?" Damned if she didn't lick her lips.

"You're a long way from your territory." Ronnie stepped to the side, tried to get around her and her white girl dreads.

"Mr. Ron, do you know this person? Is she a friend of yours?"

Ronnie said no, but it was drowned out by Annie's laughter. "Mr. Ron? That's a good one. Wait 'til I tell everyone." She laughed so hard she bent over, head hanging down.

Ronnie moved further away from her and pleaded with her eyes at Patrick. "She is not a friend of mine. You're a friend of mine. And," she edged to the street as if the physical distance would add weight to her words, "if she ever comes by again, you should probably call the cops."

Patrick was a sweet guy, always nice and polite to her, but now he drew himself up to his full six feet three inches, his chest expanding and shoulders broadening, and he edged into Annie's personal space, looked down at her, and closed the gap between them until she walked away. When she was halfway down the block, she turned around and held up each hand, giving them the finger, or rather two fingers, yelling, "Call this, ya mofos." Which didn't make any sense. Ronnie gave Patrick a glance, and she could see a smile tugging at the corner of his lips, even as his eyes narrowed, watching Annie as she went.

"She needs a bath." His voice was low, and he shook his head back and forth. "If she comes again, I will tase her."

* * *

Damn damn damn. Well, she hadn't lied. She never lied. Ronnie climbed into the backseat of her employer's car. Patrick asked if she was her friend, not if she knew her. She was never a friend of hers, just someone she and her brother Matt had fallen in with when they were first on the streets, when the crusties felt like a family. Until they didn't.

Next to Ronnie, taking up the whole rest of the seat sat a solid grey plastic tub, the kind someone stored stuff in they didn't want to look at anymore. Marc better not have seen Annie. She didn't think Patrick would ever say anything to J.A., but Marc might.

"Start loading up." Marc made a U-turn at the light, headed uptown. "I got you a bunch of smaller bills and hundreds, so it isn't only twenties. Mix them all up." He looked at her in the rear-view mirror. "And take the bands off the stacks."

*Duh-uh.* He must think she was an idiot. She pried open the lid and, in spite of herself, gasped. The thing was completely full. Packs, lose bills, jammed in there like they were nothing special, like trash, practically. She sucked in a breath, a mixture of crisp paper and oily dirt hitting her. Marc laughed, and it was not a very nice one.

"I knew you were too green behind the ears." He said some things to a cab that had pulled out in front of him. "I told Mr. Anthony you weren't ready for this."

Ronnie tossed the lid into the back and got to work. One stack of the hundreds was ten thousand dollars, so she split it in half between two of the shopping totes, messed and crinkled it, and added two stacks of twenties and a handful of the smaller bills. Why had she ever thought she needed the duffle bag?

"And don't think of taking a cut. We know exactly how much is in there."

Ronnie peered into the bin, all the loose bills, a lot of them folded into tiny squares, the kind that fit in the palm of your hand or in the watch pocket of your jeans. She doubted they knew how much, but she couldn't let that comment slide.

"I don't know who you think I am," she stuffed another shopping tote, "but I am not a thief." She stared at the back of his head with as fierce a look as she could dredge up. "These are just pieces of paper. He pays me plenty and I have nothing to spend it on." She wished she'd worn gloves, her hands clammy and grimy already. "I am not in the least bit tempted." She wiped her palms on the seat. These were her only pair of jeans.

* * *

"Look, Marc," she said to the back of his head after the fifth bank. Or maybe sixth.

His eyes in the mirror found hers.

"Don't you ever get hungry?"

He shrugged at her, one shoulder going up, then down.

"I'm starving. And I might faint in one of these bank offices, and what use would I be then?" Or she might make a mistake and John Anthony would fire her ass and then Mateo would—

Marc stopped the car, and Ronnie looked around. They were now all the way downtown, and Marc had parked halfway down the block from a taco truck. She had her hand on the door, about to open it, when he said, "No eating in the car. There's a park further down on Lafayette. Foley Square. I'll pick you up there."

* * *

She loved the al pastor, such a great spiciness with all the flavors, offset by crisp lettuce, a squeeze of lime. Ronnie sat on a bench facing Lafayette, not wanting to miss Marc when he came by for her. The sun filtered through the leaves overhead, and she settled back, face up to catch a few rays. Her Styrofoam box sat on her lap, piled with napkins, but her hands still felt a little sticky, and she examined a napkin in case there was any life left in it.

"Hey Frank." A familiar male voice floated toward Ronnie, and she started, glanced around.

Pete elbowed Frank, Frank looked away, mouth set and grim. She made herself busy with her taco box, pushed the napkins around, closed it, an orange smudge from the al pastor on the lid.

Ronnie leapt off the bench away from them, searched for a garbage can, walked as fast as she could. She scanned the street, prayed Marc hadn't chosen that moment to be waiting for her, but there it was, the black Range Rover, sitting high, idling at the curb a little way up. She had to go around it on the street to get in on the side that didn't have the plastic tub full of money. Angry, she jerked the door open, jumping in and shutting it as hard as she could.

"What did they want?"

"This place is crawling with cops. How could you bring me here, with the courthouses and police stations all around?"

"Who were those two men?"

"What men?" She was going to kill Frank. Or Pete. Maybe both.

"What did they say to you?"

"Nothing."

"I saw them looking at you."

"Maybe they were deciding what to have for lunch." Ronnie yanked on her seatbelt, taking a long time to find the slot so she didn't have to look at Marc. "How long have you been here? I was done hours ago." She looked out the window. "How many more stops?"

Marc put the car in gear, looked over his shoulder for an opening in the traffic, gave Ronnie a glance as he did so. "Until the money runs out or the banks close." The car moved along, Marc checking the GPS for the next stop. "You know, Mr. Anthony asked that I report to him everyone you talked to, don't you?"

Nice. Here's Frank telling her how important it was to keep this job and he's the one screwing it up. "So what," she said to her tinted window. "Every bank customer service person at all these branches that *you've* chosen." She pried off the lid of the bin and began filling the next shopping bag. "The taco truck guy who didn't have much English." She stared at Marc's headrest. "And no one else." She took up the next bag to fill it. The money would now smell like her tacos. "If you want to make something up about some guys in a park, go ahead. I just listed everyone I talked to today." She put the full shopping bag at her feet. "Oh, and you. I talked to you."

* * *

At their weekly meeting, Ronnie got mad all over again, letting Frank have it. She ranted on, about how the gallery owner told J.A. about "Tom Roberts," about how Marc saw them. "You need me to keep this job, right? I'm no good to you dead in the East River somewhere, am I?"

Frank didn't say anything, just sat there like a lump, watching her. She stopped talking, figured she'd made her point, and leaned against the bench with her arms folded across her chest. She wouldn't look at him, glared out across the Hudson at New Jersey, the sun making diamonds on the water, the Circle Line chugging along full of tourists.

He cleared his throat. "Sorry about that. I was more surprised than you were when Pete saw you. But it sounds like you handled it nicely. Tell me," he settled around in his seat as if ready for a long story, "what do you know about Marc? What kind of guy is he?"

The tourist boat made its way down the Hudson, smaller boats zooming past. "He's just a guy." She crossed her arms. "You met him."

"Okay." Frank looked out at the water, too. "Do you know his last name?"

"Don't you? You spent the whole afternoon with him. And Barbara. You could've asked Barbara."

Frank gave a grunt. She cut her eyes to him without moving her head. Maybe she'd pushed her luck, talked back too much.

"Okay. I can see you're mad at me." Frank put his hands in his trouser pockets. "But I do need your cooperation. And I think you'd rather have this job in a penthouse than idle your hours away in a prison cell."

She let out a long breath that blew her bangs off her forehead. "No one seems to have last names except Lisa Cranberry." She shifted on the bench, turned her face up to the sun, closed her eyes. "Like she's really proud of it, name plate on her desk as if strangers come by all the time and no one would know who she is."

Frank turned toward her on the bench, put his arm across the back. So buddy-buddy. "Okay, this next week, I want you to find out as much as you can about him. He's your new best friend. Where does he live, how he came to work for John, what does he like to have for lunch, is he married, kids, the whole thing. And a last name. Think you can do that?"

"He'll think I'm hitting on him."

"So?"

"Gross."

"You could ask Lisa about him."

"She'll think I'm hitting on him."

"So?"

"Jesus, Frank. I'm your man undercover, not your prostitute."

Frank sat silent, and she sneaked a peek at him. How would he take that? His mouth made a grimace, lips pressed together, corners pulling back.

"And as my man undercover, I need you to get information for me any way possible." He studied her, and she turned away to look over the water. "Any way that doesn't draw any more suspicion to you. I would think you'd be good at it."

Ronnie crossed her arms, slid lower on the bench. She should get some sunglasses. "What I'm good at is lifting wallets and running, not schmoozing and chatting people up." She sat up straight again, and he shifted in his seat. "That's what Isabelle was good at, not me. You should be using her if that's what you want."

Frank stood, gave a quick glance around them, put his hands in his pockets. "Well then, maybe you should channel Isabelle for this. You have your assignment. See you next week."

Ronnie opened her mouth to protest, then checked over her shoulder. How did a big guy like that disappear so quickly? Maybe he should be the one lifting wallets.

# Chapter Ten

Why Pete couldn't wake up on his own was beyond Frank. Like he was a teenager, growing so fast he required all the energy he could store up every night. Pete rolled over and put his pillow over his head. Frank pulled it away, along with his blankets. This was the third night Pete slept on his couch, the trek to his house in New Jersey too long, he said. Frank went over and raised the blinds, though not much sun came in. He poured Pete a cup of coffee and set it on the coffee table in front of him, sat on the table, and studied him. A dusting of pale stubble, lines etching his cheek from the wrinkles in the pillowcase, his T-shirt stained on the front.

"I gotta get in early."

Pete cracked open one eye and closed it again.

"You still have my extra set of keys. Lock up, will ya?"

They were actually Cathy's set, taken from her along with everything else when she went through the intake at the rehab facility. Before she ran away. He shut the door, not quietly, and took the stairs down to give himself time to leave the apartment behind, face toward work. He always considered that couch Cathy's, since that was where she slept for his divorced-father weekends. And where she went cold turkey. He thought she had the flu (*in August?* Susan's voice rang out), but when the hallucinations started, he raced her to the ER, and that was where they learned she was addicted. He banged out the front door of his building and down the stairs, turned left, headed to Third.

He felt it even now, that punch in the gut when the nurse said the words, the way Susan wouldn't meet his eyes. Because he knew they stopped the pain killers, she was back at school, recovered from the accident, except for a little hitch in her gait sometimes.

He stopped for the light, waited to cross. Goddamn hit and run driver mowed down his daughter in the crosswalk. The commuter crowd gathered at the corner, some stepped into the street as if they could make the light faster that way. He wanted to grab them, shout at them, tell them the whole story about his daughter, how she ran away from rehab, how she lived on the streets now, how he couldn't find her.

He walked downtown. Maybe he'd take the Lex at the next station. He could hear Cathy pretend-yelling at him, *The 4/5/6 Dad. You're so old-fashioned. No one calls it the Lex.* He spent as much time as he could searching for her, but mostly he sat tight. Like she would just show up. Maybe he should visit Leo again, hang around at night. For some reason, he didn't want Pete to find out, so he didn't go out these last couple of nights. He knew Pete would have his back, the whole Bureau had his back. They were his family, but this felt so private. As if, somehow, if he shared it with everyone, she would be diluted, fade away, leave him, and become theirs. His phone buzzed, and he put it to his ear without looking to see who it was.

"Why didn't you wake me?"

"Pete. Jesus. Short of dumping a pitcher of cold water on you, I couldn't wake you. I tried."

"Where are you? Wait up for me, we can go in together."

"This isn't high school, Pete." Frank was already at Grand Central and decided to take the train the rest of the way. In the large main concourse, the masses of people streamed at him as they made their way to work, and he threaded his way through. He used to love this. "Listen, Pete, buddy, you know you're welcome to stay as long as you need to…" He angled with the crowds for subways, a momentary bunching together a dress rehearsal for the commuter-hour sardine-packing on the subway, people so close he smelled them.

"No, that's okay, Frank. I'll bug someone else for tonight."

Frank heard water running, the toilet flushing. "No, Pete, that's not what

I'm saying. It's just—" Music from the earbuds of the woman next to him came at him, a clattering, metallic sound, and he eyed her, wondered how she stood it. "Listen, we'll talk at lunch. Whatever it is, I've got you. You know that."

* * *

Frank fired up his computer and checked the calendar, hoped nothing was on today, hoped he could distribute flyers of Cathy instead, take care of that so he could focus on the criminals the Bureau cared about. He read it twice and swore under his breath. He had somehow mixed up the weeks. That wasn't like him—he usually kept his calendar in his head. Today was his day to testify for the case code-named Operation NAME OF THE ROSE. They called it that because the criminals had used a florist to deliver the drugs, and he'd been tapped for it because they traced the money to terrorists. He shut down his computer, and took his sport coat, headed out. He might regret that he hadn't worn a suit today.

What was wrong with him? He'd distracted himself with the excitement of going undercover as Tom Roberts. And now he was headed to court in his blazer, and with this high-profile case, there were sure to be a lot of onlookers and even more journalists. He loved working on that case, undercover, long hours, the knowledge that the work was vital, the criminals off the street, the citizens safe. He made his way over to the courthouse, the sidewalk not as crowded this time of the morning, briefcases and heels, suits and accordion files. He had the best job in the world. He pursued the criminals, untangled the knot of how to catch them, and how to make the charges stick. At the curb, he waited for a break in the traffic. It wasn't just the end payoff, he also got the adrenaline rush from the undercover work, the secrecy, the getting in, working on the inside, fooling everyone around him. Then, coming home, shedding the persona along with the outside world, sure the good guys would win, and sure that he was one of the good guys. He just needed to keep his eye on his desk job, too.

* * *

Pete handed him his sandwich, unwrapped his own and took a huge bite before his butt even hit the seat. They had put Frank in a tiny room away from the prying eyes of the reporters who seemed to be everywhere, on the stairs, in the halls, in the elevator. Frank peeled back the paper on his ham and cheese, rye bread, and plenty of mustard. The bright yellow oozed over the crust, and Frank wrapped it up again, returned it to the bag.

"Isn't that what you asked for?" Most of Pete's words were garbled through his mouthful, his gesture with his sandwich hand at the bag the clearest indicator of what he said.

"No, it's fine. Not hungry, I guess."

Pete swallowed, took a slug of his drink. "You can't be nervous, the number of times you've testified."

Frank got up and stared out the narrow, dirty window. The green leaves hid most of the park from his view, a lawyer in a suit and tie hurried to the steps. He should've worn a suit. He surveyed his blue blazer, khaki pants. They'd have to do. At least he had the tie Pete had brought. "The AUSA asked if I left something out." He turned to see Pete ask a question with his eyebrows. "Since they didn't take a deal, wanted to go through with a trial."

Pete attacked his sandwich again, wiped his mouth, left a dab of mayonnaise on his cheek.

"Don't ask me anything until you finish chewing. Please."

Pete's jaws ground away, his eyes on Frank the entire time. "Frank, what is this? You're the most straight-up SA I know. You dot every "t" and cross every "i" and you don't arrest until you got it nailed down tight."

"Yeah, well, Special Agent or not, I don't think these defendants think I'm that special, and now they'll know who I am." He pulled out his chair to sit down, but pushed it in again. "Maybe that's why they wanted to go to trial. Wanted me out there publicly." He shook his head, paced again. "These guys are ruthless. I've seen what they can do."

Pete put his sandwich down on the bag, examined his greasy, balled-up napkin, put that down, and wiped his fingers on the outside of the paper bag. "Too bad I can't testify instead. I guess it would be hearsay, though. But what if we got word to the AUSA, tell them it would compromise you, your cover—"

Frank gave a shrug, paced the room, walked the narrow space between the heavy wooden chairs and the windows. "Thanks for the thought, but it's way too late for that."

"Is there something else, Frank? Something that happened—no, but I know you. You follow the rules even as a UCA. Not like some."

Frank kept pacing. If he got outed as an undercover agent, and someone, somehow, alerted John Anthony…aw nuts. Too far-fetched. He stopped pacing, shook out his arms, stood tall.

"So just stage fright, right? You got this. You can do it. You know this case like the back of your hand."

The door opened, and the court officer called in, "Special Agent Franklin Jankowski."

As Frank headed to the door, he threw Pete a look, but his partner concentrated on his sandwich, a lot of it on his face again. He'd try to live up to Pete's belief in him.

* * *

While he walked through the park on his way back to the office, the back of his brain automatically assessed the people around him, categorized them, dismissed them. It had done that in the courtroom, too. While he addressed the jury, his radar had been out, a habit so ingrained he did it without skipping a beat while he testified. Mostly, there were reporters, the artist sketching rapidly, a few court hangers-on who always showed up, retirees with a lot of time on their hands, but he didn't clock anyone who looked like they would be a threat to him later, who would keep him from future undercover work.

His brain told his feet to stop, and he surveyed the scene. Annie. The unmistakable blonde dreadlocks in a group of crusties, the obligatory dog with a bandana around its neck, the sign asking for money, perversely announcing it was for booze. She was nothing but trouble, and he walked again, picking up the pace as he heard "Whoa, Bro, wait up" behind him.

The reek of her reached him before the rest of her. He kept going and damned if she didn't come up in front of him, danced backwards while she faced him, forced him to a stop.

"Spare change, bro?"

"I thought you left town." In fact, Frank had counted on it. Annie was part of the reason he had three locks on the door to his apartment. She seemed to show up everywhere.

"Eh. Texas is too hot in the summer. What's that?" She pointed to his hand.

He had forgotten he held the uneaten sandwich from lunch, and he raised the bag to her eye level. "If I give you this, will you leave me alone, not follow me, not show up at my apartment, not—"

"You still living in the same place?" She smirked at him. At his scowl, she said, "Naw, don't worry about that. Too many walls. I like to live free."

He handed her the sandwich and walked away, but she was still with him, right next to him. The animal smell and maybe some Patchouli oil hung in the air between them. Good thing there was a shower in the Bureau workout room. He might need one if she came any closer. He realized he held his breath, and he turned his head away to inhale.

"Hey, bro, still looking for your daughter?" Her tone was almost kind, defiance gone, and he gave her a quick look but didn't answer. "I could help again, if you want. I mean, 'Mr. Ron' must be too soft by now, living up there on Park Avenue. Doorman and everything. You need someone who knows the streets."

"You seem to know a lot about what everyone's doing. Ever considered a job in law enforcement? Or as a CI, a Confidential Informant?"

She snorted at that and pulled Frank's sandwich out, let the bag drop on the walkway.

Frank bent down and picked it up, looked for a trash can. "Gee, Annie, I'd think you'd have more respect for your surroundings, especially as this is like, what, your living room?"

Annie gazed around her as if seeing her surroundings for the first time. Or like she was stoned. Frank walked again, and Annie kept right with him, chewed away.

"Do Confidential Informers get paid a lot? Hey, you got something to drink?"

Frank shook his head and veered over to a trash can, waved the yellow jackets away so he could deposit the crumpled bag. He resumed his quick pace, and Annie kept up with him. "Sometimes they get paid. Why, what do you know?"

Annie shrugged, dropped the sandwich wrapper, stopped to pick it up. She still held the trash when she caught up to Frank. "Nothing. Snitches get stitches. But I'll help you look for your daughter, and maybe you'll give me another sandwich like that, for my payment. For my help."

Frank didn't say anything. He knew the payment she exacted would not be that cheap.

"When're you going out again? I'll go with you, show you the places only crusties know about, places runaways like to hide."

"Thank you, but no. Last time you helped, it didn't really work out, did it?"

"Are you going tonight?"

"Annie, please. I don't need your help. I located her dealer, and I think that's a better approach."

"Bro." Annie socked his arm, but it wasn't as playful as her grin seemed to indicate. "Way to go. Who is it? I'll go with you. I know how to talk to these guys."

Frank shook his head.

"Look, no offense, but you look like a cop."

"Annie." Frank shook his head again. He stopped at the curb to wait for a break in traffic. "I am a cop." He said that more to himself than to her. "And I need to return to work. Some people work for a living..."

Annie was poised at the curb, ready to dash across the street.

"...so they can earn money and pay for sandwiches. Which they give to people like you."

She held his wrist tight, and he pulled against her, but she headed into the street, taking him with her.

"What the—Annie." Frank had to shout over the traffic.

The horns and squeal of tires drowned out her laughter, but he planted his feet and broke her grip with a quick self-defense move against her thumb. She darted across the street, gave the finger to the honking cars. The sandwich wrapper fluttered down. The wind picked up the greasy paper, turned it this way and that, plastered it to a windshield. He did not need Annie back in his life. She was too dangerous, too much of a leech.

* * *

As much as he wanted to spend the rest of the day looking for Cathy—without Annie Anarchy—he did need to move this case ahead. He and Pete met in the break room, a slightly depressing interview room repurposed and decorated with a coffee pot and a vending machine that expelled snacks most of the time. One of the overhead lights buzzed.

Frank laid out for Pete all the research he had done on Marc, the juvenile arrests for petty crimes, never sealed because of later arrests as soon as he turned eighteen. As far as he could tell, Marc had worked for John Anthony for at least six years. His mother lived in Queens, same address as Marc. She had sued her former employer for an unsafe work environment, claiming that her cancer came from the chemicals they'd made her use as an office cleaner. Looked like the lawyer raked off most of the settlement, and she was on disability.

"I went to see her." Frank drummed his fingers on the table.

"Oh yeah?"

"Yep. Pretended I was doing a background check on a neighbor boy who was Marc's age. Turns out they were best buddies and she was quite chatty about it, painting the juvenile delinquents as 'boys will be boys.' She's in a pretty bad way."

"How so?"

Frank described her slow movements, the oxygen canister she dragged around as she got him instant iced tea and pink iced animal crackers he had politely refused. "And she thinks he hung the moon. Says he's doing so well, buys her things, takes good care of her. Biggest TV screen I've ever seen, right there in the cramped living room. Among all the cat hair."

"She's on oxygen, and she has cat hair all over the place?" Pete got up and went to the vending machine. Swiped his credit card and punched in some numbers. "When's the last time you had animal crackers?"

"Not since my mother would greet me when I came home from school. Third grade."

Pete banged on the front of the machine.

"So," Frank found a napkin, wiped off the table. "I think that's our way in. His mother." Pete sat down again, having finally beaten a bag of potato chips out of the machine. "You think that's enough?"

Frank balled up the napkin. "From what she said, he must be as devoted to her as she is to him. And you know how these guys are about their mothers."

Pete crunched, nodded. "Be a shame for her to lose him."

"Bad as he is, she wouldn't want anything to happen to him."

# Chapter Eleven

Not much happening today. Ronnie wiped down a counter that didn't need it. She supposed she could rearrange the refrigerator shelves or something. She dried her hands on a tea towel.

"Marc is taking us shopping. Be ready at 10:00." Barbara came through the swinging door, heading straight to the refrigerator and found herself a bottle of water.

"Us, ma'am?" Maybe the shelves didn't need rearranging.

"Have you got an appointment or something? Another job?" She gave Ronnie a wink and turned to leave. As she went through the kitchen doorway into the dining room, Barbara added, "I need something to wear for tonight, for our dinner party."

Ronnie trailed after her, running a finger along the sideboard. What did that gang of maids do twice a week anyway? "Which restaurant are you going to?" Not that she cared.

"Oh, Kerry's doing it. He has a lovely meal planned." Barbara headed out into the foyer.

Ronnie caught up to her as she went up the stairs. "It's here? How many? What time?" She looked over the dining room. She'd have to check the silver, order a new centerpiece, shake out the tablecloth…

Barbara stopped halfway up the curving staircase and peered over the railing at her. "Didn't anyone tell you? An intimate dinner for ten, cocktails at 7:30, table seated at 8:15. Kerry's making his signature ossobuco."

"But—"

"I know, I know." Barbara turned to go up the stairs. "We're not supposed to eat veal, but can it really hurt to have it once in a while? And he's such a genius with it. Mmmmm-mmmm."

"Well, I just need to make sure everything's ready, and—"

"Oh, don't worry, it's not as if I've invited the crème de la crème for tonight. Just some of the artists, a gallery owner or two, that lovely Tom Roberts I met at Calfrida's the other day." She kept moving up the stairs, and Ronnie's eyes followed her as she turned at the landing. "John doesn't much go in for it, but after all those business dinners I had to sit through, he can certainly..." Her voice faded completely as she went down the hall on the second floor.

Holy Toledo. That bitch Lisa probably wanted to trip her up by not telling her. Gallery owners. She had to tell John—and why didn't Frank say something—he probably thought she already knew and wondered why she hadn't said anything—Frank undercover at a dinner party déjà vu all over again, and how could she get everything ready and stand around holding Barbara's shopping bags today. No way.

Ronnie raced to her room and closed the door, leaned against it as she pulled out her phone, opened to text, her finger hovering. Nothing she texted could get her an answer that would help right now. She shoved the phone back into her pocket and paced for a bit, three steps covering the room. Like a jail cell. Well, she knew how to serve Frank and pretend she didn't know him at a dinner party, but this whole gallery owner stuff. She'd better check in with John.

She hit the servants' stairs, clattered up them like she was possessed, her feet suddenly hushed on the thick carpeting when she came out on the second floor. Lisa's office door was open slightly, and she knocked as she swung it the rest of the way open. Lisa startled, a photograph falling out of her hand and into her lap. She rushed it into her paperback as a bookmark and glared at Ronnie, her eyes darkening. Who was that man in the photograph? Ronnie shut the door behind her, came to the edge of the wooden desk. She leaned over her.

"When," she hissed at her boss's personal assistant, "were you going to tell me about the dinner party?"

Lisa's teeth clicked together when she closed her mouth, and her cheeks flushed as she stared at Ronnie.

"And," Ronnie went on, "did you even bother to tell Mr. Anthony that the gallery owners were invited? Maybe you thought you'd play a joke on him, too." Ronnie turned sharply to the door, hand on the knob as she heard Lisa's desk chair slide back.

"I would never play a joke on him. Not John. And you can't just come in here—"

Ronnie let go of the knob and faced her, glad to see she wasn't all put together the way she usually was. A weird curl stuck out of the side of her head as if she'd hair-sprayed only that bit and now it protested.

"I certainly can come in here." Ronnie pointed a finger at her. "You deliberately didn't tell me about that party, and now Barbara knows that and soon John will too." She opened the door this time, pulled it almost closed, then stuck her head back through, made her voice low. "Don't fuck with me, Lisa. Not ever."

* * *

When Ronnie asked John if he had a minute, he swiveled from his screen, a scowl left over from whatever he worked on. "I have just a minute." He swiveled back to poke the keyboard, watched the screen, then faced her. "What seems to be the problem?"

Ronnie sat in the cushioned chair in front of his desk and blew out a breath, her bangs fluffing then settling. "Um, I'm just hearing about this dinner party tonight. Which is not the problem, not the main problem. Um," she cut her eyes to him, then studied the edge of his cherry wood desk in front of her. "Did you know Mrs. Anthony has invited the gallery owners, along with the artists, for this?"

John picked up the gold letter opener, passed it from one hand to the other, the jade handle appearing, disappearing. His birthmark began to darken. Ronnie followed the opener like it was a pendulum. Pretty soon, he would have her hypnotized, then he might ask her questions, then he'd find out—

She stood up as if the chair was suddenly electrified, backed away from it.

"I thought you should know. I mean, she just told me, and I wasn't sure…"

He put the letter opener down on the blotter, gave it a short pat, swiveled back to his computer screen. "You were right to mention it." He tapped his keyboard, but Ronnie couldn't see what was on the screen, the privacy cover keeping it dark. "Did she say which ones?"

Ronnie shook her head, then related the conversation, including the ossobuco.

"Well, that will at least make up for the conversation I'll have to sit through. Kerry makes a mean ossobuco."

Ronnie made sure that was the end of the conversation, then turned to go, her mind already listing off the things she would need to take care of, questions to ask Barbara.

"Hold on a minute."

Something in his voice made the hair on the back of her neck stand up. She turned from the door in slow motion. John had the letter opener again, and this time stabbed it over and over into the blotter.

"I'm hearing things from Marc." He looked her over as if to see how she was taking that.

Her heart beat so fast she was afraid he could see it pulsing in her neck. She stayed by the door. "Sir?" She hoped it sounded like she was bored.

"Marc. He said some cops recognized you at Foley Plaza. He thinks you're spying on us."

Ronnie willed herself to go stand behind the chair she had sat in when all she wanted to do was go out the door and down the elevator and into the street. But she had to convince John, so she could keep this job, so she could come through for Frank. She liked this job, anyway. John pulled the letter opener out of the blotter and kept it in his palm while he watched her, silent.

Ronnie drew herself up, expanded her chest, tried take up more space in the tiny office. "Am I supposed to answer that?"

"Do you have an answer?"

"How can I have an answer to something I have no idea about?"

John's birthmark darkened again. Maybe he was getting mad at Marc and not at her. He fiddled with the letter opener, turning it over and over. He raised his eyes to her without moving his head, wrinkled his forehead. "Why don't you tell me what happened?"

"I was starving, it was two o'clock, and I asked to stop for lunch. He chose the place. I got a taco and ate on a bench in Foley Square like he told me to. He said he'd pick me up there. So if anything is suspicious, it points to him since he chose the place."

"And the two men?"

Ronnie blew out her breath. "I have no idea about any men. He said he thought two guys were looking at me, but I never saw any two guys. So," she paused until J.A. raised his head, his eyes on her, "why would he make me have lunch right next to police headquarters? Foley Square is in the middle of all the courthouses, all the cops walking through there."

"I'm well aware of where Foley Square is."

"Maybe he was trying to get me in some kinda trouble. Get me arrested. What happened to the butler before me? Did Marc try to get rid of him, too?"

The chair squeaked as John sat back, the gold blade lying in the middle of the desk blotter, the carved jade handle dull in the light from his desk lamp. They both stared at it. She gripped the back of the guest chair, waited for him to speak. Evidently, he wasn't going to answer her. She was not going to beg, not going to plead with him that he had to trust her. But he did have to. She couldn't go back to living on the streets, this time avoiding an arrest warrant on top of figuring out how to feed herself, where to spend the night. She'd gotten used to sleeping in a bed. She swallowed.

"Sir."

He looked up. Curiosity, not anger in his eyes.

"You hired me to do a job, and I'm doing that job. Whatever you ask me to do, polish your shoes or take something to a gallery, I do it. No complaints, no deviation from your instructions. It wouldn't occur to me to do something other than what you've asked. You're the boss, and I'm the employee. Simple as that."

His eyes widened, and maybe she'd gone too far, pushed it over the edge.

But she had to defend herself. She crossed her arms over her chest and stared at him. He broke his gaze. Cleared his throat.

"Look." John's hands worked at themselves without the letter opener to play with. "I don't know what to think about Marc, I'm just passing on what he said. I do know that Mateo likes what he's heard about you, and I know I can at least trust you with a backpack and a briefcase full of money. So far, you haven't been tempted by the deposits you're making, and if I can continue to trust you, then Mateo will, too."

He swiveled back to his screen as if it had called his name, and Ronnie left as quietly and as quickly as she could. Better be the last she'd hear about that.

* * *

By the time Ronnie found Barbara in the library, her heart beat was almost back to normal. She pulled out the small leather-bound notebook, ready to jot down her employer's every word. It was more for effect, a signal to her brain to shut out the scene in John's office, focus on acting the model employee she'd sworn she was.

"I wanted to make sure I get everything exactly the way you like it. Are we doing a tablecloth, or place mats, and if place mats, the lace ones or the boards with the botanicals? Place cards? Shall I write them, or you? Which napkins, and which china? And should I let Kerry choose the wine or did you—"

Barbara closed her magazine and returned it to join the array on the coffee table in front of her. "Inside Drew's Sad Split" shouted to Ronnie upside down, a woman with her hair parted down the middle covering up most of the word "People."

"Well, you are thorough, aren't you?" Barbara tilted her head at Ronnie as if she saw a new side of her. She went through her various choices but got stuck on the china. "I can't remember which service I left for John here. Let's go look."

Ronnie followed her to the butler's pantry, the glass-fronted cupboards running all the way up to the high ceiling. Barbara, not needing a stool, took down one plate and then another, held them at arm's length as if the distance helped her imagine them on the table. She had a square plate in her left hand, white with some raised pattern, a round black pattern with gold whooshes in her right.

"I'm surprised I left him so much of the bone china." She handed Ronnie the black and gold one. "I usually like to have the bone at the Hamptons house. I swear, all those ladies sneaking in to turn over and read the plates before lunch."

After Ronnie asked her a few more questions, the flowers, the candles, the bar set-up, Barbara finally said that clearly she had too much to do and let her off the hook for shopping with her. Phew. She would now have the time to sparkle up the silver with the Windex and iron out the lace place mats. And put up her feet before the fun began.

* * *

At 8:30, Barbara's eyes found Ronnie's, her eyebrows raised for a quick tick before she turned back to Frank—Tom Roberts—and laughed at something he said. Ronnie disappeared to check on Kerry. She pushed open the swinging door, and a wet dish rag hit the door jamb next to her. Kerry slumped on a stool, stared at the stove top.

"Are you drunk?" Ronnie lowered her voice. "Are you goddamn freakin' drunk?" She kept her voice low but fierce. "This is how the famous Kerry makes ossobuco? Go sit the fuck over there in the corner."

Ronnie moved aside knives and cutting boards, a half-full wine bottle which had left red rings on the marble, finally found the scribbled menu. She plated the starter—roasted shrimp she dotted with cocktail sauce, threw some parsley confetti over—then laid out the plates on an enormous serving tray.

"Get your act together, Kerry." She backed through the swinging door. She'd probably get the blame, not the sainted Kerry, if this dinner party was a disaster.

* * *

Ronnie came through for the main course, but Kerry was no better. She wrestled him into the servant stairs, told him to go sleep it off upstairs. She plated the ossobucco, arugula and grapefruit salad, two crusty rolls. The bones on the plates stared at her, googly eyes in the glistening meat. Smelled like heaven. Maybe someone was a vegetarian, and she'd get the leftovers. As she made her way around the table delivering the main course, two gallery owners seated across from each other were arguing with a lot of hand motion about post-post-modernistic pseudo-something-something. Through the noise, she heard from down the table "Operation NAME OF THE ROSE." Frank started, though he covered up the movement by leaning away from the table so Ronnie could set down his plate. He turned his back on the guy talking about some trial and said something to his dinner partner.

Back at her station, Ronnie leaned against the wall, butler-invisible, ears tuned to the trial conversation between one of the artists and John. She stayed on alert to the whole room in case she needed to butler someone, but her ears zeroed in on the conversation while her eyes roamed the table. Frank seemed a little jumpy about this rose thing, so she wanted to pay extra attention.

Randolph Eckerty, the guy who painted "Snow on Ice" that Frank and Barbara had competed for at the gallery, was still talking to John. She caught some words, "testifying," "money laundering," "undercover." The artist raised his voice. "You don't think he looks like him?"

"I'm afraid I'm focused more on the London Financial Times than the New York Post." John's eyes were on Frank, and he narrowed them at him.

The two gallery owners stopped their discussion-argument, and one of them said, "He does, sort of. Were you testifying at the trial, Tom?"

"Trial?" Frank gazed around the table as if he'd just come out of a long movie to find it was still daylight. Ronnie began to clear, maybe she'd distract everyone, but her stomach churned, and she didn't trust her hands to pick up the loaded tray yet.

Conversation stopped, everyone waiting for his answer. Frank glanced around as if to find the guy who had asked the question, but John turned to him. "Randy thinks you look like the undercover agent from the NAME OF THE ROSE trial."

"Really? You mean I have a Doppelganger?" He beamed at John. "I was an only child, but I always wanted a brother. A twin, now, that would be something."

"Have you been following the trial?"

"No, not really. Not my thing. This ossobuco was thoroughly delicious. Better than any restaurant."

"They only had the courtroom drawings, so you know how that goes, but something in the eyebrows, the jawline..." Randolph sketched the air over Frank's face.

No way she was going to watch Frank anymore. She might throw up. She picked up the water pitcher and looked for water glasses to fill, not making eye contact with anyone. Barbara glanced up when she got to her place and whispered that she should bring in the dessert. Ronnie straightened up and said, "Ma'am," then felt John's eyes on her from down the table and gave him a quick look, ready to go to that end for whatever he wanted. His head was tilted to the side, like he thought if he looked at her hard enough, he could read her thoughts. She hurried to finish clearing, snaking her arm between the guests, dreading when she'd reach John. The conversation had thankfully turned away from Frank and on to something arty she couldn't understand. But if John didn't stop watching her every move, she might drop a plate. She moved as quickly as she could without actually running.

She made it into the kitchen without spilling or breaking anything. She couldn't start shaking now. She had to pull it together. Double time she piled the dishes on the counter, got the lemon mousses out of the refrigerator, lined the crystal parfait glasses up on the tray. At least Kerry had taken care of those before he passed out. She shook out her arms, trying to release the trembles. She hit the start button on the coffee maker, then picked up the tray. She turned so she could back through the swinging door, then stopped when it bumped into her. She butted it again but the door wasn't giving and she turned around to see what stopped it. John Anthony pushed the swinging door open and nearly made her flip her tray over. She backed away and rested it on the counter. She still held the handles, and she looked over her shoulder at him.

"Are you looking for Kerry?"

John Anthony opened his mouth, closed it, his eyebrows meeting in confusion. "Kerry? Why would I be looking for him?"

"Kerry passed out, and I told him to go upstairs and sleep it off. That's why I had to serve so late." Ronnie picked up the tray to go out the door, but John still blocked it.

"We have to talk." John stared at her.

"Okay, sure. But I have to serve." She lifted her load at him as if he hadn't noticed the lemon mousse in the glasses, candied peel curling on the surface like yellow moss.

Her boss smiled at the dessert, then dropped the smile. "You seem nervous."

Ronnie shook her head. "I'm trying to get through a dinner party without a chef, and not have the guests know that there's a problem." She rested the tray on the edge of the counter.

"This guy, Tom Roberts. You looked a little pale, green even, when Randy said he looked like the undercover agent from the trial."

"I don't know what you're talking about. When I serve at a dinner party, I'm watching everyone to see what they need, what I can do to make the dining experience as seamless as possible. I don't listen to the conversation. And speaking of seamless, I've got to get these served." She lifted the tray. Thank God her hands didn't shake.

"Hold on. One more minute. Are you sure you don't know this guy? This guy, who may or may not be an agent, is testifying at the trial. If you were me, wouldn't you be a little suspicious that he shows up when you and my wife are touring galleries?" He took a step toward her, and she took a step back, the lemon mousse like soldiers on the tray between them. "And then he gets invited to a dinner party and is recognized by a portraitist who knows faces? Recognized as the undercover agent who busted a money launderer. Why wouldn't alarm bells go off?"

She cleared her throat. "You know more about it than I do. I'm not you, so I can't say if I'd be suspicious or not. I'm a foot soldier taking orders, and Mrs. Anthony has asked that I bring out the dessert. Those are my orders right now."

"And," he said as if she hadn't spoken, "to go further back, one day my butler doesn't return to the house, but you show up, having just worked for someone arrested by the FBI. Maybe you're here because you're working for the FBI." His eyes looked like they might shoot things at her. "For all I know, you're wearing a wire right now."

In the silence following his accusation, the murmur of the dinner party came through the door, a laugh, the clink of silver on china. She put down the tray and stood as tall and as wide as she could, stared at him. She loosened her tie, pulled it over her head, put it down on the counter next to the desserts. She faced him again and got to work on the top button of her shirt.

His eyes widened, and he took a step back. "What're you doing?"

"I." Unbutton. "Am." Next button undone. "Showing you." Pretty soon, he was going to see she was too flat-chested to wear a bra. "That I'm not wearing a wire." Her fingers were on the next button.

"I think I've seen enough to believe you."

She rebuttoned quickly, reached for her tie.

"At least on that score. I'm still not convinced you're not working with this Tom Roberts guy."

She flipped her collar up and tightened her tie, centered the knot, folded the collar down. She shook her head at him. She didn't think she could say anything without making him even more suspicious. She hated lying.

"No? Then it'll be a cinch for you to prove that to me."

Now what. She didn't trust herself to speak. The coffee machine gave a small beep. At least the coffee service was all laid out.

"Okay. You're going to follow him out the building, you're going to mug him, rough him up a little, then bring me proof. Film it."

She cleared her throat. Looked at the desserts, no longer so appetizing.

"I've never mugged anyone in my life."

"Are you saying you won't do it?"

She'd never heard his voice sound so deadly. She shook her head. "He's such a big guy. I think I'll need a weapon."

He went to the coffee maker, poured it into the ornate server. "That's your problem."

She picked up the dessert tray once more, and John had the silver tray with the coffee and cups. She turned her back to the door and watched her tray so she wouldn't have to look at him. What the fuck. She hated violence.

* * *

Ronnie slipped back into the kitchen after doling out the dessert and pouring the coffee. And avoiding looking at Frank. She picked up the house phone, hit the button for the desk, Patrick answering on the third ring. She whispered into it. "Dude—hey, um—"

"Mr. Ron? Hello? I can't hear you. Everything all right?"

Ronnie looked around the kitchen. She opened the service door, went onto the concrete landing, stretching the curls out of the wire connecting the receiver to the base on the wall. She closed the door as much as she could, the garbage smell of all the cans on all the floors hitting her. "Patrick. Everything's fine. But, I mean, did you say you had a taser?"

Patrick breathed into the phone.

"Well…can I borrow it?"

"I don't know what you mean. Those are dangerous. And illegal."

Patrick paused so long Ronnie pulled the handset away from her ear and looked at it. Like that would tell her anything. Far away words came out of it, and she put it to her ear again.

"…leave my desk, I am not responsible for what you may or may not find in the drawer."

* * *

Ronnie hit the sidewalk, out of breath but with the taser tucked into the waistband of her butler trousers. All the way down the service stairs, she had prayed that Frank wasn't taking an Uber or a taxi. That he felt like walking on this fine night. She didn't even know which way he would've gone, but she had a feeling he lived south of the penthouse, so she took off in that direction. And prayed again, he hadn't yet crossed Park Avenue to head east. Her lungs screamed at her, and tears of sweat ran down her face, the cool spring air only a little relief.

She had to catch up to Frank, let him know what John was making her do, that she had to record it for him on her phone. Doormen watched her as she approached, her loud dress shoes tap-tap-tapping. She toyed with the idea of approaching him from behind, not telling him it was coming. Just to mess with him. Yappy dogs on leashes jumped, and their owners stepped back, pulling the dogs with them. But that would be too mean, and even though he could be a hard ass, he didn't deserve that. She had no idea how much damage a taser could do, but it must do something if the police liked it.

He had to be nearby—she had run down those stairs, sure she wasn't much behind the elevator from the penthouse. Why couldn't those freaking dinner guests push the button themselves. She stopped at the cross street, her breath ragged. Maybe he'd crossed Park here. Her light changed, and she stepped into the crosswalk just as a dark car edged into it. She slapped the hood to emphasize that it was in her space. That was Frank, wasn't it, down—what the—the car bumped her and she hammered with her fists, glared at the driver.

Fuck. Marc glared back at her. Waved his phone at her. She was going to lose Frank. Marc was going to keep her from passing John's test, and then what would happen to her?

He rolled down his window, yelled out it. "Keep going. I'm filming it for the boss." He wagged his phone again.

She ran, pumping faster as the countdown for the crosswalk neared zero. She thought she'd seen him go down that street, empty this time of night. She looked over her shoulder for the dark Range Rover. Maybe she could zoom past Frank, warn him somehow.

She headed down the street and heard a car behind her. Yup. Marc. So she really did have to go through with it. Where was Frank? There. Halfway down the long block, tall guy ambling east, broad shoulders, short hair cut. She prayed he wouldn't turn around, wouldn't know it was her. The idling car couldn't mask the sound of her shoes. Maybe she should take them off so Frank wouldn't hear her coming, wouldn't turn around and say her name.

He was still a ways away from the corner, so she put her foot on the bumper of a parked car to get to her laces. Even though the whoop of a siren was somewhere else in the city, she started, had to stop herself from bolting. Marc rolled down the passenger side window, the fumes from the engine swirling around her. He yelled something, maybe *hurry it up*. As fast as she could, she finished untying her leather butler shoes, tied them together, and threw them on her shoulder. She wanted to give Marc the finger, but she couldn't risk his telling John. After all this, John freakin' Anthony better well trust her.

She ran. Her shoes banged against her, and her breath came hard, Marc and his sinister car just over her shoulder, Frank whistling three buildings away. Fire escapes gleamed in the streetlight, a rat raced in front of her. Her target was several strides in front of her now. Would Marc's car make him turn around? She pulled the taser out of her pocket, put a hand on her shoes so they stopped hitting her chest. She'd never shot anything. Nothing like a gun, no paint gun, no air gun, maybe a Nerf dart gun. How close did she have to get to him—he was turning, he must've heard her. She pulled the trigger.

A loud pop, the crackling as the wires went zinging into his shoulder, his arm, his back. He let out a yell, a roar, and he went down, twisting, maybe trying to see her. She ran. She crossed around the Range Rover, crouched behind a car on the other side. She could hear Frank swearing, Marc's car still there. She crept along, but she couldn't see anything, parked cars hiding Frank on the sidewalk. Why was Marc out of his car, a thud, a shout, Marc back behind the wheel and racing away.

She inched her head up. Frank was standing, twisting around, probably pulling the barbs out. That had to hurt. She'd never heard anyone yell like that. Like an animal. He moved to the middle of the street, looked east, like he thought about running after Marc's car. Maybe she should inch away, head away from him while his back was turned. Hunched over, she headed west, her shoes swinging. She hugged the cars, maybe she could stand up soon, run before he saw her. This crouching and running was hard, and she steadied herself on the next car, setting off the alarm. Damn damn damn.

She stood up, Frank already coming toward her. A window went up across the street, and then the alarm cut out. Frank did not look happy. Ronnie checked up and down the street. No sign of Marc. "Frank..." Her voice was hoarse, barely a whisper. She tried again. "I'm sorry—I had to—he made me..."

He was nearly past her, and he hadn't said a word.

She grabbed at his arm. "But—"

He stopped. Shook off her hand. Looked through her like he didn't even know her. In a fierce, low voice, he said, "We can't be seen together." In a louder, meaner voice, he said, "I don't have any money on me." And he continued walking, his footsteps echoing, fading away.

# Chapter Twelve

What the actual fuck. He would deal with her later, find out what this was all about. And who the guy was that kicked him in the ribs. Goddam. The last thing he expected was to get tased. The longest five seconds of his life. Worse than during training since he wasn't prepared for it. Ronnie looked miserable, but she wasn't the one who'd lost all control and hit the cement. His forehead throbbed where he'd landed, and he felt around, his fingers coming away with blood on them. He tried to shake everything out as he walked, loosen every single muscle that had tightened with the electricity. He would deal with Ronnie tomorrow. Or let her stew, wait for the regular weekend debrief. Goddammit.

* * *

No way he could run today, and somehow he convinced Pete that they could just walk around the reservoir. He didn't want to tell his partner what happened last night. Seemed like an admission of weakness, a failing, even though he knew it wasn't his fault. Though if he hadn't been at the penthouse, would she have tased him? He was still angry with her, reminded every time his ribs screamed at him. Why was it always the ribs?

Pete speedwalked ahead, his wiry body slicing past the 432 runners on the reservoir path this sunny Saturday morning. Frank lengthened his stride, but didn't pick up the pace. Last thing he needed was the impact on the cement jarring his ribs and possibly puncturing a lung.

After a week and a half on his couch, Pete's work clothes hung in Frank's closet, the weird green stuff he drank for breakfast center stage in his refrigerator. An easy friendship, easy partners, easy roommates. Maybe he shouldn't be keeping the tasing from him. Frank tried to lose himself in the rhythm, swinging his arms, breathing, but it wasn't the same as running, the steady strike of shoes on the path, his lungs and heart working together, his mind on his stride, his form, with no room for thoughts.

Pete veered away in front of him, stopping at the fence overlooking the water. Frank stopped beside him, rubbing some of the sweat off his face with his T-shirt-covered shoulder. His and Pete's breathing nearly in unison.

"She wants me to move out."

Frank could barely hear him. "Let's walk and talk," was all his brain came up with, but it was enough for Pete, and they moved to the side of the path.

As the sweat dried and their breathing slowed, Pete talked, describing the twelve-year descent of their marriage, the way they used to look at each other over the heads of their children at the table, then the way they stopped looking at each other at all.

"Even if I didn't have an active case, I'd find some reason to work late."

Frank nodded. Listened. Made an uh-huh noise.

"And she said that even when I was home, I wasn't there. Not paying attention to her or the kids."

"Married to the Bureau."

Pete gave Frank a quick look. "Are you bugging my house? My phone?"

Frank laughed, though not because it was funny. "That's what Susan would say to me. Over and over and over again."

"You never told me that."

Frank shrugged. "I thought that's what every spouse thought. Let's go to that place on Madison, the one with those great bagels."

Pete's face lit up. "Last one there buys." He took off faster than Frank thought his partner capable of.

* * *

Pete was already seated at a table outside when Frank got there. Of course, the seat he left for Frank shimmered in full sunlight, Pete cool in the shade. Frank's wrought iron chair encroached on the sidewalk, people passing by a little closer than he'd like. He angled his chair so he straddled the corner of the table, and watched the street for a beat. He never got tired of people watching, all the different shapes and sizes, trying to guess what they did to earn money based on their dress, the way they walked. He adjusted his baseball hat. Rude to leave it on at the table, but he had the sun as an excuse. And it hid the bump on his forehead.

The waiter set down their plates, Pete having gotten something that seemed too big to take a bite out of, oozing with melted cheese, piled with bacon, a fried egg or two curling at the edges in a brown lace. Frank's smoked salmon and cream cheese smiled on the plate, this restaurant getting the perfect balance between them, topping it off with a few tendrils of purple onion, thinly sliced tomato, capers sunk into the cream cheese so they couldn't roll away.

"Pete," Frank took another bite. "I'm sorry you're going through this. You know you can stay as long as you need to." He picked up his bagel and took a bite, people-watched while he chewed. "I told you about the dinner party, right?"

Pete, his cheeks bulging, shook his head. To get Pete's mind off his troubles, Frank told the story as if it were the funniest thing, the conversation stopping, all eyes on him, John Anthony staring him down, Ronnie looking like she might throw up. "So there I am in the spotlight, mapping out all the exits, and the artist says—"

"Tom? Tom Roberts?"

A woman's voice rang out, and they both turned toward it, Pete finally shutting his mouth, which had hung open the entire length of Frank's story, his breakfast sitting on his plate. She came up to their table, breaking the invisible barrier between the diners and the public. Frank put his bagel down, angled his head to see the woman. Damn. What a small town this could be.

"Uh, yes...Maggie. What a surprise." He took up his napkin to clean his right hand and half rose out of his seat, extending it for a shake.

"Oh, don't let me disturb your breakfast. Really, sit down. I was just passing and I had to say hello. I never see anyone I know in the city." His dinner partner from the other night turned her gaze on Pete, and Frank introduced them, calling him "Jim Jones," the first name he could think of, unfortunately.

She gave a little laugh as she shook his hand. "Rap or Kool-Aid?"

"I'm an actuary, actually. Do you have life insurance?" Pete's voice was a monotone. Even Frank didn't want to listen to any more of it.

"So nice to meet you. I've got a lot of errands to run still, and my husband has this thing this afternoon…" She gave them a little wave as she turned away, *lovely to see you* trailing after her.

"You know," Frank picked up his bagel, "actuaries don't sell the insurance, they—"

"What the *what* was that?"

"You sounded like you were trying to sell her life insurance, and I was explain—"

"Frank, I'm pulling you out. Right now." Pete seemed larger, broader, taller in his seat. And he stopped eating, his plate cradling a quarter of his breakfast, his napkin crumpled beside it.

"What are you talking about? It's nothing I can't handle." Frank popped his last bite into his mouth. Leaned back in the tiny chair, crossed his arms, and stretched his legs onto the sidewalk.

"You. Can't. Handle." Pete's words like bullets. "Frank." Pete paused until Frank sat up and faced him. "Frank." He repeated it as if to be sure he was with him. "This isn't about you. I don't care about you."

"Thanks a lot."

"What I care about is that you're endangering Ronnie. A civilian. I don't care how street smart she is. She hasn't had the training you have, and you've put her in there with the Mataderos Cartel, the most dangerous, most heinous cartel in all Latin America. And you seem to think it's all too funny." Pete's eyes dark, his jaw set.

"You can't pull me. I'm just getting started. Look, nothing happened. I asked if they thought I had an evil twin."

"And what happened then?"

Frank shrugged. "They just talked about something else, something in the art world. Ronnie took her tray into the kitchen and then brought out dessert. Lemon mousse. You would've loved it."

"What did John do? Was he happy with your answer?"

Frank shrugged. "Seemed to be. He went into the kitchen and came back out with her, carrying the coffee."

"That's it. Consider yourself pulled. I'm your case officer, and I'm pulling you. You have no perspective on this, and you're endangering your CI. Frank. *He followed her into the kitchen.* Do you really think he thought the butler needed help serving?" Pete pulled two twenties out of his running shorts pocket, tucked them under his plate, the edges fluttering as a car passed on the street. "What did she report about what he said to her in the kitchen?" Pete stood, his chair scraping on the cement, a sharp jangle emphasizing his question.

"Nothing. We're not due to meet for another few days."

"Jesus, Frank."

Frank didn't feel like craning his neck to look at his partner.

"This isn't like you." Pete headed for the sidewalk.

Frank looked at the money, figured he should leave the rest of the tip, but all he had on him was a credit card, and it seemed like a lot of effort to pull it out, wait for the guy to run it. He joined Pete, and they walked side by side.

"You meet up with the target's wife on a whim," Pete's voice low, "the Bureau has to scramble to put together your cover, and now you've endangered a very valuable CI."

Frank's bagel lay heavy in his stomach.

"What were you even thinking?" Pete lengthened his stride, increased his pace, and Frank let him go ahead. He watched the dark T-shirted back of his partner, then began walking. In all their time together, he'd never seen Pete pay for a meal. He looked back at the restaurant. Might as well go back and leave a better tip.

* * *

Laundry day today, and by the time Frank wandered back to his apartment, no Pete, but a pile of sweaty running clothes reeking on the bathroom floor, so he threw those in the hamper too. He was glad he didn't have to deal with Pete. That was unfair, yelling at him like that. Overly cautious, even, and Pete would squelch the case. His case.

He stripped off his T-shirt and shorts and threw them in the hamper, turned on the shower, looked at his face in the bathroom mirror while he waited for the water to get hot. The road rash on his forehead looked worse. At least the baseball hat covered most of it up, so he didn't have to lie to Pete.

He'd spent a lot of time putting this case together, and he'd spent a lot of time with Ronnie. He knew her better than Pete did, and he knew what she could handle and what she couldn't. In fact, he thought as he stepped into the shower, she usually surprised him with how quick-thinking she was, how she always landed on her feet, and how she took everything in stride. She was a superstar. Why couldn't Pete see that?

* * *

Down in the laundry room, piling his sheets, Pete's sheets, all the towels, and the contents of the hampers into the miraculously empty machines, Frank couldn't stop thinking about what Pete said. He couldn't pull him. This was his case, his CI. He hadn't really put Ronnie in danger, had he? Maybe she'd tased him because she was mad at him, but then what had she said...*he made me.* She was apologetic, not mad. Oh shit. He stood up, paced. Why hadn't he remembered that? Too angry with her at the time to pay attention—what was wrong with him? He *had* put her in danger, made John Anthony suspicious, the guy in the car most likely one of John's guys, there to confirm what she'd done.

The washing machines chugged to a stop, each one in turn. He pulled someone's dry clothes out, dumped them on the table, moved the wet loads into the dryers. He had to sit down. He should be protecting his CI. He'd been so eager to be out in the field again, like old times, the fancy dinner party, Ronnie serving. It made him feel alive, made everything else seem so mundane and boring. And he'd screwed it up. He pulled his phone out. If Pete were pulling him, was he allowed to even text her? He texted Pete instead.

*Should we pull her too?*

Frank sat on the bench and stared at his phone. He hadn't sent the text yet. If Pete said yes, then Frank would've single-handedly screwed up the case. Royally. Well, not asking the question wasn't going to change the outcome. He hit send.

His eyes traced the worn brick of the floor, the cracks and stains. The dryers stopped, one after another, with a hard, insistent buzz as if each agreeing he'd fucked up. He pulled the first load out. What the hell was this? His sheets had huge blue streaks, the towels too. He pushed aside the stranger's load on the table and plopped down his supposedly clean laundry. This looked like ink. He stuck his head in the empty dryer. A cheap ballpoint pen. Ink all over the drum, and now all over his and Pete's clothes.

He wanted to hit something.

He headed back to the apartment with the ruined laundry, past the garbage and recycling chutes, the big compactor churning away at the garbage. He heard some clattering and watched as someone's recycling came down the chute and into the big blue bin. Too bad no one incinerated anymore. He'd get real satisfaction watching all this ruined laundry burn up.

* * *

His phone buzzed as he crammed a reluctant pillow into a case. He threw the half-covered pillow onto his bed and pulled out his phone.

*Case has barely started*

He returned the phone to his pocket. Case has barely started and he'd already messed it up. But if Pete didn't think she was in that much danger, then why should Frank get pulled? He left the laundry. He'd fold it later. Another text came in.

*Unless you know something I don't*

Like he could see into his soul. Frank never kept things from Pete, never screwed up a case, never made mistakes like this. He had been so restless, so eager to dive into another world, get away from the worries about Cathy, if just for a minute. It had felt so right jumping at the chance when Ronnie texted about the galleries, Tom Roberts talking art with the wife of the money launderer, rubbing elbows with the art world in the fancy penthouse.

Maybe he'd kept the tasing from Pete because he knew in his heart of hearts that it was a bigger deal than he wanted to admit to himself. Dammit. He called his partner.

* * *

He found Pete at the bar eating peanuts so fast he hardly had time to shell them. The shells that hadn't hit the counter littered the floor around his stool, mixing with the sawdust and other peanut shells. Fire inspection must love this place.

Pete nodded to him, went back to watching the soccer game, and eating peanuts.

Frank didn't like sitting with his back to the rest of the room, but the place was pretty empty, and they were the only ones at the bar. He asked for an iced tea, and when the bartender left, Pete said, without looking at him, "I'm listening."

Frank sucked in a breath. Let it out. Told him. How he was minding his own business, happy to be undercover again, the street empty, a car idling somewhere, then turning to look who was behind him, and zap! the barbs going into him, the five seconds of complete agony, hitting the ground. Pete recoiled, like he could feel the barbs too, the sidewalk on his face.

"Wondered what happened to your forehead."

"Then the driver gets out of the idling car and kicks me. Hard. Before I could even get up. Puts his phone away. Drives off."

"And? Where's Ronnie in all this?"

"Up the street, setting off car alarms. She's the one that tased me."

"And you know this because..."

"She was apologetic, said he made her do it."

Pete swiveled, faced Frank. "You spoke to her? You went up and spoke to her after the guy—"

Great whoops came from around them, and Pete's head whipped back to the screen. "Dammit. There goes that bet."

Frank drained his iced tea. "Pete. Please. Have some faith in me. I walked past her, told her we couldn't be seen together."

"And you think he was filming it for proof for John Anthony?"

Frank nodded. "Had to be." He used the tiny bar napkin to wipe off the counter in front of him.

Pete watched the TV screen, yelled at the guy who had missed the goal. He turned back to his partner. "All we can do is ask her. She hasn't texted you, has she?"

Frank shook his head. Turned his glass around and around, seeds from the lemon soggy on the cubes.

"Okay. I'm guessing that she passed his test and everything's all right, since we haven't heard from her. We have to expect that she'd get a few tests here and there, especially with Tom Roberts—"

"I get it. I get it. I fucked up and I'm off the case. You don't need to rub it in." Frank pulled out his wallet to leave a tip. "I just wanted to give you that information."

Pete eyed the dollar bill on the bar. "You're not off the case. You're still working it, you're just not handling Ro—" He glanced around, lowered his voice. "—her. Plenty more to do otherwise." He studied Frank's face. "We're still a team."

Frank grunted, slid off the stool.

"Right? Still a team?"

"I gotta go buy some sheets."

* * *

He put his gun on his hip and found a light jacket to cover it. Shame since the weather was so nice, a polo shirt being plenty for today. But he was used to it by now, and since he was going to pass out flyers in the less friendly places, he should have his gun.

He went out the door, pausing to throw the deadbolts. He needed something to distract himself from the case, the tasing, the risk to Ronnie. He headed down the stairs. He would never want to use the gun, of course. Prayed he wouldn't find himself in that kind of situation. Besides, way too much paperwork. Merely insurance. Had to have it, but never wanted to need it. Searching for Cathy, he hadn't covered Central Park as well as he should have, so he headed for the Lex. Maybe he should start calling it the 4/5/6, invoke Cathy, bring her closer to him. He'd get off at 103rd, make his way west, find some street kids to give the flyers of Cathy to. Some days it seemed hopeless, the city so vast, the kids such wrecks. He tap danced down the steep steps to the turnstiles, the cooler air welcome on his face, gritty as it was.

* * *

A gang of kids littered the steps at Duke Ellington Circle, and Frank pulled out Cathy's picture, held it in front of him as he approached, a white flag signifying he wasn't their enemy. He stood on the walkway looking up at them. All the usual words—I'm looking for my daughter, have you seen her, could you really look at the picture, we love her, we just want her safe—the kids jeered and chanted, shook the hat at him, asked for money. The dog with the bandana looked mangy and Frank entertained the idea of scooping it up, taking it home, giving it the care it deserved.

"What's your dog's name?"

Several voices answered. "What's it to you?" "Dawg." "Food ain't cheap."

He reached into his pocket, pulled out a five. "Does that girl look familiar to you?"

One of the kids, the greasiest one, grabbed the puppy and crowded Frank. "We'll sell it to you. Fifty bucks."

Frank backed up, put the money in his pocket.

"Hey, wait! Is that guy a cop?"

"Run!"

A head full of white dreadlocks bounced his way. "Well, that got rid of 'em." Annie Anarchy gave him her loopy grin. "What're we doin' today?"

"Annie. Was that you who yelled *cop*?" Frank carefully folded the flyer, stuffed it into his jacket pocket. He made his movements deliberate, because if he didn't keep his hands busy, he might reach over and strangle her. "I wanted to canvas them, see if they'd seen Cathy."

"I can help. C'mon over here." She tugged on his arm, headed for the Gorilla Cheese truck. Of course she did.

He took his arm back. "Annie, why don't you tell me first if you've seen my daughter."

"I can't think on an empty stomach. C'mon, dude."

He was too tired to deal with her today. "Annie, here's a twenty. More than enough to cover a meal. And if you want to help me, you can take this flyer and ask around. But I'm going to canvas on my own, and if you hear of anything, you can call me." He gestured at her with the flyer, gave her the twenty only after she'd taken the piece of paper with Cathy's picture.

Annie pocketed the twenty faster than he thought possible, then her hand darted into his windbreaker and grabbed the rest of his flyers. She took off, an evil laugh bouncing behind her in rhythm with her white-girl dreads.

He rezipped his jacket. She'd zoomed away so fast he could no longer see her.

# Chapter Thirteen

T*his is Uncle Pete,* the text said. Must be spam or a wrong number. Ronnie was about to hit the delete button when another message came in. *I got a new number.* Shit. Pete. Weird that Pete was texting her. *Eye in the Sky 3:30, Loews Lincoln Square Snape's last movie meet me there?*

She put down her book. *See you there,* she texted back. Why was Pete texting her? Was Frank really hurt? He'd walked away all right. Maybe he was mad at her. But this was days early for the debrief. Something had to have happened.

She glanced at her book. Barbara had said she was welcome to read anything in their library, and "Gone Girl" had caught her eye, and now she couldn't put it down. She had thought it would be about a runaway teenager, like she could help Frank better if she read it. But so far, it was about a husband who probably murdered his wife, and she couldn't wait to see how he did it. She could get a few more chapters in before she had to leave.

John Anthony had seemed happy with the footage Marc had given him, his birthmark a soft pink when he'd congratulated her. Evidently, Marc had gotten good footage of the whole thing, though why did he have to kick him in the ribs? She winced. Like she could feel it in her ribs, too. After Frank had passed her and wouldn't talk to her, she had had to take her socks off, they were so shredded, and put her shoes on over her bare feet for the walk back. She left her socks on top of a garbage can at the front of a brownstone.

No way she could read this book now. It was Frank's fault she had to tase him. What was he doing here anyway? And he'd just been at a big trial, and there's a drawing of him in the paper. Damn. She paced the tiny room, peered out the dirty window into the narrow airshaft. Maybe she'd just go a little early, walk a good part of the way. Damn Frank. Everything's fixed with John, and now it's all messed up with Frank. And what did Pete want anyway?

* * *

They sat in the balcony, the place everyone went who wasn't there to watch the movie. The floor was sticky, and Ronnie bet it wasn't only from Coca-Cola. She pulled her feet up to the edge of her seat, wrapped her arms around her knees.

"Where's Frank?" She whispered at Pete. This was the first chance she'd gotten to ask. When she'd seen him out front, he gave her a sideways, favorite-uncle hug, paid for her ticket, and they talked about nothing while he bought popcorn and drinks. They went up to the balcony and sat in the top row, the seats slammed up against the wall. "Has something happened? Is he okay?" She rested her chin on her knees. She wasn't going to look at Pete. Tasers didn't do that much damage, did they?

Pete had just tossed a handful of yellow popcorn at his mouth, most of it making it in, and he shook his head as he chewed. He swallowed and glanced around them. "He's fine. Don't worry. It's just that he needs to lay low. He's been compromised. At that dinner party."

"So I can't meet with him anymore?" Maybe that was a good thing. He'd seemed pretty mad when he walked past her.

"Don't you like me?"

Some teenagers settled into the front row, put their feet up on the railing so no one could get past them.

"Seriously," Pete went on, "we can't take any chances. Did anyone follow you here?"

She shrugged next to him. "I don't think so, but how am I supposed to know?"

"Good point. So what did John say to you in the kitchen, when he followed you in after the artist identified Frank?"

Ronnie told him how he said if she were him, wouldn't she be suspicious. That she said she wasn't him, she was a foot soldier taking orders, and she never listened to the conversation anyway.

The lights in the theater dimmed and music blared, loud even here at the top of the balcony.

She leaned toward him. "And he accused me of working for the FBI. Because I showed up right after Isabelle had been arrested."

"How'd you answer him?" Pete smelled like fake butter.

The trailer started up, and when blood splattered a bearded Joaquin Phoenix, she thought she heard Pete say "Good one."

She leaned back in her seat. She was not going to tell him about the tasing. No way. "He accused me of wearing a wire. So I started unbuttoning my shirt right there in the kitchen."

"You did?" Pete stopped chewing. "And?"

"I think he got embarrassed." Ronnie ate a few kernels of her popcorn. As gross and satisfying as she thought it would be.

"Tell me about the tasing."

"Oh." She didn't mean to say that out loud. She sipped her drink. Watery Coke. Great.

"You have to tell me everything." He eyed her. "Why would you forget to mention it, especially since Frank knows it was you?"

She shrugged, slid down in her seat, knees over her face.

"Never mind. Just tell me what John said." Pete crunched some more popcorn.

She told him how John wanted her to prove to him she wasn't working for the FBI, mug him, bring him proof.

"So he gives you the taser..."

She swallowed. "Well, no..." she spoke to her knees. "I got that from the doorma—"

Pete held up a hand. "No, don't tell me. It's better I not know about that. Just the illegal activity John engages in."

"Suit yourself. You said I had to tell you everything."

"And that was John's guy who kicked him in the ribs?" Pete's straw sucked air at the bottom of his cup.

"The driver. Marc. I guess he filmed the whole thing, and John Anthony seems to be happy with me now."

"Good." Pete rattled the popcorn bucket. Looked in, then set it down on the floor. Wiped his hands on the seat.

They watched the rest of the trailers, and when the music started for *Eye in the Sky*, Pete asked her if she was any closer to nailing him on the source of the cash.

She shook her head, told him she'd try to find a way to ask John something about what he does all day.

The music was way too loud. Pete leaned over. "Okay. Just keep doing what you're doing. We won't meet on a regular schedule for a while, but when you have something to report, text your Uncle Pete." He told her the new codes to memorize, then settled in his seat to watch the movie. "And Ronnie."

She looked at him. Didn't like the way his voice sounded.

"You need to tell me everything. Trust me, the way you trust Frank. I don't care about the tasing. Maybe he even deserved it, putting you in a situation where John Anthony had to make you pass a test."

She nodded. Poor Frank.

"Okay? We okay?"

She nodded again. Slouched down.

"Are you going to finish your popcorn?"

* * *

They sat through the whole movie together, for appearances, Pete said, though Ronnie suspected he really wanted to see the movie and she heard him suck in his breath when it looked like the little girl was about to get blown up. He gave her another uncle-hug out on the street, said loudly to let him know if she wanted to see another movie, then turned and left.

He wove his way among the people, picked up speed, and left the theater crowd behind him. Loneliness came out of nowhere and wrapped around her, and she went in the opposite direction of Pete so she didn't have to watch him disappear, leave her behind. How the hell was she supposed to grill John on where his money came from? She floated, seasick, like she'd been cut loose and sent drifting.

* * *

Ronnie moved the feather duster along the bookshelves, stopping every so often when a title caught her eye. She shoved the duster into her back pocket, pulled out a bright yellow book about a girl with a tattoo. She flipped it over to read the back cover.

"What are you doing? We have maids for dusting!"

The fierce hiss almost made her jump, but she wasn't going to let Lisa see that. She put the book back on the shelf, hoping she remembered where it was so she could come get it after Lisa went home. She turned to face her. "What's up?"

"John—Mr. Anthony said to order lunch from Ustinov's. Do it now. Dover Sole. Go, go." She made shooing motions with both her hands. Her eyes looked a little crazed, and her breathing was a little fast.

"Hold on. What's going on? Lunch for how many? Does he want a salad, dessert, or just the fish?"

Lisa flashed her an annoyed, panicked look and turned to go. "I don't have time—"

Ronnie grabbed her arm, and Lisa whirled on her so fast that Ronnie took a step back. But she still held on to her arm. "If Mr. Anthony has sent you as the messenger, then you better make sure you get this right. Because you'll be blamed, won't you?"

The flush crept up Lisa's cheeks, and she tugged on her arm. "Let me go." The words came out through her teeth, her jaw clamped so tight Ronnie thought her teeth might crack. "What do you know about John'll do anyway?"

Ronnie dropped her grip and moved to stand between Lisa and the door.

Lisa looked around her like she was trying to figure out her chances of an escape. She pushed her hair off her forehead. "Mateo is coming. Lunch on the terrace. John wants the whole thing, salad, fish, dessert."

Ronnie nodded. "See, that wasn't hard. What's Mateo like? What should I expect?"

"Nothing. You'll barely see him. He doesn't like servants, so you should just disappear." She looked Ronnie over like she wanted her to disappear right now. She made a wide circle around her and threw over her shoulder, "Chill the Montrachet Grand Cru from the cellar. Oldest year, he said."

* * *

Mateo Rosas de Flores was a large, handsome man, dark hair slicked back, curling a little behind his ears. Per instructions, Ronnie was at the elevator on the second floor to greet him, take a coat or whatever, show him to John's office. He wore perfume, or cologne, she supposed you called it when a man had it on, and when he handed her his light coat, she noticed his fingernails were covered in clear nail polish. She forced herself not to react, laid the garment over the chair that stood guard at the elevator doors, led him down the hall. She had no idea men got manicures.

John leapt up from his desk, more animated than Ronnie had ever seen him. "Ah, Mateo. ¿Qué tal? ¿Cómo estás?" As Ronnie shut the door, she saw them hold each other's shoulders, kiss the air on either side of their cheeks. Oh boy. Not what she expected.

A couple of hours later, John buzzed her, said they were heading to the terrace, and she put a large tray together, glad she didn't have to walk the thing up three flights of stairs. The intercom rang again, and she had an impulse to ignore it, but she came back into the kitchen, put the tray down, pushed the button.

"Sir?"

"Bring a plate for yourself. Mateo would like to get to know you."

Shit. The last thing she wanted to do was have lunch with Mateo. Jesus. Okay, okay. Whatever this was, she could handle it. She had to handle it. *You're the first person who's gotten in there.* Frank's words echoed in her brain.

So she would make sure she stayed in here—or she would make sure she got out of here alive. Focus on one thing at a time.

She always ordered extra when the Anthonys got delivery, and now she knew why. She made the tray even heavier with another glass and bottle of water, another serving of the salad, Dover Sole, and flourless chocolate cake. She didn't know why she plated lunch for herself. She couldn't imagine taking one bite.

Once she figured out she wasn't in trouble, she actually enjoyed Mateo. He seemed more like a professor or something, only in a very expensive suit. Not someone scary running a drug cartel. You always think of those guys with gravelly voices and ugly scars, but Mateo was charming, smart, a good listener. Like she imagined a neighbor might be like. Or a friend. He and John talked and laughed, Mateo telling about a trip to Europe he just returned from, the shopping, the eating, the drinking. He described in detail the fabric he had a suit made from, the wool so fine it was like silk, the exquisite red lines that ran through like a secret, the way it draped and moved with you, even better than your own skin.

John seemed to have forgotten about the fork in his hand, his lips parted as if by inhaling all the words, he'd be wearing the suit, too. Mateo described a white truffle crème brûlée, the perfect crack of the caramelized sugar, the creaminess, the hint of muskiness that made the wood nymphs appear. Ronnie could see them as they danced, the curve of a leg, streamers of silk behind them, wrapping around—

"So you worked for this, this Isabella before coming here?"

Ronnie nearly jumped, then she felt sad that she couldn't dance in the woods a little longer. She let her eyes focus on Mateo. "Isabelle, yeah, Isabelle Anderson. Have you heard of her?"

Mateo gave John a look as if he needed help translating.

Her boss gave a short nod. "That socialite over on 83rd? I told you about her, I'm sure of it. We donated heavily to her foundation." He wiped his mouth with his napkin, dropped it in his lap. "And she donated back to ours." He picked up his fork, stabbed around in his salad.

Mateo turned to Ronnie with a big smile on his face. "Ah, that Isabella. I thought she sounded familiar. How long were you together?"

He made it sound as if they were lovers. Ronnie cleared her throat. "Um, I worked as her butler for maybe six months, before—well, she—the—"

"The FBI shut her down," John finished for her, looking at his plate.

Mateo took off his sunglasses, and his eyes grew wide as he glanced between the two of them. He looked at John. "And this one," he gestured with his sunglasses toward Ronnie, his eyes still on her employer, "just shows up here?" He turned his head to examine her.

Maybe he couldn't hear her heart hammering away.

Mateo put his glasses back on and aimed them at John. "I know you showed me the tape, the mugging. And you are satisfied that she isn't working for them?"

John looked her over with a frown, like she'd spoiled his day. "She's passed all my tests." But to Ronnie he didn't sound a hundred percent sure.

"How is it that the FBI didn't catch you as well? Don't they like to take everyone, no matter?" Mateo leaned forward, as if to take in every syllable, every breath.

Ronnie put down her fork, wished he would talk about his trip to Europe instead. She settled in her chair, elbows on the arms, as relaxed a posture as she could pull off. "They questioned me at the time. Of course they did. But," she widened her eyes, held up both palms, "I had no idea what Isabelle Anderson was up to. I was no help to them because I didn't know anything." She shook her head regretfully. "Nothing at all." She picked up her fork and hovered over the fish. "So they let me go." She looked at her plate. "They had to."

Mateo laughed a warm, infectious laugh that made her smile. "Even I believe you." He laughed a little more, though it sounded a tiny bit fake, like maybe he didn't really believe her. He stopped laughing, his perfect eyebrows coming down, his mouth neutral. "But, they must be watching you, no?" He looked to John. "Why wouldn't they be watching her?"

"We've looked for them. Especially since she came aboard." John's eyes never left Mateo.

Ronnie's fork froze, then she cut a bite, watched the tines sink in, and hoped they hadn't noticed. Jesus.

J.A. went on. "And there hasn't been any increased activity since then." He moved his plate away and waved Ronnie off as she pushed her chair back, started to stand. "Besides, we always assume we're being watched no matter what. And so we're always very, very careful. You'd never think I was anything but a successful money manager." He took Mateo's plate and his own, put them on the tray by the door. He took the three plates of cake and dealt them around the table. "Coffee?" he asked Mateo.

Ronnie picked up her half-finished plate, got up. That was her cue. She cleared the rest of the table quickly and quietly, glad to have something to do, glad to have the Mateo spotlight off her. She brought them each a cup, left the silver pot in the center of the table, the sunlight winking off it. She retreated, leaning against the windows in the shade next to the table holding the tray.

"John, my friend, tell me, what do you think about gold?" Mateo sounded like he was asking John's opinion on the lunch.

John straightened up, put his fork down as if afraid it might shatter. He cleared his throat and took up his napkin, wiped his mouth for longer than necessary. His hand trembled as he placed the white linen on his lap.

"Gold?" He aimed his sunglasses at Mateo. "Barbara loves gold. You should see the earrings, the necklaces, the bracelets."

Mateo gave him a look over his own sunglasses as if that might help John understand him better. Ronnie saw his green eyes searching, searching. But he didn't say anything.

"Me?" John's voice rose. "What do I think about gold? As an investment? Sell some stocks, buy some gold, an anchor to the volatile markets? Maybe. But gold has been going up, you know. Remember when it was at two hundred dollars? And then it took off, though not like Bitcoin, but maybe we could—"

Mateo grunted, frowned to himself, took a sip of coffee, the cup ringing when he set it down in the saucer. Ronnie tried to butler-disappear, focus on the conversation so she could report it to Frank. Or Pete. The color had drained from John's face, his birthmark almost disappearing. Even if she didn't understand what was going on, she had to memorize everything they said.

"Not, my friend," said Mateo, "as an investment." He wagged a finger back and forth, a gold chain on his wrist catching the light.

John poured Mateo more coffee, topped off his own cup, but didn't pick it up. "How do you get around the regulations? There are worldwide reins on the mining, the refining, the selling, you know that."

"I also know there are always ways around any regulations. Especially in Mexico." He pronounced it "meh-hee-co" and Ronnie practiced that in her head, decided she liked the sound of that better, it seemed gentler somehow.

"So, you mean, along with—as a companion to—" John waved around, and his nervous hand arrived palm up at Ronnie. He dropped his hand, kept staring at Mateo. He must've seen something in his face because his tone changed, his voice higher, and he spoke faster. "You'd never leave the U.S., would you? Our friendship, our business. Haven't we done a good job for you? Fairer than most, you always receive the money in your accounts in a timely manner, the collections taken care of, nearly invisibly. And Ronnie—"

Ronnie launched herself off the windows, put her hands behind her like a soldier at ease. She wished he hadn't pointed her out again.

"Ah, Ronnie. Come sit down again with us." Mateo smiled, put his hand on the back of the chair next to him. "Tell me," he watched her settle in, "what have you been doing for John, for me?"

The sun was hot on the legs of her dark pants, and Ronnie had a sudden urge to pour the ice water on herself. She reached for her glass, took a sip of water, put the glass on the table. She looked a question at her boss. John almost wriggled in his seat, like a kid in school who had to go to the bathroom, but he gave her a small nod, so she faced Mateo, made sure to look him straight in the eye, or rather, straight at his expensive sunglasses. "I've been buying paintings and depositing money. Every week, without fail. Marc, the driver, takes me to the galleries, I hand over the briefcase, a painting or a sculpture shows up at the house." Mateo nodded, seemed to be thinking.

"And? The deposits?"

"Marc and I make the rounds, deposit various amounts, always under $10,000. I bring the receipts back to John, and what happens after that is up to him. And to you."

Mateo's sunglasses gathered up the sunlight, seemed to get darker the longer she spoke.

She swallowed and willed herself to keep her face aimed at his, to not squirm. Not like John.

"And you are never tempted, all this cash in your pockets. That's a lot of money."

She shook her head.

"A young person—you have dreams, things you desire to own. Cash like that can go a long way toward your dreams."

In the silence as they waited for her answer, a horn honked far below them, street sounds, city sounds muted but never gone.

"My dreams? My only dream is to keep my job. John pays me very well, and I save all of it since I don't have to buy food or pay rent."

Mateo nodded at her as if she had said something very wise. If only she could see his eyes, understand what he was thinking.

"And, I am not a thief."

At this, Mateo gave John a look with an eyebrow raised over the frame of his Ray Bans. John raised one shoulder.

"You need to know, Señor Rosas de Flores," Ronnie went on, hoping she pronounced it correctly, "I am very loyal. Very. Maybe there isn't much you can count on in your world, but you can count on me." She wanted to flop in her chair, get the focus off her, but she sat up straighter, her eyes steady. Even though Mateo's manner was calm, his voice reasonable, Ronnie didn't want to find out what he was like when he smelled weakness.

He nodded at her, then asked, "How many accounts do you visit each week?"

She shrugged, looked over at John.

"There are forty, forty-one accounts around the city."

"And how often are you making these deposits?"

"Every two weeks. Twenty banks one week, the rest the next. They're all over town, so it takes all day." Maybe that was enough to get the spotlight off her.

"So. Two hundred thousand dollars a week." Mateo aimed his gaze at John. A silent conversation seemed to go on between them, and John looked unhappier the longer it went on, his birthmark now dark on his cheek. Ronnie felt like kicking the table leg.

"You see what I mean, don't you?" Mateo's voice was quiet, reasonable. His sunglasses still aimed at J.A., he said, "Thank you, Ronnie. You've been very helpful."

Ronnie scooted the chair back, the metal on the decking clattering like machine gun fire. She lifted the chair up and placed it under the table.

"This has been delicious, thank you." Mateo put his napkin on the table and looked all around as if noticing the rooftop for the first time. "It's very nice up here. And quiet. You'd hardly know you were in a city." He turned to look all the way around over one shoulder, then turned the other way. "Though I suppose others could look down on you from their rooftops. Maybe I should get one of these, a penthouse, a rooftop garden, a butler."

Ronnie cleared, placed forks and knives on plates, moved as precisely as she could, when all she wanted to do was race through the door and down to her room. Bolt herself in.

John's voice was back to normal. "That could certainly be arranged. I was thinking that real estate might be a great way to keep things clean, though it would have to be something you'd flip, not something you'd want to live in. I could show you some offerings I have in mind in my office, if you'd like."

"Business, always business. Too bad your office isn't up here, out in the sunshine."

# Chapter Fourteen

Frank paced the tiny office, paused to look out the window, the stretch of buildings to the south. He tried to pick out the FBI building but had to give up.

"Frank, sit down. We're early. She'll be on time." Pete opened the small refrigerator under the counter.

"What if she's followed?"

"When she stops at the security desk for her visitor's badge, they'll hear her asking for her Uncle Pete's insurance office, and they won't be able to keep following. Christ, we've been over this." Pete pulled some bottles out of the refrigerator, put them on the coffee table. "All of a sudden, you're worried about her?"

"And you're not?" Frank sat down and got up again, paced.

Pete shook his head. "Her text said it wasn't an emergency. Frank, just sit down willya."

"I-I just—I'm—"

They both turned to the sound of someone coming down the hall, calling out "Uncle Pete?"

For a quick second, his partner's face melted in relief, then Pete gave a nonchalant shrug like everything was normal. "In here, oh niece o'mine," Pete called out as he went to the door. He looked both ways down the hall and pulled her in, shut the door. Her eyes widened when she spotted Frank, and she took a step back.

"Don't worry, I'm not mad at you."

She gave Pete a glance.

"He knows all about it."

Her brows knitted, then she shrugged, looked around the bare office. "What is this place?"

"Here, sit. Take a load off." He gestured to a chair. "Whaddya got for us?" They all moved over to the crammed set-up in the corner, furniture that had seen its best days at Headquarters, relegated to offices like this when a new SAC moved in and redecorated. Pete gestured at the water and Coca-Cola in the middle of the table and asked if she wanted something else.

Ronnie picked up a Coke, twisted off the cap, and drank half of it on her way to sitting down. Pete and Frank settled in and leaned toward her.

"Okay, okay, guys." She looked at them in turn, and they sat straighter, not invading her space quite as much. "Look, I don't know what it means, but the way John reacted made me think you'd want to know."

Frank searched her face, but she seemed calm, relaxed. She wiped her mouth with the back of her hand, and Pete got out his notebook, jotted something down.

"Mateo came for lunch—"

"We know that." Pete's pen hovered over the notebook.

"Then my job is done."

Frank could've told Pete that would irritate her. "Go on." He nodded to Ronnie. "We'd like to hear what happened."

She surveyed Frank, lingering on his forehead. "You okay? I'm so sorry. I didn't know what else—"

"He's fine. He's a big boy, now tell us why you called this meeting. Please."

She threw Pete an annoyed look and turned to face Frank. She relayed how Mateo asked her to join them for lunch, how he asked her why she hadn't gotten arrested, how John said they were always watching—

"We've seen them. We know they're there. They just haven't seen us."

Ronnie drank the rest of her soda, put the bottle on the table. "That's what John said, they hadn't seen an increase in activity since he hired me. Why didn't you tell me they were watching? I almost jumped out of my skin."

"Which is why I didn't tell you." Frank stopped himself from patting her arm. "I wanted you to act normal, like you had nothing to hide."

Pete cleared his throat. "Is this what you wanted to tell me? That you're being watched by us?"

Ronnie spoke to Frank, "The thing that got J.A. all excited was that Mateo said he was thinking about getting into gold."

Pete wrote something down. "That's all he said, 'I'm thinking about getting into gold'?" He aimed a look at Frank. "Didn't you teach her about relating this verbatim?" He turned to Ronnie. "That means tell us—"

"I know what it means. Jesus. How long is this going to take?"

Frank softened his voice, told her she was doing a great job, mentioned again how she was the first person they'd gotten in there, how she had to be their eyes and ears, how every detail was important, even if she thought it wasn't, even if she thought they already knew it.

"Y'mean like the Dover Sole? The flourless chocolate cake?"

Pete licked his lips, reached for a water bottle. "Yeah, like that, the food from Ustinov's. Was it any good?"

"I don't think we need to know what it tasted like, Pete. That won't come up in court."

"I'd like to know."

"He thinks with his stomach," Frank told Ronnie.

"First good thing I've heard about you." Sounded like she meant it.

They got her to go over the whole conversation, tell them John's gestures and body language, Mateo's, everything about that day.

"And that's what you told him?" Pete looked at his notebook. "'I'm not a thief'?"

Ronnie sent Pete a silent *duh-uh*, and Frank asked her, before the two of them could get into it, "What did you make of Mateo, what kind of guy is he?"

Ronnie shrugged. "He's really nice. Not scary at all. Seemed genuinely interested in what I had to say. Would rather talk about crème brûlée than business. You should've heard the way he described the hotels he stayed in, the fancy—"

"Now don't go falling in love with these people." Pete put down his notebook.

"I'm not falling in love with anybody. Jeez."

"Just remember you're working for us."

"Oh, you're paying me? Not John? With Mateo's money."

"If you want," Pete went on, "I can show you pictures of the kind of carnage the Mataderos Cartel is capable of. They're particularly fond of using acid. While the person is still alive. You see, they—"

Ronnie paled, so Frank interrupted. "We made the job available to you, Ronnie. And remember we got the okay to let you keep what they're paying you, so when this is all over, when you get what we need to make the case, you'll have saved up a lot. We're the reason, the real reason you're there. And so in a way, it is as if we're paying you."

Ronnie crossed her arms and stared at the floor.

"And this assignment you're doing for us is like paying you by not putting you in jail."

Ronnie spoke to the table. "It's just that he was so nice. No way Mateo would do something like that, is all. I'll bet all his suits are custom-made."

"Paid for by hooking people like your brother, Frank's daughter—"

Frank shot Pete such a sharp look that Pete seemed to flinch.

"So that's what they're selling? Heroin?"

"Heroin, cocaine, methamphetamine. Why, what did you think it was?" Pete tucked his notebook in his jacket pocket.

She shrugged one shoulder.

"Ronnie," he paused until she looked up, "don't lose sight of why we're doing this, of who these people are and what they've done."

She nodded, turned to look out the window like his gaze was too intense. "I guess."

Her voice was low, and they both leaned forward to hear her.

"It's so much easier to do my job if I don't think about the drugs."

"Look at me," Pete said. "Yes, you need them to think you're a part of everything they do, that they can count on you and trust you. But never forget who's actually buttering your bread. Okay? Got that?"

"Jeez. Okay, okay. How could I possibly forget with you reminding me all the time?"

Frank walked her to the elevator, leaving Pete to clean up the little office. He had to assess the mood of his CI, because no matter what Pete thought, she was still his.

"You good?"

Ronnie's eyes flicked to his forehead, then met his. Nodded. Though she didn't seem sure. "What does that mean, Mateo getting into gold? Why would John be so upset?"

Frank punched the down button for her. The elevator hummed as it rose. With anyone else, he'd change the subject, tell her not to worry about the case details, but he needed Ronnie to feel she was part of the team, part of their team and not the criminals'.

"We'll figure this out. It may mean we'll need to act faster, that Mateo won't need John any longer, gold being a great way to clean a whole lot of cash all at once. But it could also mean an even better opportunity, though we don't want to lose sight of John. Good work on this. Keep letting us know what's going on, especially on that angle."

The elevator closed on Ronnie, and Frank stood for a minute, the steel doors so pitted and scratched, his reflection was like a ghost. He knew she had to do whatever it took to stay in there, to get them the evidence so they could make the arrests, hopefully get Mateo as well as John. He rubbed his forehead. Too bad it involved a tasing and a rib kicking.

Pete joined him in front of the elevator, punched the down arrow. "I think you gotta lay low for a while."

"Lower than I already am?"

Pete nodded. "If these elevators came out facing the lobby, I'd tell you take a different one so no one saw you."

They listened to the machinery pulling the little car back up to their floor. "You know what this means, don't you?" Frank leaned against the wall.

"That she lied to them about not being a thief?"

They both got on the elevator, both reached for the button at the same time. Frank moved to the back, crossed his arms. Let Pete run the show.

"Think she got my point about the acid?" Pete punched the "L" button and leaned against the wall, a wobbly image of them coming together as the doors closed. "And that we're the good guys?"

Frank nodded. "I hope so. And I think we can help her tightrope that fine line between convincing them she's one of them and remembering that she's actually loyal to us." He cleared his throat. "But what I'm really worried about is Mateo getting into gold, loading up fake Brinks trucks with US dollars, taking them over the border. He won't need John, and we won't have enough on him to arrest him or Mateo. So poof. There goes your case."

"Our case, you mean."

"Seems like it's now your case. Your case, your CI, your neck on the line."

"Is that what's eating you? Seemed like just now we were a team. Pulling together to work this case, arrest the criminals, rid the world of evil." He looked Frank over on the last word like he was thinking of applying it to him. "You're the one who went all rogue on me, leaving me to scramble to cover your ass. And then you get made and you know I had to pull you. But you think you still should be undercover eating caviar and drinking champagne out of someone's stiletto, running your CI with your free hand."

The elevator chugged uncertainly, bouncing as it stopped at the lobby, hesitating before opening the doors. Frank stayed where he was. This didn't feel like team spirit to him.

"Never mind that you put *your* CI at risk." Before Pete exited the elevator, he punched the B button. "Go on down to the basement so we're not seen together."

Pete left, and the elevator waited there, waited for its next set of instructions. Frank hit the "B" button again, and the doors juddered closed. Why would Pete say that, that Frank thought he should still be under cover? One tasing was enough, thank you.

He didn't think John Anthony had enough manpower to be following him everywhere. Though they could've followed Ronnie. But—oh well, maybe Pete was right, they should play it safe for a little while, maybe get someone to counter-surveil his apartment, make sure no one's watching it, don't see Uncle Pete going in the same building as the now-under-suspicion Tom Roberts. But would they still be mistrustful of Ronnie after they'd gotten proof of her attacking him?

Frank made his way down the little hallway under steam pipes, ducked his head in places. The door let him out in a narrow alley where a garbage truck idled, diesel fumes hitting him as he came out. But more efficient for John Anthony to keep watching Ronnie and watch their own building rather than find Frank at his. Even so, maybe Pete shouldn't be staying at his apartment. He'd figure out how to mention it so that his partner knew it was for the safety of the case. Guess he really did screw this all up.

* * *

"I got the word, let's go." Pete slid his desk chair back and stood.

Frank logged out of his computer and got his blazer, followed Pete out of the hallway, both of them quiet. Ronnie must've texted with a pickup time.

"Lunch?" Frank asked.

Pete nodded, pushed the "down" button, looked out the narrow window, few buildings this tall nearby. "Lunch" meant Marc would pick Ronnie up right before noon, giving him and Pete plenty of time to get to the garage where Marc retrieved John Anthony's black Range Rover.

* * *

Like any good driver, Marc's habit was to be early, and today was no exception. Frank and Pete stayed in the shadows. "That's the guy who kicked me when I was down."

Pete narrowed his eyes in Marc's direction. "Didn't I tell you that's what Ronnie told me?"

"Maybe you forgot because you thought I'd kick him back today." His ribs still hurt sometimes, but at least he could laugh again.

The attendant made a call, and soon they could hear a screech of tires as the car made its way down the ramps, the garage like a six-story pinball machine. Another parking attendant, a pipsqueak with a broad smile, pulled up with a chug as he slammed the gear shift into park. John Anthony must need to get the tires replaced often. Maybe the gearbox, too.

Marc got in and as he paused to turn left, Frank and Pete hit the back doors at the same time, each opening, getting in and closing the door, a choreographed dance. Marc was quick. He had turned around and pulled his gun out at the same time, Frank and Pete barely settled in.

"You need to get out of my car," a set of eyes and a barrel said to Frank. The eyes widened.

Pete, having squished between the door and a large plastic tub, was out of Marc's line of sight, and Frank was gratified to see he had already unholstered his gun. He put it to the left side of Marc's head. Marc's eyes widened even more, then narrowed with hatred.

Frank grinned at him. "Maybe you could just drive. No need to get John Anthony's car all messy, do you think?"

Marc's eyes strained at the corners, probably trying to see Pete. It seemed like he was calculating various scenarios, eyes darting around, then he took Frank's advice, dropped the gun, and faced the steering wheel. The gun lay on the passenger's seat next to Marc. Frank took his own gun out and prayed it wouldn't come to that.

"I must not've kicked you hard enough." Marc growled, the deep rumbling like a far-off train.

"Maybe I'll get a chance to pay you back."

"Just drive." Pete sounded annoyed. "You can tell your boss there was traffic." Pete lowered his gun. "I've got this aimed at your heart," he added. "If you have one."

Frank told him to drive around Central Park. That way, they could stay more or less in the neighborhood, so Marc didn't get too antsy. Despite the tough talk, they needed him. "How's your mother doing?"

Marc looked at Frank in the rear-view mirror. "I knew I didn't like you the first time you got in my car." If looks could kill.

"Terrible disease." Frank made a few ticking sounds as if he really were worried. "And," Frank turned to Pete as if cluing him in, "I hear it's the rapidly progressing kind. You know what that's like."

"What is this?" Marc asked with a low growl. "Who sent you?"

Pete spoke up. "Aw, c'mon now, Marc. You don't have to be like that.

We're here to help you."

"Could you keep both hands on the steering wheel, please?" Frank said. "Thank you. As my partner says, we're here to help you." Frank looked out the window as they went past The Plaza Hotel, the carriages in a jumble out front, tourists climbing in on this sunny day. "So you can keep taking care of your mother. She only has you, right? Shame if something happened, if she had to go into one of those horrible state-run facilities."

"Nothing's going to happen to me." Marc took a deep breath, expanded his chest, probably trying to look bigger, to reassure himself he could handle whatever was coming.

Pete took over. "We'll make sure nothing happens if you work with us."

"I already have a boss."

"Oh, sure. John Anthony will continue to be your boss, of course," Frank said. "Pay you in cash and everything."

"Who are you? Cops?" He looked in the mirror again, checked the traffic to his right, and made the turn, headed uptown around the park on the west side. He gave a snort. "I don't care about cops. How 'bout I pull over up there, let you both out."

Pete looked at Frank. "We're not cops, are we?"

"Technically, no, we're not."

Marc put both hands on the steering wheel, said nothing. Okay, big guy.

Pete took his turn. "We're FBI." He grinned, though the driver couldn't see him. "I'm Special Agent Pete Johnson, and this is Special Agent Frank Jankowski, and you're—" Pete paused while Marc made a noise in his throat, "in a lot of trouble."

"Federal prison for decades kind of trouble," Frank added helpfully.

"You have nothing on me. I just drive for Mr. Anthony. I go where he tells me to go." The light at 72nd turned green, and he leaned on his horn, earned a cabbie salute from the driver in front of him.

"We've been watching you for a very long time, and we all know that's not entirely true, is it?" Frank leaned forward through the gap, his voice as mean as he could make it. "You also kick people in the ribs when they can't defend themselves. Like a coward." Frank leaned back, threw Pete a look.

"You go to warehouses with no one in the car, dontcha, Marc?" Pete seemed to enjoy this a little too much. "You meet other people there, put plastic tubs in the backseat of the car," he patted the one next to him, "pick up the butler, drive to banks."

Marc didn't answer, seemed to be forcing the creases out of his forehead, but his grip on the steering wheel tightened.

Frank picked up the narrative. "We don't know why the butler has to have so many bank accounts, but we can guess. And we'd probably be right. But we'd like to keep you around, so you can take care of your mother."

"Wait a minute. I knew I'd seen you together before." He glanced over his shoulder at Frank. "You guys were in the park that day." He turned back, inched the car forward, saying to the mirror, "She's working for you, isn't she? I told Mr. Anthony he couldn't trust her."

"Trust who? Lisa Cranberry?"

"No. Ronnie. The butler."

"The butler's a girl?" Pete's eyebrows raised in a question.

"Looked like a guy to me," Frank said. "Didn't he look like a guy to you, Pete? Narrow hips, flat chest, short hair?" Frank addressed the back of Marc's head. "You've only seen me, with Barbara Anthony. And flat out on the sidewalk that night." He poked the back of Marc's arm with his gun. "No way you know Pete here. You're getting rusty, Marc." Frank shook his head back and forth like it pained him to think that Marc might be mistaken. "It must've been two other guys."

Marc's neck turned red, but he didn't say anything.

"At any rate, you're going to be our eyes and ears. You're going to wear a wire and you're going to help us in our case." He paused, let it sink in, let Marc understand all the ramifications. "We have enough on you already to arrest you." Frank craned his neck, looked out the window. "You can go back to the East Side at 96th."

Pete tapped on the plastic tub. "What's in here, anyway?"

Marc grunted, kept the car nosing through the uptown traffic.

"But," Frank made his tone agreeable, "we'd rather not. Arrest you, that is. Your mother needs you." When Marc still said nothing, Frank tsked. "Such a sweet old lady, too. Adores you." Frank said to Pete, "She has this big gold locket she wears all the time. Picture of him, picture of her."

The back of Marc's neck was nearly purple. He took his right hand off the steering wheel, went for the gun on the passenger seat.

"Both hands on the wheel," Frank barked, reaching around the headrest and retrieving Marc's gun. "And we all know this isn't the Sopranos, protect you like you're family. You'll barely be in your holding cell before someone takes care of you. They won't even wait for arraignment. And your mother... I hate to think what they would do with that loose end." Frank released the cartridge as well as the bullet in the chamber to the floor. He dropped the empty weapon at his feet, bullets and gun nestled together. "You should be more careful, Marc. This thing could kill someone."

The traffic began to move, and Pete holstered his gun. "We could get out and walk."

"Nice day today. Marc. Let us out up there, would you? Here's my card." He let it fall to the front seat. "Of course you won't tell John Anthony, because that'll paint you as a snitch, whether you're working with us or not. And I know I don't have to tell you not to run." Frank opened the car door. "Because you know we're watching you and you know we'll arrest you before you've finished packing your suitcase." He got out but didn't shut the door, stuck his head back in. "Call me before you make your next trip to the warehouse. We'll get everything installed so you can keep feeding your mother that chicken soup from Arnold's." Marc started but didn't look at him. "Best soup in five boroughs." Frank closed the door.

Marc's car left them with a squeal of tires, but the traffic only allowed him to go a couple of car lengths, and Frank and Pete stood together and watched him go, Pete grinning.

"Twenty bucks says it'll take him two days to call you." Pete's eyes followed the car.

I'll take that," Frank walked, aimed for the park, the shade on the walkway a bit too cool. He hurried his pace. "That way I'll win if he comes in sooner, and I'll win if he waits longer." They split apart to let a stroller pass them, came back together. "But I don't think he will. The guy's really devoted to his mother."

"Is that really true, they'd kill him rather than protect him, not make sure his mother's safe?" A bicyclist whizzed past them, and Pete stopped to watch him as he went down the path. "I thought they had special paths for those guys." He walked again.

"As I said, that's only in movies." Frank headed north on the path, Pete following like they'd agreed out loud. "And if you're high up in an organization." They could grab the C going downtown, ride it all the way back to the office. "But these guys—you've seen it. They'd rather torture and kill than have someone like Marc hanging around."

"And we put Ronnie in there..."

"Well, at least she'd proven herself to John Anthony." Frank rubbed his forehead, glad it was nearly healed.

# Chapter Fifteen

Ronnie moved handfuls of dirty bills from the plastic tub on the seat beside her into a canvas bag and tried to pretend this was like every other weekly smurfing run she and Marc made. The tension radiating off Marc made her wonder if he was safe behind the wheel. In the front seat, next to him, Mateo asked him question after question, he giving a nod or a shake of his head as if that would end the conversation sooner.

She whispered the count of the small bills to herself, rubber-banded them into packs, reached for the next handful. Mateo turned all the way around to look at her through the space between the two front seats. His head took up the whole gap, and Ronnie hoped Marc didn't have to slam on the brakes because Mateo wasn't wearing his seat belt. His green eyes were like a coiled snake's.

"Tell me again, so I understand, how it is that all this money," a chin jut aimed at the plastic bin next to Ronnie, "my money, isn't going into your account. Maybe you split it between two accounts." He leaned a little away and held out his hand flat, palm up. "One John knows about and one," he turned his hand over, "he doesn't."

"We're not depositing to accounts today." Ronnie started the count over. He didn't respond, and she finished the count, banded the stack, and showed it to him. "We're smurfing today, smaller amount, more stores to go to." She looked out the window. "Hey, you missed one. We could've stopped there."

"We're not stopping until I say we are." Mateo closed his mouth, eyes on her movements.

Marc sucked in his breath. Didn't let it out.

Ronnie counted, banded.

"When I'm satisfied, then we'll stop," Mateo said. "So my English must not be very good. What is this *smurfing*?"

Ronnie explained to him how they went to different stores that sold the preloaded Visa or Mastercards, paid cash—she wiggled a pack of dirty bills at him—and bought the cards.

"Why is it called that?"

She shrugged, counted out another handful. "I dunno. Not my word. I just buy the cards. For you." He didn't stop watching her, but no way would she let him think he scared her.

"So, I ask you again, how is it we know you are only buying the number of cards you say you are, not buying extras, keeping them?"

Ronnie leaned forward, when all she wanted to do was fling herself through the door and away from Mateo. "You don't. It's called trust. You trust me. I trust you. To trust me." She held his eyes a whole lot longer than she wanted to, but this was important, no backing down, no sign of weakness. "Besides," she went on, "Marc said you all knew exactly how much was in here." She slapped the plastic lid of the grey bin, a dull smack. "So all John has to do is total up the dollar amount of the cards I give him and add to that what's left in the bin and see if it's how much you started with."

Mateo pulled away and examined Marc's profile. Marc gave a tight grimace and stopped at the corner, waited to turn right. But he didn't look at Mateo.

"You don't trust her either." Mateo watched out the windshield like he could wait for an answer forever.

"It's what I told her on the first day."

"And?"

Marc inched the big black car into the crosswalk as if he could hurry up the light. His knuckles turned white on the steering wheel. "No reason to doubt she's doing what she says she's doing." It was the most words he strung together so far, and as if he realized his mouth still worked, he added, "What John told her to do, to take care of things for you and nothing else."

Marc turned up the fan on the dashboard, angled the vent towards his face. She went back to working on the cash. If Mateo would just let her do her job, he would see that he could count on her. They better stop soon. Take all day to get rid of this tub. Maybe she'd luck out and they'd find a block with a lot of places so she could walk it. Get out of this car.

Marc hit the brakes, and Ronnie took a quick look out the windshield. He took one hand off the steering wheel, wiped it on his pants. Did the same to the other hand. She piled her stacks into a shopping bag, a white one with a store logo on it. She had learned to wear gloves for these trips, the dirt in the sink when she washed her hands after the first time, making her want to gag. Who knew where all this had been, especially with the junkies...

"How do you pick which stores?" Mateo braced his hand on the dashboard.

Marc shrugged, tilted his head at the GPS map lit up between them. "Drugstores, Targets, fancy grocery stores, they all sell them." Marc turned left, hit the gas to avoid getting T-boned by the oncoming traffic. Though maybe he'd like to have a car hit Mateo, bam, right into his door, the airbags deploying...

"And how much can you buy before they report it?" Mateo appeared unfazed by the traffic dangers. Like he knew he couldn't die.

Marc shrugged again, slowed down to look for a place to park. "'bove my pay grade. Get out here," he tossed over his shoulder to Ronnie. "Circle the block. Come back."

He must've thrown some more words in there, filled out the sentences, but those were all she heard, and she figured the car, not her, would circle the block. Fine with her. She snatched up the shopping bag and leapt out, felt Mateo watching her as she went. How surprised would he be if she skipped like she was a seven-year-old, not a care in the world. Well, not when *she* was seven. The air in the car was thick and full of an animal smell the air conditioner couldn't get rid of. She was glad to be outside. Maybe Mateo would get bored and ask Marc to drop him off somewhere while she bought the cards with the cash. His cash.

* * *

As she entered the store, she went straight to the cashier where the cards were displayed. Just her luck, a long line. She waited in it, tried to decide whether she should leave and go to another store, risk another line, or stay here, what with the time she already stood here. She blew out her breath, her bangs fluttering off her forehead. It was going to be a long day if every store was like this.

She glanced into the shopping bag as if the packs of money might have disappeared when she wasn't looking. Mateo was right, this was a lot of money to a girl like her, but there was so much of it, almost like it wasn't real.

Ronnie came out of the door, her head turned up the street to look for a black car sitting high with the windows darkened. She looked the other way. Maybe there was another store to go to before the car came around.

"Where are you going?" A hand grabbed her arm, and she wrenched at it as she started to run. The hand squeezed tighter, and she realized it was Mateo. She stood still. His light cologne filled the air between them. "I knew all that money was too much temptation." He took the bag from her, letting go of her arm.

"These are the only cards?"

She nodded.

"Did you buy others and put them in your pocket?" He looked her over as if he had X-ray eyes.

"No. Of course I didn't." She rubbed her arm where he had held her. She stared at him. "Go ahead, check my pockets." She had on skinny jeans, and she knew anything in her pocket would be obvious. She turned all the way around for him.

He nodded at her, handed her the shopping bag, headed down the street. "This is very time-consuming."

"Here's another store we could go into. That way you can see how it works." And why you can trust me.

Mateo went to several stores with her, at first he watched the transactions, then after that, took a pack of money from her bag, asked the cashier for more cards than the limit allowed, tried to charm the guy, explained he had a big family, all those nieces and nephews, and the cousins, "You would not believe all the cousins, and their—" And at that point the cashier would give up and let him buy all the cards he wanted, the people in line behind him grumbling and the cashier working quickly, looking past them for the next customer.

* * *

They got through the bin faster than Ronnie could believe, ended up on the west side, somewhere between the Village and Chelsea, all cobbled streets and low brick buildings.

"Ah. The meatpacking district." Mateo smiled out the window.

Marc flinched. Maybe he was thinking about meat hooks and bone saws. She was thinking about the meat part, like a big juicy hamburger, one of those crusty buns, a pile of lettuce—

"Stop. Right here." Mateo grabbed the door handle. "There's a beautiful restaurant here, on that corner, just there."

Marc had to idle in the middle of the narrow street, and Ronnie looked up ahead. Maybe they could find a bodega or something where she could grab a candy bar while they waited for Mateo.

Mateo opened his door, turned to Ronnie. "Come on, you come too, and I'll show you. You won't believe it. Like eating in a fairy garden, all the trees, the fountains, the lights." He looked like a kid at Christmas. She threw a glance at Marc, but he looked relieved rather than left out, so she decided not to feel sorry for him.

She joined Mateo on the sidewalk where he folded crisp hundred-dollar bills and put them in his trousers' pocket. Where was this beautiful place? "I hope they aren't too fancy. I didn't really dress for it."

They both looked over her outfit, her black loose-fitting T-shirt, black skinny jeans, black leather wing tips. She bent to retie one of the laces. Probably disappointed him.

"You're fine. You're with me." Mateo walked toward the corner. "And because you're with me, they will think the cotton is silk and the denim is linen." He gestured for her to go first through the door, and she squared her shoulders, decided to move as if she wore something expensive, something Barbara Anthony would have in her closet.

Mateo handed out his folded hundreds to everyone who looked official, to the doorman, to the Maître D', the manager. He handed out bills until the staff found them a table, even though they didn't have a reservation.

He was right. The whole restaurant was a fairy forest, trees everywhere like live umbrellas, tiny lights nestled in, and a constant sound of water trickling. Damn if the waiter didn't fluff out her napkin and put in her lap for her. She almost snatched the cloth away from him, not realizing waiters did that for you.

Mateo's eyes twinkled, a smile playing at the corners of his mouth. His green eyes were dark now, the skin around them pale and somehow a little too soft. He picked up his menu, ran his eyes over the dishes, put it down. A waiter rushed up before Mateo even glanced around. He ordered, listed so many things Ronnie couldn't keep track of, let alone find on her own menu. How could he possibly eat so much? She put her menu down and opened her mouth to give her order, but the waiter whisked her menu away with the tiniest bow. She watched his back as he made his way between the tables and plant life.

"I ordered for both of us. I hope you do not mind."

What would he say if she did mind? She gave a half a shrug. "You seem to know what you're doing." Better be something like a hamburger coming her way.

"So. We had a good day today, didn't we?"

She nodded, watched their waiter pour sparkling water into their glasses. Another waitperson came up and showed Mateo the label on a bottle. He nodded at her, and she uncorked it, poured the nearly clear liquid into the tallest wine glass Ronnie had ever seen.

Mateo swirled the wine in his glass, held it up, took a sip. He looked so happy, Ronnie almost wanted to see what it tasted like. He continued talking, "It's good for me to get on the ground sometimes, see what the soldiers are doing."

"We covered a lot of places today. Got done in record time."

"It is a lot for one person. You don't mind it?"

Ronnie looked around. Maybe fairy lights would cheer her room up. "It's my job. I just do what I'm asked to do." She sipped her water. "And I like staying busy, having something to do."

"And you like to help, no? Take care of others?"

Someone brought them a breadbasket, and Ronnie thought her stomach might eat itself. Mateo held it out to her, and she chose one of the slices, all big holes and a hard, dark crust. The butter curled up like snails in a silver dish, and she put one on her plate. The perfect softness for spreading. She sat against the banquet as she ate. Mateo looked amused, like he would give her whatever she asked for.

She finished chewing. "I never thought of it like that. I guess so. Though I think most people should take care of themselves." She looked at the breadbasket. Maybe she'd wait and see what he'd ordered. "Oh, I forgot…" She reached behind her and pulled out the small leather notebook she tucked in her waistband, in the small of her back where someone else might keep a gun. "I need to record how many—"

"What is that? Let me see it." Mateo held out his palm like she was supposed to drop the little white notebook into it. And everything had been going so well, too. She ignored the palm and held it out so he had to take it from her.

He flipped through the pages, paused at some, went to the next one. "What is all this?" He angled it this way and that as if he could break her codes by looking at them sideways. He turned the notebook upside down and shook it. What did he think was going to fall out?

"John said I could keep track of the banks, which weeks I go to which one."

Mateo raised an eyebrow at her.

"You can't go every week. Or on the same day. They get suspicious."

His eyes were steady on hers.

"And I need to record what we did today, how many stores we went to, where they were."

"And where is that information in here? And what are all these other words?"

Ronnie drained her glass. "The other words are from my last job, and the dates and numbers are there, in the back. Turn it upside down."

"And John looks at this every time?" He set the book down next to his lineup of forks.

She nodded. "He knows all about it. Checks it. Makes sure I'm not writing anything that would make sense to anyone but us."

Mateo slid the book across the table to her just as three waiters arrived to deliver the food, pour more wine for Mateo, refill Ronnie's water glass. The table was crammed with boards of baguettes, fresh fruit, plates of smoked salmon, cheeses, artichoke hearts.

"Are you sure…" Mateo picked up his glass, and Ronnie braced for the next test question. "Are you sure you do not wish for some wine, or maybe champagne?" Mateo broke off a piece of bread, reached for some cheese. "You are so young-looking, I forget you are old enough to drink in this country."

Ronnie reached for a bunch of grapes, put some brie on her plate. "No, thank you. I never drink. Ever. But I don't care if you do."

Mateo took a delicate bite of his bread, a sip from his flute, chewed, looked away as if the better to concentrate. "The flavors, so delicate, the sour of the bread, the sharpness of the cheese, and then the sweet bite of champagne."

Her mouth was full, so she nodded as she chewed.

"Never tempted?" He asked her. "Or you used to and now you can't? Or are you religious?" This last question made him cock his head as if he'd find that interesting if she was.

She shook her head, swallowed, wiped her hands on her napkin, glad they stopped talking about her notebook. "Let's just say," she pulled a grape off the stem, "my father did enough drinking for all of us." She didn't realize she was going to tell him that. She never talked to anyone about her family, but the words just popped out. He nodded as if she'd said something incredibly wise.

More food arrived, salads on tiny plates, some traditional lettuce, some curls of green things, some with croutons, some with discs of fried Parmesan. Mateo wouldn't let them clear anything, and they watched as the waitstaff moved plates around, fit everything in like a mosaic.

Mateo tasted from one of the dishes, closed his eyes as he chewed. Ronnie got busy putting some leaves on her plate. All this emotion over food made her want to hurry the meal up. She looked over the table, calculated how many people on the street the leftovers could feed, wondered what Mateo would say if she asked for to-go cartons, if she could carry that many cartons in one trip.

In the end, Ronnie did get her hamburger, but she was so full she only took two bites. She had so looked forward to it, and when the plate finally sat in front of her, she was no longer very interested.

"What are you thinking?" Mateo's rumbly voice interrupted her.

"Nothing." She looked up at him. "I mean, it's just, it's—all this food."

"Heaven, wasn't it? We shall have to try another restaurant together."

"Um, you don't think Marc—"

Mateo signaled a waiter. "Ah. Poor Marc. He does not seem himself, does he?" The waiter rushed up, and Mateo made a writing gesture in the air. The waiter raced away with a *right away, sir.* "I think that may be dangerous for my business, this nervousness of Marc."

# Chapter Sixteen

After a couple of agents did countersurveillance outside Frank's apartment for several nights, they'd seen no activity, from Mateo's people, nor anyone else. So Pete was once again sleeping on Frank's couch, and Frank was once again sneaking into his own apartment so as not to wake him.

Frank was exhausted, but keyed up, the long walk home from Leo's corner energizing him rather than preparing him for sleep. He'd studied the dealer from across the street, the customers coming up, the brief exchange, Leo always in motion as he stood, looking past the guy he handed the drugs to, hypervigilant. Frank examined every female, even those walking by with dogs, grocery bags, arm in arm with someone. The Lord above knew how other parents found a way to deal with this, the not-knowing, the imagining, the desperate hope. All Frank knew was that he had to keep trying, keep looking, wear out his shoes handing out flyers.

He rolled over, the lights from the city coming in around the window shade. What could he glean from watching Leo, and how could that help him find Cathy? If you took away the Rasta hat, cleaned him up a little, you could put him in nicer clothes, and he would seem nearly like any other salesman. He had a product, people wanted to buy it. He was efficient, didn't waste time with chit-chat. Frank punched his pillow, rolled over again. God, what was wrong with him? Leo was scum, he was a dealer, he was between him and Cathy. He had the local cops on his payroll, and he was supplying horrific drugs to the weakest and poorest in the city. If he were that efficient in getting these people into detox...

He felt a little insane when he thought about Cathy. He couldn't marshal his thoughts, form a coherent plan. He could work a case and catch all the criminals, but he couldn't find his daughter. The city was so vast, the places she could be so myriad. All he could do was just keep plugging away at it and pray that something happened. Leo calling originally had been a lucky break, but he was at his mercy. If he pressured him, as he wanted to, Leo could just shut him down. His only lead.

Should he involve Pete? He was reluctant to, and he didn't want to explore why. Might not reflect well on him. Pete would have his back, he knew that. He would be all in on looking for Cathy. Somehow, this seemed like a private thing, his own quest, his to endure alone.

* * *

They met Marc in a rest stop several miles from the warehouse, behind the convenience store where the weeds were busy snagging trash, and Frank felt as if he could catch something merely with a glance at the cracked cement. The driver sweated in the early morning damp, the tang of nerves hit Frank as he performed the intimate job of wiring him up.

"Are you normally this jumpy?" Pete leaned against the Bureau car, arms folded.

Marc didn't answer, took a step back, rubbed his palms on his black tab-collar shirt.

"Don't undo the tape, man."

"Okay, you remember everything we said?" Frank spoke to him softly, like Marc was an alley cat he was trying to catch.

Marc nodded.

"Remember, you want them to say something about the drugs. Ask them a question, like how are sales going, something like that."

Marc's eyes darted around.

Frank stayed still until Marc met his eyes. "Think you can do that?"

Marc gave a short nod, race-walked to his car.

Frank was beside him before he could open the door. "Meet us back here after. That's important. You got that?"

Marc looked like he might lose his breakfast. Or piss himself.

"You can do this. Simple. Just like any other day, right?"

Marc got in the car, and Frank patted the top of it, and Marc took off.

"Twenty bucks says—"

"Whose side are you on, anyway?"

Their car waited to enter the traffic, the blinker echoing Frank's heartbeat.

"You don't know which way I was betting."

They sat in the van with the tech guys, wanting to hear it firsthand, wanting the case to wrap up before Mateo put everything in gold, wanting the evidence on the first try. The space was crowded, and Frank could smell someone's breath mints. Too bad they didn't all have breath mints.

"I don't like how nervous he was," Pete said to Frank, and the tech shushed him.

They heard the door to the warehouse open, and everyone quieted in the van, even Pete. The voices said "sup" to each other, and Frank picked out two others besides Marc's. Either they had come in a back door, or they had arrived before the van. It didn't matter, really. They wanted the top guys, not the street level. That was up to the locals, though from what Frank had seen between Leo and those local cops, he questioned how interested they were.

"This it?" Marc's voice was muffled, thuds and shuffles in the background.

C'mon, Marc, you can do it. Bring us the words, that's all we need. The criminal source of the cash.

"What're y'trying to say? That's it, same as always," said one of the others.

"Business alright?"

Good boy, Marc, just like we told you.

"How come you're asking all these questions? Take it and go." Same guy, no word from the other one.

"Well, you see, Mateo's in town and—"

"We know. We always know. Maybe more than you know, we know." The voice was louder, maybe he'd come closer.

"Okay, okay. Never mind."

Something screeched against the wire, and everyone tore off their headphones, the techs glaring at them as if it was their fault. One of them gave them a question with her eyes, and Pete shrugged at the same time Frank nodded. All they could hope for at this point. The camera trained on the door showed Marc leaving the warehouse, lugging a grey plastic tub.

"He's sweating through his blazer. Even we can see that." Pete stood next to Frank, eyes on the screen. "I'm praying it was too dark for the other mooks to notice."

Frank and Pete drove over to meet up with Marc as they had told him, to retrieve their equipment, and to assess their inside guy. He had taken off the jacket and now wiped his forehead with his shirt sleeve as he got out of the black Range Rover. He swiveled his head around as if he thought someone was going to jump out of the bushes.

"You did good. Nice job. Next time let's—"

"Uh-uh. No next time. They said—" Marc reached inside his shirt, but Pete stopped him with a hand on his arm.

"I'll do that." Pete unbuttoned the top buttons on Marc's shirt. "Next time, don't rub that plastic bin all over the mic. We nearly lost a tech because of that."

Marc's eyes were a mixture of fear and misery as he stood still and let Pete pull the wire off him. Frank stepped closer, made his voice gentle. He was the Confidential Informant Whisperer. "It's okay. You did good. We need a little more discussion of the drugs next time. How did these guys seem to you? There were two of them, right?"

"Two. Yeah. Same two every time."

"Names?"

"Mutt and Jeff." Marc looked back and forth between them.

Pete took out his little notebook and wrote in it.

"We don't do names." Marc's voice was hoarse. "That's just what I call them."

Pete asked, "So then what do you call—" but Frank cut him off.

"Good, good. Any chance you're driving Mateo today? Picking him up somewhere, dropping him off?" They already knew the answer.

Marc backed away from them. "No way. I'm not doing that. I can't. They could be watching me right now. They'll kill me. I gotta go."

"Hold on." Frank put a hand on his arm. "You're doing great, and we're watching for them, believe me." Frank kept his voice low and gentle, reasonable, a discussion of topics they all agreed on. "Look, you're no good to us dead, so we won't let that happen."

Marc reared back, but Frank held on to his arm.

Maybe he shouldn't have said that last bit. "We won't have you wear the wire this time. We need you to let our tech guys do a few things to the car."

Marc shook his head back and forth over and over like he was in a horror movie, and soon his head would turn all the way around.

Frank released his arm. Looked him over. The van arrived. "Ah, here they are." Frank jutted his chin to the street.

Marc jumped, then relaxed. Must've realized it was the tech guys coming. The three of them faced the van as it rolled toward them.

"No way I can do this." Marc slumped, a rag doll about to hit the ground.

Frank had his arm again. "That's okay then," Frank nodded to the tech. "We'll wire you up again. But," he reached toward Pete to take the listening device, "don't let your seatbelt interfere with it, and don't let Mateo know you're wearing it."

Marc's scalp released more sweat, and he rubbed his sleeve on his forehead again. "What will they do to the car?"

* * *

"I've seen jackrabbits calmer than that guy," Pete looked over the roof of the Bureau car as they each opened their doors. Tech had put everything in place in the Range Rover in record time.

"When have you ever seen a jackrabbit?" Frank pulled out his keys.

"Maybe we picked the wrong guy." Pete climbed in.

Frank got behind the wheel and turned the key. "I don't think we had a choice. If Mateo gets into the gold, then John's out of a job, and it'll be tougher to land him."

"But if Marc is so nervous, what if he doesn't say anything in the car to Mateo. Think saying Mateo's name at the warehouse will be enough?"

Frank put the car in gear and followed the van out from the rest stop. "Let's go back to the office. Steve can listen to it, and if he thinks it might be enough, we'll check with the AUSA." He merged into the traffic and got up to speed. "Does it seem to you," he honked as someone drifted into his lane, "that it's always the big tough guys that melt into puddles the fastest?"

* * *

After work, Frank stopped at Macy's and bought three dozen men's white socks, along with T-shirts and underwear. Tighty-Whities better be okay. Steve, the money laundering consultant, told them merely the mention of Mateo's name wouldn't be enough, not in this country. The day wasn't overly warm, and so he walked across town, the shopping bag bumping his legs. They would need more, need Marc to somehow mention for the tape the source of the cash.

As he neared the neighborhood of the Port Authority, he slowed his pace and examined every young woman, tried to keep an open mind, heard Ronnie saying, *the streets change you*. But these kids, the ones he could tell were runaways, they looked too dirty, too strung out, too hopeless. Cathy was cheerful, a twinkle in her eye as she teased him, a slight smile as she argued a point, lectured him on the world as she saw it.

"Got somethin' for me?"

Frank pulled the shopping bag closer to his body, cursed himself for allowing his usual radar to disengage. He took a step away from the voice, assessed the person it came from.

"Annie."

"That's a big shopping bag, Bro." The crusty girl angled her head to get a look inside.

Frank started walking without answering, and she kept up with him. "Last time I saw you," he picked up the pace, "you took all my fliers and left." Her blonde dreadlocks bounced beside him. "Did you even hand them out?"

"I can help carry your bag for you."

"Look, Annie, there's nothing in the bag for you. I'm on my way to Benedict House. Maybe you'd like to go with me, check in, secure a real bed for tonight." And a shower.

"I'll walk with you and wait for you, but I'm not goin' in there. Uh-uh. Too many walls, too many rules." She got in front of him and walked backwards so she was facing him. "But whaddya got in there that's not for me?" Her pupils dilated, and he wondered if it was from the sun.

Frank tightened his grip on the handles. "It's men's underwear. For the shelter. Not for you, not for your friends." He felt a little mean, but Annie wasn't easily dissuaded, and not easily annoyed. "And I don't need you to accompany me. I'm fine." Polite hints didn't work with her.

"Still haven't found her?"

Frank shook his head, moved the bag to the other hand.

"Talk to her dealer?"

He shook his head "no" as they paused at the corner. "Benedict House is in the next block, so I'll leave you here."

"Frank. Hi. Who's this?" His ex-wife, Susan, joined them.

"She's just leaving."

"Frank, that's not very nice." Susan turned to Annie, who grinned at her. "I'm Susan. I volunteer at Benedict House. Are you on your way there too?"

The light changed, and they crossed the street together. Frank tried to outpace them. If Susan wanted to make friends, far be it from him to stop her. Annie asked if there was something to eat there, if they were giving stuff away. He'd warn Susan later about the wiles of the Crusty Girl. In fact, if Susan were going to Benedict House, he didn't need to be there.

He slowed and thrust the bag at Susan when she caught up to him. "Here, this is for the shelter. I gotta run." And he did. He ran. Though he didn't for a moment think that Annie couldn't find him again.

* * *

"What was that all about?"

# CHAPTER SIXTEEN

Frank stirred his coffee, put the spoon down, took a sip, set the mug down, and said to his wife, his ex-wife, "Did she hang around long?"

Susan gave him an exasperated look. She had asked him to meet for coffee the next morning. She wanted to talk to him yesterday, she said, but he disappeared.

"Who is she anyway. And dare I ask, how you know her?"

Frank lined up the flatware, made sure each handle was even with the next. He cleared his throat. "Well—"

Susan held up a hand. "Never mind. If you can't tell me, you can't tell me. But I hope she's not a CI."

"Oh? Why's that?"

"Doesn't matter." Susan looked away, out the window.

"No, really, I'd like to know what she seemed like to you. I thought she was awfully observant."

"When it suits her. When something's in it for her. I found her untrustworthy, though she seems to have a good heart. But that's not why I wanted to talk with you."

"Okay." Frank stiffened, braced for whatever it was that she had to tell him so badly.

"No, it's not like that." Her voice softened. "I wanted to hear how your search is going. I look at every single young girl who comes in Benedict House, and I can't stand the idea of Cathy out there, sleeping Godknowswhere, doing Godknowswhat..."

"I know, I know. There was someone over in the East River Park who appeared to know Cathy from the picture I showed her, but she and the guy she was with bolted, and I haven't found them again." He turned his knife over, then over again. He found her eyes. So much pain in them. His eyes must look the same. "I just keep handing out her picture."

Susan nodded.

"And waiting for her dealer to call. If he is her dealer and not stringing me along for the twenties I keep handing him."

"Tell me about him."

Frank described Leo, where he dealt, the park behind him, the way the cops left him alone. "He seems to do a thriving business, and no one is stopping him."

"Well…I guess in a way that's good for us if Cathy comes to him and he lets us know."

"If, if, if…"

"I know it's frustrating, but don't give up, Frank, not now. So this Annie person, would she have any ideas about finding Cathy?"

"I tried that. She's better at finding me, no matter where I am. She just shows up. And she'll find you, too, if you get close to her."

"Thanks for your concern, Frank. I'll take double precautions where Annie's concerned. I thought she might…"

"I know. I had thought so too."

They sat in silence for a few minutes. Susan looked at her watch, said she had to get back, don't get up, he should stay and finish his coffee. "And let me know, please, if Leo calls you." She put her hand briefly on his shoulder as she went by, and he sat with his cold coffee until he could no longer conjure up the comfort that gesture had given him.

# Chapter Seventeen

Ronnie's head was about to explode. Shoddy work drove her crazy, and these maids were the worst she'd ever seen. In the library, she followed them, dusted as fast as she could behind them as they chattered and chattered. Obviously, they had no idea that she was the one who could fire them. The elevator doors squeaked open, and she went to see who Patrick sent up without alerting her.

"Oh, Mrs. Anthony. I thought you had a lunch?"

Barbara Anthony put her tiny purse on the console next to the elevator and kicked off her shoes. "Have we got anything here? Leftovers from last night?" She headed off to the kitchen, and Ronnie poked her head into the library.

"That's Mrs. Anthony," she hissed at them. "Get to work or she'll make sure you're not on this job again." The three women stopped their chattering in whatever language it was and stared at Ronnie. "I mean it. I'll call your boss." Evidently, they knew that word because they stopped talking and flapped their rags around. Ronnie raced into the kitchen.

"I can put something together for you," Ronnie said as she came through the swinging door. Barbara sat at the island, held a cold pork chop by the bone, a bottle of Perrier at her elbow.

"What has happened to Marc?" Barbara put the pork chop down and picked up a napkin.

"Wasn't he driving you?"

"Have you had lunch? No? Why don't you grab yourself something and sit down? I'm not in the mood to have someone hovering, watching me eat."

While Ronnie made herself a peanut butter and banana sandwich, Barbara told her how Marc had arrived late, how he looked like he'd slept in his clothes, how the car reeked of stale alcohol and cheap cologne.

"And he'd put up one of those horrid Christmas tree 'air fresheners.' I couldn't stand it."

Ronnie poured herself a glass of water and sat cattycorner from her boss's wife. She took a big bite of her sandwich, enjoyed the sweet softness of the banana next to the crunchy saltiness of the peanut butter, the way the bread—

"I had to cancel lunch. So embarrassing."

Ronnie swallowed the bite. "You canceled?"

"What else could I do? Tell the biggest gossip on the Upper East Side to get her own Uber because my driver was too hungover to find his way to her condo?"

"Oh. I am sorry." Ronnie sipped her water, picked up her sandwich and studied it, planned the next bite. "But what about Town Cars? So you didn't have to miss your lunch."

Barbara put down the now stripped pork chop bone with a frown. "Heavens. I haven't called for my own car in twelve years. And Lisa didn't answer her phone, or his. Straight to voicemail like I was a telemarketer. On every line."

"Oh." She should've put more banana slices on her sandwich. "Patrick?"

Barbara shook her head. "I was too far away by then. It was all a disaster. A complete you-know-what show. I had to have that lunch with that influential socialite, to work on—" She waved her hand in the air, like it was too much to explain. "Why is John so busy lately?" Barbara got up and put her plate in the sink. "And his door's always closed. Which I learned long ago meant 'Do Not Disturb, especially you, Barbara.'" She ran the water and washed her hands. "Really, I don't know why I'm here sometimes. It's not like I get to see him very often."

She pronounced it "off-ten." Must be how rich people were supposed to say it. Ronnie practiced it in her head a couple of times.

"Couldn't you talk to him?" Barbara asked. "Isn't that your job anyway?

Staff supervision?"

"I'll talk to him," Ronnie put the sandwich corner on her plate. Never mind which "him." Barbara didn't need to know that Ronnie didn't supervise Marc, or even know how to call him. She'd never questioned it before, but maybe Mateo was the driver's real boss, and that was why she only dealt with the useless gang of maids that came in twice a week and mostly giggled. Marc had been acting funny ever since Mateo had gone with them to the banks. Maybe Mateo had scared him at some point, and now he was blowing it because he couldn't handle it. Mateo was elegant and charming, all good manners and whatnot, but sometimes he made her think of a beautiful snake, slithering along in quiet danger.

Lisa came through the swinging door, saw Barbara, and stopped. Her mouth made an "O," and she went to the refrigerator, opened the door, and spoke into it, "So many people here. Funny how I lose track of who's coming and who's going."

Barbara was silent until Lisa's head was out of the refrigerator, until she finished unwrapping a deli package of sandwich meat, and said to her, "Especially funny when you're the one who owns the penthouse, and your own husband won't answer your calls." Lisa colored and busied herself making a sandwich. "Nor his assistant."

"I didn't get any calls," Lisa said into the mayonnaise jar.

Barbara made an impatient sound, just shy of a snort. "I need to speak with him. And so I will."

She was halfway through the door when Lisa yelled, "No! He's with a client. You can't—"

"I can't?" Barbara's face was sculpted from ice. "My husband, my house?" Barbara had one arm on the swinging door. "And you're telling me I can't?"

Lisa finally looked at her, but she didn't say anything.

"Which client?" Barbara's words clipped out like she couldn't believe she had to ask.

"An important one. A very important one." Lisa's voice was pleading, begging, like she would get fired if Barbara barged in there. "His most important one."

Probably his only one. Interesting that she didn't say who it was.

"Ronnie." Barbara sounded like she couldn't say one more word to Lisa. "Please take care of the issue we discussed. And let me know when I can speak to my own husband, will you?" She went out the door, and Ronnie watched until it stopped swinging.

Lisa shot a look at Ronnie, then at the door as if Barbara might still be there. "What? What issue?" The words hissed. Ronnie gave her a shrug, put the plates in the dishwasher, and went through the servant's door toward her room. If Barbara wasn't going to tell Lisa, then she wouldn't either. That was an interesting exchange. She felt like she missed some important piece of information that would explain what exactly had just happened, but it wasn't her business.

Boy, Marc sure was screwing up, the business John worked hard at keeping away from his wife spilling into her life. Barbara asked questions like a master interrogator, and she was sure John wouldn't want her prying into Marc's life, find out what had spooked him so badly. She mentally checked herself over, wiped her mouth, smoothed her already smooth shirt. Marc was a key part of what John did for Mateo, so maybe Mateo should hear about it, too. Sooner rather than later. She went up the uncarpeted back stairs like a thief, a quiet contrast to all those sharp, loud voices that had filled up the kitchen. Plus, she didn't want Lisa to run up the stairs after Ronnie, spitting and scratching.

* * *

John's voice sounded annoyed when she knocked, but when she said her name, he sounded less annoyed, told her to come in. Three bottles of red wine sat on the corner of his desk, the labels creamy with a jumble of gold letters. In a black swirl underneath them, "John Anthony" shouted out. Mateo sat easy in the larger armchair, his legs crossed, his ankles bare above thin leather shoes which might have been made of crocodile. Or sharkskin.

Mateo tilted his head and looked her over as she came in, as if she had come to see him. He smiled at her, gestured to the other, less comfortable chair.

"Thanks, but this won't take long. Um, but can I ask, do you have a vineyard?"

Mateo laughed, and John gave her what he must have thought was a smile, though his birthmark was almost the color of the wine.

"I always bring this to him when I come because I can't believe someone else has his name." Mateo's eyes twinkled at her. "But what a good idea. Maybe we should buy the vineyard."

John got the letter opener and twisted it into the ink blotter on his desk.

"I thought you would want to know that Barbara, Mrs. Anthony, canceled her lunch because Marc was such a wreck that she was too embarrassed for him to pick her friend up and take them to the restaurant."

"She told you this?" John didn't look up.

Ronnie nodded. "She thinks I supervise the staff, and she said you were busy."

"How is Barbara these days?" Mateo picked up an ashtray from the tiny table at his elbow, put it down. "I haven't seen her since she was at the bank."

John didn't answer him, so Ronnie plowed ahead. "She also wanted me to find out when she can talk to you."

John nodded. "How did she describe Marc?"

Ronnie told him what Barbara had said, seemingly hungover, his rumpled clothes like he slept in them, the pine tree air freshener. At this last detail, each man made a frown, like that was the worst of all.

"Okay." John picked up the receiver from the landline on his desk. "You were right to tell me right away." His birthmark had darkened more. "Oh, and tell Barbara I'll be through here—" he raised his eyebrows at Mateo, though Mateo stayed silent, "—this afternoon, maybe around four."

Ronnie gave a short nod to each of them and left. Ooh boy, she was glad she wasn't Marc right now.

* * *

The next morning, Ronnie stood next to Patrick at the curb, the sun already hot. Maybe she should race back up and change into a T-shirt. As she waited for Marc, Patrick talked about climate change, how the summers began earlier and lasted longer, how humans were destroying the planet, how maybe one of these Ebola things should come along and wipe everyone out.

"Bro, everyone? You and me and the Anthonys? Everyone?"

Patrick looked down at her without moving his head, eyes nearly shut. "Everyone. We weren't supposed to be this many. Now we're all over, like, like—"

"Like ants? Like cockroaches?"

Before Patrick gave her an answer, Marc screeched to the curb and waved a beckoning hand at her like it was on fire and he was trying to put it out. She and Patrick exchanged a look, though what Patrick was thinking, she had no idea. He got to the car first and opened the rear door for her, like she was royalty. She saluted him, and then she leapt in, the door barely closing before Marc tore off.

"Hey man, where's the bin? Aren't we going to the banks?"

Marc said nothing as he wove through traffic, honking and slamming on the brakes, barely missing, by her eye, several bumpers. She put her seatbelt on and closed her eyes, but decided that was worse. If this was going to be her last car ride ever, she wanted to see her own death as it happened. She gripped the armrest and stiffened her feet against the floorboards.

"What the hell, Marc. What's wrong with you?"

Marc's hair stuck up in odd places, the air full of stale alcohol and sour breath. No Christmas tree air freshener, though. He turned on 55th and braked hard, a FedEx truck blocking the way. He let loose such a long string of swear words that Ronnie wanted to write some of them down.

"Get out. Tell him we're here." Marc leaned on the horn and yelled through the windshield at a guy taking his time loading up his dolly.

"Who? Where are we?" Ronnie had to shout over his shouts.

"Mateo. St. Regis. Go, goddammit!"

Ronnie found Mateo in the lobby, on the phone, not looking happy. When he spotted her, though, his face brightened. He looked away and frowned, said something into the phone. After a bit, he poked at it and pocketed it. She told him Marc had hit traffic. Once outside, they spotted the car inching toward them behind a taxi and a stretch limo big enough to hold most of the Rockettes. Mateo, in his pale linen suit, strode towards the Range Rover, and Ronnie tried to peek inside the limo as they passed, hoping to see a leg or two high-kicking.

As she climbed into the backseat, Marc said something to Mateo, but she only caught "warehouse" and "quick." Mateo stared straight ahead, arm on the dash, his silence scarier than anything he might've said out loud.

The warehouse was half an hour away, and the more traffic Marc encountered, the more sweat he wiped off his face. Finally, the traffic thinned, and they turned into an area with a bunch of warehouses, Marc punching in a code for the wide gate. He parked them at the end, in front of a chain link fence, weeds growing up through the metal, trash stuck in the holes, a plastic bag fluttering, cigarette butts in a pile near a sign that said Keep Out, the letters pierced and rusted from bullet holes.

"Right back." Marc left the car running, shut his door on them, on the air conditioner.

Mateo watched Marc, and Ronnie did too, tracked him as he went alongside a huge warehouse, lights on in the middle of the day. The building was old, tiny windows, a lot of them broken, no other human activity. Marc turned the corner and disappeared. Between two buildings off to her right, the water glittered, big barges slowly chugged along, stacked high with shipping containers.

"What is this place?" Ronnie finally asked, though she thought she knew. She just couldn't stand the silence.

Mateo cleared his throat, angled in his seat with his back against the door, giving himself a view out the windshield and at Ronnie. "This is where he picks up the money. So we can go to the banks again."

"Oh. Huh. I never thought about where it came from. So they bring it here for him? Do they work for you?"

"Everyone works for me," Mateo said on an exhale. He made it sound like that wasn't necessarily a good thing, but for him or for them, Ronnie wasn't sure.

The silence dragged on, but before Ronnie thought of something else to say, Mateo spoke.

"He seems very sweaty. I think that he has been overly nervous lately." His voice was soft and measured, like he was talking about a chess move. "Not like you. You seem…cool. As if nothing bothers you. Does anything ever bother you?" He turned his head to take her in fully, green eyes on hers like he was truly interested. He darted his eyes out the driver-side window and back to her.

"Only when my loyalty's questioned."

"Ah. Yes. I admired that spark." He shifted in his seat as if to get more comfortable. "When we do what we do, this business, your coolness is what we need. Not all this," he gestured to the driver's seat, toward the warehouse, dropped his hand. "This sweat."

"So, you're pretty high up, huh? In this business?"

He sighed. "My family. I was born into it. Sometimes I think I was born into the wrong century."

Ronnie didn't know what to say to that. So she didn't say anything.

"He is taking far too long," Mateo said.

Ronnie shrugged. Seagulls landed near the water, several fighting over something, a fish maybe, one slightly bigger one coming up, tearing off a hunk, and flying away.

"What were you born into?" Mateo's voice brought her back into the car.

"Me? What was I born into?"

"Is my English not very good?"

"No, I—" She thought she'd insulted him without meaning to, then she saw the twinkle in his eye, the smile at the corners of his mouth. "I wasn't born into anything. Youngest of three brothers. Got all their hand-me-downs."

"Your mother dressed you like your brothers?"

"She died when I was really little. So." The gulls picked at the last bits. Fish didn't bleed much.

"So, a large family. Lots of aunts and uncles and cousins?"

"Nope, just us. Wish I did have some cousins around."

Mateo turned in his seat so he faced her. "No? No uncles? Are you sure?"

A rushing in Ronnie's ears shut everything else out, and the car felt really, really small. No twinkle in his eyes this time. She willed her eyes to stay on his. She might strangle Pete the next time she saw him, if there was a next time.

"Are you talking about Uncle Pete?"

He watched her like a panther.

How the fuck did he know about Pete? She tried to pull on the coolness he admired. "I won't ask how you know about him, but he's not my uncle." She broke his gaze to look, unseeing, out her window, as if the conversation didn't matter. He couldn't see how hard her heart was beating, could he? Couldn't hear it from the front seat.

"And yet you call him 'Uncle.'"

"We've always called him 'Uncle.' He's just this guy who lived on our floor. He's known me since I was little."

"And he works in an insurance company."

Ronnie faced Mateo, held his eyes, tried to keep every emotion out of them, tried to act like a kid who wouldn't know what the family friend did for a living. She shrugged one shoulder. She couldn't read him. She prayed her answers were enough. When he finally stopped looking at her, she figured, she prayed, that meant she had passed that test, so she said, "What do you think is going on in there?" She gestured toward the warehouses, the buildings Marc had walked past. "Is it supposed to take this long?"

"You've never been with him before, picking up the money?"

Ronnie shook her head. "Tub's always in the car when he picks me up."

"So. First, he is unable to drive the lady of the house. Then he changes the routine. He takes a long time to complete the errand. And he's sweaty." Mateo angled the air conditioner vent away from his face. "What does that say to you?"

"I'll go check on him. Do you know who he was meeting?" Ronnie pulled on the door handle, hot air seeping in.

"The guys who have the money."

"Do you know how many guys who have the money are in there?"

"Do you have a gun?"

"Only a knife."

"I do not even have a knife. I usually have no need to have anything."

* * *

The door to the warehouse hung open a little, a rusty metal door, banged up like it had been used for a basketball backstop, and she pulled on the handle, the metal shrieking. Something made her pause, made her take a step away from the darkness inside. Her skin tightened with the silence. She sucked in a breath. No animal life outside, nothing scurrying past her, as if they had sensed something too. Even the breeze had stopped. She inched forward. Maybe she should let Frank or Pete know—know what? That this place made her nervous? That seagulls fought over a dead fish? She let her breath out, and even though Mateo couldn't see her, she tried to be cool, as if he were watching.

The door screeched as she opened it wider, an echoing throughout the building as she went in, looked around, let her eyes adjust. Light came in from the upper windows, several floors up. She shivered. The space was dark and cool and dusty, and smelled like something was rotting in the corners. She moved further in, abandoned pallets with machinery, packing material strewn on the floor. She inched around a pallet piled high with sealed boxes. No voices, so she probably didn't need to hide. She risked a peek into the big room.

A lump, a dark lump on the floor. Her eyes got used to the dark, the lump big enough to be a body, it was a body, had it moved, was it Marc, was he—a moan came from it and she rushed over. There was blood. A lot of blood, his eyes were open. Was that moan what people said, that last whoosh of air right before someone dies, but he blinked. Did he blink? She didn't want to lean closer, the animal smell, heavy, sticky, metallic, but he blinked again. He was still alive.

She knelt, scanned him, nothing registering. Why did he have to wear all black? "What happened? Where's the blood coming from? Are you hurt?"

She had no idea why she was whispering, except he wasn't talking, and maybe the guys with the money were still here somewhere. He moved a hand, and she saw a hole in his dress shirt, another, and another. "I'm calling 911," she told him, pulled out her phone, clicked it on. Where's the frigging icon to dial? He was saying something. She leaned over, trying to poke at her phone and listen to him at the same time.

"Then," he squeezed out, "you're stupider" he swallowed, a dry swallow, "than I thought."

She sat back on her heels, put her phone in her back pocket. She looked him over to figure out where to apply pressure, try to stop the bleeding. "What happened?"

"They jumped me." He stopped moving his lips.

"We need to get you to the hospital. I'll get Mateo, we'll get you to the car—"

In the dark dank warehouse, a breath like a sigh, a smell of shit, and Marc wasn't moving. He would never be moving again. Ronnie backed away. Her pants felt heavy, and she looked down at them, at her hands. Even in the weak light, she could see that it was covered in Marc's blood. What should she do? Her body started trembling. Should she close his eyes, but she was shaking, she didn't want to touch him anyway. She backed away, keeping her eyes on him. She whipped around. What if they were still here? She hadn't seen anyone leave, what if—

She ran. Out the creaky door, the sun hitting her, the musty, weedy smell of abandoned concrete, the screech of gulls, the black Range Rover looking like a tank, the windows so dark she couldn't see if Mateo was still there. She wanted to run forever, past the car, out the gate, into the street. What if something had happened to Mateo, too, while she'd been in there?

She opened the back door and jumped in, slammed it, saw Mateo out of the corner of her eye before she opened the door again and threw up on the concrete.

When she finally pulled herself back into the car, Mateo handed her a handkerchief, soft and white and large. He handed her a bottle of water. She swished her mouth out and opened the door again to spit, didn't look at the barf. Oh God, don't heave again. She poured the cold water on her head, not caring that it ran down, soaked her shirt. She shook her head like a dog and closed the door. She tried to give him back the handkerchief, but Mateo told her to keep it.

"You will have to drive us, I think." His words were calm, reasonable. Just another ordinary, goddamn day.

She scooted over on the seat, the door with no barf outside it such a long way away. Her bloody hand slipped off the handle, and she tried again, this time practically falling out of the car. She could just lie down now, close her eyes...and see Marc, all that blood.

Mateo opened his door. Looked at her for several seconds, closed it again. She managed to walk around the front of the car, opened the driver's side, and slid in behind the wheel. She put both hands on the steering wheel the way Marc did, turned to Mateo. "I don't know how to drive."

"I never drive," he said, as if that settled it.

Her hands shook as she turned the key, tried some things she'd seen Marc do. Horrible sounds, like the engine was going to start throwing things. Mateo made suggestions of what to try, and they inched and bucked their way away from the warehouses. She found the brake pedal and threw Mateo at the dashboard. He didn't say anything, put his seatbelt on. She got up to ten miles an hour, and he told her they should probably get further away from this area.

At the gate, there were so many cars streaming past them. How did anyone ever make the decision to pull out in front of an oncoming car? Mateo looked out his window. Maybe he thought the same thing. She sat so high up, the car taller than the rest like it had suddenly grown, the humming of the engine filling her ears, the steering wheel shaking as she held on tighter, her hands shaking, maybe her hands were making it shake, the trembling going down her arms and then her whole body was shaking, the world outside the windshield turning dark until the only thing she saw was the lights on the dashboard, signals from another world.

Mateo was reaching over her, unbuckling her seatbelt, but he reached over her from the door side, the door open, when had he gotten out of the car, he was taking her arm, guiding her out, her knees buckling, so he had to walk her around the car, hold her up until he put her in his seat, buckled her in, closed the door with a firm click. She fumbled at her door, finally found the window button, rolled it down, and leaned her head out, the air cooling her scalp.

"Wait here. I'll be right back."

She had no idea they'd gone anywhere, that they'd stopped. He'd left the car running, she could hear that much. She peeled open one eye and saw a car next to them, an empty, white car that looked so ordinary she wanted to cry. She raised her head, closed the window, the tinted glass turning the ordinary everyday car grey. She never cried.

She put her head back against the rest and closed her eyes. She didn't know how long he had been gone, how long she sat there and shook, her hands palm up in her lap. She kept her eyes closed, she couldn't look anywhere because all she saw was blood: on her hands, on her pant legs, on the dash. When she stared out the windshield, she saw Marc, the dark of his clothes, the dark of the blood on his clothes, all melting into the dark of the warehouse.

The driver's side door opened, and she shrank back. Mateo got in and handed her a white bag, orange and pink lettering running up, whiffs of sugar and bakery. He put a cup of coffee in the holder on the console between them.

"You must eat. Sugar is good for the shock."

Ronnie turned to look at him, hoping she didn't see blood on him too.

He took the bag from her and pulled out a glazed donut, held it out for her to take. "Your first body?"

She nodded her head "yes," then shook it "no." He raised an eyebrow at her. "All that blood," she whispered. She didn't want the donut, but she took a bite anyway. And another, and Mateo peeled back the tab on the coffee lid, handed her the warm cup. She didn't know when she had finished the donut, but the coffee was creamy and sweet and hot, and she sipped while Mateo took out a bright pink iced donut, covered in a rainbow of sprinkles. She reached out for it, the birthday cake she'd never had. She dropped her hand.

"What is wrong?" Mateo angled it toward himself, examined it.

"I'm not supposed to eat in the car."

# Chapter Eighteen

Ronnie peered at her phone. Why hadn't her alarm gone off? She launched herself out of bed, into the bathroom. She always set her alarm, what was wrong with her? Oh. The blood, the donuts, Marc, Mateo, the guys coming to drive them back. John told her to take the day off, take it easy, she'd been through a lot.

She peeked into the hamper, her clothes from the day before stiff, a rotten, almost sweet smell. She couldn't puke again. She went back into the bedroom, maybe she should try to go back to sleep, but she knew it was no use. Once she was up, she was up. She could use the sleep though. She raked her fingers through her hair, peered at her eyes in the mirror. All night she'd been awake more than asleep, the images of the day before racing through her head. Her eyes looked hollow, sunken in.

She dressed, pulled on jeans and a T-shirt. A surprise day off school, like when her brothers woke her early to play hooky. But this wasn't something to celebrate. In fact, it felt a little like punishment, especially since John had told her to lay low, not go anywhere for a little while, and she had no idea what to do with herself.

She scrolled through her phone while she ate at the island in the kitchen, searched for any mention of a dead body in a warehouse. She took a big spoonful of Cinnamon Toast Crunch. Must be Lisa's cereal. Far too sweet for her, and the sugar made her heart race, her head throb. Way too much sugar in the last twenty-four hours. She brought her bowl to the sink, dumped it out, the soggy cereal a lump in the drain. She'd make herself some eggs, something solid. She pulled out the carton, a mix of brown, green, blue, and white eggs, all very pretty, all normal-looking. She wanted to throw them on the floor, watch them crack, ooze out, one after another. She put the carton back in the refrigerator and sat down on the stool at the counter.

Her phone buzzed in front of her, jumping on the counter with the vibration, the screen lit up with a text message. She snatched it up. Uncle Pete.

*How about lunch today?*

She put the phone in her pocket and went into the butler's pantry. How about not. She decided all the silver desperately needed polishing, carried trays and coffee services into the kitchen. No way she had time for lunch with all this to do.

* * *

"Oh! John said you had the day off."

Barbara's voice surprised Ronnie, and she dropped the small plate engraved with initials and a date she had been working on. The clanging of the silver bounced around the kitchen, her nerves jangling with the sound.

Ronnie slid off her stool. "Can I get you something?"

Barbara waved her away. "No, I'll rummage around for something for lunch. I'm not in the mood to wait for something to arrive here. I'm far too hungry, and the food would be lukewarm anyway. I swear I don't know how John can exist on either takeout or nothing." She brought out a few covered bowls and peeled back the plastic wrap, bending over and sniffing at them.

Ronnie sat back down and finished the plate, gathered everything up to rinse and dry. She'd do the rest later.

"So you're not taking the day off?"

"I dunno. I just like to be busy. I don't know what else to do with myself."

"Come with me this afternoon. I have a few errands to run, maybe we'll go to some galleries, too. I could use the company."

* * *

Ronnie didn't want to run errands with Barbara, but how could she say no. She couldn't tell her John said to not go anywhere because Marc—she shook her head as if she could erase the images from yesterday. She knew the boss' wife had friends, but she seemed lonely anyway. She must be really lonely if she had to ask the help to go shopping with her. Barbara hadn't said to wear her butler uniform, so it wasn't like she wanted to show off that she had a servant to carry packages.

They waited for the car, Barbara chatting away and Patrick standing straight and tall, at the ready to open the door for them. How many rich people only had friends they paid, like a butler, a masseuse, a personal trainer, a secretary, a decorator? A dinner table full of those people—what would that conversation be like?

"Ah, here he is."

Ronnie took a step away, thinking she meant Marc. Her heart raced and she looked around, eyes darting between the street, the sidewalk, Patrick, Barbara. But of course it wasn't Marc, it would never again be Marc. She might throw up.

Barbara must've noticed her hesitation because she told her she had to have Lisa order the town car, some problem with the Range Rover. Barbara got in on the curb side, so Ronnie went around the street side and opened the door to the back seat. She caught Patrick's face, frowning and shaking his head like he didn't approve. Of what, she would probably never find out.

The driver took them to store after store, Ronnie going in with her while she selected a special perfume in one, her must-have mascara in another, hand-made soaps in a store where Ronnie's eyes watered. She excused herself, stepped outside, and away from the heavy perfumes. Someone called her name. Must be for someone else. She didn't know anyone—

"Ronnie, it's Uncle Pete," called the voice, and Ronnie's instinct was to run in the opposite direction. "I've been trying to get a hold of you." He closed the gap between them. "Is your phone dead?"

No, but Marc is.

"Ah, Ronnie, shall we—" Barbara noticed Pete. "Hello, I'm Barbara Anthony." She didn't offer her hand, just peered at him as if she could read his life story in his face.

"Pete Johnson. Ronnie's uncle. Well, not her real uncle, just a family friend, you know, but I've known her all her life and—"

"So very nice to meet you." Barbara looked over his shoulder to the street. "We—uh—have a few other places we need to go. So we'll be off."

"Well, actually, I was kinda hoping I could steal Ronnie for a few minutes. I've been trying to reach her, and I think it's fate we ran into each other here. I've got something I need to discuss with her, so if you don't mind..."

Ronnie looked back and forth between them, wondered which one would be worse to go with. She gave up. Today was a dark, useless day, and she would do whatever they decided between them.

Barbara's face contorted, then quickly relaxed. "Here's my driver." She walked toward the black sedan, which sat, double-parked. "Ronnie," she said over her shoulder, "it's your day off. Maybe you should go with your uncle instead of on these boring errands with me." She stood by the car as the driver slipped around to open the door for her. She gave them a little wave. "Have fun, you two."

Pete grinned his goofy grin at Ronnie. "How about we go to my office? Not far from here. You look like you could use a Coke."

They didn't say a word as Pete led them the several short blocks to the office building, past the security and up the elevators. He opened the office door for her, and Frank sprang up and came toward her as if he wanted to give her a hug. She stiffened and took a step back. If anyone touched her right now, she'd end up on the floor melting. Then disappearing.

"How are you holding up?" Frank gestured to one of the chairs at the coffee table.

"I'm fine. Really, I'm fine." Ronnie stayed near the doorway.

"You look pale."

"Wouldn't you? I gotta go."

Pete came up next to her, herded her into the seat, handed her a can of Coke. She looked at it, the red bright in her hand. He took it from her and opened it with a sprfft, the bubbles rising out of the opening, popping, and filling in the silence. A bead of water wandered down, distorted the curly top of the "C."

"I'm thinking we need to pull you out." Pete sat in the chair on the other side of her.

She tipped her head back and drank, her eyes finding Frank as if the danger lay with him. She put the can down. "I'm fine. Fine. Fine. How many times do I have to say it?" She wiped her mouth with the back of her hand, tried to slide the little armchair away from them, but it stayed in place. "And anyway," picked up the can, put it down, "how do you know something happened? Did you bug me without me knowing?"

"Never mind that," Pete picked up his notebook.

"Why don't you tell us what happened?" Frank's voice was gentle. "Go through the whole thing."

So Ronnie went through the day, how Marc showed up late and a wreck, how Mateo said he was sweaty. She stopped when she got to the part inside the warehouse. She looked at her hands, rubbed them on her thighs.

"You didn't see anyone in the warehouse?"

She shook her head *no*, said to her hands, "it was dark."

"I know this is hard," Frank leaned toward her, put a hand on her arm. She pulled her arm away, rubbed it like she could remove his touch. He didn't lean back again, stayed close to her, talked in that kind, soft voice. "We need to know everything, though, how Marc looked, whether he was still alive when you got there, if he said anything."

Ronnie jerked against her seat, crossed her arms. "I said I was going to call 911, and he said I was stupider than he thought."

"Those were his last words?"

"No, he said something like 'they jumped me.'"

"How many were there?"

"How the hell am I supposed to know that? No one was there when I got there. I already told you that." She sucked in a big breath. "They plugged him good, though, I thought I saw three places, three holes, I tried to stop the bleeding, but I couldn't, so much blood, I tried, I tried…" She stared at her palms as if the blood still covered them.

"We're going over the warehouse now, see what forensics we can pick up."

"Wait. How do you know where—" She looked first at Frank, then at Pete. "You knew where I was that whole time, and you just let it happen? Why didn't you keep Marc from getting..."

"We couldn't have stopped that," Pete told her. "We're not that magical. But we know Mateo was involved. He called them when you left the car to look for Marc."

"What the—you're bugging the car? So why didn't you come and pull me out if I was in so much danger? Whose side are you on, anyway?"

"We didn't hear the tapes until this morning. And you have an emergency extraction code you could've sent us."

Ronnie snatched up the Coke again, but it was empty. She put it down with a clink. "Mateo was nice to me. He took better care of me than you guys did."

"You feel safer with him than you do with us?"

Ronnie nodded. "Right now I do. Yeah."

Frank looked over her head at Pete.

"What?" Ronnie swiveled, looking back and forth between them. "I do. Not like you did anything when you realized Marc had been—Marc was—when they'd—" She wished Frank didn't watch her so closely, like she was some delicate thing about to topple over or blow away or shatter into millions of pieces.

"Maybe you're right." Pete closed his notebook. Frank looked up at him. "Maybe we can make this work."

Frank didn't say anything, but it seemed like there was a whole silent conversation going on between them. Slowly, he nodded, faced Ronnie. "Mateo may be feeling extra protective of you right now, so you may be safer now than before. But we should receive daily reports from you." Frank cleared his throat. "You take the trash out, right?"

"Why are you even asking? Seems like you already know. The garbage chute's right outside the kitchen door."

"Okay. You're going to start keeping a journal." Frank pulled out a spiral-bound notebook from a briefcase on the floor at his feet. "You're going to write in it every night." He opened it and put it on the table in front of her.

"I don't care what you say on this page, but on the one after it—see, they're lined on one page, blank on the next—that one is ours and you're going to rip it out and throw it away. It'll look like it's blank. You'll be able to see each word as you write, and then they'll disappear, the page empty. You'll throw the page down the recycling chute every morning. Got that?"

"They don't like me writing things down."

Pete took over. "So, on the page that's yours, don't write anything down about what's going on in the Penthouse or with your job."

"That's my whole life right now. What am I supposed to write about? Lunch with Uncle Pete?"

Pete ignored that. "How 'bout, you met a guy. You'll write about him. You can—what? A girl? You met a girl you like?"

"You guys are creepy."

Frank explained that it would be natural for someone her age to write about a new love interest, that she could start slow in the journal, the meet, then a call, then a date, then—

"Really creepy. And if I ever did have a 'love interest,' it would be a guy, for your information. Jeez. How do you two think of these things?"

Frank sidestepped the question. "On our page, I want you to write down every single thing that happened that day, what John had for lunch, who came to meet with him, what kind of mood he was in, anything at all that he said."

"Okay, yeah, yeah. An essay every night." She leaned back and let out a breath that fluffed her bangs. "I left school for a reason."

"What do you think made Mateo decide to have Marc killed?" Pete asked her.

"How should I know that?"

"Well, how did Marc seem these last few days?"

"I told you, he was a wreck. Barbara had to cancel lunch the day before because he was late and the car reeked of alcohol."

"I wish we'd known that. That's exactly the kind of thing you need to write down for us." Pete wrote something in his notebook like he thought he should demo it.

"You really think Mateo ordered it? And then sent me in? Why would he do that? Was he trying to kill me, too?" She stood. She had to get out of here.

"It's okay." Frank put a steadying hand on her arm.

She looked at it until he removed it.

"Sit for a minute longer. He wasn't trying to kill you too because he told the guys to leave."

Ronnie sat down and folded her arms. Might as well hear him out.

"It's possible Mateo wanted to show you what he was capable of, that he suspected Marc, and he wanted to send you a message too."

"Marc had been so nervous. Why would Mateo want to send me a message?"

"Maybe because he wants to involve you further in his organization? He seems to like you, like your spunk and your demeanor." Frank's eyes softened at her.

"Whatever that is. Well, I got the message."

"And you still feel like you can be at the penthouse, report to us?"

"Write a book every night about what John has for breakfast? That sounds boring, not dangerous."

"Here, let me have your phone." Pete held out his hand. She gave it to him, and he poked at the screen. "Okay, Linus is already in here. Your new boyfriend's name is Linus."

"That is way too creepy."

"Well, it already goes to Frank, so might as well. You can text him when your relationship with Linus gets to whatever stage it is when people text. Meanwhile, we'll intercept the journal pages—throw them away sometime after 7:30 in the morning, but before anyone's around. And use this pen, only this pen. It disappears on the blank pages, shows up on the lined ones." He handed her the pen. "How'd you guys come up with 'Linus' anyway?"

"Because if I ever do meet someone, there's no way they'll have that name."

* * *

The Coke had made her feel better, but she would never tell Pete that. The pen and notebook were awkward in her hand, but since they were presents from her Uncle Pete, she guessed they wouldn't seem suspicious to anyone who might be watching her. She looked around the subway car, but damned if she knew what Mateo's watchers would look like. Too tired to even stand, she fell into a seat, and now she examined the notebook on her lap. The cover was stamped with his supposed insurance company name, the notebook saying, "Let us start protecting you now" under the same logo as on the pen. They'd also given her a few more codes to memorize, some of which she changed to emojis. She could deal with this better if they, especially Frank, weren't fussing over her so much.

Right now, she liked Pete better because he had been a hardass, not making a big deal once he'd opened the Coke for her. She felt someone watching her, and she stood as if her stop was next, moved to the door, and leaned against it to better scope out the whole car.

The train rumbled along, and she grabbed the pole just as she spotted him. He gave her a smile and didn't look away. Couldn't be someone following her because he would've looked away. The guy got up, sort of unfolded himself, and he was so tall, several people gave him a glance as he left his seat. Ronnie looked at the floor, but then he was hanging onto the pole in front of her and saying something. She couldn't hear him over the train, and she turned around like the doors were going to open any minute. In the glass of the door, she saw him behind her, her head coming to his chest, his eyes looking down at her, his mouth curved up. Who was this guy?

He tapped her shoulder. "I was just wondering if you're a writer."

She turned around. Her station better come up soon. Everyone knew you didn't talk to someone on the subway. Someone else waited at the door, and she'd have to shove them if she wanted to get away from this guy. She squeezed into the corner, looked him over. He seemed harmless enough, but wasn't that how they got you?

He gestured with his chin at her notebook and looked the question at her again.

She shook her head "no," the train slowing for the next station, her legs tensing, ready to run as soon as the doors opened. He was kinda cute. She looked up at him. "Your name isn't Linus, is it?"

* * *

The walk from the subway station seemed much longer, the hill to Park Avenue steeper, the sun hot on her head. She ran a hand through her hair as she waited for the light to change, wiped it on her pants leg. She squinted at the building on the corner. Probably Patrick sat inside, in the cool, dark lobby, the fan on his desk aimed right at his face. She'd stop and talk with him a minute, his pleasant mood a good distraction from all that tension coming off Frank and Pete.

The sun beat down, and she fluffed out her T-shirt. Maybe she should get sunglasses, some cool-looking shades, maybe like Mateo's, all wrapped around and dark as sin. The light changed, and she walked faster than she felt like, so she didn't get stuck on the island between the four lanes of traffic. Why John had to live on the widest avenue in the city…the light turned to flashing and she hurried across, hitting the corner just in time to see Annie coming up the stairs from the service entrance to the building. Ronnie picked up her pace, hurried to the front entrance. Great, now Annie was dumpster diving at her building.

Patrick came out to stand under the awning, like he felt Ronnie coming. She gave him a wave, hoping Annie hadn't seen her, hadn't rounded the corner onto Park, had turned the other way to go back to the park, back to her crusty friends. Ronnie didn't dare look back. She'd zip into the lobby just in case, and if Annie was behind her, the doorman would stop her. Patrick gave Ronnie a smile as he opened the door for her, then looked past her with a frown. Annie must've followed her.

"Yo, Duuuuuude." Annie sounded wrecked, the words sliding out behind Ronnie, thick and low. Maybe that was what she was doing on those steps to the basement, taking in some substance Ronnie didn't want to guess at. She ignored her, giving Patrick a look meant to say *sorry* as she went through the doors. She was almost at the elevator in the back of the lobby when

Patrick came through the double doors, and she turned to say something to him. Annie flopped in his arms like a rag doll, her grey skin and dirty dreads out of place in the lobby, gleaming with marble and polished brass.

"What the—"

How could she be walking down the street one minute and passed out the next, her head lolling, dreadlocks brushing Patrick's pants.

"Call 911!" Patrick lay Annie down on the thick carpet in front of the doors. He straightened her out, pulled on her legs and arms, said her name, shook her shoulders.

Ronnie couldn't find her phone, she moved underwater, the grit of the hot day, the smell of that morning with her brother slamming into her. Something was wrong with her, she had to call, here was her phone, but it was useless, the screen blank, unresponsive, no matter how many times she poked at it. She was helpless what could she do? Patrick's fist hovered over Annie's nose, a thumb pushing down on the thing in his hand. Narcan. If only she'd had Narcan that morning, but no, that was different. Her brother was already dead when she woke up in the alley where they slept, the cardboard bed already hot from the summer sun.

Someone, two someones came in through the door and stopped. Two pairs of sunglasses, two custom-made suits, two pairs of thin leather shoes.

"Maybe," a deep, gentle voice said, "Park Avenue is not so fancy after all."

"Patrick," John Anthony's voice higher, "Why didn't you open the door for us? Who is that? Ronnie. Did you bring her here?"

"Did you call 911? The Narcan only lasts so long." Patrick aimed the question at Ronnie, ignoring John and Mateo. He moved Annie onto her side, tucking her hands under her head, bending her knees, watching her face.

"I—my battery must be dead. I'll use your desk phone." Ronnie moved around Annie and Patrick, toward the doorman station, but Mateo held out an arm, stopping her.

She opened her mouth, searched Mateo's face, looked at her boss. John watched Mateo like he couldn't have an opinion until Mateo spoke.

"She is a friend of yours?"

Ronnie shook her head at Mateo. "No. I mean, I know her, but she's not a friend. But the phone—mine's dead—I need to—she needs help."

Mateo turned his head slightly to the floor where Annie now sat up, dazed but breathing, her thin T-shirt patterned with dirt and food and God knew what else. Mateo wrinkled his nose. "Patrick, get rid of her. She does not belong here." He strode to the elevators and stood still as if John or Patrick would come over and punch the Up arrow, as if no one had anything better to do right now. Patrick led Annie to the bench against the wall, kept a hand on her shoulder, to prop her up or keep her from running, Ronnie wasn't sure which.

"John," Ronnie pleaded, "We can't just—"

"You heard what Señor Rosas de Flores said." John's voice tightened, the words barely making it out of his mouth. He went to the elevator, pushed the button.

"Sir," Patrick's deep voice glided across the marble floor. "She needs the attention of medical experts."

Mateo, not John, turned from the slow elevator, aimed his sunglasses at Patrick. "She needs to leave this building. You understand? It is not my concern what you do with her. Put her on the street, put her in a cab, put her in the dumpster. She is not worth any more of my time." The elevator chugged, squeaked to a stop, the doors finally opening. Mateo got in, John following. Before the doors closed, Mateo's words floated out: "Or yours."

They both watched the doors close, but neither one of them moved, Patrick still standing next to Annie. Ronnie's head clouded, Mateo's words a jumble. She couldn't believe it, he must have said something different, he must've meant—

"What the fuck." Annie's voice echoed like there were four of her. She tried to stand, but Patrick's hand on her shoulder kept her down. "Who was that guy?" She still looked like a wreck, but now she looked like a wide-awake wreck.

"These are probably his drugs in your system." Patrick jutted his chin at her. "What did you take?"

Annie looked back and forth between Patrick and Ronnie. "What are you talking about? I got these off some guy in the park. Not some guy in a suit who wants to put me in a dumpster. Let me go. I'm fine." She stood, wobbled, bent, and spewed all over the dark green carpet that made the path from the door to the elevator. She collapsed next to the barf.

"Ohmigod do something!" Ronnie reached over the wooden barrier at Patrick's station, searched for the phone, didn't see it, pushed things off the desk, if she could just—Patrick's large hand landed on her arm, stopped her from finding the phone. Whose side was he on, was he really not going to help Annie, let her die in an alley, so scared of Mateo that he would just let her—"She's a human being! Patrick!"

She flung off his hand and went to Annie, maybe she had a phone, she looked like she was dying, the grey skin, the blue lips, no, this couldn't happen again, Patrick there, pushing her away, Ronnie fighting back, Patrick's arm stiff, holding her away, he was going to smother Annie, kill her right there in front of her—"No! Don't! Patrick!" He got between her and Annie, and then she saw it. Another Narcan, he was giving her more Narcan, and Ronnie stepped back. The color returned to Annie's face, and she sat up in a whoosh, clawing the air, clawing at Patrick.

"Take her," Patrick said to Ronnie, "I will clean this up. I called a car. Take her to the hospital. There it is. Go. Now."

Ronnie held Annie's wrists, and pulled, pulled her out the door, the noise from the street, the horns, the brakes, the rush of the traffic slamming into her ears. A black sedan, a gypsy cab, pulled up and Patrick appeared next to them, opened the back door, said something to the driver, pushed Ronnie in after Annie.

"I'll call to tell them to expect her. Do not wait with her. Do not give them your name or your address."

Ronnie stared at him, the pieces coming together, the realization that Annie would live. She put an arm on the door so he couldn't close it yet. "Patrick. Wait, I don't have any money. I can't tip the driver."

A small smile played on his lips. "Mr. Anthony has tipped him already. I put it on his account."

She must've looked surprised. Or scared.

"He'll never know." Patrick closed the door, patted the roof, and the car angled into traffic.

# Chapter Nineteen

After Ronnie left, Frank and Pete moved around the little office, cleaning up, getting the space ready for whoever used it next.

Frank brushed invisible crumbs off the table. "Think it'll work? Think she'll be okay?"

Pete put the water bottles and soda cans in the tiny refrigerator next to the credenza. "Frank, if you have any doubts about this, let's pull her now. We'll start over, nab John Anthony some other way."

"No, no. I think she'll be all right. I just wanted to hear you say it."

Pete straightened up, looked Frank over. "She's tough, and she knows how to take care of herself. Plus, Mateo seems to have a soft spot for her." Pete tied off the bag of trash and scanned around the office, went to the door.

Frank followed.

"Hell, I have a soft spot for her." Pete turned off the lights, locked the door, headed for the elevators. "How does she do that, d'ya think?"

Frank had studied people endlessly for this job. In fact, thinking about what made people tick had been a fascination for him long before he became an agent. But Ronnie's appeal was something he was still trying to parse. The elevator arrived with a squeak, the doors opening slowly, and they both got on. Something in the combination of naiveté and street smartness, the seeming vulnerability in her slight frame, combined with the self-sufficiency—

"So...I'm thinking maybe we could get an apartment together." Pete didn't look at him.

"What? Where'd that come from?" Frank eyed his partner as the elevator came to a stop on the ground floor. "I didn't realize our relationship had gotten to that stage."

"Very funny. A two-bedroom. One for you, one for me."

"I don't know. I need to think about that."

They headed out the doors, turning left as if they'd agreed out loud to take the 4/5/6 back to work. "I don't know what there is to think about. I mean, aren't you tired of me on your couch?"

"You're welcome to stay as long as you need to."

They turned down Third, the subway entrance on the next corner. Frank got behind Pete to let a jogger pass them.

"That's just it," Pete said. "I don't need to anymore. I mean, I need to find an apartment, and I thought we could share the rent. I figured we get along. So."

They each fed in, then retrieved their MetroCards at side-by-side turnstiles, headed together down the next set of steps, the damp tunnel air coming at them as they descended.

"I'm sorry it's not working out with you," Frank said once they were on the platform.

"I thought we were friends." Pete stared straight ahead.

"Marriage is more than just friendship."

"We're not—oh jeez, I thought you meant—oh. So when you said, 'it's not working out,' you meant my marriage, not my sleeping on your couch."

Out of habit, Frank scanned the people waiting for the subway, standing or sitting, some alone, some together, near the platform, or off to the side. He peered down the tunnel, probably caves he should explore between the stations. A group of young people joked with each other, two girls chattered away, took pictures of each other. But no Cathy, no teenaged girl with a ribbon holding back her dark hair, a teasing smile.

The train came into the station, and they paused as several people got off, an older woman having trouble with her folding shopping cart. Frank helped her lift it up, and she glared at him as if she thought he was going to steal her groceries.

"I guess," Frank grasped the pole between them as the train started up, "I keep thinking that Cathy'll just show up some day." He felt Pete studying him, but he didn't want to meet his eyes. "Just walk in, dump her backpack, and flop down on the couch. And if I moved, if I wasn't there when she tried to come back, come home..." Frank swallowed. "It's like giving up, like I'm saying she's never coming back."

* * *

At the office, he and Pete each sat in their cubicle, each clicking away on their keyboards, catching up on the paperwork, all the necessary minutia so once they'd landed the criminal, the AUSA had what they required to make the case stick. He felt restless, and he doubled down, telling himself he couldn't get up until all the forms were done. He wanted the routine to anchor him, force his mind away from Cathy, what she was doing, what was happening to her. He used to do these forms in record time, loving the routine of it, the way the recap and detailed listing of the case so far let him see what further things the case required. But now he found it tedious and stupid. What was wrong with him? Like his whole world went sideways after Cathy ran away.

He took in a deep breath. He needed to put Cathy in the "personal" compartment in his brain, focus on the "work" area now. He couldn't do anything to find Cathy right this minute, and he had to concentrate on his cases.

He had another case that was at a standstill, and he reviewed those files, a habit he'd developed to see if anything new occurred to him. Fresh eyes. The case had come his way through the money laundering aspect, and it concerned a man in his thirties who quietly scammed women online. He was careful though, the fake profiles the Bureau put up not engaging him at all. It appeared that he had to initiate contact, and, according to the woman who brought him to their attention, he spent a long time with his victims, drawing them out with flattery and love poems until, it seemed, they would do anything for him, addicted to his attention. The victim who came forward had already been scammed, that avenue wasn't much use to the Bureau, her profile name deleted by the time her son insisted she report it.

He sighed, clicked the file closed. There was no end to the creativeness of the criminal, and while he always liked picking apart the knot, the challenge of making the case against them and catching them, sometimes the endless stream of bad guys got to him. Whack-a-mole. Once in a blue moon, they got lucky because the criminal was stupid and did something stupid, but usually they were smart, and when the Bureau closed one avenue, another popped up, especially in cyberspace. Or the interwebs, as he used to say to tease his daughter, always able to get a rise out of her at his supposed ignorance and backwardness. He could still hear her voice saying, Daaaaaad!

He stood and stretched, rotated his neck, and loosened his shoulders, checked his watch. Close enough to call it a day. He needed to move anyway, let his body work while his brain was busy. Pete swiveled his head at him, not breaking his rhythm on the keyboard.

"Done already? I didn't know you typed that fast."

Frank wiggled his fingers at him. "Fastest in the Bureau. Commendations and everything."

Pete snorted and looked at his screen. He hit the "enter" key with a flourish, clicked his mouse, and closed everything down. "Where are we going? Wanna grab a burger somewhere?"

* * *

Seemed like Frank was always watching his partner eat. Pete'd gotten dessert on top of the burger, fries, and salad. Should he be worrying about Pete's wallet along with his waistline? But the guy never gained weight, was always hungry.

"You ever get checked out for a tapeworm?" Frank watched the fork of chocolate cake travel from his partner's plate to his mouth. Frank had gotten coffee, not decaf, thinking he would head out with the flyers again. No Ronnie to help him look now. "We're sure," Frank made sure no one was anywhere near their booth, "aren't we, that leaving her in there was the right move?"

They had been partners so long that Pete didn't have to ask him for proper nouns instead of pronouns. He nodded. "Plus, she's got the extraction codes. You know we can be there in minutes."

"What if somehow she's in trouble, she can't text Linus?"

"She's a cat. She always lands on her feet." Pete scraped the plate with his fork, not one crumb left.

"Maybe you're pregnant. Eating for two."

"Besides," Pete looked around, as if contemplating more dessert, "Mateo seems to really like her—that lunch he took her to, leaving Marc in the car—almost like he thinks of her as family." Pete held up a finger for the waiter. "And we'll get the first report in the morning, we'll get the guy to read what she wrote the minute he's out of there."

The waiter came over, and thankfully, all Pete asked for was the check. Frank wanted to pick up the flyers, go back out, not sit in here spending money with Cathy on the streets somewhere. At least it was summer…

"She'll be okay, Frank. Really. Wanna go get a nightcap at the place over on First?"

As they headed to Frank's apartment, he told Pete he wanted to go distribute the flyers, and Pete was all over it, offering to go with him, help him look, brimming with ideas of where to go. He was practically jumping up and down, he was so excited.

Frank didn't say anything, and Pete kept babbling, but Frank tuned him out. He had to think about this a minute. The runaways were skittish, and if two big guys approached them instead of one, they might run. On the other hand, two people could cover more ground, put more copies of her picture in more hands. But would he be giving up, announcing to the universe that he couldn't find her by himself? He was her father, he knew her best, he should be able to find her. Of course, he had enlisted Ronnie to help him before, so how was Pete different? Because he was "Uncle Pete," a father figure competing with him for Cathy's attention? He was an idiot. And he didn't mean Pete.

They changed into clothing that hopefully didn't scream "cop," though loose enough to conceal their guns. Frank took up stacks of the flyers, Cathy's face smiling at him, that little faux dimple winking. He studied the paper as he waited for Pete to come out of the bathroom. He never wanted this picture to become so familiar to him that he dismissed the image, stopped looking at it, stopped seeing his daughter.

They hit the Port Authority, a place teeming with kids, full in the winter for the heat, full in the summer for the air conditioning. They showed them Cathy's picture, group after dirty group, some of them keeping it. They went down to the levels below, went to every corner they could find, left the flyer on a bench next to an old woman who was asleep, in the hat for collecting money for someone who rapped with a mic, with a juggler who recited long poems and the Articles of Confederation on the next level. An emotional roller coaster. The hope when they approached a kid, the disappointment when she wouldn't look at them, swore at them, walked away. The hope again when someone studied it, kept it, promised to keep a look-out for her.

"So this is where you go all those nights?"

"I try to go out as often as I can."

"What about Times Square?"

"We could go over that again. I should get some tape, put her picture up on the lampposts again."

"Don't give up, Frank."

"Never."

For efficiency, they split up at Times Square, so many people, even this late at night. The district had been cleaned up quite a lot over the years, making it safe and more appealing to tourists, so Frank went down side streets, around the blocks, ended up once again in the lights and the crowds, kept an eye out for Pete. Guys in red jackets sold double-decker bus tours, and he talked to one of them. He was nice enough, but he had a job to do, and he said frankly he never looked at the people, just called out and told them where to buy tickets. Plenty of tourists, a lot of languages in the crowds, but no runaways, singly or together, no homeless groups sitting on their backpacks next to a dog in a bandana.

He called Pete's cell and met him under the Lion King billboard, the brightness creating daytime at their feet. "I think it's hopeless here." Frank gestured around them. "It's getting late anyway. Maybe we should head back. School night and all that."

"I saw a group of kids down on 45th, past Seventh, showed them the picture. They kept it, but Frank, they said no one they'd run into would look like that unless she was a tourist they were panhandling."

Frank grunted and began walking. They headed to 42nd Street to take the S train, shuttle service to Grand Central. They split up around the crowds of tourists, the barkers, a man covered in silver paint moving like a robot.

On the platform, waiting for their train, Pete spoke again. "Frank, I haven't seen Cathy in a while, maybe not since this picture was taken, but I'm thinking you might have a better chance with a more recent picture."

"That's my favorite picture of her, the way her eyes twinkle. I thought it really showed her personality."

"Her personality, the way it was when she was fourteen. Before the addiction, before the streets."

"You don't need to remind me of that. I'm well aware."

"I'm sorry, Frank, but it needs to be said. If you've got a picture of her with all the black makeup you told me she'd started wearing, when her hair was messier..." Pete pulled out a flyer, and they both studied it. "I mean, c'mon, she's not wearing a blue ribbon like a brunette Alice in Wonderland now. She's on the streets, she doesn't have access to a daily shower or maybe any shower. And she's doing drugs and godknowswhatelse to buy drugs and—"

Frank turned away. Pete's words hit him like a fist in his gut, and he didn't think he could take any more. Maybe he should leave Pete here, walk home alone, the rhythmic beat of his footsteps drowning out what his partner had said.

He hadn't clocked that he'd moved until he heard his name and felt a hand on his shoulder. He shook him off, kept going, up the stairs, into the night, down the sidewalk, leaving behind the lights, the tourists, the barkers, the horns, trudged uptown on the quieter streets until they were too quiet, his footsteps echoing off the buildings as if calling out *come mug me I'm alone.*

He put each key in turn into the three deadbolts on the door to his apartment. The door didn't open, so he began the process again, halfway through when the bolts clicked, and the door swung open. Pete had beaten him there. He welcomed Frank into his own apartment, the look on his face morphing from worried to relieved to apologetic.

"Frank. I'm glad you're back. Look, I didn't mean—I was only trying to—what I meant was—"

Frank came all the way into the apartment, forcing Pete to take a step back. He stopped in the middle of the room, disoriented. Was this his apartment? "Pete." The sound was hoarse, like it wasn't even his voice.

"Can I get you something? Water, something stronger?"

Frank turned and stared at him. Who did he think he was? "This is my apartment."

"I know that. Of course it is." Pete studied his face. "Oh. Do you want me to leave?" He went to the couch, Cathy's couch, pulled up the blanket, folded one corner to the next. "I'm sure I can find someplace this time of night, some cheap hotel, maybe the couch in the insurance company office, maybe—"

"Pete, shut up, will ya? You're babbling." Frank sat down on the couch, on top of the blanket, pulling it from Pete's hands. Pete sat too. They were each silent, Frank's hands shoved into his hoodie pockets, Pete fiddling with something on the coffee table. "I'm not kicking you out."

Pete let out a long whoosh of breath. Stopped fiddling.

"It just seemed weird you offering me something in my own apartment." Frank went to the window. Looked out. Saw nothing.

"Oh, of course. I get it. But why did you walk away, leave like that? I was talking about Cathy, and you just left."

"That's why. You were talking about Cathy. Talking about my daughter like she was some strung-out hooker, filthy and smelly and, and…"

"And living on the streets." Pete went into the kitchen, a cupboard opening, the faucet running.

He came into the living room with two tall glasses of water, handed one to Frank. Frank put his on the coffee table. "Like that'll solve anything," he said, almost to himself.

Pete drank, the glug of his swallowing going on forever until Frank thought he might knock the glass out of his hand. His partner set it down on the table and turned toward Frank. Frank watched him out of the corner of his eye but didn't move, stared at the table in front of them.

"Okay, Frank. No bullshit. I think we need a Come to Jesus Meeting, and since I'm the only one here, I'm the one who's going to have to deliver it."

Frank shifted but didn't get up.

Pete sucked in a long breath. Let it out. "You're going to listen to this even if I have to handcuff you in place." He paused, evidently waiting for something, maybe acknowledgment from Frank.

Frank grunted.

"Okay." Pete's voice was low, but firm. "I think the reason you're not finding Cathy is that you keep looking for the little girl in the photo." He paused a beat, like he wanted it to sink in. "You can't believe that she would've changed, you can't see her on the streets because you still think of her as that cute fourteen-year-old smiling and laughing." He cleared his throat. "Frank."

Frank finally looked at him but had to look away again. He knew Pete saw the pain in his eyes.

"She is most likely strung out and filthy like those runaways we saw tonight, doing whatever she needs to do for the next fix. No, no, hear me out. She's no longer your daughter because she is now an addict, a daughter of the heroin, probably barely aware of who she is and what she's doing."

Frank launched himself off the couch. This apartment was way too small, no place to go, to get away. He paced behind the couch, but that was a ridiculous three feet, and he finally stopped in front of the window, raised the blinds to look out, pretended he wasn't inside. Pete moved around behind him, a clink of a glass in the sink.

"I. Think. I. Know. My. Own. Daughter." He bit off each word as if the force of it would make it more true. He turned from the window to see where Pete was. "Better than you do."

Pete held up his hands, palms out. "Hey, hey, don't shoot the messenger.

I'm saying that the person we're looking for isn't really Cathy. She's a runaway teen addicted to opioids. The drugs will have taken over and changed her. As will the streets." Pete went over to the couch and straightened the blanket over the cushion, tucked in a corner. "And I think you'll have a better chance of finding her if you keep that in mind, stop walking by the dirty strung-out ones, accept that as bad as they seem, they still could be Cathy."

* * *

For three days, Frank tried to avoid Pete. Not easy since they were partners, since he saw his snoring body tangled in the blankets on his couch every single morning. How could Pete say that to him? She was his daughter, not Pete's. He knew her like he knew the back of his hand. His heart knew her. When he got the text from Leo, he didn't tell him. Nor Susan. Like it was his own private thing, and telling someone might jinx it somehow.

Tonight was hot, the air pressing down, everyone out, walking aimlessly as if looking for a party. The world was upside down, night acting as day, people outside who should be in, everyone awake when they should be sleeping. Frank had tried hard to dampen his excitement when he got the text saying Leo needed to meet with him. He must have Cathy finally. She would finally come home, safe, his daughter once again. He might never stop hugging her.

Leo motioned with his head to the bench behind him, but Frank couldn't sit. His restlessness kept him moving, and he circumscribed the bench, shoved his hands in his pockets. All he wanted to do was grab Leo and make him tell him where Cathy was. Pin his arm behind him, force him to the ground, Frank's knee in his back...Frank unclenched his fists, shook out his hands. No reason for violence. This had to finally be good news, he just knew it.

Leo approached with his head down, told him it was his dinner break, and he should follow him.

Since when had dealers unionized, won scheduled breaks? Frank looked around, some skanks eyeing Leo walking away as if he were their last hope. Must not have gotten the memo. Frank hurried to catch up. "Where is she? Where's my daughter?"

Leo said nothing, kept walking, head down.

Frank grabbed one of his sagging shoulders, spun him around. "Tell me. Just tell me where she is."

Leo shook his head, his eyes fleetingly sad, before he gave him a hard stare. He shook his hand off. "Just follow me."

This didn't feel right. Frank stopped, watched Leo making his way up the street. Was Leo going to dinner, or taking Frank to Cathy? Were Leo's shoulders sagging because dealing was exhausting work, or because something else was going on? Frank mentally shook himself. This had to be good news, everything else a distraction. After all this time, the late-night searching, Pete's lecturing—he was due. Cathy's ordeal finally over, theirs again, living her life as a normal, New York teenager. He caught up to Leo.

The dealer stopped in front of an entrance so dark, so narrow, so easily missed. The black lacquer shone, a small gold knob in the center, no sign, no hint of what was behind it. Leo turned the knob, the door soundless as it opened. Low lights deep inside made it impossible to see anything. Leo stood back, waved a hand between Frank and the open door. "Go on in." He didn't meet Frank's eyes, just backed up, headed up the street.

"Wait—where is she?" He might strangle Leo.

The drug dealer didn't answer, just kept walking.

Frank looked at the doorway. What would Cathy be doing in here? As a precaution, Frank unsnapped his holster but didn't take his gun out. He peered in. A clean, earthy smell of sandalwood, of thick carpets, of wealth floated in the air. "Cathy?" He edged in, the place hushed. He reached for his phone and the flashlight feature, a voice stopping him.

"Mr. Jankowski. Right this way, please." The slender man dressed all in black walked further into the dark, and Frank stayed close to him in case the man disappeared into the shadows.

Frank's senses were on high alert, even though this seemed like a very high-end restaurant and not a greasy alleyway with thugs waiting for him.

But thugs, obviously, could be anywhere. They turned a series of corners until the man stopped at the end of a short hallway, slid aside a heavy door on well-oiled tracks. The man gestured for him to go in, and Frank put his hand inside his light jacket, peered into the room.

"No need for guns, I do not think." Mateo Rosas de Flores did not rise as Frank came in.

What the actual fu—the young man expertly frisked him and removed the gun before his brain got through all its questions. "You can't take that. I'm a—it's a—"

"You will have the return of your gun, Special Agent Frank Jankowski, when it is time for you to leave. Please sit. Sake?" A gold-capped black bottle sat in front of Mateo, little ceramic cups on a black tray next to it.

Frank shook his head, remained standing. How the hell did he know he was an agent? "Why am I here?" He tried to keep his voice calm and firm. As if he could be in command of whatever this was. "Leo said—"

"Leo said you were looking for your daughter. Please have a seat."

The round table had three other chairs, and though Mateo gestured to the place on his right, Frank pulled out the chair opposite him. He held onto the back and didn't sit. "What have you got to do with my daughter? What's going on here?" Mateo must have people everywhere.

Mateo seemed not to have heard him. He unscrewed the gold cap on the bottle, poured out two cups. He held his to his nose, closed his eyes as he moved the cup around. Eyes still shut, he sipped, set the cup down, opened his mouth, and breathed in. When he finally opened his eyes, they seemed to be seeing something not in this room. The ritual almost made Frank want to taste the stuff, but he was too angry, too focused on not letting that anger cloud his judgment. And he didn't want to drink anything Mateo offered him.

Mateo's glance lingered on him, then moved to the chair. "Please. Let us be civilized. I have done you the honor of talking to you myself. I believe I have—as you say—all the cards. So please be civilized, return the honor and sit, enjoy the world's most expensive sake, see why it is so renowned." He moved the second cup to the middle of the table.

"First, tell me what you know about my daughter, and then I'll decide if I'm going to sit with you." If it came to that, he could use this chair as a weapon.

"I will tell you when you are seated."

Maybe the sake was heated, he could throw it in his eyes. He reached for the cup, Mateo's satisfied nod in his peripheral vision. It was room temperature. He set the cup down, pulled out the chair, sat away from the table, ready for whatever might come next.

"Thank you. Please, be my guest, enjoy my hospitality."

Frank brought the cup to his mouth, tipped it, wet his lips, nothing more.

"I have a few requests of you, and once I am satisfied, you will have your daughter."

Frank's cup hit the table, and he stood up, the chair tipping over. "What? Where is she? Tell me now!"

The door slid open, and a man filled the opening, stayed there. Mateo did not acknowledge him. "I am sorry. I have daughters, and I can imagine what your daughter means to you. All those nights you went looking for her. And your wife..."

"You leave her out of this."

Mateo suggested he pick up his chair, once again sit down. After Frank righted the chair, the door slid closed again, but Frank had no illusions the guy had left. Mateo sipped his sake, poured himself another cup. Finally, he repeated that he wanted something from Frank in exchange for Cathy, and added, "She is safe, and she will be unharmed. We are keeping her on a maintenance dose, and, depending on how long it takes for me to be satisfied, we will begin decreasing it, wean her off so that she will no longer be addicted when we return her to you." He shook his head, as if to himself. "Though Leo said she was a good customer." He sighed. "Well, we have others."

"I need to see her. Now." Frank glared at him. He had to show some strength. He was not rolling over for this motherfucker. Ever. He would make Mateo tell him where she was, the whole Bureau would rescue her, and kidnapping would be added to all the charges against Mateo. "Bring me to her."

The door slid open, the young man who had shown Frank in carried a tray, silently put down small dishes, two pairs of chopsticks. He left without a word, without looking at either of them. Mateo gestured to Frank, then to the dishes.

Frank continued to stare at him. "I need to know she's safe, that you haven't done things to her. That she's not terrified because of your thugs—"

Mateo shook his head at Frank, plucked a mini rice ball out of one of the dishes like he'd been born with chopsticks in his hand. He popped it in his mouth, closed his eyes. Frank looked away from the indulgent display. "I gave the strictest orders." Mateo waved his chopsticks at Frank. "My men know what happens to them if they don't follow my orders exactly. So. She is safe." He slid chicken and charred peppers off a skewer onto his plate. "She is comfortable, she is not terrified. She had the use of a shower, has been fed. I bought her new clothes. She was told she could have anything she wanted to eat, and do you know what she chose?"

Frank clamped his mouth tight. He didn't want Mateo knowing he was desperate to hear every detail about his daughter.

Mateo dabbed at the corner of his mouth with his napkin. "Anything in New York City, any restaurant, anywhere in the five boroughs, any price, and she asked for a Shake Shack Avocado Bacon Burger." He shook his head slowly as if in wonder. "Those burgers must be very unusual." He plucked up the thinly sliced pickled ginger, dipped it in wasabi, placed it in his mouth. "I am treating her very well, Mr. Jankowski. She is very safe. Not in danger as she was before."

Frank's phone buzzed in his pocket. He ignored it. Nothing could interrupt this.

"Go on. Look at it. I asked the men to send you proof."

Frank tore his phone out of his pocket, poked at it in the dim light. A picture of Cathy, skinny, but clean, a burger in front of her, a milkshake in her hand, her mouth open to take a sip. The emotions rushed in, threatening to overtake him, his eyes barely seeing the room around him. He clutched his phone like he was hugging her. He forced himself to breathe, measured breaths, in and out. He returned the phone to his pocket because otherwise he would stare at the screen and lose all rational thought. He needed to compartmentalize the personal, become an agent again. Assess the situation and take every advantage he could. His phone buzzed again. He retrieved it. A close-up of a man standing behind Cathy holding a newspaper up over her head. He enlarged the picture. Today's New York Post.

"Okay." Mateo sipped his sake. Put the cup down. "We have Cathy, and you see she is safe. And now this is what I want from you."

Frank stood. He would get the Bureau to analyze the photo, figure out the guy's clothing, find all the shadows, and listen to—"I need to see a video of her. Hear her say in her own words that she hasn't been mistreated." Then they could listen...who was he kidding? The noise from all the millions of apartments in the city sounded the same. And they could be keeping her anywhere, not just in Manhattan.

"I will see what I can do. Meanwhile, this is what you will do for me. And if and when I am satisfied, I will return her to you."

Frank could feel the heat creep up his neck. This sonofabitch. He needed time to think this through. "Leo works for you? He turned Cathy over to you."

Mateo cocked his head as if curious, maybe analyzing why this was important to Frank. He gave a small smile. "He works for us. And we know you have sold his drugs for him. What would your precious Bureau say to that? You were not on a case, you were not undercover, you exchanged money for my drugs, and narrowly missed getting arrested. So." He sat back. Steepled his fingers. "You've already done work for us. Now you will do more." He cleared his throat and laid out what he wanted. Which was everything. Notice of all the cases involving him, advance notice of raids, court cases dropped, regular reports on all FBI thoughts and actions where it concerned the Mataderos Cartel.

With each demand, Frank wilted a little, then straightened up in anger. He felt like he was on a yo-yo string. He should walk out. But Cathy. No doubt, Mateo would kill her. But would he anyway after Frank did his bidding? No way he could be a snitch. A double agent, as it were. Revealing everything.

Helping this horrible criminal continue his heinous activities. He couldn't. Mateo was a foreign national. This would be treason. Did he have a choice? He had to find out where Cathy was. And he had to get the Bureau's help to do that. And if they arrested Mateo before he found Cathy—oh God. He couldn't even think about that.

"You are in shock, I think. It is a lot to process. But you should partake of the sake. It will help."

The ceramic cup was in his hand and to his lips before he realized he'd reached for it. It tasted sweet, a little fruity, a little nutty, and it went straight to his head. He put the cup down a little harder than he meant to. Was there something else in this besides the alcohol?

"There. Is that not lovely? Did you get the caramel notes? No? Maybe another?"

Frank shook his head again. He reached for the bowl of peanuts, saw in the dim light the flakes of red pepper. Better not be too hot. He tossed a handful in his mouth. Fuck the chopsticks.

"We will meet again. Soon. I will send you the address, the time. And you will tell me all that you have done for me in order to earn your daughter back." He pushed his chair away from the table and stood. "It will be nice for you to have her home." The door slid open before he got there, and Frank sat stunned, watched his bespoke-suited back retreat into the darkness.

# Chapter Twenty

Watching Lisa stomping ahead of her, Ronnie decided she must be part dragon. Like she could see the nasty smoke curling around her after she had roared her fire at her. Ronnie followed for several blocks up Park Avenue, then over to Fifth. Lisa was mad because John said to take Ronnie with her, so she refused to speak, walked so fast ahead of her that Lisa might as well just flat out run. They both arrived at the doorman at the same time anyway, but Lisa had probably enjoyed her scaly solitude, knowing Ronnie was behind her. Lisa spoke to the doorman, pushed her thick curly hair off her forehead. She breathed hard and her cheeks flushed. Probably the most exercise she'd gotten in months.

They had to ride the elevator together, and Ronnie examined Lisa's reflection in the doors. She stood tall, stared straight ahead, eyes not moving, but Ronnie had no doubt she saw Ronnie relaxing against the corner of the elevator car. She'd bet anything Lisa wished she could slump against the wall, take a load off those stacked heels.

They came out at the penthouse and even Lisa sucked in her breath.

"Whoa." Ronnie went past her to the windows in the great big living room. "How much time is he going to spend in this place?" The windows gave her an amazing view of Central Park, above the trees, above everything, the apartment buildings on the west side distant, friendly.

"Not my business and not yours either." Lisa pronounced the last word "eye-thur."

Ronnie decided not to practice it in her head. She didn't need to imitate Lisa.

"Are you taking notes?" Lisa's tone was superior, like only little people like Ronnie took notes for grand people like her.

John had sent them over to Mateo's new penthouse to figure out what he'd need to get the place ready. John would hire an interior design firm, and he wanted to give them some direction before they started. They wandered the rooms, Lisa commenting and Ronnie taking the all-important notes. The kitchen was a big shiny affair, all marble and stainless steel, glass-fronted cabinets full of dishes and stemware. At the other end of the room, a heavy curtain marked off a table and chairs, an upholstered bench along one wall matching the flowery drapery.

"Isn't this the coziest little nook. Can't you just picture the family in here for breakfast, the children gathered around..." Lisa pulled out a chair, the seat of which matched the curtains and the bench.

"Does he have children? Will they be here with him?"

Lisa waved a hand at her like she was being silly.

"I'm not kidding," Ronnie shut the notebook. "We should know this, because if his family isn't going to ever be here, he would hate that setup."

Lisa turned on her like she'd drowned her kitten. "What are you talking about?" Her whole face was flushed, and not from the walk over here. "Of course he'd love it. Who wouldn't?" She wriggled in the chair and faced the table like she thought Ronnie was going to bring her lunch.

"Mateo likes to be served, and he doesn't like to be in the kitchen where all the work gets done."

"What do you know about it?"

"I've spent some time with Mateo and I've gotten to know him a little. He'd rather have his meals in the dining room, the more formal the better."

Lisa barely spoke to her the rest of the tour, all three floors, up the stairs, into the closets, out on the rooftop. "I suppose you're going to tell me he would want to get rid of all this furniture up here," Lisa swept her arm to include the wrought-iron tables, and chairs so fancy they looked like should be in the living room.

Ronnie shook her head. "No, he'd like this just the way it is."

On the elevator ride down, Lisa fumed, crossed her arms, stared at the carpeted floor.

"Look, Lisa."

She didn't look up at Ronnie.

"We have to work together on this, so we might as well talk to each other. Why are you so mad at me anyway? What did I ever do to you?"

"You? What did you do? You waltzed in here and changed everything. Wrecked my life, and you wonder why I'm mad at you?"

"What are you talking about? You've been a bitch to me ever since you hired me." Ronnie stared at the back of her head, Lisa's curls like snakes. "Why did you hire me anyway, if you hate me so much?"

"I didn't want to," Lisa said to the floor of the elevator. "John said I had to, said your background was what he required." Lisa stared at Ronnie in the reflection of the doors. "Everything was perfect before you got here. I had John all to myself, and Kerry would leave me something for lunch, and I had the best job ever, and then you come along and Kerry gets fired and suddenly you're the favorite and I never see John and—"

The elevator hit the ground floor, and Lisa stalked out, didn't acknowledge the guy at the desk, practically ran up the few steps to the door. Ronnie checked the doorman's name tag, thanked him by name, told him they'd probably be back soon.

She caught up to Lisa on Madison where she waited for the light to change. She stayed alongside her, matched her pace, and when they more or less had the sidewalk to themselves, she grabbed her arm, made her stop. "That's what you want? John all to yourself, just a little family of two? Does Barbara know that?"

"She was never here until you came along and she decided she had to spend so much time with you." Lisa tried to go past her, and Ronnie blocked her way.

Ronnie looked into her eyes until Lisa turned as if to go. Ronnie grabbed her arm. "Wait a minute." Ronnie shook it like she needed to wake her up. "You're in love with him." She tightened her grip. "You are, aren't you?"

Lisa opened her mouth, like she was going to deny it, then her face contorted until it crumpled, and tears streamed down her cheeks. It was all Ronnie could do not to walk away, or grab her again and shake her, tell her to pull her big-girl panties up and pull herself together. Instead, she leaned against the wall of an apartment building, crossed her arms, turned her head away a little to give Lisa time to recover.

Lisa wiped at her face, first one hand, then the other, then both. Her head was down as if she thought her hair would give her some privacy.

Ronnie said nothing.

"Why don't you go away, go back where you came from, just leave?" Lisa's face was red, blotchy.

"Then you'd have to hire another butler." Ronnie took a step toward her, and Lisa turned away. "And maybe the new butler wouldn't be as nice as I am."

Lisa snorted. Swiped at her nose.

"Why do you want to be involved in all this anyway? You know what he does, don't you?" Ronnie moved to make more room for someone walking past.

"I don't care about any of that." Lisa sniffed. Looked around like she was calculating escape routes. "What about you? You do all that stuff for him, all cozy with Barbara. Why don't you just go back to your own family?" If looks could kill.

"You okay to walk now?" Ronnie was not going to tell Lisa she didn't have a family to go back to. "I kinda think we might have a lot to do. Isn't he coming back next week?"

Lisa sniffed and snuffled beside her as they made their way to Park Avenue. Maybe she should lead Lisa by the hand since she stumbled once or twice, like she needed help walking.

"Look." Ronnie waited for the cars so they could cross the street. "I won't be here forever. Hang in there, and maybe you can be the star again. Have John all to yourself."

"Where are you going?" Lisa's voice sounded hopeful.

They turned the corner at Park, the sidewalk so much wider, the traffic loud, a horn beeping. Ronnie shrugged. "Nowhere right now, but you can count on me not always having this job. Hey, Patrick." Ronnie stopped to chat with him, knew Lisa would keep going. She'd rather stand with him under the awning in the heat than ride the tiny elevator with the meltdown disaster named Lisa Cranberry.

* * *

"Let me see your phone."

He'd never asked to see her phone before. "What're you looking for? Maybe I can help." Ronnie pulled the phone out, unlocked the screen, hovered a finger over it, eyebrowed a question at him.

"May I have it, please?"

She put it on the desk in front of him.

"What are these pictures?" He swiped away.

It was all Ronnie could do not to snatch it out of his hands. "That's to show the designer what they're taking out and redoing for Mateo's penthouse."

He turned the phone this way and that, peered at the screen. "Is the decorator redoing the closet? Or do you have some other reason for taking this picture?" He looked over the phone at her, his birthmark darkened.

"Jeez, John. After all this time, you're still suspicious?"

He held on to her phone like it was his.

"Look. Lisa asked me to take pictures of the closet in case Mrs. Mateo needed a different layout or something."

He swiped at her screen. "You don't have many contacts. Who's this Linus person?"

What the—play it cool, play it cool. "John. Can't I have a private life? He's a guy, just a guy. Y'know, like guys and girls together?"

John poked at the screen, held her phone to his ear. He listened while he looked at her. She heard Frank's voice, a tinny echo, saying, "Ronnie. What's up?"

He ended the call and handed it to her.

"Great, now he thinks I hung up on him."

John rolled a silver-sided case out from behind his desk, laid it flat on the floor. "Take this down to the Waverly." This was a suitcase, not a briefcase, wheels, pull-out handle, everything. "Mateo owns the studio now, but Nigel still runs it. He's expecting you. Lisa's called the driver, so you'd better hurry." He glanced inside, shut the top, clicked the latches, spun the dials next to each one. He sat back down behind his desk, studied her.

She grabbed the handle and nearly let go, it weighed so much. She didn't want to think about how much money it held.

"Wait."

Ronnie stopped. Now what. John didn't say anything, so she turned around, stared at him. He played with the jade-handled letter opener, twisted it, turned it over and over.

"You know you can't bring people like that to my building."

"People like what?"

Silence. Flip. Twist. Flip.

"Oh. You mean you think I brought Annie—"

"Mateo has strict rules for his employees. No users, no dippers, no cheaters, no liars." John Anthony looked up from his lethal toy.

Ronnie wondered if he ever threw it.

John cleared his throat. "Mateo was saying he wanted you more involved, but after seeing that piece of trash in the lobby, he wasn't so sure."

Her face flushed. If Annie lost her this job…but why would she want to work for someone who ordered another person thrown in a dumpster? She couldn't get fired before Frank made this case. This was a nice gig, easy hours, nice room, good pay. She needed to see this through. She slid the handle back into the suitcase, a firm click.

John's eyes widened, and his eyebrows rose.

Ronnie moved the suitcase away from the door, put her hand on the knob. What if he called her bluff? She looked over her shoulder at him. Would Frank have another job for her? At least Frank thought Annie was a person. But if she stayed, got deeper into Mateo's organization, maybe she could help Frank and Pete take the whole thing down.

She faced John, folded her arms, leaned against the door.

John watched her, head tilted.

"John. Look, it's one thing to take a briefcase," they both looked at it, "or a suitcase, to an art gallery. I don't know what's in it, and I don't care. My job is to follow your orders."

He took up the letter opener, his face relaxed like he thought he'd won this one.

"But it's another to work for someone who kills people for no reason, who says to throw away a girl who did nothing but OD—probably on his drugs—"

"In the lobby of this building." John's voice cut like a shard of glass.

"So you agree with him. You would say the same thing: throw her in the dumpster." Ronnie turned the door handle. "I think I'm going to be sick. I can't run your errands today."

"Hold it."

Ronnie didn't turn around, but she heard the jab, jab, jab of his letter opener.

"Can I explain something to you?" Jab. Jab. Jab. "Look, sit down a sec." He watched the letter opener as it sank into the blotter. "Not that I owe you an explanation, I pay your salary, that should be explanation enough."

Ronnie sat in the guest chair, but on the edge of the seat, let him know she was ready to bolt at any wrong word.

He let out a big sigh, stopped playing with the jade-handled weapon. "I've been working with Mateo a long time, first at the bank when we all thought he was a legitimate businessman. I mean, he is, but that's only because he has to put his money somewhere to clean it. Which I found out once I left the bank to open my own business with only one client: Mateo Rosas de Flores. By then, I was in too deep with him to refuse, or to leave, to get out."

Ronnie crossed her arms. Was she supposed to feel sorry for him now?

"He was good. Oh boy, was he good. He led me along, introduced me to all the lovely things a lot of money buys, the incredible restaurants, custom shoes and suits, the places to get away to where your whim is someone's sole job to cater to." His head went back and forth, a slow movement like he wished he were there right now.

"He seduced you."

John startled like he forgot she sat in front of him. He narrowed his eyes, then gave a small shrug. "Yeah. I guess that's the right way to put it. But now I can't leave. Do you know what happens to people who want to get out?"

"Like Marc?"

"Yep. Or worse than that." He turned back to his computer screen, hit the space bar. "So," he said, still looking at his screen, "what Mateo wants, says, or does, has to be okay, no matter what I think. And if you don't take that suitcase to Nigel, I'll have to tell Mateo that he can't trust you, and I worry that he'll think you're a little too far into this to be allowed to leave."

"Okay, John."

He cleared his throat but didn't turn to face her.

"I'll take this suitcase down to Nigel. I'll do this today and tomorrow and forever, but you need to tell Mateo that he has absolutely nothing to worry about where I'm concerned. You'll tell him that you stand behind me 100% and he never has to question my loyalty, my honesty, my behavior, again." She grabbed up the suitcase and opened the door before he said anything else, before she said anything else. "And neither do you." She dragged the heavy thing across the carpet, shut the door, didn't dare look back.

In the elevator, she let out a long breath and pulled her phone out of her back pocket. She sent "Linus" a text. *sorry butt dial* Which, for once meant what it said, that everything was okay, and she hadn't meant to call him. She'd write in the journal tonight what had happened so they didn't get all panicky and ride in here to rescue her. But she hadn't told them about Annie, and no way she was going to now, about her almost getting her in trouble with Mateo, about having to stand up to John.

* * *

She waited with Patrick, a town car nowhere in sight. She felt wrung out from that conversation, and she had a long day ahead of her. First time anyone said Marc's name, John acknowledging it without a flicker. Weird how no one else ever mentioned Marc, no pretend story about why he wasn't there, like everyone knew that everyone else knew, but no one saying anything. Not even Patrick. They stood together under the awning, though it was still hot, the air thick. She'd be glad when August was over.

"Everything okay with your friend?" Patrick's voice was deep, pleasant.

What? Oh, Annie. "Bro, let's talk about something else. I just got an earful because Mateo thinks I brought her here. How many people do I have to tell she's not my friend?"

They faced the street in silence, but she didn't think Patrick was mad at her.

"So," Ronnie peered up the street, "lucky you had that Narcan. Didn't think this was the kind of building where the doorman would need a supply of that stuff."

Patrick shook his head. "You'd be surprised."

"Why did you tell Annie that Mateo sold her the drugs?"

Patrick looked uptown with her, Park stretching its wide avenue forever north. "Mateo's people work the Upper East Side, Central Park, down to midtown on this side. Stood to reason."

"Do you work for Mateo?"

"Everyone works for Mateo."

"Have it your way." Maybe she should get a cab, make Lisa reimburse her. From her own pocket. "But, can I ask you, does it bother you that he makes his money selling drugs that wreck people's lives?"

"Does it bother you?" The words came out low and even, not really a question, more of an answer.

Ronnie was about to give a one-shoulder shrug as if to say nothing bothered her, but images of her brother had been with her ever since Annie had OD'd. Annie, her brother, Frank's daughter. She shivered, the involuntary kind that the neighbor lady would say was someone walking over your grave.

Patrick sighed. "I wanted to get out, but you can never get out. I guess Mateo saw something in me, so he got me this job. Where he can watch me."

A group of kids piled out of a car halfway up the next block, laughing, greeting the doorman. Even from here she could tell their clothes were expensive. Maybe they bought from Mateo, too.

"You were selling?"

Patrick nodded. "Not proud of it, but I figured they would buy from somewhere, so they might as well buy a clean product from me." He nodded his chin at her. "But you. It's not too late. You could get out, you haven't been here long, you could leave, start again, work for someone else..."

Nice dream. But she couldn't tell Patrick that they were in the same boat. Frank got her this job like Mateo got Patrick his job, and she couldn't walk away any more than he could.

The black Town Car slid up, the driver popping the trunk, but Ronnie told Patrick she wanted to keep the suitcase with her, and she dragged it onto the seat as she got in. Patrick closed her door, went around and closed the trunk, tapped on it to let the driver know he could leave. That tap-tap reassured her, like he summoned a protective spirit. Ronnie looked at the silver suitcase next to her. She certainly hoped so.

A plastic partition divided her from the driver like in a cab, but unlike in a cab, this one was tinted, and no advertising, no air holes, no license displayed. Out her window all the traffic, the buildings, the sidewalks, everyone going about their business like it was any other day, like Marc hadn't died in that warehouse. And around the penthouse, it was as if poof! he'd never existed. Just bam, another driver, another black car. John hadn't said when she'd be smurfing or doing deposits again. He'd just given her this suitcase full of—she didn't want to think about it.

If a briefcase full of hundreds held two and half million (she'd looked it up), and this suitcase could hold like six briefcases, then...she'd have to go back to school to figure that one out.

They slowed for a light as they headed downtown, and a bicyclist stopped beside them, looked into the backseat as if he could see her through the tinted glass, see into the suitcase. She held on to the handle of the thing.

"The doors are locked, right?" Ronnie asked the driver. She looked at her door but didn't see the lock button. So dark in here with all the tinted windows and black leather. She scrabbled at it, at the molded plastic at her door, but she couldn't find anything, couldn't feel where to lock the door.

"Hey!" She tapped hard on the divider separating the front seat from the back.

The driver reached up and slid the window open without turning around.

"There's a guy on a bicycle staring in here. How do you lock this door?" The bicycle-riding Peeping Tom was still beside the car. Every door clicked. Better be locking, not unlocking. The driver slid the window closed again. She felt for a door handle to test but there wasn't one. What kind of car was this? Did Lisa do this, ordered a car for her that was actually a prison, told the driver…naw, this had to be J.A.'s, Mateo's new driver. She knocked at the partition again, but the light changed, and he drove, not hearing her, or pretending not to.

The bicyclist kept up with them as they made their way in the heavy traffic. Maybe John Anthony had sent him. Maybe this was another test. How could he keep looking at her and not run into something? Who was this guy? Her heart beat faster, up in her throat, the tingling around her eyes, her brain shutting down. She belly-breathed, in, out, short inhale, long exhale, *you're fine you're fine it's okay it's okay...*

She needed her brain working, needed to figure this out. First, the driver was heading downtown, in the direction of Waverly & Waverly. Second, he might be just a bicycle guy, or maybe someone Frank and Pete sent. She sat up straighter. Okay, that's good, that would be good if he was FBI. Third, maybe town cars sometimes came with partitions and no handles in the back, or maybe Lisa thought it was funny, a joke, not a danger. She thought she'd been pretty forceful with John, pledging her loyalty. Again. *Breathe.*

Maybe a car like this was for her protection. From what? More like imprisonment. Maybe the driver was kidnapping her, he was going to take the suitcase full of money, and once he had it…there had to be a handle, why was she not seeing anything on the door? Was she about to meet the same fate as Marc? But why, what had she done? But then what had he done?

With the flat of her hand she skimmed the door again. Why hadn't she seen it before. There was the handle, which she tried, confirmed the door was indeed locked. And right next to it, a little lever to lock and unlock her door. She let out a long breath. This job was going to kill her. Scratch that. Bad juju. Be the wreck of her.

The car turned west, hopefully to head down Eleventh, which was the most direct way. No sign of the cyclist, so maybe that was paranoia too. But whoever heard of a town car with a partition?

* * *

Inside Waverly & Waverly, Ronnie paused in the cool. The place was fancier than ever, more employees, more art on display, more security. And no customers. Ronnie rolled the suitcase into Nigel's office, and his eyes widened, part greed, part fear, licked his lips as his breathing increased. His pupils were so dilated his eyes looked black.

"Well now." He rubbed his hands together and reached for the suitcase. The air in his office was suddenly stifling, and she told him she'd be going unless there was something he wanted her to give Mr. Anthony.

Nigel started as if she'd woken him up, then recovered himself, put one hand in his pocket. But they both knew she'd seen him. "Is he still requiring receipts?" He scanned her up and down like she suddenly smelled bad. "With this new arrangement?"

"I haven't been told otherwise. Have you?" Ronnie turned to go. "See you next time."

"How soon will that be?"

"Your guess is as good as mine."

"He knows, doesn't he, that these things," Nigel gestured at the suitcase with a roll of his wrist, "take time? I'd like to have that one empty before the next one comes along."

Ronnie shrugged at him. "I have no idea what John knows and what he doesn't. I do what he tells me to, and if tomorrow he tells me to bring another one of those down here, then that is what I'll be doing." She left Nigel looking around his tiny office as if imagining stacks of hard-sided silver suitcases.

She turned right out the door and walked uptown. Good, no car. She needed the walk, needed to shake off the day so far, get rid of all these people in her brain. Mateo, Annie, Frank, John, Lisa, Pete. Even Patrick.

But she liked Mateo, liked his custom suits, the way he tilted his head and actually listened when she talked, liked his descriptions of food from all over the world. Her shoes tap-tapped as she strode, the rhythm of it, the movement let her mind work the kinks out. But damn this was getting dangerous, and the way he talked about Annie. Would he talk about Patrick like that, or her. He liked Patrick, that was something. She was pretty sure he liked her, made her feel better after the warehouse, after Marc. But Pete had said Mateo was the one who had him killed. How could you be a killer and talk about white truffle crème brûlée?

A guy across the street started up a saxophone. Just walking along playing a saxophone. She wished she could float away on that music right now. Maybe she should've let Frank and Pete pull her out, but it seemed like they wanted her to stay in, make it work. She thought Frank liked her, wouldn't put her at risk, but he was always threatening to throw her in jail, so how much did he like her? She couldn't have made their case for them yet, so she had to stay in, even if it was risky. Could she get out, run, take the next suitcase, and go…where, where did people go? All she knew was this city, and where she grew up, and if she went home, Frank would find her, and if she stayed here, Mateo would really find her.

A drip ran down the inside of her shirt. Far too hot, the air thick and muggy, the walking now more uncomfortable than calming. So, where was that car when she needed it? No way she was walking back to the gallery. She pulled out her phone, and it started ringing.

"Lisa," she said into it, "where's my car?"

"Where the freak are you?"

Ronnie looked around, told her the intersection.

"What the hell. Wait until J.A. hears about this. He told me to tell that driver not to lose sight of you. You're in it now."

Sounds like you're in it. "Listen, Lisa, just call them and tell them where I am. It's not my fault he wasn't there, and I started walking."

"You—"

Ronnie cut her off. "But maybe it's your fault for not giving the driver thorough instructions."

She heard Lisa huff like she was about to blow fire, like she wanted to say something but was so mad she couldn't form the words.

Ronnie hung up and waited for the evil black town car under the shade of an awning. At least the air conditioning would be nice.

# Chapter Twenty-One

That bastard. Mateo Rosas de Flores was all Frank could think about. That and how he was going to deal with this. Once again, he'd been avoiding Pete as well as he could while he tried to figure this out. The morning was easy, Pete, a heavy sleeper and a late one, too. He felt like a cat burglar as he slid the deadbolts open oh-so-slowly and tiptoed out each day. He couldn't walk all the way to work—it would be tough on his shoes and take at least an hour and a half. But he could walk part of the way, let his mind work on this while his body moved.

August hit him in the face as he came out of the door and down the steps. He had to arrest Mateo sooner than soon. Could he get that done without telling Pete? What would happen if he told him? Would Rick, the boss, have to know? He was already sweating in his sport coat, but he couldn't take it off, have someone shout "gun!" when they saw the holster. Though since this was New York, maybe they'd just cross to the other side of the street. But if he arrested him before he found Cathy, why would Mateo tell him where she was? He loosened his tie, avoided a dog walker with five dogs stretching their leashes. He would not have anything to hold over him. Because Mateo would not be shaken by the arrest. He would get his pack of top-priced lawyers to get him released. And he would still have Cathy.

Someone on old-fashioned roller skates aimed toward him, her purple cape floating behind her. Did he believe Mateo when he said Cathy was safe, not harmed, getting fed? He'd looked at the pictures obsessively, and he wanted to believe they were real. Plus, the Shake Shack detail. The two of them would go as a special treat, Cathy always ordering the Avocado Bacon

Burger. Every time. No way Mateo could've known that.

A line formed halfway down the block on Third and Frank got in it. Best coffee and croissant from the tiniest shop in the city. Hardly wider than a person, the space forced the guy to spin around in place to bag up flaky croissants and dispense coffee, cream, and sugar on the side. He worked quickly with no changes to what he offered. Good business model, perhaps. Maybe Frank should quit the Bureau and open a place like this. He could hide out and not have to think about anything. Except Cathy.

He got two croissants in case Pete wanted one. Who was he kidding, of course Pete would want one, even if he'd had a full breakfast. He continued heading south, his footsteps drumming *Cathy Cathy Cathy*. He had to stop walking, pray for an air-conditioned subway car so his jacket had half a chance to dry out before he got into the office. He clattered down the steps, the air more humid, a wet dankness, the garbage, urine, metallic smells strong. And, though it didn't seem possible, it was even hotter down here than on the street.

He had to figure this out, but really, he already knew what he had to do. The train blew in, stopping with a screech of brakes. It was so damn full already, and Frank wasn't in the mood to press against all those bodies, spill his coffee down the front of his white shirt. He backed up, away from the crowds on the platform who were barely letting people off, then pushing in. He sipped his coffee. He told himself he needed to understand all the ramifications of what he had to do next, but deep down, he knew he was just delaying the inevitable. Because he was furious to be in this position and terrified for his daughter.

* * *

Famous for the lousy food, Jack's also had very private booths and extra privacy due to a dearth of customers. Frank and Pete went there if they had something they needed to discuss outside the office. Of course, the bad food didn't stop Pete, and he had a mouthful of a grey burger in a flat bun. Frank laid out the whole scene for him, hoping that Pete would be done chewing by the time Frank had finished relating what Mateo had said.

"Frank. I wish I'd gone with you. Maybe we could've—"

Frank shook his head. "Believe me, I looked for anything I could've done. You should've seen the size of the guy on the other side of that door." He brushed non-existent crumbs off the table. "All I wanted to do was grab Mateo's elegant neck with both my hands…but Cathy. He has Cathy. Here're the pictures he sent."

Pete wiped his hands on his paper napkin. Left it balled up on the table. He took the phone and swiped between the two pictures. "I hate to ask this, but someone has to." He handed Frank his phone back. Waited 'til he held Frank's eyes. "Do you believe him?"

"Believe that he has Cathy?" Frank waggled his phone. Put it in his pocket. "Seems real to me. And the Shake Shack order—"

"Frank." Pete's voice was softer, his eyes narrowed as if willing Frank to listen. "I meant, do you believe he'll return Cathy to you?"

The floor moved under him, and he gripped the table edge. Looked around. New York didn't get earthquakes. They weren't over the subway. The air rushed in his ears, and he couldn't hear anything else.

Pete reached out a hand like he was going to pat him or something.

Fucking better not. "I—I—yes." Frank swallowed. "I believe him." He finally met Pete's eyes. "Everything he said seemed real, giving her a shower, buying her clothes, letting her eat anything she wanted."

"Tell me about his demeanor when he said those things."

"Like…like a kindly uncle, watching out for his family. I don't know. You know." Frank held his hand palm up, gestured to Pete. "You know, like honor among thieves, like his most important tool is his word. Whether he keeps it and punishes his men and their families or holds up a promise he makes…just seemed like he was absolutely sincere."

Pete studied Frank's face for a beat. "Okay." He nodded. "We've got to get the Bureau involved. All the resources. Kidnapping." He glanced into his glass, rattled the ice cubes, set it down. "You say Leo, the drug dealer, brought you there? Do you think he handed Cathy over?"

Frank picked up a ruffled potato chip off his plate. Turned it over. Set it back down.

"Frank?"

"I can't get the Bureau involved."

Pete took a huge swallow of his drink, crunched on the ice cubes. "Why might that be?" He picked up the balled-up napkin, examined it all over, put it down. He ran his thumb and forefinger down the corners of his mouth.

Frank lined up his knife and spoon, parallel to the table edge, moved the knife a sixteenth of an inch. Moved the spoon. His world was narrowing, squeezing him, he couldn't take a breath. He had to. Breathe. He couldn't look at Pete, didn't want his partner to see the emotions swimming in his eyes.

"You can tell me, Frank."

Frank didn't look up.

"Frank, it's me. Uncle Pete. We're partners. Whatever is going on, you can tell me, and I'll always have your back. You know that."

Someone passed their booth on the way to the bathroom. Frank paused until his peripheral vision confirmed the guy was gone and the door firmly shut. He looked at Pete without moving his head. Blew out a long breath. Began talking to his plate. Told him all about his second meeting with Leo, how he'd been forced to deal for him, how the locals nearly arrested him until Leo saved his ass. How Mateo knew about it. So, he had a double whammy against him: Cathy and his job. His career.

Pete was silent for a few beats, and Frank risked a look at him. He had a big smile on his face. What the hell.

"I love that you said that. *I'm Leo tonight.* Because you are a LEO."

Frank shook his head at him. He was in the worst place he'd ever found himself, and Pete thought it was funny.

"You know. Law Enforcement Officer?"

Frank might reach over and wipe that grin off his face.

"Okay, sorry. Too soon." Pete moved his plate to the side, like the server would actually come by and take it away. "Why would that come up? Mateo might try to use it once we arrest him. But it would be your word against his. And the locals? They wouldn't speak up because it would highlight their graft. If Mateo is suspicious and sends an anonymous tip, we could have an internal investigation, but how could anyone prove it?" He paused until Frank met his eyes. "I think you'll be good, Frank. And if anyone tries to bring it up, the excitement and near chaos surrounding bringing in the head of the biggest, baddest cartel will supersede it. Drown it out. It'll get lost while we line everything up to send Mateo Rosas de Flores to supermax." He looked around, then lowered his voice. "We may have to tell the AUSA, though, y'know, so Mateo's defense team doesn't blindside him." He sat up straighter. "But we'll deal with that when the time comes."

Frank listened while Pete outlined how it could play out, Frank acting as a double agent, the Bureau putting everything on hold so Mateo thinks Frank is coming through for him. Meanwhile, the machinery of the Bureau is in high gear, zeroing in on figuring out where Cathy might be, based on the pictures. Who the guy is holding the newspaper.

"That part bothers me."

"Which part?"

"Why would the guy show so much of himself? The watch, the suit, the room behind him…why would Mateo let him? Unless…unless…" Frank decided not to say anything more in case his voice betrayed him further. He swallowed. Took a sip of water.

"Because Mateo doesn't know what we're capable of. How useful those details are to us. Don't worry, Frank. We're the best law enforcement agency in the world. With all the tools we have, we'll get Mateo and get Cathy before those assholes know what hit them. Mateo can trade in his John Lobbs for plastic shower shoes."

Now there's an image he could hold on to.

"We'll find stuff you can feed them, Mateo thinks you're doing what he's asked, he's satisfied, gives you Cathy and we nail his ass. Then we get to add kidnapping of a minor, false imprisonment, threatening a federal officer to all his other charges. As a start."

"Sounds like you're happy he's kidnapped my daughter." Frank turned over the knife at his place setting, turned it over again.

Pete held very still across the table from Frank.

Frank finally looked at him. He'd never seen anyone look so hurt. "Forget I said that. I know you're on my side. Never mind."

Pete slid out of the booth, waited for Frank. "Let's go talk to the Big Guy. Too much time has passed already."

* * *

Frank and Pete had to wait an agonizing couple of hours for Rick to be free. Now that he had broken the dam, as it were, with Pete, he was impatient to talk to the boss, and it took all of what was left of Frank's willpower not to barge into his office and demand to be heard. He wandered over to chat with another SA, shooting the breeze, learning about the intricacies of the case he was immersed in. Something about encrypted cellphones. The complication of it kept Frank's mind busy and off Mateo for fifteen minutes. Finally, he heard Pete call his name. Heart hammering, he didn't wait for Pete, got to the office door ahead of his partner.

As Frank laid it out for Rick, beat by beat, excluding the drug dealing, the Big Guy listened closely and without fidgeting. Frank had never seen him sit this still, his hands on the arms of his chair. Nothing on his face gave Frank a clue as to what he was thinking. Frank came to the end, and the silence in the office made him want to yell.

"Well. I see how it is. And you know, you've given me no choice." He gazed steadily at Frank.

Well, fuck. Frank sank into his chair, expelling a long breath like a punctured balloon. He looked at Pete. He knew this would sink his career. The FBI was all he knew. All he cared about. Why had he listened to his partner?

Rick reached for a paper clip and unfolded it. Tried to fold it back. "Okay. The Bureau has your back. We're family. We'll talk to the AUSA, we'll talk to the Chief of Police, everything will look like everyone backed off him."

Frank sat up and threw a silent question at Pete. Pete gave him surprised but encouraging eyebrows. Tilted his head at the Big Guy, who started talking again.

"You'll meet with him wearing a wire—"

Frank found his voice. "Uh, sir, respectfully, no way. No wire." He cleared his throat. "These guys are ruthless. They'd probably smell it before I got near Mateo, and then—we told you what they do to people, right? The acid—"

The boss nodded. "What about a pen, a cufflink, a flag lapel pin? We still got those, I'm pretty sure."

"Boss." Pete leaned forward. "Mateo is the kind of person who would notice changes in Frank's sartorial accoutrements."

The Big Guy nodded. Picked up a pen. Put it down. Nodded again. "Okay, you have the full force of the Bureau on this. We'll make those pictures top priority, analyze the hell out of them. You meet with him again, tell him all the things you've done. Tell him you've done what he's asked, so you can get your daughter back." He leaned back and looked Frank up and down. "What is it?"

Frank cleared his throat. "Well, what if—if he asked for something more? Like, I dunno, a prisoner freed, someone killed." Frank saw his hands gesturing helplessly, and he dropped them. Shoved them into his pockets.

"Frank. We've got you. Don't worry. You can agree to it and report that it's in motion, but it takes time. We can disappear someone. Hide them. Lay low and then arrest them once we have Mateo and you have your daughter." He leaned back in his desk chair, the springs in the seat protesting. "You have the whole Bureau to back you. Let Mateo know you'll be his bitch." He stretched out the last word like he enjoyed the image. "And then we'll nail the hell out of him."

* * *

Inside the discreet hotel, expensive lighting showcased a world of white and gold. Hushed carpets, forgettable artwork, pristine wainscoting, a staff to match. Frank thought he might throw up. Mateo had summoned him, and no case he had ever worked on had given him this much anxiety.

As instructed, he handed his ID to the efficient front desk clerk, who checked something on his computer, handed it back. The guy thanked him in a hushed tone, nodded toward a uniformed man waiting at a far elevator. The man was clearly not a bodyguard, if anything his build was slight, his manner deferential. Frank wished he hadn't left his gun at home.

The elevator took them quickly to the top floor, opening out on more whispered white and gold. Frank stopped to get his bearings, the elevator guy waiting for him. It was impossible. Every wall, every corridor, every door looked the same, and Frank didn't know if he were headed east, west, or any point in between. But what he did know, as he followed his guide, was that he was headed into hell.

Mateo sat with his arm across the back of a white couch, a low glass table in front of him, the metal holding it up continuing the gold theme. His unbuttoned suit coat gave Frank a look at an expensive shirt, his initials embroidered near his waist: MGRF. Mateo Guillermo Rosas de Flores. Head of the largest, most evil drug cartel in the western hemisphere. Even the name of the cartel, Mataderos, spoke of evil, of slaughter, abattoirs. He did not rise to greet Frank. A silvered coffee pot and two tiny cups sat in front of him on the table, a basket of biscotti next to them.

"Come in, Frank. Please sit down. May I pour you *un café expreso*?" Mateo did not sit forward, did not reach for the elegant coffee server.

Frank went to the windows, floor to ceiling, heavy drapes tied back with thick gold cords. At least he knew now he was facing north, the patch of Central Park stopping the buildings and streets. What should've looked like a city oasis, a green idyll, appeared, at this distance, like a festering scab interrupting the busyness, a sad place where no buildings grew.

"Everything you've asked for has been put in motion." He spoke to the triple-paned glass, the fog of his breath quickly dissipating.

"Ah." Mateo's voice was melodious, a timbre suited for the stage. "Business right away. No pleasantries, no small talk. So very American."

"I'd like my daughter returned to me."

"Tsk. If I am returning her, as you say, wouldn't I be returning her to the streets? And you would be continuing your endless search."

The sound of pouring, the aroma of coffee came to Frank, and he almost turned around, the desire to taste the delicious promise so strong. "How do I know—" He swallowed. "I need to talk to her, make sure she's okay."

"I do not think you appreciate the favor I have done for you. Finding her, cleaning her up, feeding her, keeping her safe."

Frank's fingers curled, and he focused on relaxing them. Too bad he hadn't brought his gun. He was so sure he would be frisked, his gun, his phone taken from him. He trusted it was still recording, could pick up the sounds from over here at the windows. Maybe he should have that "*expreso*." He approached the low table, sat in a wing chair that nearly swallowed him; it was so soft. He moved to the edge of the seat and reached for the pot.

"It is done, I am afraid." His green eyes seemed genuinely apologetic. "Now, since we are talking business, you can tell me everything that is 'in motion' as you say."

Frank knew the whole coffee pot thing was a power play on Mateo's part, but it irked him, especially since he now desperately wanted an espresso. He cleared his throat. "I'll tell the AUSA we're dropping our investigations—"

"And he will tell your boss you said that?" Mateo watched him steadily, like he studied him, like he would start reading his thoughts.

"No, no. The guy's a friend of mine. I'll tell him in a way that he won't feel a need to deal with the boss."

Mateo raised an eyebrow. He put his demitasse to his lips, eyes still on Frank. Sipped. "And your current investigations? How will you make those go away?" His voice was so calm, like they were discussing nothing weightier than the commodity price of sugar.

"Well, it's not that hard, but it'll take a little time. Evidence will get lost, some of it will get tainted." He released the next finger from his fist. "Second, witnesses will change their statements, refuse to testify, disappear."

"And your partner, your boss, they are happy with this?"

*Nice try.* "They know nothing about it. This is all me." Frank settled back against the armchair, tried not to look at the silver squat coffee pot. He had to talk to Cathy. He had to force Mateo somehow.

"Will that be enough? Taking care of these witnesses, the evidence?"

Frank nodded at him. "You have to let me see Cathy."

"Nothing more needed to do than that?" He set the cup down, a clink of fine china. "The boss will not notice?"

"I'm also very good with the keyboard." He flexed his fingers, held them in the air as if typing. "Now. About Cathy. I've done my part."

Mateo wagged a finger like he was a naughty boy. "Americans are so impatient."

Frank lunged forward, hands on the table. "Now wait just a goddam moment!"

Mateo hadn't even flinched at Frank's sudden movement. And his voice was still calm, measured. "I have a few more questions." He paused, studied Frank. "Tell me, you are still building a case against John Anthony? That is why you were there, befriending the wife, enjoying a meal with the artists? And you are still doing it. The case is 'ongoing' as you say?"

Frank's palms started sweating, and if he removed them from the table, the evidence would be there on the glass. He reached for a napkin with one hand, put the napkin on the table, picked up a biscotti. "No."

"No?" Mateo tilted his head slightly, a cat waiting to play with a mouse.

"I admit I was stupid, blew it. Got caught. I told my boss there was nothing there, we were mistaken in pursuing it." He bit into the biscotti and wished he had coffee to wash it down. A crumb better not get stuck in his throat. He coughed into his napkin. "So he *is* part of your organization. We were right about John Anthony? He's laundering your money?"

Mateo continued to watch him, said nothing, as if Frank hadn't spoken.

"I've answered your questions. I've done what you've asked. Now you need to give me Cathy. Where is she?"

"Thank you very much for this visit. I will be in touch with you again. At that point, we will have proof that everything your agency is pursuing has been dropped. I suggest, if your daughter is so very important to you, you will hurry it along." Mateo didn't move. He did not take his eyes off Frank.

Frank had never strangled someone, but he wondered what it would feel like. His fists clenched, unclenched. He got up, sure Mateo had noticed. He imagined slapping the cuffs on him, tightening them, the metal biting into his pampered flesh. That image would have to last him until it could actually happen. Halfway to the door, his phone buzzed.

"There is your proof of life."

Frank resisted the urge to pull his phone out, dive into the most recent picture of his daughter. When he reached the door, he heard the unmistakable sound of liquid pouring, the smoky coffee smell following him into the corridor.

# Chapter Twenty-Two

Nothing in the office felt normal. Everyone looked up at Frank when he came in, nodded, said *hey buddy,* came to his desk to show him what they'd been working on. Sometimes Frank wanted to tell them to all go to hell, to work this like any other case, go back to giving him a hard time. Because of the lack of routine, of normality, the kid gloves made him so jumpy. Reinforced how skewed his world had become. He wanted to take three showers in a row after meeting with Mateo. Even though he wasn't truly working for him, he had to act as if he did, and he felt slimy, felt like throwing up. He ran four miles more than he usually did, but everything was still upside down after his breath, his pulse, returned to normal.

The second picture of Cathy was vital to him, but not very helpful to the Bureau. Same angle, probably same guy standing behind her, new date on the paper. But the agents were enlarging, analyzing, pulling whatever data they could from the file. They categorized the color of the wall behind her, the color of the guy's skin holding the paper.

Even Pete, who should know better, was a little too solicitous. He gently patted Frank's shoulder. He actually whispered. "Rick wants to see us." Maybe he should tell Pete to go without him, he could sit at his desk, find another case to work on, throw himself out the window.

Rick started right in. "The AUSA is on board with us. Luckily, they've got nothing they're ready to indict, on Mateo or any of his lieutenants right now. I've had a chat with the Chief of NYPD, and everyone here is lying low. Tell me what's new with you."

Though their boss offered the chairs, Frank remained standing. He always stood to give the Big Guy an update, and he wasn't going to change that now. He related his meeting with Mateo, how he was waiting for proof. He left out the espresso and biscotti. The tech guys had the recording, but it was probably more useful to the final case than to finding Cathy. Unfortunately.

"What more does that guy want? Christ. Frank, please sit." Rick waited until Frank relented, perched on the edge of the chair as if he had so much to do he would dash out as soon as the meeting was over. "Frank. I gotta ask this. You know I do. What if—" He reached for a paperclip, unbent it, worked the pieces back and forth. "Look. Do you trust him? Honor among thieves and all that?"

"I suppose I'm the thief as well in this case?"

Rick worked at the paper clip.

Frank cleared his throat. "I think I do. Though, is he stringing me along, or does it make sense that he still has no proof other than my word that we're laying off him?"

The two halves of the paper clip went into the trash can, and the Big Guy picked up another one. "Good question. But what about once you bring him proof. Do you think—will he keep his word?"

Frank blew out a long breath, sat back in the chair. No way he would look at Pete. "Actually, I do think he'll keep his word." *And why was that?* He examined his hands. "There's something about the way he treats our CI, and the way he says that his word is so important. Like it's his only real currency. I suppose saying it's a gut feeling is a little lame. But yes, I do trust him on this." He finally looked at Pete, who nodded reassuringly.

"That makes sense, boss." Pete's matter-of-factness made up for Frank's flimsy gut feeling. "He's not some glib talker. He's calm, he's serious, like he wouldn't say anything he didn't mean, couldn't come through on." Pete shifted in his seat. "I can totally see why Frank would trust him about Cathy."

Until his daughter's name was said out loud, Frank could almost think of this as just another case. At least they weren't calling her "the victim."

Rick stopped torturing the second paper clip. Nodded. "Okay. I think it's time to get this on the ground level. I'll tell everyone to casually mention it to their informants. They'll—"

"But, boss." Pete leaned forward over the desk. "If they're not on a Mateo case, then what good will that do?"

Rick did not look happy at the interruption. "All those weasels all talk to each other. Word will get around quickly. I mean, what better gossip than that the Mataderos Cartel is among the untouchable? Protected, as it were, by us?" Those last words sounded bitter.

Frank and Pete exchanged looks. Could work. Frank stood. "That sounds great. Thank you. Do you want me to draft that 'official' email to the rest of the field office saying that we will no longer be pursuing any cases against Mateo, his lieutenants, the cartel in our jurisdiction?"

The Big Guy nodded. "Make sure you add the invisible text indicating the falsity of it, and I'll put it on my letterhead and sign it for distribution." He ran his thumb up the corner of a pad of sticky notes, did it again. "Then, of course, someone will print it out, show it to a criminal or two."

The Big Guy abandoned the sticky notes and pulled a folder from his inbox. "And I'll tell everyone to let their informants know. We'll get that bastard, Frank. Don't worry."

* * *

All the informants had been met with, a word casually dropped here and there, the signed letter stating that the Mataderos Cartel was no longer an organization of interest, slyly handed off to a middle-level lieutenant in a rival gang. The office was buzzing like everyone was on a caffeine high, and they seemed to be turning back to their other cases. They'd done all they could for Cathy, and now it was up to Frank.

And all Frank could do was wait. He didn't want to wait, but he couldn't upset Mateo by demanding another meeting. He had to wait until word filtered up to Mateo, until he had the proof he needed, and he would release Cathy, and Cathy would be home, buried in her phone until Frank took it away, told her they were checking out the new pop-up museum in an alley in SoHo.

The buzzing of his phone nearly made him jump, and he looked at it where it vibrated on his desk.

"Jankowski." The display showed "No Caller ID," but Frank knew who it was, and he wouldn't give him the satisfaction of hearing the desperation in his voice. It was all about power with these guys.

"Señor Rosas de Flores will see you at 2:00. He says you have all the details."

"What details?"

"Thank you, sir."

"Wait—"

Pete appeared at his desk and put a coffee down, the steam rising from the chipped rim like he was in Dante's Inferno. "What's the news? Was that—?"

Frank nodded. Pushed the coffee to the side of his work area.

"Well, that's good, right?" Pete went around the partition, his desk chair giving a little squeak as he sat down.

Frank stared at his monitor, watched the logo swirl around. "Something doesn't feel 'good' about this. I think Mateo would've called me himself if he was releasing Cathy."

Pete's chair rolled on the plastic mat, and Frank could feel his eyes on him. "Want me to go with you? Together we could make him tell us. We still remember our training. We could—"

Frank shook his head. Couldn't look at Pete.

"We still think he'll keep his word, don't we? That nothing's happened..." Pete's chair rolled back to his desk, and the coffee cup hit his desk with a clink. "Frank, c'mon, let's get some air. I think we could both use it right now."

* * *

This time, when Frank showed his credentials to the desk, the man with the polite undertone picked up the phone, pushed some buttons, listened, then hung up. He told him the doorman would take care of him.

Doorman. Did that mean he would be taken to Cathy? That he'd gotten it all wrong, that he'd let the anxiety of dealing with Mateo cloud his perception? The doorman had on a uniform that had to be hot, especially standing on the sidewalk all day. But he looked cool, detached, professional. He nodded to Frank, then went to the street and looked down it. The guy didn't raise his hand as he would for a cab, didn't even nod, but here came a sleek black SUV, shiny and silent, and the guy opened the door and held on to it. Continued to stare down the street.

Frank stuck his head in, met Mateo's eyes, then scanned the back seat.

"It is just us." Mateo's voice was melodic, reasonable. "I am showing you something today. Please." A command, not a plea.

As soon as the door was shut on him, the car moved, glided rather, heading west. The interior was cool, dark, hushed. Frank didn't put his seatbelt on. "I hope you're bringing me to where you have my daughter." They sat side by side, a console between them, a crystal glass with ice and bubbles breaking next to Mateo. Frank swallowed. "I've done everything you asked. I've jettisoned my career to save my daughter. I know you're a man of your word."

They were on the West Side Highway now, seagulls careening and squawking, the piers rushing by.

"You do not have to ask if I will keep my word."

"Then I'm here because you've gotten your proof, you're aware that the Mataderos Cartel is now untouchable by any law enforcement agency within our jurisdiction. Free to operate all your illegal activities anywhere." Frank made himself focus on regulating his breathing. He couldn't believe he had to say that out loud.

"Thank you. It is nice to have it spelled out so perfectly. This is why we are visiting the west side. The Mataderos would like to operate, as you say, over here." The car stopped in a no-parking zone, the engine silent. "We will walk."

Columbus Circle was busy as usual, dog walkers, women in suits and scuffed flats, men on their phones, a guy in a giant orange hat weaving through the pedestrians and cars on a unicycle. And under the statue of Columbus, the unmistakable activity of selling drugs.

"I am expanding the business. They" Mateo nodded at the guy standing under the statue "will be my dealers instead." They waited for the light to change, horns honking, the squeal of bus brakes, the whoosh of the release of air. Once they crossed the street, their fellow pedestrians dispersing about their day, Mateo spoke again. "When you show me proof of the death of Alberto Morales, then I will release your daughter. She is bored. Restless. It is time. I can give you one week, because I know these things can take time."

"Wait just a minute. I'm working alone here. How do you expect me—"

Mateo turned away, began walking around the circle, away from Central Park, Billionaire's Row looming from a couple of blocks away, all glass skyscrapers and expensive condominiums. As he strode, everyone got out of his way, his confidence and entitlement a force even New Yorkers didn't want to challenge.

He didn't look around when Frank caught up to him. "You are a professional. I know your agency knows everything about him. He is sloppy, unlike I am, and you must have people inside the organization. It will be not as hard as you think." The black car was now double-parked, the subtle headlights on, linked together with a straight line between them. It looked otherworldly. "I will give you an extra week." Mateo's stride was long, slower than the average New Yorker, but his command of the sidewalk unmistakable. "And after those two weeks, I will cease having them inject your daughter. She will be in agony. And you will be responsible for that pain."

Frank stopped walking. If he stayed with Mateo, he might begin removing the sleeves of his expensive blazer and wrap them around his throat. Mateo was good. He knew just where to stick the metaphorical knife in and twist. The thought of Cathy in the throes of going cold turkey again, her skin on fire, every nerve ending electrified. He waited until Mateo got in the car, then turned around, pulled out his phone, dialed Pete.

* * *

Pete had been able to get an appointment for the end of the day with the AUSA, and they sat in his office now, catching him up to speed, nudging him toward the same conclusion they had come to. Mateo may have merely guessed they had a guy on the inside, but he was right. They had CIs and a UCA, and this would make the plan easier to carry out, especially given the time frame. Frank's stomach clenched at the thought of Cathy going through withdrawals, and he focused on the conversation to block out the image.

"So you think it's doable? That fast?" Pete watched Michael, the AUSA, intently. A pile of case files was at his elbow, and Frank concentrated on trying to predict when it would topple. He was afraid to hear the answer. The application to the US Marshals usually required time to work out the security measures, a background check for WITSEC, and it could often take a while to put the whole process in place.

Michael cleared his throat. "We can get them to put him in the Emergency Witness Assistance Program. I can say there's a life at stake—"

Frank's startle made Michael stop talking and regard him.

The AUSA turned to Pete. "Is he going to be okay?"

"Do you have a teenaged daughter?"

"Let me put the question another way: Can he be professional about this?"

Frank got up and went to the window. He may have brushed the stack of files on his way. They needed the AUSA on their side. But what a dick.

* * *

Frank was on his morning run when his phone buzzed. He didn't usually bring it with him, but he had been lately because...because of Cathy. He stopped near the water, the gulls crying, and he was half-afraid to answer. "Pete. What's up?"

"They got him. Michael will meet us upstate. How soon can you be ready?"

Forty-five minutes later, they were in a Bureau car, Pete yelling at the traffic. Frank would rather be driving, but Pete had checked out the car, picked him up once he'd showered. He aimed the blast from the air conditioner away from his face. "So run it by me, will ya? Maybe it'll take your mind off all the brake lights."

Pete leaned on his horn. Emitted a few choice epithets.

Though to Frank, it looked like it was his fault. Frank gave him a shrug like whaddya gonna do. "So, how did they pick up Morales?"

"Turns out we already knew from our informants that Morales visits his old neighborhood every Sunday, without fail."

"And you got him there."

"Who's telling this story?"

Frank settled back in his seat. It would be a long drive upstate, and he might as well let Pete take his time. Maybe it would make him a better driver. Seems the hot shot drug lord of the Upper West Side couldn't resist showing off for his neighborhood every week, making a big production out of his visit, distributing things like $150 shoes, giving sob stories money to cover the rent, advising kids to stay in school and learn accounting and business so they come work for him.

"And he never varies the route he takes, so sure that no one would challenge him in his own neighborhood. There's one place, an abandoned building right before he turns the corner to go to his mother's apartment." Pete flossed his way into the next lane and Frank held on tighter to the oh shit bar above his window. "So the undercover Agent was in the bottom apartment area, wanting to talk to him. He came down the steps—he didn't want to at first, but our guy persuaded him—and then we grabbed him, hustled him through the building, out the back, through the vacant lot and into the waiting car."

"Nice." Once they crossed the George Washington Bridge, then made their way to I-80, the traffic eased, and Pete relaxed a little. Frank let go of the bar above his window. "Think the AUSA will convince him to let us kill him?"

"You talk like that, he'll never do anything for us."

"You know what I mean." Frank watched the traffic. "If he's so arrogant that he never varies from his routine and he has to stand out as the big man from his neighborhood, maybe he'll still think he's invincible and won't go into WITSEC."

"Twenty bucks says as soon as he hears Mateo's name, he'll cave."

"The make-up people on their way?"

"Hot off the set."

"What? We're using outside people?"

"Frank, you think one of our Special Agents has that talent? Of course we're using outside people. All signed and sealed. They won't talk. It's good business for them. We pay well."

Frank drummed his fingers on his knee. "Then the guys will Photoshop the guy into some dark alley or something?"

"Well, except that it's our software, much better, much, much harder to detect. It'll be brilliant."

They crossed over the Hackensack River, the slow water flat and grey, warehouses built right up against it. "We have to go to west-nothing, New Jersey, for this? Don't we have a place any closer?"

"Frank, this was a hurry-up operation. You get what you get." Pete cut his eyes to him, looked back at the road. His voice softened. "Hey, I get you're nervous, impatient. You want every 'i' crossed and 't' dotted. It'll be fine. This is the Bureau."

* * *

They finally got off the highway, made some turns, turned at a bait store, and bumped their way down a dirt road. The trees closed in, the road narrowed, wide enough for just one car. No better security than nature. He couldn't even spot the cameras in the trees. The road ended at a tiny cabin with no fewer than four other cars parked every which way in the dirt. Cigarette smoke from the makeup people waiting to be called in covered over the damp air, the piney outdoors smell.

Inside, the shades were shut, the air redolent with flop sweat and gun oil and dust. A few fishing rods were on a rack by the door, but Frank knew no one who came here ever fished. The AUSA, Michael, sat deep in a couch that might've been new in the early 70s. Alberto sat across from him over a scarred, low coffee table, glasses of water at hand. Two agents stood behind the moth-eaten armchair Morales occupied.

This guy's cooperation stood between Frank and his daughter. Morales looked belligerent, defiance and fear flashing in his eyes. Pete put a hand on Frank's arm, and Frank looked at it. He hadn't realized he'd moved. He met Pete's eyes. Maybe he hadn't moved. Maybe Pete just knew him that well. It meant as much to Pete as it did to Frank.

"I ain't no snitch. No way. You take me back and I'll visit Mom as per usual. No one will know. Except that rat who's working for you. Him I'll kill."

Maybe they didn't need his cooperation. Maybe Frank would drive him back to the city, and they wouldn't need the makeup people either. He could do it himself…Frank stepped back. Went to the kitchen area, ran the water in the sink. No glass. He cupped his hands and drank, then splashed some water on his face.

"I'm not sure you understand your position, Mr. Morales." Michael opened a very thick folder, kept it on his lap, his knees raised because of the low couch, the contents of the folder hidden from view. "We have a lot on you already." He turned a piece of paper over. Then another. "Hmmmm. Too bad about the witnesses to the shootings." His eyes moved from the folder to the scumbag Morales. "Too bad for you, I mean." He shut the folder, set it on the couch next to him. "So, your choice is to either be arrested, kept most likely without bail, due to the heinous nature of the charges. Or, to cooperate, tell us everything about your operation, your suppliers, your lieutenants, everything. And then you go into the Witness Security Program, also known as Witness Protection, and you will be safe. If we let you back on the streets, it'll be a race between your people and the rival drug lords who kills you first. I can't imagine they would do it quickly. Can you?"

Morales put an angry look on his face, but Frank could see the defeat, the anxiety in his eyes.

Michael leaned forward, rested his arms on his knees, clasped his hands. "After we confirm what you've told us, we'll run an obituary, false news reports, possibly with a gruesome picture for some internet-only outlets. Everyone will know you're dead. Only the US Marshals will know that you're not. And you, of course. They'll bring you back to testify, but we'll conceal your identity for that."

It sounded so reasonable, Frank was almost tempted to go into WITSEC himself.

Morales' pride couldn't let himself go down without a fight, and he began trying to negotiate. Frank knew this would be a long process, the AUSA pretending to cede ground, then walking it back, Morales pretending to fight, knowing he had no choice. No doubt the prosecutor would let him have a thing or two, like protection for his mother, which they would've been prepared to give him all along.

Frank threw a look to Pete. He didn't feel like listening to all the back and forth, and he indicated the door with his head. Pete gave him a slight nod, and then they were both out, standing in the dirt in front of the house, the sky paling beyond the tall trees, the cigarette smell still in the air. The people leaning against their cars popped up when Frank and Pete came out, relaxed again when they realized who they were. Or who they weren't.

Obviously, Michael was running this show. He and Pete were along for the ride, making sure all the nails were securely in the coffin, as it were. Plus, Frank needed to make sure the trauma makeup person got everything right.

"Do you think just bullet holes will be enough?" Frank surveyed the woods. Maybe no safer than the city streets. "A lot of blood and bruises would be nice. Like he got roughed up and then killed."

"Is that your practical side speaking or your revengeful side?"

"Let's go ask the makeup person what they can do." Frank tried to pick out which one she was.

"Nannette?"

"You know her name already?"

She was talking with a female agent when they approached. She was tiny, like a ballerina in a box, but the way she assessed them as they approached made Frank feel he'd like to stay on her good side. Pete asked her about her skills.

"I can do whatever you want. I could make it look like a chainsaw got to him, if you wanted. But that might take a long time. Plus, you guys said I have to clean it off, too, right?"

"I don't care if you clean it off. Remind him what could happen."

"Maybe we should just have strategic bullet holes, like a professional forehead double tap. Hands zip-tied, a little bruising on his arms and face. Blood on his shirt." Pete pantomimed his description, even putting his hands behind his back, patting his shirt.

"Easy Peasy. He'll have to live with the blood on his shirt, though. I can't clean that off without a washing machine."

"How'd a nice girl like you get into this business?"

Frank eyed his partner. Seemed genuinely interested rather than flirtatious.

"Boredom. Plus I wanted to scare the crap outta my mom when I was a teenager."

"Did it work?"

"Grounded for a month."

"That seems a little harsh."

"Gave me time to perfect my art."

"Can I hire you for Halloween?" Pete grinned at her.

"Booked solid for the next ten years."

* * *

Pete had just started talking about sending someone for hamburgers, or pizza, or anything, when the U.S. Marshal came out and told them they were ready for makeup. They all filed in, Nannette carrying a bright red toolbox.

"Okay, Frank." Michael stacked up his file folders, opened his briefcase, shoved them in. "It's your show. Tell us how you want him to look."

"Like he got roughed up, zip-tied, then shot in the back of the head." He'd forgo the chainsaw.

Nannette worked quickly, creating cuts and bruises at lightning speed as if it meant nothing to her and she wanted to be out of there. The transformation was brilliant. If Morales wasn't actively looking around the room, he'd swear the guy was dead. Frank wished he were. Wished he could do the same to Mateo.

They asked Frank how to pose him. He counseled them to zip-tie his wrists first, then lay him down. The guys who would be altering the photograph had some suggestions, discussed the puddles of blood they'd add, how the lighting would work. They stood over the body, took pictures with a very fancy-looking camera.

"Wait a sec."

Everyone looked at Frank.

"Shouldn't I just take it with my phone? And a flash? I mean, we're assuming this'll happen at night, in an alley, right? And all I'd have is my phone."

Morales started shaking, tried to get up.

"Quit it. You're dead."

He pissed himself.

One of the agents said, "There's a little realism for you."

Frank held his breath against the stench, took a couple of pictures leaning over him. Checked them, nodded around the circle, and went to the door. Opened it. He'd spent far too long in this tiny cabin.

One of the Photoshop guys came out to check the pics. Gave his approval.

Frank and Pete were silent for the first half of the way back.

"Think Nannette is single?"

"I think she's too much for you to handle."

"I wouldn't mind being handled by her."

Frank didn't think either one of them had their heart in the banter. Why wasn't he more elated. "That guy gets to live, free, guest of the government."

"Worth it for Cathy?" Pete used his turn signal this time, though Frank wished he'd allow a little more room between the cars. "Plus, we get his whole operation."

"And Mateo gets to take over."

"We'll get him, Frank. Don't you worry about that."

* * *

The tech guys worked quickly, for once the slow wheels of the bureaucracy not hampering them. The results were fabulous. Frank almost checked his phone to see if he'd actually taken the picture at the cabin and not in the city. The lighting was seamless, a flash on the ground around him, the trash completely believable in the alleyway. He could almost smell the rot. These couple of pictures taken at different angles, the false news reports, and the fact that Alberto Morales had actually disappeared, had to convince Mateo.

Frank left word at Mateo's hotel that he wanted to meet.

Almost immediately, his phone rang. One of his henchmen. Send the proof to this number. Mateo will call you. You don't call him.

Frank sent the pictures, began pacing the office. Who was he kidding? Mateo needed Frank to know that he was in power, so no way would he release Cathy immediately. He felt like he was in Dante's *Purgatorio*, being endlessly tortured with Cathy just out of his grasp.

# Chapter Twenty-Three

Ronnie knocked on the door to John Anthony's office and waited for an answer. She reached for her phone to text him a message instead of knocking again, then she heard a muffled *come in.*

"Ah, Ronnie." He smiled. "What can I do for you?"

"I wanted to let you know, Mateo asked me to drop by his penthouse. Go over some things, he said."

John's birthmark went from a pale pink to a light red as he frowned. "Doesn't he know *I* pay your salary?" He toyed with his letter opener, and they both watched it spin flat on his desk blotter.

"I don't know what he knows and what he doesn't, but I wanted to tell you before I went over there."

"You two are getting quite chummy, aren't you?"

Ronnie didn't think she was supposed to answer, so she fixed on the letter opener instead. He set it spinning again.

"Well, he likes you, which is a good thing, I suppose." But John sounded doubtful.

The gold and jade object slowed down, and John didn't touch it again, concentrating on it like it was an oracle. When it stopped the gold point aimed right at her.

"Just don't take over my job." His birthmark was almost purple now, and Ronnie hoped the color was from anxiety about his relationship with Mateo and not anger at her. Because she hadn't done anything but follow his orders.

She cleared her throat. "I'm pretty sure he wants to talk about curtains.

And I'm also pretty sure that's not what he needs you for." She turned to leave.

"Hold it."

"Sir?"

The birthmark was fading a little, his face like one of those dyed carnations, fake-looking. He stared at the bookshelves, frowning. "Uh..." Seemed like she could see gears churning, a scale weighing what he was about to say. "Yeah. Okay. Could you do me a favor?"

"Anything. Of course."

"When you get there, I mean before you get there, maybe in the elevator, could you call me and then don't hang up? Just put your phone in your pocket and leave the line open?"

Ronnie nodded at him. Who didn't he trust, her or Mateo?

"I may be busy later." The side of his face darkened again. "So I want to hear it in real time." He picked up the prized letter opener and put it in his leather pencil cup. "Y'know, rather than wait for when you get back."

She decided the birthmark also darkened when he was lying. She hoped he never played poker, unless he liked losing. She gave him a thumbs-up and left.

* * *

Mateo welcomed her in like she was one of his many nieces he hadn't seen in a long time, a big hug, a few pats on the shoulder, offers of something to drink, to eat. He settled them out on the terrace that surrounded the first floor. She'd been right, he wouldn't get rid of the outdoor furniture, a match to the ones on the rooftop terrace. The afternoon sun made the cushion nice and warm, and she was so comfortable she could take a nap. Over the railing, the park glowed green, the people tiny, the trees ringing the west side, the Dakotas' pointy roofs like soldiers.

Mateo brought out Cokes for each of them, little plates, and cloth napkins. Ronnie had told him a Coke would be fine, so what was up with the plates and napkins? He came back out with a huge pink bakery box, set it on the glass table between them. He untied the string around the box. A few grease spots decorated the pink, which meant lots of buttery, flaky things inside. Her stomach growled.

"From the best Mexican bakery in the city. Have you ever had pasteles? Tortas? No? No galletas? Pan dulces? Ah. You are in for a treat." He piled some on a plate and handed it to her. No way she could eat all this. Cookies and donut-looking treats covered in sugar, a large, pink, puffy thing, a little cupcake.

Mateo did most of the talking while she did most of the chewing. Maybe she would jump ship and work for Mateo. John didn't seem to care about food at all. Mateo told her stories from his childhood, all the different pastries, and when they had them, the traditions behind them.

"Maybe my favorite was Pan Muerto, for the Day of the Dead."

Ronnie put down the cookie she'd just taken a bite from. Wiped her fingers on her napkin. "What? What is that? You celebrate death?" What was John thinking of this conversation? She leaned forward. This was fascinating.

"Ha. No, little one, we celebrate those who have died, not the death itself. In this country, you like to celebrate youth, you like to pretend that people never die, constantly try to prevent it. We know it is part of life, and we honor the dead, ask them to come and visit that day so we can feed their souls, remember them, tell each other stories about them." Mateo gazed out over the balcony as if lost in those stories.

She looked at his profile, imagined him as a small child, indulged, no doubt, by all the aunties, older sisters, grandmothers.

"Ah. Well." Mateo stirred himself, looked over at her. "You are a good listener, has anyone ever told you that?"

Ronnie shrugged. "You tell good stories."

"I always enjoy my time with you. In fact, I think it is thanks to you that I understand better what my operation looks like on the ground." Mateo closed the box of pastries, put his napkin on his plate. "Tonight, you will go with me to the warehouse, and I will introduce you to the men. Normally, I would just send you, but I want them to know how important you are to me. That you are under my protection. And that you are taking over the collection of the cash." He took off his sunglasses to study her.

Taking over collecting the cash because Marc couldn't anymore. Hadn't Marc been under his protection? Maybe he was until he wasn't. She didn't think she had a choice in this, even though he waited for her response. She carefully put down her napkin and swallowed. She gave him a nod. Stood up, stacked the plates.

He waved his hand, told her to leave them. "That is not your job in my house."

As Mateo walked her to the elevator, he told her, "I would like to bring you more into my organization, have you more involved. I have seen you in different situations, and I think you are ready." He must've seen something on her face because he asked her, "Do you not think you are ready?"

"No, I'm ready." I was born ready. "I was just wondering how I'm supposed to pick up the cash when I don't know how to drive."

Mateo pushed the button to take her down to the lobby. "Ah. Practical. I like that. Already thinking ahead. This is what I mean. This is why you should have a bigger role." The elevator opened, and he held his hand over the door closest to him. It bumped against him, then stopped. "Do not worry. We think alike. I have a new driver, and you will meet him tonight." Ronnie got in and turned to face the door, face him. "Be ready at 9:00. I will pick you up. No weapons."

* * *

She checked in with J.A. as soon as she was back. "You get all that?"

He motioned her in, and she sat in the other chair, not the one Mateo always sat in, as if he would join their meeting. Or was already here.

John picked up the letter opener, stabbed over and over into the blotter. His birthmark was purple. Ronnie shifted in her seat. She did everything he told her to do. So why did she feel like she was in trouble?

"I'm trying to figure out what this means," John didn't look at her, kept stabbing.

Ronnie stared at the letter opener too, the motion kind of mesmerizing, hypnotizing her until an image popped up of the point going into someone's skin, *her* skin, and she tore her eyes away. She busied herself looking around the office, the diplomas in frames, a bookshelf with financial texts that would instantly put her to sleep, a painting leaning against a wall still in its gallery wrapping.

"If he wanted to promote you, why didn't he talk to me first? Why is he leaving me out of this?" Stab. Stab. Stab. He finally met her eyes. "And when the hell did he hire a driver? Why didn't he ask me to do that? What the hell." John stared at her so long, he must've thought she knew the answer.

"I don't know. I really don't. I just do whatever you tell me to, and now, I guess, whatever Mateo tells me to."

"That's what I thought. All this time you've been getting so buddy-buddy with Mateo, riding with him, having lunch with him, going over to his penthouse." He sat with his arms folded, his face nearly half black now. "You've been planning this all along, haven't you? Getting close to him, getting rid of me." His eyes blazed at her. "The gold was your idea, wasn't it?"

"What? What're you talking about? No, no way. I don't know anything about any gold. I'd never met Mateo before he said that, and it wasn't my idea to have lunch with you guys that time. I would've rather eaten by myself in the kitchen and not mix it up with you two. None of this was my idea. It was all Mateo's, if it wasn't yours." She realized she was leaning forward as if she could force the words through the air, make him see she was telling the truth. She sat back. "I thought I was supposed to go along with whatever he wanted, and if that meant lunch, or pastries at his penthouse, then I figured that was part of my job." She stared at him, and he sat and blinked at her. Where was that letter opener?

He sat a long time with his eyes on her. She refused to look away, refused to squirm, though she hoped he couldn't see her gripping the arms of the chair tighter and tighter. She let go and wiped her hands on her pant legs.

"Look, John. I'm not that smart. I'm the cog that helps all the machinery work. You tell me to turn, I turn, help you do your job. I'm a soldier on the ground, not some masterminding general."

"But this going with you to the warehouse. He's never done that before, never shown the dealers someone working for me was under his protection. That I know of." His birthmark grew darker. "Maybe he's grooming you to work closely with him, be his right-hand man. I thought I was his right hand. But now he's cutting me out." He stood up. He gripped the letter opener in his fist, and Ronnie leapt up, her chair tipping.

"John." Ronnie caught the chair so it didn't go all the way over and stood behind it to keep it between them. "John. I don't know how to make you see I'm not part of this. I just follow orders. John, please. Can you put the letter opener down?"

He looked at her like she was crazy. She pointed to his hand, and he looked down at it as if he hadn't realized it was part of him. He put the letter opener on his desk, the blade pointing at Ronnie.

"I don't know what you're worried about," he said. "I'm not violent, not like some people. Some people you have a date with tonight." He turned away from her as if there was something much more important on the credenza behind him. "Maybe we should make it a double date. I'll come too. Me and Lisa, and then it'll be a real party." He shivered, all over, like he'd seen a ghost. Or something worse.

He had no idea how thrilled Lisa would be if he asked her. "You *should* come too. See what it's all about. See there's nothing between me and Mateo. But maybe leave Lisa here. Those warehouses are pretty gnarly in the daytime. Imagine what they're like at night." Whether they were done or not, Ronnie knew she was and turned to go. After she opened the door, she paused and looked at him. "Why d'ya think he said 'no weapons?'"

* * *

After Ronnie left John's office, she went to her room, bolted the door and put a chair under the knob for good measure. She didn't know who she was afraid of, but it made her feel safer. She paced the tiny room. She wasn't equipped to referee an ego fight between John and Mateo. Jeez. She hoped John decided to stay home tonight so she didn't have to deal with him wrestling her for Mateo's attention. What a baby. Wasn't her fault Mateo liked her, wanted to promote her. If John wanted the truth, she didn't want the promotion. She liked living in this fancy house, polishing silver and polishing shoes, holding Barbara Anthony's shopping bags, and following the maids around, watching them not clean.

She plopped down into the small armchair near the window. The idea of going back to that warehouse, or to any warehouse finally hit her, and she willed her body not to tremble. In a funny way, she wished they'd gone straight from Mateo's, so she didn't have to think about this for the next few hours. Think about getting deeper into the organization, about what Mateo had in mind for her. *No weapons.* Must mean she should have a weapon at other times, but her flick knife probably wouldn't cut it. Sometimes, it's better not to have any weapon at all.

She leapt up, paced around, went into the bathroom and back out to cover more space. This was too much. She hadn't signed up for this when she took this job. Damn. She almost forgot this wasn't her real job. She needed to text Frank, tell him and Pete what was happening. She couldn't wait to write it on their journal page. Not that they could do anything, but this was a big step, and she didn't want them yelling at her that they should've been told. Last thing she needed was someone else yelling at her.

She pulled out her phone and sat on the edge of her bed, the springs creaking. She typed in 'Linus,' looked at the box to fill in. How could she let them know all the stuff that had happened in the last few hours.

*So Sorry!* She typed. *Can't make it tonight. Boss's boss needs me to do something*

She erased *do something* and pecked out *go with him. Sorry came up all of a sudden so*

So now what...

*maybe tomorrow*

She threw the phone on the bed, snatched it up again, peppered the message with emojis, a sad face, a shrug eyeroll, sunglasses face at the end. Those should be enough to let them know how big of a deal it was. She tossed it on the bed again and got up. What to do to fill the time until nine. Food was out of the question, her stomach in knots. Oh, man. Probably

John wanted something to eat and wanted her to make it or get it for him. Maybe he could get it himself for once. He hadn't said anything, but then, he probably had other things on his mind.

The house phone hung on the wall next to her door, and she picked up the receiver, punched the button for his office. He didn't sound very happy when he answered, but she ignored that, asked for instructions for his dinner. Silence. Breathing. Maybe his stomach was in knots, too.

"Omelet."

Maybe it wasn't in knots. She guessed this meant he wouldn't go with them tonight, and now she felt a little disappointed, as if his being there would've meant nothing scary would happen. She let out a long breath.

"Don't you know how to make an omelet?"

She had forgotten he was still there.

"I-I do."

"I'll be down in a few. Show you how it's done."

She started to hang up the receiver when he spoke again. She put the phone to her ear.

"Um, listen. Sorry about earlier. You're doing great. Glad you're working for us."

She looked at the receiver, which now blared a dial tone at her. Wow. First praise he'd ever given her. Like from his deathbed.

* * *

The kitchen was big, the ceilings high, the white cabinets gleaming, and it had never seemed so cozy to Ronnie as she sat at the counter and John Anthony chopped and whisked and sizzled the butter and taught her how to make an omelet. She knew how, but his technique was different, and she leaned over to study how he patiently lifted the edges all around, the bright yellow going from liquid to solid. He put the shredded cheese, and the sautéed onions, and then the ribboned spinach leaves on at just the right moment, shook the pan a little, lifted it off the stove, tossed the eggs in the air. They both watched the omelet fold itself over and land back in the pan.

He smiled. She could get used to a life like this.

"Maybe in your next life you should be a chef."

He dropped the smile, and she wished she hadn't said that. He cut the omelet in half and served up two plates, handed one to her. "You mean after Mateo no longer needs me?" He didn't bother to sit down as he sliced into his creation with the side of his fork.

She took a bite. She'd never tasted anything so delicious. The butter, the melted cheese, the spinach, so perfectly cooked. "That's not what I meant at all." She took another bite, but this one didn't taste quite as good. She put her fork down.

"Maybe I'm not as great a chef as you thought I would be."

"No, this tastes great. It really does. I just—"

"Sorry, didn't mean to bring that up." He sighed, took another bite, chewed. "But, when Mateo no longer needs me, he may think I'm a liability."

She looked a question at him.

"I know too much." John set his plate down, maybe no longer hungry, too. He got busy around the kitchen, put the frying pan, the knives, the cutting board in the sink.

She watched him for a minute until she realized where she was, who she was supposed to be. "Let me do that. You cooked, I'll clean." She slid off the stool and picked up her plate. They worked together until the kitchen was all put back together, as if no one had ever been in it.

John stood by the sink and dried his hands on the dishtowel longer than seemed necessary. He looked around like he didn't know where to put it. Ronnie held out her hand, and he gave her the damp towel. "That's why I think I'll go with you tonight, show Mateo I can do more than just sit behind a computer. Show him I work at the ground level too."

* * *

John paced as they waited for Mateo's car. He insisted they go down early, and here they wilted in the evening heat, not looking at each other. She'd realized when she got back to her room after cleaning up from dinner that she had forgotten to hit the send button on her text. She'd also had to erase all the gibberish that had been written in the box by her pocket. Probably didn't matter when they got it. Not much they could do with that information at this point. The Bureau moved so slowly, and all they knew at this point was that she'd be with Mateo. And now John, if Mateo let him go with them.

* * *

The silence in the car was about to kill her. She and John were in the back seat, Mateo next to the driver, where he seemed to like to sit, captain of the ship, arm on the dashboard as if expecting them to crash at any minute.

"I am wondering what you believe you will see." Mateo's voice was soft and low.

John squirmed next to her, like a kid called on in class. The air inside the car felt thick. Maybe she should roll down her window, the night air coming in, cooling her face. She could pretend she wasn't in here, maybe on the Circle Line, going up the Hudson…

"I wanted to see where you were taking my butler tonight." John's voice was a whine, a complaint, a brittle defiance. Ronnie mentally closed the car window. What was Mateo going to say to that?

"Your butler." Mateo finally turned his head to look at John in the back seat. "Are you in the habit of owning people?"

"I pay her salary, give her a place to live. Feed her." He said the last two words as if that were the biggest expense of all.

Mateo glanced at his driver, braced himself on the dashboard again. "You pay her with what money?" He asked the windshield. "Whose money bought your penthouse? Your food?"

John didn't answer, his breathing a ragged sound like he was angry. Or scared. Finally, he said, so quietly he might not have said it, "We used to work together."

Mateo let out a laugh, and it filled the car, going up and down like a song. "That is it? You feel left out, like we will not let you play in our game?" He turned fully around, his head between the two front seats, and he wasn't laughing. "John, you will always be in the game. You will never not be. Even if you wanted out, you will never be out. You understand this?" Mateo studied him until he nodded "yes."

Out her window the buildings passed by, the streetlamps made a pattern of light and shadow, a bicyclist in a hoodie passed them headed the wrong way. Maybe she'd always be in this game, too.

Mateo launched into stories like none of the previous conversation had ever happened, like they were at a cocktail party and there was nothing else to do but listen and be entertained. The best Wagyu beef in Tokyo. The most delicate Bearnaise sauce in Paris. A pasta in Florence that brought him to tears. The finest tailor in London, and the loftiest down comforter in Zürs.

"John," Mateo said, "if you knew you would not eat anything more, what would you choose to be the last thing you tasted?"

Silence from the seat next to Ronnie.

"The very last thing you held in your mouth?"

John didn't even fidget.

"I've often thought about it," Mateo went on as if it weren't a one-sided conversation. "Maybe a glass of the best champagne. Or red wine so dark you would think it was blood. And beef so rare it is weeping as you slice into it—ah," he interrupted himself, "here we are."

They glided up to the gate, and the driver leaned out his window to punch in a code. The night air, thick with humidity, came in the car, along with the salty smell of the water, and a rotten, garbage odor. When the driver rolled his window back up, Ronnie got a whiff of nervous sweat, a tang that took her back to middle school and acne-pasted boys.

"John, I think it best that you stay in the car. We will be only a minute, while I introduce the men to Ronnie."

John made a strangled sound, but no words came out.

Ronnie focused on breathing normally as she and Mateo walked together to the warehouse, the exact same warehouse she'd gone in to find Marc. She put her hands in her pockets as if she was merely on a stroll, easy-peasy.

Her phone was in her right front pocket instead of her back one, and she held it to keep it from hitting her leg as she walked, but gave up and moved it to her back pocket. Their shoes crunched on the paving, echoing off the building as they got close.

Same kicked-in metal door, same long squeal as Mateo opened it, gestured for her to go first. She didn't want to go first. But Mateo stood behind her holding the door, and she went into the warehouse, trying to move like no big deal, like she did this all the time. The last time she'd been here, Marc was dying on the floor. Seemed like she could still smell the blood.

As they came in, Mateo called out, "I am bringing someone for you to meet." His voice was deep and commanding, echoing across the space. They came around a stack of boxes, three guys tensed, one with a gun out. He quickly put it away when he saw Mateo with her.

"Jefe," he said, a nod of respect to Mateo.

Mateo laughed. "Ah, but not 'El Jefe.' He got himself imprisoned." He closed the space between them with two long strides and motioned to Ronnie to stand beside him. "I want you to meet someone new," he told them, his hand on her shoulder.

"I'm Ro—"

"No names," Mateo said, his voice gentle, firm. "Faces are enough. Pull your hood away so she knows who you are." Mateo tapped a grey plastic bin on the table in front of the men. It was like every bin Marc had put in the back seat for her. "This is it?"

The guy who had drawn the gun, the guy with the hoodie, took a half step forward. "No. There's a ton of these. You haven't picked up in too long."

One of the other guys spoke up. "We've been watching them pile up. We've been thinking about how much's in there."

"And now we are picking it up. You can help us carry them to the car," said Mateo, reasonable, calm.

"We've been thinking."

Mateo studied him. Said nothing.

"We do all the work. Give you all the money."

Mateo gave a little nod. Still said nothing.

"We're thinking, there's so much money here." He waved an arm as if the entire warehouse was filled with grey bins. "You would never miss it."

Mateo gave him a smile that had no warmth in it. When he finally spoke, his words were low and even, casual as if he were describing the plot to a movie to pass the time. "We pay you the most for the work you do. No one else will give that large a cut."

The hoodie guy shifted his feet, looked away.

"I could give you a bin." Mateo's open hand gestured at the grey plastic, and three pairs of eyes jerked to it. "You could take it home, split it up, buy the cocaine and the steak dinners, the high-class whores and the expensive champagne. Until it ran out."

Their faces looked hopeful, almost happy.

"And then," Mateo paused, and they looked like trained dogs, waiting for the command, the treat. "Then, you should tell each person you care about how much you love them, what they mean to you, how much you will miss them."

Their eyes widened, one hand reached behind a back but didn't come out again.

"Because after tonight, after your big party, after you spend all my money, those you love will wonder where you are and why my men have picked them up. Why they are hanging from rafters," Mateo looked up at the warehouse roof, "skin peeled off, but they are not yet dying. Only bleeding, the blood dripping...dripping...dripping..."

Ronnie didn't mean to—it was involuntary, the step she took back, away from Mateo and the silky words that were so horrifying. But the movement made the guy bring the gun out, and he waved it between the two of them as if he couldn't decide. Everything inside her loosened, and before she knew what was happening, she was on the floor, in a heap, the warehouse watery around her. She tried to pay attention to what was going on, but all she heard in her head was Mateo's terrible words, and all she saw were bodies hanging from ceilings like carcasses in a meat locker. She threw up.

# Chapter Twenty-Four

Frank crouched in the dark behind a stack of boxes. Someone vomited and he tilted his head for a better view of the group in the warehouse, three unknowns, Mateo, damn. Ronnie wasn't there. Where was she? If something happened to her...his heart hammered and he willed it to slow, willed the calm needed for the tense situation. There she was, on all fours, then standing. Mateo moved so that he was between her and the thug with the gun. Frank scanned back to the gun guy, his own gun aimed at him, ready for a kill shot if it came to that.

The other agents in the warehouse had a man they trained their guns on. When the tactical team sneaked in, which they should be doing any minute, they would cover the guy in the hoodie with their guns, everyone breathing and waiting for the signal. Frank had assigned himself and Pete to Ronnie, and he knew Pete was watching the gun guy, too. As Frank held his breath and watched him, he nicknamed him Mr. Hoodie. One guy sported an impossibly white T-shirt, the other a pearl snap short-sleeved number.

He felt as if even the warehouse was holding its breath, the dusty, oily thickness waiting, watching. His brain cast a spotlight on Mr. Hoodie, the thin light from overhead putting the rest in shadow. Even as he watched Mr. Hoodie intently, he was also keenly aware of the other people, the flash of Mateo's white linen suit as he moved to the grey plastic bin, Mr. Hoodie not giving way, not ceding to Mateo, the tension among them charged, rising.

The tactical team checked in, having gotten in place silently. Frank whispered a short countdown, then everyone moved at once, an army of guns aimed on the group. Dark blue windbreakers swarmed, shouts of *Guns down! Hands up! On the floor now!* T-Shirt and Pearl Snap swiveled their heads around like they thought they would run, and then they got down. Mateo took a step back from the onslaught of agents, a scowl, then a look of disbelief as he picked out Frank.

Mr. Hoodie snatched Ronnie by the collar, yanked her to him, aimed his gun under her chin, the path of the bullet if he pulled the trigger straight to her brain.

Frank sucked in his breath, a sharp sound echoed among his agents. Everyone, everyone froze, guns still aimed. Mr. Hoodie held Ronnie close to him, a slight smile, actually a smirk, and his dead eyes told Frank it would mean nothing to him to pull the trigger, that all the emotion was with the agents. Mr. Hoodie had pulled the ace card and changed the entire game. And he knew it.

"I have the shot lined up." The whisper in his ear was soft, professional.

Everyone stood by, waiting for the command from Frank. Ronnie squeezed her eyes shut, then quickly opened them wide, blinked rapidly like she was clearing away fog. Frank had seen Ronnie in all kinds of situations, had seen her street smarts in action, true bravery as well as bravado, courage, strategic retreat. But he had never seen fear in her eyes like this. He forced himself to analyze the situation, to not look at Ronnie because he needed to be detached, unemotional. Giving in to his desire to rip Mr. Hoodie's head off would just as surely get her killed as if he'd pulled the trigger himself. He whispered to the team, "Do not take the shot."

Frank took a step closer to Ronnie. "Put the gun down." Mr. Hoodie jammed the gun into her neck. "Easy now," a baby step closer, "You're outgunned here." Frank kept his voice even, reasonable, as if recommending his favorite dish off a menu. He held the man's eyes, but his peripheral vision detected a movement in the shadows behind Mr. Hoodie, and Frank said under his breath to his team, "No one move." He needed to ascertain if there was a bad guy they didn't know about or if it was one of theirs. If someone looked, it would alert Mr. Hoodie.

"I think I have the advantage." Ronnie's captor changed his grip from her shirt to her hair, grabbing tight enough to move her eyebrows up and make her gasp.

"Let's talk this through." Frank took another short step as Pete came out of the shadows, straight behind Ronnie and Hoodie, out of Hoodie's line of sight, as stealthy as a cat. Pete's gun at the man's temple, just like that, grabbing the guy's gun hand before he could react.

"Eight and eleven. Go!" Frank said to the group, and two agents zoomed in, put Mr. Hoodie on the ground, his arms at his back, a knee to hold him, Pete's foot on his head to keep it on the floor while the other agent secured his wrists with a zip tie. Ronnie took two wobbly steps back, and Frank gave the go-ahead for the rest of the team, who came out of the dark, half of them holstering guns, working quickly, efficiently to handcuff everyone, including Ronnie. He hoped the woman working on her wrists wasn't zipping it too tight. Ronnie looked a little green in the fluorescents. But she was safe.

They placed everyone on their knees, spaced apart in one long line, except for Mr. Hoodie who was still on the ground, his cheek still attached to Pete's heavy shoe. Mateo, next to Ronnie, whispered something to her. He appeared calm in his fine linen suit as if he were used to kneeling on a cement floor with his wrists tied behind him, looking down the barrel of a handgun held by a female FBI agent. Ronnie searched around her, eyes darting as if to parse the scene, to find something she knew. She hadn't spotted Frank, he guessed.

"What—" Ronnie blurted out. "Where's—"

"No talking," the agent watching them said.

Mateo said something to her again, a ventriloquist whisper, and she gave him a quick look, her face a mixture of relief and fear, if that was possible. She leaned slightly toward him, said something back to him, the conversation between them now unobserved by the agent guarding them.

Frank let out a long breath. His team had done their part, the rest up to the Evidence Response Team, and the Crime Scene Investigators, who were either waiting outside or on their way now. The tension in the air dissipated, efficiency, teamwork replacing it now that the shitbirds were neutralized. Two agents seized each suspect, one on each side of them. They left the warehouse to separate them, put one in each car, speed off in the big black Chevys, take them downtown to process.

Pete snapped up Mateo, dragging him forward before he found his feet. Pete paused to let him get grounded, no doubt knowing that if Mateo fell, he would go with him.

"You lied to me." Mateo's voice was far from hurt. It sounded vengeful.

"You should've returned my daughter to me."

Ronnie's mouth hung open, her eyes wide, her head going back and forth between Frank and Mateo. Before she could say anything, Frank got a hold of her arm and she flopped like a rag doll, as if she didn't know how to work her feet.

He righted her, trying to thread the line between gentleness and believability. "No talking," he stared straight ahead, his voice official. "We're going to do this nice and smooth, no resisting arrest, no trying to run." He waved off another team member who had come to help. He had to play this right so that no one, not even the other agents knew she was the CI. Ronnie sagged, and he helped her along.

The summer air hit them, warm even at night, their shoes crunching on the litter, broken glass, and God knew what else, Ronnie walking more and more on her own. He gave her arm a little squeeze. She'd be okay, she'd bounce back the way she always did. Frank opened the door of the big black car, a hand on the back of her head, ducking her in.

She hung her head as he pulled the seatbelt around her, clicked it into place. She never looked up from the floor. Frank shut her door, climbed into the driver's seat, started the engine. "Let's wait 'til Pete gets here, then we'll explain everything." He looked for her in the mirror. "You okay?"

Before she could answer, Pete got in the backseat with her, per protocol. Frank looked a question at him in the rear-view mirror. He gave him a thumbs-up. Patted Ronnie's shoulder.

Frank inched his way toward the gate, watching for a break so they could leave while the other teams arrived, the ones who did the real work of bagging and tagging and sniffing around, amassing the evidence so their case would be tight, would hold up if no one pleaded out. The locals, with every light flashing, had blocked the street, some of them coming through the gate to be a part of the scene, others keeping back the news crews who were arriving.

No one spoke until they were clear of the chaos, then Frank said, "That went well. Thanks for the heads up, Ronnie."

"Wait, what heads up? I forgot to send the text. What're you guys doing here? Aren't you going to cut these off me?"

Pete patted her shoulder again. "We need to keep up the pretense a little longer. For your safety. They're not too tight, are they?"

Frank explained that they would take her in, book her, make sure Mateo saw she was being arrested too, then pull her out for interrogation and whisk her away, losing the arrest paperwork.

"Jeez. I don't know what was scarier, the gun to my throat or worrying that you'd forgotten I was your CI and you were arresting me."

Pete held a bottle of water to her lips, and she was able to swallow a lot of it.

"How did you guys know to come here?" She wiped her mouth on her shoulder. "I mean, I barely said anything in my text, and then I forgot to send it, and then—it wasn't John?" She shook her head at Pete when he asked her if she wanted more water.

"What wasn't John?" Pete capped the bottle of water.

"He wasn't the snitch? Mateo said he had to have been the one, because he wasn't there."

Frank laughed and looked over his shoulder at Ronnie. "Sweetheart," he drawled, "*you're* the snitch."

* * *

Everything at HQ went as they'd hoped, parading Ronnie past the holding cells to the last one, Mateo eyeing death threats at Frank. But he saw Ronnie, saw them manhandling her. Saw her again as they took her supposedly to the interrogation room. Frank waited for her at the end of the hall, watched her give Mateo a look, hopefully one that added to the verisimilitude. After the escorts left, they turned off the camera, the recording equipment, the lights, whisked Ronnie away, and back into their car.

They settled in at "Uncle Pete's office" for the debriefing, Pete pulling out Cokes from the tiny refrigerator, Frank grabbing the coffee pot. He went down the hall to fill it with water, the silence in the building a little eerie but also a little comforting, giving them a safe haven to debrief, decompress. And after Mr. Hoodie had held a gun to Ronnie, the need to decompress was so strong. He mentally shook the scene off. He needed his professional distance to finish this up tonight. There'll be plenty of time to wallow in the emotions later.

He had been so torn, professionally and personally. He knew they had to go in when they did, arrest Mateo, extract Ronnie. But Mateo still held Cathy, and everything within him screamed. Pete had given him a look, and Frank nodded to him. He could be professional. But where was Cathy now? How was he ever going to find her?

He headed back to the office with the coffee pot full of water. Straightened his shoulders. They still had a lot of work to do, and he would tuck his daughter into the box marked "personal," and maybe he and Pete could figure this out later.

He opened the door. At least they got Mateo. And the agents had been at John's penthouse when he'd sneaked back in. Frank had warned the team that Mateo thought John was the snitch, emphasizing the need to put on extra precautions for tonight. No sense losing their key witness.

On the drive back into midtown, Frank and Pete's phones each dinged, the arrest team reporting that when they'd woken Lisa up, she'd put up a fight, screaming through the apartment door at them until they convinced her they'd break it down if she didn't open up. *Hellcat* was the word they'd used, and they didn't mean a car. Frank and Pete had a bet going on how quickly she'd cave, rat out the whole operation, and this resistance boded well for Frank's bet.

In the morning, a pair of Special Agents would have a talk with Barbara at the house in the Hamptons, a property soon to be owned by the Federal Government, along with the penthouse and whatever else the AUSA had decided was purchased with proceeds of criminal activity. Michael had agreed to cordon off Ronnie's room, not include it as part of the inventory of proceeds. Frank was pretty sure Barbara played no part in her husband's illegal activities, but they would nail that down officially. John Anthony's world was getting smaller by the moment.

The lights in the office were low, only desk lamps and table lamps lit, no overheads. Frank poured two packets of coffee grounds into the paper filter, flipped the switch. They needed the double dose of caffeine tonight, and since the coffee tasted awful with a single packet, how much worse could a double be? Pete opened drawers and cupboards next to him, finally locating a cache of granola bars and chocolates.

They spent the next couple of hours debriefing Ronnie, taking notes even though they were also recording. Call him old-fashioned, but Frank liked having a notebook in hand, a pen jotting away. Made him think better. They covered the same ground, over and over, asked the questions in a different way, made her back up, fill in details, tell the story again and again until they seemed to be losing her.

"Now it's my turn."

They each paused in their writing, looked up at her.

"I want to know how you got there, how you knew where to go. I mean, what made you think that tonight would be the night you would arrest everyone?"

Frank looked at Pete. She had zeroed in on the exact issue they'd discussed, Pete sure that they had to act. Frank, as a father, had been dead against it, all chance of getting his daughter back locked up along with Mateo. Frank the agent knew this was the chance they had to take, prayed they could use it to their advantage as they piled up the charges against him.

"All the emojis." Pete's grin was lopsided. "I knew how serious it must be for you to put all those in there. I knew we had to act quick."

"But how did you know where we were going?"

"That's easy." Frank put down his pen, leaned back in his chair. "After all this time, the watchers finally had something to do, to follow you as we gathered the rest of crew."

"But so how did you know how many people to bring, how many you were going to arrest? And how'd you get there so fast?" Ronnie opened a granola bar. Set it down.

Pete answered before Frank, and he leaned back to let Pete tell it. Let him have his own moment of glory since Frank, not Pete, had actually run the operation. "We figured that if you were going somewhere with Mateo, it was most likely a meeting, so we had everyone ready, just in case."

And, Frank knew, if it weren't a meeting, they would need just as many people to keep Ronnie safe.

"Okay." Ronnie nodded to herself. "And how did you get there so fast?"

"We got a silent escort, care of NYPD. You guys were probably carefully going the speed limit, and we went a different route, all lights flashing until we got close. As soon as you guys went in, we pulled the cars in and raced inside."

"But your timing was perfect."

"That," Pete took a sip of coffee, "was sheer dumb luck."

Ronnie's eyes widened, and a leftover fear came into them.

Pete's eyes twinkled at her. "Sheer dumb luck that you butt dialed 'Linus' and left the line open the entire time."

* * *

Even with all the coffee and Cokes, they napped some in the office once they'd gone as far as they could with the debrief. Frank and Pete agreed without words to give Ronnie the couch, they in the chairs, stretching their legs across the round coffee table from opposite sides, arms folded, chins on their chests.

Pete's phone woke them, the team reporting in. The morning light came in the office windows, a dull, dusty yellow promising a very hot day, a last kick of summer. Ronnie sat up and raked her fingers through her hair, saw Frank, gave him a little wave.

"But what about all my stuff?" She ran her tongue over her teeth. "I don't even have a toothbrush. If I'd known, I would've packed my backpack."

"And Mateo would have wondered why you needed to bring jammies and all your suits to a meet with the cash boys."

She rolled her eyes at him and headed for the door and presumably the Ladies. He called the team and gave them additional instructions that Pete hadn't. Pete headed over to Ronnie's couch like he thought he could cram in a few more minutes' sleep.

* * *

They sat in a booth at one of Frank's favorite diners while they awaited the agent bringing Ronnie's possessions. He'd double-checked with her on where the team would find her things, and Frank was struck by how few possessions someone could have and still call it a life. He supposed that's what living on the streets taught her.

Luckily, they'd found a booth by the window, and they had slid in like they did this all the time. Pete and Ronnie had ordered the same thing, lots of eggs, bacon, hash browns, toast. They were each going after their breakfasts like they hadn't eaten in weeks and didn't expect to eat again soon.

"Wonder what they're serving Mateo this morning." Frank swallowed a spoonful of yogurt.

"His lawyer didn't get him out? He spent the night in jail?"

"Yep," said Pete around a mouthful. "No nice linen suit or leather shoes in there. No Ray-Bans or silk shorts, either."

Frank studied Ronnie. "You look sad."

She shook her head. "I don't think I'm sad about his being in jail. Especially not after what he said to those guys in the warehouse." She picked up a piece of bacon with her fingers, crunched on it, then wiped her fingers on a paper napkin. "Maybe I'm sad because I liked him up until then. But the way those words came out, so calm and reasonable, but so…graphic. Like I could see the bodies…" She shuddered.

She sat back and looked out the window, and Frank looked too, the people passing by, a car waiting in the middle of the street with its blinker on as another car maneuvered out of a parking place. Just a normal day, people going to work, getting groceries, meeting a friend, not one of them aware that the FBI, Frank and Pete, and Ronnie, too, had just taken out a major player in the most evil drug cartel in Mexico.

"So, is that your secret? Your superpower?" Pete jammed a part of his toast into his mouth.

"What are you talking about?" Ronnie balled up her napkin and put it on her plate.

"Is that how you get everyone to like you? Because you like them, even if they're responsible for torturing people for fun?"

"I don't get people to like me, I take them as they come. I don't care if they like me or not. Whatever." She waved a hand.

Pete looked across the table at Frank. "Superpower."

"Lisa didn't like me."

"Her loss."

"Hey, what about her? What's going to happen to her?"

Pete smiled at his plate, piled hashbrowns mixed with egg yolk on his fork. Could he really fit the whole thing in his mouth. They both waited while Pete chewed, swallowed. "Frank's going to lose the bet."

"You guys have been together way too long." Ronnie shook her head at them. "You speak in code like an old married couple. C'mon, really. Is Lisa—"

"She's having the same breakfast as Mateo right now, and Pete has bet me on how quickly she'll break down and tell us everything, make a deal."

"How much is the bet?"

"The usual," Pete said. "Twenty."

"Which way are you betting?"

Pete told her he was betting it would take three hours from when she sat in the interrogation room, and that Frank thought it would take longer.

Ronnie reached into her pocket and pulled out a twenty, unfolded it. "You're both wrong." She smoothed out the bill. "She'll go right away, under three, way under."

Pete and Frank looked at the money in the center of the table, then looked up at her as if they were controlled by the same puppeteer. Pete reached for the bill as Frank said, "We're not taking your money."

"No. I'll be taking your money. And I could use it right now, since I'm unemployed, thanks to you."

Pete pulled out his wallet and selected a twenty, which he laid on top of Ronnie's. Frank did the same, squaring the corners into a neat little stack. Pete asked her why she thought Lisa would break so quickly.

"Because. She's in love with John." Ronnie picked up the money, folded it, and leaned to one side to put it in her back pocket. "All you have to do is tell her John is singing and has sold her out. That she was the first person he sent down, even before me."

"That's my girl." Pete slugged her shoulder playfully. "I don't think you'll be unemployed for long, will she, Frank?"

Frank toyed with the idea of letting her watch them question Lisa, thinking she might enjoy that. But Pete must've seen something on his face because he shook his head at him ever so slightly.

"What?" Frank took a spoonful of fruit and yogurt.

"Bad idea."

"Jeez, just a thought, not an action." Frank put down his spoon. "Are you the thought police now?"

Someone tapped on the window, and the three of them turned to see who it was. The agent held up Ronnie's backpack, then her dark green duffle bag, and Frank gestured to her to come in. Ronnie looked relieved as she watched the door, then got up to meet the woman and take her things.

"Special Agent Williams." Frank nodded to her. "This is Ronnie, and you know Pete. Thanks for gathering her possessions. How're things at the penthouse? Do you have time for some coffee?"

She said hi's all around, told them they could call her "Jeri." She shook her head "no" to the coffee and remained standing. "Everything is getting bagged and tagged, except for her things."

Ronnie unzipped her backpack, looked in. "Did you see Patrick? The doorman?"

Jeri opened her mouth to answer, but Frank beat her to it. "Don't worry. We'll be questioning him."

"That's not what I meant." Ronnie gave him a frown. "I just meant I didn't get to say goodbye." She dug into her pack. "And by the way, he has nothing to do with any of this."

"Then we'll find that out when we bring him downtown."

"Can't you just talk to him at the building? He hasn't done anything. He doesn't—"

Well, this was new. "I didn't realize you were running the case." Frank leaned in, eyes on Ronnie's. "What is he to you anyway? He was never in any of your reports."

Ronnie shook her head at him, busied herself with her belongings in her backpack.

Jeri cleared her throat. "Well, if that's all, I'd better get back."

Ronnie thanked her, and Pete and Frank nodded their goodbyes.

"What the—how did this get in here?" Ronnie put a green-handled letter opener in the middle of the table.

"That's not yours?" Pete picked it up. The gold of the blade glowed in the morning light. The three of them stared at it, hypnotized, Pete twisting the blade back and forth as if it were an ancient relic.

"It's John's," Ronnie said, "from his desk. He was always playing with it. Why would they put it in my bag?"

"It must've been in your room. They wouldn't have given you anything that wasn't. Everything else is either evidence or otherwise seized." Pete handed it to Ronnie and raised an eyebrow at Frank, who gave a slight shrug. "I don't think either one of us saw anything in there that wasn't yours." The letter opener disappeared, and Ronnie zipped up her backpack.

"Before the check comes and we have to get back to work," Frank moved his bowl and silverware to the end of the table, "there's one more thing we need to discuss."

"That sounds official." Ronnie picked up a piece of toast, then put it down.

"Well, Pete and I are going apartment hunting, and we think you should too."

"No way I'm living with you two. I'd go crazy."

"No, that's not what I meant."

The check came, and Ronnie reached into her back pocket, but Frank slapped his hand over the flimsy paper. "It's on the Bureau. Working breakfast." Of course, Pete didn't make a move for the check, as always happy to leave the paperwork to Frank.

Outside the diner, as if there hadn't been a break in the conversation, Pete turned to Ronnie. "But really, we think you should get your own apartment, and we'll help you look."

"Apartment? What? I can't afford something like that." She slung her backpack over one shoulder, picked up the duffle bag. "Can't I stay at the creepy hotel apartment until the next job comes along?" She switched the duffle bag to the other hand. "Hopefully a job that doesn't include handcuffs at the end of it."

"We'll work out something temporary." Frank patted her shoulder. "But you can definitely afford it. If you've saved everything you earned while you were employed, then you'll be able to pay rent if you're careful with your spending."

"And," Pete chimed in, "we got the okay to give you first, last, and deposit as a way of saying thank you.

"Keep you on our side." Frank grinned.

Ronnie's jaw fell open, and she stared back and forth between them. She closed her mouth and swallowed, then opened it again, an "O" of disbelief.

He and Pete stood side by side, taking up most of the sidewalk, grinning idiots. Ronnie took a step back, and another, a pedestrian, scowling and maneuvering around her. Before she turned around and walked away from them, Frank saw her eyes fill, emotions working away on her face, flushing her cheeks. Her head turned, and bangs followed, and she was gone, melting into the crowd as she headed uptown.

* * *

Back at the office, he and Pete each clicked away on their keyboards, getting the paperwork ready for the AUSA. But the front of Frank's brain was occupied with Cathy. Where was she? What was happening to her? They'd had to go to that warehouse, arrest Mateo when they did, even if he hadn't given him his daughter as promised. But dammit…word was that Mateo, or rather his lawyer, had been attempting to use Cathy's whereabouts as a bargaining chip. The AUSA wasn't biting for now, but Mateo maintained his silence. Surprise, surprise. A stalemate. Frank felt gut-punched, a real physical pain in his core.

He had held out unreasonable hope that the tech guys would find something, as thorough as they were. But nothing could be got from the two digital photographs, everything too generic. Without Mateo to protect her—and Frank trusted him on that—instructing his guys on how to treat her…oh, God. He couldn't think about that. His stomach in knots, sweat breaking out. He stood up so suddenly his chair tipped over. Pete's keyboard stopped clicking.

"Frank? Everything okay?"

Frank didn't trust himself to speak. He picked up his chair, set it down with exaggerated care like it might explode. "I-I can't. Not with Cathy…God knows what's happening to her."

"Send me what you're in the middle of. I'll finish it. Do what you need to do, Frank. I got you."

"Thanks, Pete." He cleared his throat. "But…I think I need to stay busy. You know."

He sat down. Pulled out his keyboard. Stared at it. He slammed it back in. Dammit. He pulled the keyboard out again and sent his files over to Pete, told him over the divider he was going out to get some fresh air. Pete seemed to know enough about Frank not to try to come with him.

* * *

Leo's corner—not a corner, his sidewalk—looked the same, the world going on as if nothing had changed, as if no one had been arrested and Cathy hadn't been kidnapped. Well, there was one thing about that equation he could change. He strode quickly to Leo, scattering pigeons and customers. Leo put his hand behind him and faced Frank with angry defiance in his eyes. Before the scumbag could pull his gun, Frank grabbed his wrist, spun him around, cuffed him. His prisoner yelled out, but Frank didn't need to listen to him. He dragged him back into the trees away from the sidewalk and flung him to the ground.

"Where is she? Where are they keeping her?"

Leo let out a moan, and Frank flipped him over, put a foot on his chest. "Dude," Leo's eyes pleading with him. "Dude. You don't need to do this."

"You're right. I don't. In fact, I think I'll take you downtown and put you in the cell next to Mateo and get word to him that you're ratting him out." He pressed his foot down on his skinny chest.

"Oof." The air went out of his lungs.

Frank eased off slightly.

"No, Frank, that's not what I meant." Leo's voice was raspy. "I've been looking for her." He coughed. "When I heard Mateo'd been arrested, I-I was worried."

"Really. Since when do you care about your customers so much?" Frank took his foot off Leo's chest, rested his hand on the butt of his gun.

"Can I sit up, please?"

"Sure, go ahead." Frank watched Leo squirm on the ground, roll to his side, try and fail to get to his knees. Finally, finding it more sad than amusing, Frank grabbed him by the shoulders, dragged him up.

Leo looked up at him. "I didn't want Mateo to have Cathy. I didn't want to do it." He shook his head. "But I didn't have a choice. He basically owns everyone, and do you know what he'll do to you if you tell him 'no?'"

Frank grunted. "I can guess."

"So you know I had to." Leo wiggled his hands behind his back. "Can't you take these off of me?

"You're not going to try to run?"

Leo shook his head several times as if that would make it even more true.

Frank retrieved his handcuffs and watched him while he rubbed his wrists. Leo asked if he could stand up, and Frank nodded. Watched him.

"Like I said, I've been looking for her. Because without Mateo there to threaten his goons …" He eyed Frank like he was contemplating whether to say it or not. "...who knows what they'd do."

Frank covered up his shudder by crossing his arms over his chest. Kept his eyes on Leo.

"His organization is a mess. I've been talking to everyone I know, but no one knows anything. They're sending someone else up here, from Mexico, but they have to tread carefully—it's not like Mateo's dead. He'll be out soon and then angry if someone truly takes over."

This was information they could use. Maybe Leo could be part of their team in the future. Frank cleared his throat. "Why don't you tell me where you've looked, and we'll look somewhere different."

Leo glanced side to side like he thought someone could hear them. He shook his head. "I never thought I'd be cooperating with a 5-0..." He looked Frank up and down like he might've changed in the last five minutes.

Frank reached for the cuffs and took a step closer to Leo.

The drug dealer, his only link to his daughter, put up his palms, an "okay, okay" motion at Frank. He made excuses for not having that much time outside of his "work," then mentioned a few places, a few people he talked to. Said he'd rather not give their real names since they were friends of his.

Someone ambled toward them, looking like they needed a fix. Frank stowed the cuffs. "Noted. Now, I'm going to call you every day, maybe several times a day, and you'd better pick up every single time. Got that?" He waited until Leo nodded. "I put a lot of the blame for this on you, since you're the one who turned her over to Mateo."

"Dude, I already blame myself. She didn't deserve it. Not like some—most—of my customers." He looked over his shoulder at the guy coming toward them. "Speaking of which..."

Frank watched him sell the guy his drugs and then return to his sidewalk to sell more drugs. He shook his head at himself as he walked in the direction of the F train. Now his only lead on his daughter was a goddam street dealer.

* * *

After three agonizing days filled with paperwork and begging agents to ask their informants again for any information, his personal phone rang, Leo's name blazing on the screen. He pushed the button to record the call. Just in case.

"Jankowski."

"Frank. Leo. I wanted to let you know I—"

"Where is she?" He hadn't meant to shout. He lowered his voice. "Do you finally have a lead?"

"Frank, Frank. I'm telling you. I took her to the ER. They let her loose, and she was ODing. So I thought that best. Rather than hooking her up."

"Which one?" Frank was already out the door and pushing the down button at the elevators. Pete came up next to him, poking at his phone. "Gouverneur's? Got it." He ended the call.

The doors opened, and they both got on. Pete gestured at him with his phone. "I've just called an Uber."

Frank nodded at him. Too many feelings bombarding him to speak.

"It's Cathy, right? Is she okay?"

Frank stared at the closed elevator doors, listened to the soft hum as it carried them down. He nodded again.

"Want me to tell Susan?"

Frank swallowed. "I-I'd better tell her."

"Want me to dial her number?"

Frank turned to look at Pete. He knew he was just trying to help. "It's just—I've just got all this," he waved a hand in the air, "roiling around. It's so hard." He looked at his shoes. If Pete patted him, he might slug him.

Pete put his hands in his trouser pockets. "You can do this. It's better coming from you. But she'd want to know sooner, rather than after all the roiling is done."

The elevator doors opened to the lobby, and they both made a beeline for the street, Frank working his phone as they went. Susan answered right away, and Frank told her where to meet them.

A ten-minute Uber ride wasn't long enough to unpick Frank's emotions, but fear seemed to be top of his list. Fear that Cathy wouldn't love them anymore, fear that she'd never get over the addiction, fear that she'd changed too much, fear that she'd run away again. He couldn't look at his partner.

But Pete knew him too well. As if he could read his thoughts. "Just take it one step at a time and see what happens. That's all you can do."

* * *

Susan arrived not too long after Frank had finished the paperwork for Cathy.

"They said she's nearly stabilized. They'll keep her overnight, but then we have to decide where she's going." Frank hated to interrupt his ex-wife and Pete's conversation. They looked so comfortable together.

Susan gazed at Frank for a beat. "We should talk about that. We agree on rehab, right?"

"After last time—"

Pete looked back and forth between them. "Coffee? I'm getting some for myself."

They both nodded, and Pete got up, threaded his way through the plastic chairs, headed to the coffee machine next to the nurses' station.

"I know, Frank. But rehab isn't something we can do for her. Wherever we put her, we'll make sure it's better on security than the last one."

All the images of the past year or so crowded in. The initial shock of learning of his daughter's addiction, the confidence in the rehab, the devastation when they learned she had run away. And the past year spent looking, hoping, worrying. Susan's eyes were on him. She was so assured on this—volunteering at Benedict House must've taught her so much.

Susan leaned toward him. "But we should talk about what kind. Long-term or short-term residential, outpatient. You know."

"What do you think?"

Pete made his way to them slowly, his eyes on three Styrofoam cups of coffee held out in front of him in a triangle.

Susan gave Frank a quick look, like she hadn't expected his acquiescence, his nod to her knowledge and experience.

Pete handed cups around, sat down.

Frank shrugged a little. "You've studied this."

Susan sipped, winced, set the cup on the linoleum next to her feet. "I'll talk to some people, but I'm guessing, as expensive as it might be, long-term residential is going to be what she needs, after all this time."

Frank removed the lid from his coffee, blew on it, took a sip. It was awful, but he didn't care. "I'm still adjusting to the fact that we found her. That she's in that other room, that we finally have her. After all this time."

"I know. Me too. All those hours volunteering at Benedict House, every time the door opened, every intake, every time I came in and checked the list, checked the beds, hoping, hoping, hoping." She leaned down and retrieved her coffee.

"Can we decide later?" Frank put the lid back on his cup. "Just spend the time right now getting used to the three of us together again?"

"Leave me out of this. I'm just Uncle Pete, here, minding my own business."

Susan burst out laughing. A slumped-over figure four rows ahead of them stirred, and Frank saw one or two people turn their heads. Probably no one ever laughed in the ER waiting room.

"I meant—"

"He knows what you meant, Frank." She put her cup down again and rummaged around in her purse. "Just like old times, huh, Uncle Pete?"

* * *

Frank left work right after lunch to meet Susan at the hospital. With any luck, the procedure to release Cathy would be quick, and they'd arrive at the rehab facility before the intake window closed. Susan had gotten someone at Benedict House to make some calls, and she felt confident about this facility, talked up the success rates, the quality of the staff, the proximity to the city for when they were allowed to visit.

Halfway there in a borrowed car, Cathy yelled from the backseat. "Let me out! I've got to get out, I can't do this, I'm going crazy!"

Frank cringed, pulled from his daydream of his family and their future together. He turned around in his seat to see Cathy tugging on the door handle. Who was this in the car with them, because this wild thing was not his daughter. Her face scrunched up, and when he said her name, she looked at him with such venom he felt like she'd struck him. Susan sped up, moved into the far-left lane.

"We should stop, talk to her. She's going to unlock the door any minute," he said to his ex-wife's profile. She looked in the rear-view mirror and increased the gas.

"Child-locked." Susan kept her eyes on the road.

He watched out the windshield, eyes intent on the traffic as if he could help her drive, help her deliver their daughter to safety. Susan punched the radio button and adjusted the volume, but for Frank, the noise only made the whole situation more tense. The music did nothing to cover up the yelling. How could Susan do this? The woman who had been so attentive to their daughter, listened to her, listened beyond the words to understand what she truly needed, created a closeness between them that often made Frank feel useless and left out, made Frank want to work extra hard to win Cathy over—this woman now ignored the pain radiating from the backseat, drove with her mouth in such a grim line Frank couldn't imagine her ever having smiled. Or laughed.

"Don't you even care about what's happening back there?" Frank didn't realize he was going to say anything until the words were already out of his mouth. "About what our daughter is going through right now? How can you be so cold?"

"Frank." Susan hit the horn as someone cut into their lane too close. "You have to trust me on this right now. We have to be together, united front, and all that. That's the only way it's going to work."

"But—"

"You need to understand," her voice softened, "this still isn't Cathy. She's still an addict going through withdrawals, and she will do anything," Susan cut her eyes to Frank, then back to the road, "*anything* to relieve the pain. These are the drugs talking. The addiction. Not Cathy."

He had finally found his daughter, but he had found an addict, too. He let out a long breath, kept an eye the traffic ahead of them, tried not to react as

Susan zoomed up on bumpers. "It's killing me."

"They said this might happen."

"It's worse than when she was a baby crying, and we didn't know why she was crying, what she needed."

"You never knew what she needed. Poking the bottle at her when she'd just finished eating. Never burping her after."

"It feels like we caused this pain—"

"That's right motherfuckers," exploded at them from the back seat. "You caused this. This is your fault!"

* * *

Frank hadn't realized he would feel so relieved, turning Cathy over to the rehab place. Susan had told him to call them as they drove up, tell them they would need help. Four people came quickly out the front door, official, efficient, neatly extricating Cathy from the car and away from them, strapped into a wheelchair. Someone thrust a piece of paper at them, and Susan signed quickly. One of the nurses or whatever they were jabbed a needle into Cathy's arm, and she slumped in the chair, her tangled hair hiding her face. They wheeled her away.

The intake was speedy, the woman handing them a thick stack of papers, talking the whole time, getting Susan to sign some more things, but Frank couldn't process it at all, the woman's voice sounding like the wah-wah-wah of an adult in a children's cartoon. This place was so different from the first one, less campus-like and much more institutional, no cozy wood paneling in this woman's office, no offers of coffee, tea, just get through the paperwork and go.

"We'll give you weekly progress reports by encrypted email." The woman held the door open for them.

"*Weekly?*" It was the first time Frank had spoken, and both women looked at him like he had two heads. "How about daily? I need to know daily how she's doing, when she's getting out, when I can see her…"

Susan and the institution lady exchanged looks. His ex-wife put a hand on his arm. "Frank, we'll go over this in the car. We need to let them take care of Cathy now."

"But I'm her father. We're her p-parents. We—we need to know..." He was stammering. He couldn't help it. He had just gotten her back, and now he'd lost her again. This place seemed so far away, so sterile and cold. If he could've given her a hug...

* * *

"She's safe now, Frank, that's something." Susan was in the far-right lane, going, if anything, under the speed limit, as if to balance out how fast she drove on the way there. "And we know where she is. No way she'll be running away from there."

"But..." Frank cleared his throat in an effort to make his voice work better. "The restraints...our daughter..." Out his window, the grass on the side of the road went by, the trash blowing away as they passed. "What if she never comes out?" He had whispered, not sure if Susan heard him.

She put a hand on his shoulder, then put the blinker on, slowed for the exit. Where was she taking him? For a horrible minute, he felt the way Cathy must have, trapped, taken somewhere against her will.

"Let's get you some coffee and a piece of pie." Susan stopped at the end of the exit ramp, put on the turn signal. "You've always liked Mom's Peppermill."

The diner was visible from the turnpike, a giant white peppermill on the roof, a place they used to stop on the way back from family outings.

Susan sat across from him in the booth as he ate, took sips of her black coffee, the only sounds between them the clink of her cup in her saucer and the scrape of his fork on his plate. She'd been right, this was exactly what he needed, the kind of comfort missing from that god-awful facility.

"I didn't know you could be such a hardass, Su-su." As if the old nickname might soften his rough words.

She actually beamed at him. "Thank you." She saw the look on his face and continued. "It's tough love, Frank. It's no good giving in to her. It's not what she needs."

"Spare the rod, huh?" Frank looked around for the waitress to refill his coffee.

"Not at all. It's not like that. It's more setting rules and boundaries and not budging."

"I thought you were going to ride up a few tailpipes on our way there. I should've called in some favors, gotten us an escort. Lights, sirens, everything."

"Cathy would have loved that. She probably would've thought we were taking her to prison."

"Not much different to my eye."

They paused as the waitress poured the light brown liquid into their cups, took away Frank's plate.

"Place never changes. Same weak coffee, same amazing pie." Frank caught Susan's eye. "Thank you. This was exactly what I needed."

"Sugar is good for shock."

"So I've heard."

* * *

Two weeks later, Frank sat on the hard bench in the harsh light. He mentally traced the linoleum at his feet, his eyes running over the cracks and the divots, the lines of the squares, a spot where a piece was missing, and the dirt would never get out no matter how many disinfecting mops ran over it.

"Broski! You finally brought a bag for me."

He snatched up the shopping bag and stood in one motion.

Triumph shone in Annie's eyes. "You was miles away, man. I could've emptied that bag and you never would've known it."

"What are you doing here?" Frank clutched the bag tighter. "I don't think I've seen you inside a building before." Susan came up behind her, and Frank almost fell out of his shoes when his ex-wife put her hands on Annie's shoulders.

"She's working here, now." Susan turned Annie around toward the desk and away from Frank and told her to go gather up the sheets. Her eyes followed Annie and her blonde dreadlocks as she punched at the keypad, then slouched to the back. "All of them, please." Susan shook her head, and Frank knew exactly how she felt.

He held out the shopping bag, and his ex-wife smiled and took it, looked inside. "Girl things, this time. That's interesting. And thanks, we can really use these."

"I can't believe Annie would put up with a job here. Inside and regular hours? Wow. You must've worked some real magic to get them to hire her."

Susan punched in the numbers on the keypad, opened the door, and held it for Frank. "Actually, I hired her. Want to come into my office, have some mediocre coffee?"

"Your office? You hired—I thought you just volunteered on your off hours. You work here now?"

"C'mon back. I have a minute or two. I'll tell you all about it."

The hallway was a touch bleak, institutional, though attempts had been made to brighten it up with some blue paint. Her office was small, jammed with big three-ring binders and stacks of files and piles of pamphlets, but it felt cozy and comfortable to Frank, and the ceramic mug she handed him fit his big hand as if it had been custom-made. He settled in as Susan told him about the offer of Resident Advocate, how she spent so much of her time here anyway, how she'd gone as far as she could at her day job and was ready for a break.

"I'm thinking about getting a master's in social work." Susan seemed to be gauging his reaction.

"Really? That's wonderful. I always thought you should get your masters."

"Frank, you thought I should get a master's in accounting." She pantomimed stifling a yawn and then laughed.

Frank, relieved she found it funny now, laughed along with her.

"Salary, of course, doesn't come near to matching, but I've got savings, and more importantly, I really care about what I'm doing. The work here feels so much more significant."

Frank sipped his coffee. "Uh, maybe I could, y'know, help out."

Susan raised her eyebrows.

"Money-wise." He wasn't sure if he'd said that to beat her to the punch or because of the happiness that made her eyes twinkle.

"That's not why I'm telling you this." She gave him a smile, then picked at the armrest of her desk chair. "I dunno, I thought maybe I'd sell things online or something to supplement my income. I hear macramé is coming back in style."

Frank smiled. "Never left, at your apartment." He had liked the plant hangers, the market bags, the belts she used to make. "So…Annie? Really?"

"She came in after an OD. She's pretty spunky."

"Tell me about it."

"I thought maybe if I engaged her, I could help her."

"Or she could help herself."

Susan smiled. "I do need to keep an eye on her sometimes. Especially around the donations. Speaking of which." She opened Frank's shopping bag, pulled the things out, piled them on her desk. "Interesting that now that Cathy's back, you brought things for young women."

All stacked up like that, the T-shirts, socks, and underwear he brought didn't look as generous as his receipt suggested.

"Why is that, d'ya think?" She swiveled in her desk chair to fully face Frank, her eyes finding his as if she truly wanted to know.

He shrugged, set down his mug on the edge of her desk. Posters on her office walls proclaimed Benedict House can help, her shelves full of manuals, city codes, a stuffed dog with one eye flopped next to them.

Susan hadn't stopped looking at him.

"I guess," he cleared his throat, "if I had to analyze it, I would have to admit that in a way I thought I would jinx it."

Out of the corner of his eye, he saw Susan nod.

"Like if I brought something here that Cathy could wear, then she would never come, we would never find her." He hoped his ex-wife wouldn't think that was weird.

"And now that we've found her, now that she's safe," Susan said, "you feel safe bringing things young women her age could use."

"You always did know me better than I know myself."

They sat in easy silence for a minute or two, the tiny, crowded office a refuge. Frank didn't want to break the spell, but she was probably busy, and he had things to do.

"Well, I'd better go. Pete and I are apartment hunting."

"You and Pete? Is he getting a divorce?" At Frank's nod, she said, "Oh, I am sorry. But maybe for the best?"

Frank gave a small shrug. How can anyone know what goes on inside someone else's marriage? "Well, we're going to find a two-bedroom and figure out a way to have a cozy spot for when Cathy stays. Maybe put up a screen or something so she has a little space to herself."

"That sounds nice." Susan stood up, and for a second, Frank thought she was going to give him a hug. She opened the office door for him. "But you do know, don't you, that may be a while."

He paused, absorbed her words.

She rolled her hand through the air to help with the explanation. "Before she's out, before she's back to weekend visits with you."

He left her office and aimed for the entrance. The hallway seemed colder, more institutional, less personal than her office.

"Baby steps, Frank." Behind him, Susan buzzed the door open. She said it in the same tone of voice she would say *take care* or *have a nice day*.

"Baby steps," he said back to her, but she'd already turned away, someone behind her needing her attention. He hit the sidewalk and lengthened his stride, headed east, the comforting tap of his shoes on cement, the cars rolling to a stop at the corner, the people around him going about their day, the sun at the slightest angle promising autumn soon, the flowers in the buckets at the corner grocery store now chrysanthemums instead of daffodils. Frank had always felt that the new year should begin in September.

# Acknowledgements

Authors need readers to complete their art, and I am so grateful to every one of you who bought my first book and took the time to read it and to let me know how you liked it.

The observations and ideas of early readers in my critique group made this book better in every way. I am particularly grateful to Tom Andes, Alex Baron, James Shade, and Brooke Terpening for their camaraderie, encouragement, and incisive comments. Beta readers are numerous, and I am afraid if I name them, I'll leave someone out. Suffice it to say you know who you are and I am grateful for your detailed observations.

Zech Chafee provided much needed insight into ADAs and legal maneuverings, as did Brooke. Hell, Brooke provided all the brilliant plot points that I am too dense to come up with on my own. Ellicott and Alec did a great job finding the holes. I hope I've patched them well enough to honor the time and thought you gave it.

As always, my New York sources were invaluable, and once again thank you to Helen and Russell Pennoyer, Susan Sylvan, Janet Rassweiler, Margaret and Catie Pennoyer. Thank you too, to Stephen Chapman for lessons in money laundering—every mistake mine and mine alone.

Robert, my go-to source for nearly everything street-related, gave me invaluable and sensitive insights and details, and if I left in a few things he was skeptical of, that's no reflection on his expertise.

Helen and Russell, thank you so much for throwing the best book launch an author could hope for, and to Ellen T. White for the hard work and crowd-raising she did. Jonathan and Sydney Winthrop enticed people as well, making it a completely lovely party.

I am so grateful to my family for their relentless cheerleading, for coming to my bookstore appearances, for wearing the earring(s) featuring the book cover, handing out bookmarks right and left, and getting their friends interested in reading my first book. I hope that this one will stand up to your hype!

# About the Author

Jenny Dandy is a graduate of Smith College and of Lighthouse Writers Workshop Book Project. Though she has lived and worked from Beijing to Baltimore, from Northampton to Atlanta, New York City was the place that held onto a piece of her heart. She now lives and writes in the Rocky Mountains where there is no way she could launder money for cartels.

AUTHOR WEBSITE:
www.jennydandy.com

SOCIAL MEDIA HANDLES:
https://www.facebook.com/jennydandyauthor/
https://www.threads.net/@jennydandyauthor
https://x.com/JenniferDandy?t=13GKj4XYqSNHyWHW0p7lfA&s=03
https://www.instagram.com/jennydandyauthor/
Twitter handle: @JenniferDandy
Instagram handle: @jennydandyauthor
Facebook: Jenny Dandy

# Also by Jenny Dandy

*The Brownstone on E. 83rd*

www.ingramcontent.com/pod-product-compliance
Lightning Source LLC
LaVergne TN
LVHW042113200525
811829LV00007B/27

* 9 7 8 1 6 8 5 1 2 9 5 8 3 *